THE CONTROL PROJECT

Ernie J. Sinclair

Spice Dog Publishing

COPYRIGHT ©2021
ERNIE J. SINCLAIR

ISBN-13: 978-1737293828
ISBN-10: 173729382X

Cover design by: Colette Hunt

ACKNOWLEDGEMENTS

For my mother, Celestine Gwynn, who never gave up on me. My son, Anson, who has saved me more times than he can know, and my favorite daughter, Ayla, who left us way too soon. I love you all.

This book is also dedicated to the men and women who are currently serving or who have served in the military. Thank you for your service!

A NOTE FROM
THE AUTHOR

Thank you dear reader, for allowing me to entertain you.

The premise of this story came about from all the differing opinions about how the COVID pandemic was handled as well as the subsequent vaccines.

My brain tends to always lean toward the 'what if?' scenarios when I write and that is what I am presenting in this book, otherwise, it would be a pretty boring book. What if it was all a big conspiracy and they really are out to get you? I certainly hope that everything in my book stays a conspiracy theory and never happens in the real world.

As far as I am aware, the viruses and vaccines contained within the pages of this book, have not and cannot be made using today's technology, no promises on what tomorrow's technology can do. I have taken several liberties with how human DNA and human genomes can be manipulated in order to make this story a much more entertaining read.

I enjoyed watching my characters explore this world and how they handled themselves throughout the ordeal. Characters are fun to develop, and as a writer, you never truly know what they may be thinking or how they may react to a situation until the words are actually typed out onto the screen. I found myself surprised that my original intentions for a couple of my characters were 180 degrees off of how they turned out. The good guy turned out to be a bad guy, and the bad guy ended up a good guy, how does this happen when they are figments of my imagination? There were also some twists that I didn't see coming so I hope you are surprised as well.

I have taken various liberties with the layout of some locations listed in my book to fit the story better. All the characters come from my imagination and any similarities to anyone, living or dead, is purely coincidental and unintentional. Please note that any and all errors are mine, I am only human after all, but I have tried my best to make sure I present the best possible book to you, the reader, as I can. My ultimate goal is for the characters to become your friends and for you to laugh and cry with them throughout their journey.

Please take the time to leave an honest review on whatever platform that you purchased this book from. As an independent author, I rely on my readers to help get the word out about my books to others who may also enjoy taking an adventure with me.

If you have any questions, comments, complaints, suggestions, or just want to say hi, I can be reached via email at: ernie.j.sinclair.author@gmail.com

Sincerely,
Ernie J. Sinclair

4/3/21-5/14/21

PROLOGUE

T en of the wealthiest and most powerful people in the world had gathered in secret, either in person or virtually, to discuss the fate of the Earth's population. Not an unprecedented occurrence but noteworthy none-the-less. Six were billionaires and the other four were wealthy, high ranking government officials. They had met on a semi-regular basis about the overpopulation issue since it had been raised in the early 1950s, but a final consensus had not yet been reached on how to fix the issue. They called themselves, The Core. They were the leaders of The Elite Group and had come to the conclusion that at least 95% of the world's population needed to die in order for the rest of the world to survive. They decided to call it, The Control Project.

The ten members of The Core were actually just a small representation of The Elite Group as a whole. The Elite Group consisted of members of governments, scientists, doctors, engineers, agriculture, and many other careers. The group had initially started in the 1800s as a way to gain power and control over the government to help prevent them from eroding the principles that the country was founded on. Over time, The Core modified their mission to fit their own ideologies and it became a twisted shell of what it once was, eventually spreading to the civilian population where they soon controlled everything from the stock market to the price of gas.

Worldwide, the group numbered around 500,000

people. In the United States, there were approximately 150,000 members and each was promised a place in the new world with their immediate families. Of course, the members did not know the full scale of The Control Project, only their small part in it. Many had been led to believe this was a 'just in case scenario' should a world catastrophe occur, such as a meteor hitting the Earth or another biblical flood. Had they known what it had become, many would not have approved, especially since some of their family members were on the unwanted list and would become casualties.

Several leading scientists from around the globe had theorized that the Earth could sustain a population of approximately 10-11 billion humans before food shortages would become a major problem.

The population began to grow exponentially in the 1900s and into the 2000s. The following list was presented at a conference that was attended by several low ranking members of The Elite Group.

World Population by Year
1800 – 990,000,000
1850 – 1,263,000,000
1900 – 1,550,000,000
1950 – 2,560,000,000
2000 – 6,140,000,000
2050 – 9,700,000,000
2100 – 11,200,000,000

The information was passed up the ladder until it came to the attention of one of The Core; however, they did not include the additional information that predicted the population would self-stabilize shortly after 2100 at around 10,200,000,000. Thus began the crusade to control the number of people populating the world.

In 1979, due to containing over 20% of the world's population, China implemented the "one child per family" policy, in an effort to control the growth of their population. This policy stated that citizens must obtain a birth certificate prior to the birth of their child. The citizens who agreed to have only one child would be offered special benefits. Citizens who did have more than one child would either be taxed an amount of up to fifty percent of their income or be punished by loss of employment or other benefits. In 2016, China changed the policy to two children per family due to the majority of their population becoming age 60 or older and having the lowest birth rates in decades. China would not be able to sustain the workforce required for their current aging population unless they could quickly create a baby boom or rapidly decrease the aging population. Most recently, in 2021, they raised the number of children to three per family after the census continued to show a steep decline in birth rates.

Over the years, several other tests were conducted in various parts of the world to see how the population would react to a threat on a local scale. The first global test was the COVID-19 virus in 2020 that China had released unintentionally. The Core seized the opportunity to let the virus run its course in order to study the way that it spread and how both the governments and the citizens around the world would respond.

The results of the first global test were surprising. Governments were able to have almost complete control of their citizens as long as they maintained control of the media. They could decide everything from what businesses could be open to how many people could gather for Christmas dinner. When the vaccine was released, governments could regulate not only who received it, but when and what version they received. Most countries began requiring everyone to receive the mostly untested vaccine and carry proof they received it in order to travel on public transportation. Businesses quickly followed suit, forcing those who did not want the vaccine, to have to get it in order to work or even buy groceries.

The Core now knew how they could fulfill their self imposed mission, they just needed to determine a time frame and work out other mundane details such as who would live and who would die. The die part was a surprisingly easier decision than the live part. The Core determined that the elderly were a drain of resources and could no longer contribute anything worthwhile to society. The same held true for the mentally and physically disabled as well as those who were on any kind of welfare. Convicted criminals were also placed in the die category as it cost a lot of money each year to keep someone imprisoned. On average, $40,000 a year was spent per prisoner and with almost 2.5 million prisoners in the United States, that's 75 billion dollars a year that the taxpayers spend unnecessarily.

Determining who would live was a bit trickier. The Core and many of The Elite Group would need servants and people to do other manual labor such as growing food, building and maintaining infrastructure as well as developing new technologies that would benefit them. The issue was that they could not be allowed to overstep the station in life that they were assigned. Although most would essentially be slaves, The Core would always refer to them as citizens, no need to confirm to the citizens that they were in fact, slaves. In essence, The Core wanted total control over the population. After all, they were The Core and no one else mattered.

There would be several phases to The Control Project. The first would be a virus that would target people from third world countries. A select ethnic cleansing much like Hitler had done except this one would be blamed on a virus. The second would be chemical sterilization of the welfare class through vaccines. Vaccines would also be used to finish off specific ethnic groups who managed to survive the virus. Using specific genes from human DNA, The Elite Group's scientists had been able to remove such targets with pinpoint accuracy as those with blue eyes, red hair, or even a specific person if they had that person's DNA on file. This was how they planned on taking out high ranking officials and the majority of the military. At the same time, all prisons would be locked down and poisonous gas would be released in each one. Once this was accomplished, the recruitment of slaves could begin. The Core expected the first few attempts at large scale recruitment to go poorly. Citizens would rebel but the consensus was, once the rebels were permanently eliminated, other groups would be more than willing to be recruited. After all, most people preferred not to die if given the choice.

The New World could then begin...

DAY ZERO

Dr. Jeremy Carter

Dr. Jeremy Carter was almost giddy. The virus, no that wasn't right, HIS virus was about to be unleashed on the world in just a few short hours. This was his baby, his gift to mankind. True, it was going to kill most of the planet but that didn't bother him in the slightest. It was a small price to pay to show the world his genius.

Jeremy had spent a lot of his life as a molecular biologist and virologist studying DNA and gene splicing. He had also worked alongside the Human Genome Project for a number of years. While still in college, he had been approached by The Elite Group (although he didn't know who they were at the time) and was offered a place in the organization. Once he had officially joined, he directed his studies towards virology and microbiology since viruses would become his focus for the group.

Initially, The Elite Group had him working on creating a virus that would shorten life spans. Over the years, that had evolved into creating gene specific viruses and that was where Jeremy had excelled. He loved the idea of being able to pick and choose what attributes each virus should contain depending on who the target was. Things really changed once he had figured out how to use gene splicing in human DNA to target a specific person. This involved creating a virus that basically contained an on/off switch. The default switch position would be off unless the virus found a specific gene or gene sequence in the host body which would trigger the switch to turn on, infecting the host body. This is where he shined.

His ex-wife had been the first real world test, infecting her with a strain of rabies that he had modified to be much more aggressive. First, he infected their son, with whom Jeremy had little to do with at the time, who then passed it on to his mother without even realizing it. The best part was that his son didn't even get sick, he was just a carrier, only his ex could suffer the consequences of the virus. That test went perfectly, although he had worried that children, siblings, or other close family members might also be susceptible to the active infection. A lot remained unknown about exactly how genes and DNA worked. If he had accidentally used a gene from her mitochondrial DNA, which transfers from mother to child, well then, more relatives would have probably died.

Killing off his ex-wife did create a few questions. No one could figure out how she had contracted rabies, eventually, they put it down on her death certificate as rabies from an undetermined source.

Being a self-absorbed person, Jeremy really didn't care about anyone else. It's not that he didn't like people, he just had no feeling about them one way or the other. This made him perfect for creating viruses for the Control Project. The only thing he asked was that he got to name any virus he designed and created.

He had already made around 250 of the specialized One-Offs, which is what he called the single target viruses, by using the DNA supplied by members of The Elite Group. Since the One-offs needed to be initially ingested before they became airborne, these were made in a small capsule form, designed to instantly dissolve in any liquid. For the most part, he really didn't know who these viruses were targeting since he only received a name and the DNA sample. If he didn't recognize the name, he assumed they were for members of the government who weren't with The Elite Group.

7

The World-Ender was his greatest achievement. It was a virus that targets only those whose skin pigmentation is naturally darker. He did add a small tweak to it, unbeknownst to The Core, making it an extremely contagious and aggressively spreading virus while also having a very short life span. This was against the plan but he didn't want everyone to die at once, what would be the fun in that. Testing had already been completed with excellent results for both the One-Offs and the World-Ender virus but he still had others.

There was one more round of tests to do on the sterilization vaccine that he called Steri-12, but he had been promised more test subjects within the next day or so. Jeremy had equally high expectations for it as he had for his other creations, he did design it after all. Early testing showed excellent results and a final test probably wasn't even necessary but it also wouldn't hurt. Plus, he liked to see what his babies could do.

Production of the Steri-12 sterilization vaccine had been in full swing for months so there would be enough available when it was needed. The World-Ender virus was already in the third world countries that would receive the initial infection, just waiting to be released.

It was all coming together and Jeremy was indeed giddy.

Mumbai, India

Rahul Patel's heart was pounding. He was rushing through the crowd and across the platform, trying hard to catch the train. If he missed it, he would be late to work and his boss was not a nice man when that happened. Rahul would be forced to work late every day for the remainder of the week to make up for it. Luckily, he managed to grab onto the train's railing and pull himself onto the stairs just as it started to pull away from the station.

He felt a quick sharp pain in his right buttock as he attempted to obtain better footing. Reaching back and feeling where the pain had originated from, he didn't feel anything and briefly wondered what had caused it. As more people tried to cram inside the train car out of the heat, he quickly forgot the incident while fighting his own way inside. He did manage to get into the shade, although it didn't really help that much.

Feeling good about not only catching the train but actually getting inside out of the heat, he decided that it was going to be a lucky day for him after all.

Rahul was dead wrong.

New Delhi, India

Gaurau Gaur always enjoyed walking through the market. He especially loved all of the smells associated with the variety of products that the vendors put up for sale for the locals and tourists to haggle over. He had no time for that today.

Today he was on a mission. His favorite uncle had sent him to retrieve a gift for his aunt. Tomorrow they will have been married for twenty years and there was going to be a grand party held in their honor. He couldn't wait for the festivities to begin. He found it hard to imagine being alive for 20 years, let alone married to someone for that long, Gaurau was only 14 years old after all. He was very proud that his uncle trusted him to come by himself to pick up the gift and increased his stride at the thought.

Arriving at the appropriate merchant's stall, Gaurau gave a big smile as he waved to get the vendor's attention. "My name is Gaurau and I am here to pick up a gift for my uncle. He said you would have it ready?"

"Ah yes, I do indeed have it ready for you. He has already paid for it so let me go get it." the hunched old man said, turning away as he slowly made his way to the rear of the stall.

There were an amazing amount of wares for sale and Gaurau took the opportunity to see what all was being offered. There was a large variety of handmade jewelry. He saw that most of the jewelry displayed at the front of the stall was made of cheaper material but with high quality workmanship, these he knew were for the tourists, A little further back he noticed a selection that was made using more expensive material and finer details. Gaurau was definitely impressed with the man's work. There were also clocks made of wood and copper. Gaurau could smell the hint of fresh cut wood and lacquer so knew the old man was an artisan who believed in doing everything himself and would scoff at others who sold the cheap plastic, mass produced items. He admired the fine details carved into a small clock that was near where he was standing. Gaurau was amazed at the many hours and the patience it must have taken just to make this one small clock and thought that one day, he would buy a clock from this man, that would be handed down to his children and then their children, for many generations to come. No wonder the old man's back was stooped, leaning over a table for so many hours, just to create a single clock!

The man returned with a small package, pleased to see the youngster admiring his work. "I hope your aunt likes it, I took extra care in making this special for her," the man boasted with a glint of pride in his eye, "and tell your uncle thank you for me."

Gaurau gingerly accepted the small package that he guessed was a piece of jewelry, based on the size, and carefully placed it in his pocket.

"I will sir. Thank you. You have many nice things here and I was honored to see them." Glancing down at the small clock. "May I come back at some other time to see more of your work?"

The old man straightened up slightly as a huge grin spread across his face. He was very impressed with the young man's eye for quality. "I would be most honored. Perhaps, one day soon, you would like to assist me for an hour or two. You could see how I assemble the clock or shape a piece of copper into the perfect design."

Gaurau took a deep breath and raised his head slightly. This was more than he could ever dream of. Seeing a real artist create such masterpieces. He couldn't blow this opportunity. "You are most kind. I would be honored if it's truly no trouble."

"No trouble at all. Why don't you bring your uncle to come to see me in the next few days and we can make the arrangements."

Happiness coursed through Gaurau veins like a tsunami. "Yes sir! I will do that. I must be getting back to my uncle now. Thank you again for everything."

The old man waved him off as a tourist approached the stall.

Walking with his head held high and a grin on his face that wouldn't go away, Gaurau couldn't believe his luck. He loved to learn how things were made and always knew that he would use his hands to create things when he became a man.

Quickly leaving the merchant behind, he happily made his way through the crowd, being careful to keep one hand over his pocket, clutching the small package. Thieves were always about in the market and he had learned to be careful.

Impatient to show that his uncle's trust hadn't been misplaced, he hurried on towards home. Squeezing between a tourist and a local woman haggling for a better price on some fish, Gaurau felt a small pinch in his arm. Turning around, he thought he caught a glimpse of the tourist quickly walking away but lost sight of him in the crowded market. Deciding it wasn't as important as getting the gift to his uncle, Gaurau smiled and continued on.

He didn't think of the pinch of pain again until he became ill later that evening, then he only briefly wondered if the two things were possibly related but promptly dismissed the thought. Gaurau never mentioned it to anyone before he died less than a week later. He never got the chance to return to see the artist do his work.

Cape Town, South Africa

Today was an important day for Kamran Nkosi, and he

was nervous. If the meeting went well, the promotion was almost a certainty. He wanted that promotion so bad that he could feel it deep inside his bones.

He could just imagine the satisfaction he would feel when they announced him, Kamran Nkosi, a boy from the Ghetto, as the new Vice President of Sales. He had worked hard over the years to prove himself and now it was all coming to fruition. Besides getting the respect of his coworkers, the new position would give him a large corner office, a new company car, and a significant increase in his salary. The additional money would come in handy in helping out his aging parents. They had sacrificed so much to send him to college and he had vowed that he would make it up to them in any way he could. Perhaps, now that they were getting older and he was on his feet, financially speaking, he would get the opportunity.

Fidgeting, he glanced at his watch. Seeing that he had almost an hour before the meeting with his boss and clients, he decided to get something to drink. Initially, he thought that a Coke sounded good, he changed his mind after realizing his hand was already constantly tapping his leg with nervous energy, he went with a non-caffeinated bottle of juice. Caffeine would have him bouncing off the walls and he needed to remain calm and focused. He would find somewhere that he could sit and review his notes to make sure the presentation would go perfectly. Kamran thought that it might also help keep his nerves in check.

It only took a few minutes to go into the store and purchase his drink. Making his way over to a bench that mostly sat in the shade of a building, he positioned himself on the bench and took a big drink of the ice cold beverage.

He tried to relax but his leg kept bouncing up and down like it had a mind of its own. As he opened the presentation on his laptop, Kamran decided that he would need to stay on his feet while presenting to the client in order to keep himself calm.

Deep in thought on the different ways he could improve

his presentation, he failed to notice as a woman walked past the bench that he had turned into a temporary office, and sprayed the air over his head with a small aerosol can before casually walking away.

Checking the time, he quickly finished his drink, gathered up his belongings, and headed off to his meeting. Kamran was now a walking infection, spreading the virus to everyone who breathed the same air as him.

Yes, today was an important day, but not for the reason Kamran had thought.

Oran, Algeria

Nassim Saidi was not a happy man. He should have just stayed home today.

After going out with some friends last night and drinking a wee bit much, he had forgotten to set his alarm which, by default, had caused him to oversleep and in turn, gave him no time for a shower. He had dressed hurriedly and got to work only to find an obvious stain on the front of his pants.

So here he stood, the vein in his forehead throbbing in annoyance, still tired, kind of smelly, and wearing dirty britches while his boss glared at him. He knew he was in trouble and before the day was done, would find himself in the office with the door closed. Nothing to be done about it now. He had to lie in the bed he had made, which he thought sucked.

Now some uppity tourist bitch, who probably wouldn't even leave a tip, was returning her food for the second time. This time claiming that there was a hair in it and demanding that she should get to order something different. Nassim just folded his arms and stared at her with an obviously forced grin waiting for her to shut the hell up so he could return the offending dish and put in her new order. He was finally able to get the plate of food and take it back to the kitchen where he put in the replacement order.

Usually, Nassim didn't mind the job and loved to talk to

the Americans who came here on holiday. His dream was to save enough money to move to America and open his own restaurant. He was also realistic and understood that achieving his goal was still some time away.

As he took a pitcher of water out to the dining room to refill any empty glasses, some woman accidentally sprayed her perfume over her shoulder and into his face. Although he was sure she didn't mean to make him smell like a cheap whore, that didn't make it acceptable either. He took a deep breath and shook his head, trying to calm himself while she apologized profusely before leaving him a large tip and scurrying off in embarrassment.

Now Nassim was too aggravated to function properly so he went and sat in the walk-in cooler, screaming and cursing for a few minutes to vent his frustration. A well known, at least among the restaurant industry, therapeutic method used throughout the world for restaurant workers to maintain their sanity.

After a few minutes, he had calmed down and decided that he would try to make the best of the remaining part of the day. After all, it couldn't get much worse...until it did.

Mogadishu, Somalia

Abdirisak Ali was often amazed at all the changes that the city of Mogadishu had throughout his 21 years of life. Growing up, it was war torn and terrorist attacks had been frequent. He still sported a scar on his face where he had been injured by some flying shrapnel when a car bomb had exploded just outside the market. Over the years, Mogadishu had slowly become safer. Roadblocks and barriers were built to help prevent terrorists from entering the city. Police patrolled the streets with their guns at the ready, looking for any sign of trouble. It seemed like new businesses were opening nearly every day and tourists had slowly started to return once the airlines had begun flying passengers back into the area.

Even with all the new buildings going up, there were many partially destroyed buildings still standing throughout the city. If one bothered to look, they would see where chunks of bricks and stone had been blown away with rifle fire during one of the many firefights that had occurred in the not so distant past.

Abdirisak was a rickshaw driver. It was a constant daily fight to get passengers as there were many rickshaws and tuk-tuks in the area. He did better than some since he had learned English as a young child. His mother had hopes that he would be able to go to America and make his fortune. American tourists seemed to expect everyone to know English even if it wasn't the native language. He always tried to get American or European passengers if at all possible because they usually tipped the best but the competition for their business was also fierce, for that very reason. The downside was that the tourists were targets for gangs because the general consensus was that all Americans were rich. The possibility always existed that he and his passengers might get robbed.

Today was a slow day so he decided to go down by the beach, hopefully, he could find a passenger there. As he weaved his way through the throng of rickshaws and tuk-tuks looking for a possible passenger, someone in a passing tuk-tuk sprayed a mist into his rickshaw. He couldn't go after them as he was going the opposite direction and he could never pedal fast enough to catch up to a motorized tuk-tuk anyway. Figuring that it was some tourist kid playing games, he decided to forget about it, besides he spied an American who was waving him down. Abdirisak's luck was still holding, or so he thought.

N'Djamena, Chad

Haroun Mahamat hated Chad, always the fear of death in the air but it was all he knew and all he would ever know. He understood that Chad was one of the most dangerous places in the world to live, but this is where he grew up and what remained of his family was here, so he hardly ever entertained the idea of leaving.

He had a friend who had left to go to South Africa two years ago in search of a better life. Haroun wasn't sure if he ever made it as he had not heard anything from him in all that time. Most likely he had either been killed by, or forced to join, one of the many roving gangs in the country. Leaving apparently wasn't such a good idea after all.

His wife was pregnant with their first child. Not that he would ever let it show but Haroun was terrified to bring a small life into this hell hole but what could he do? He loved his wife and if a child was what it took to keep her happy, he would gladly deal with the fear, plus he had very much enjoyed making the baby.

Haroun was on his way to the market to obtain some fresh produce. His wife claimed that the baby desired some fruit so he had no choice but to venture out to get some. He was always very aware of his surroundings and had a healthy fear of strangers. There had been many kidnappings and murders in the city and he did not wish to be included in that group. This was not a good way to live but he preferred fear to becoming seriously injured or dead. What would happen to his wife and unborn child should he get himself killed just because he wasn't paying attention he wondered, just as a man ran by and sprayed him in the face with some water.

"Damn it!" Haroun said to himself. "That's what I get for letting my mind wander. At least it was only water and not acid. Guess I got lucky."

Haroun looked around cautiously before crossing the street to the market, vowing to himself that he would be more careful...not that it mattered anymore, it was already too late.

Luanda, Angola

Some people loved to fish, Akemy Manuel was definitely not one of those people. He found it boring, smelly, and he didn't like being on a boat, yet his grandfather enjoyed it so when his grandfather asked him if he wanted to go fishing, of course he had said yes, pretending to be excited because he loved his grandfather tremendously.

They had spent the majority of the morning in his grandfather's small boat catching fish. They had about ten decent sized ones that his grandmother would fry up for the family's evening meal. Now they were headed back to the pier and that made Akemy smile big enough to light up his eyes.

His grandfather docked the boat and tied it off before handing the bucket containing the fish, to Akemy. He scrunched up his nose at the smell as he carefully set the bucket on the ground so that he could assist his grandfather out of the boat and onto dry land. Once they were both safely out of the boat, Akemy picked the bucket back up and walked alongside his grandfather, back towards their house.

"Grandfather, why do you like fishing so much?" he asked.

"Well child, the truth is that I haven't always liked to fish. As you get older, you realize that what you like to do doesn't really matter. There are many things that I do that I don't like but they are necessary in order for me to give our family the things they need, like food," he said, nodding to the bucket of fish. "Over the years, instead of dreading a chore, I made a mental choice that I would like it, no matter what it was. After I did that, I found that I actually really did enjoy doing some of the things that I thought I didn't like. Take fishing for example, I get to spend the day outside looking at beautiful scenery, no one else is around to bother me so I am able to relax, it's peaceful and I can provide a good meal for my loved ones. What's not to like?"

Akemy laughed as he pinched his nose, "The smell, grandfather."

His grandfather smiled at the comment. "It is true that fish don't smell that good but we probably smell just as bad to them. I think the good makes up for the bad, don't you?"

"Yes grandfather," he tilted his head in thought before admitting to his grandfather, "maybe fishing isn't so bad after all."

His grandfather laughed, "For only being 12, you sure are smart. Now give me that bucket, find your friends, and have some fun. Be home by dinner though," he said, waving the youngster away.

"Yes grandfather," replied Akemy happily as he handed over the bucket.

He immediately began looking for his friends. Seeing his friend Roka talking to someone whom he didn't recognize, he headed that way. Akemy ran down the dirt trail that passed as a street, curious to see what was happening. They didn't often get strangers in their part of the village.

"Hey Roka, who's your friend?" he asked, nodding at the stranger who quickly looked away.

"Oh, hi Akemy. Just someone wanting to know how to get to the pier. Okay mister, you just need to go down past that building then turn left. It will take you straight there."

Akemy was always curious and noticing something in the man's hand, he couldn't resist finding out what it was.

"Hey, what's that?" he asked, pointing at the object.

"Oh, this is my inhaler. I have asthma and this helps me breathe. Want to see how it works?" the man offered, seeing a confused look on the boy's face.

"That's okay. I know medicine is expensive," he said, shaking his head.

"It's alright. I don't need it very often so it usually expires and I end up throwing it away," he replied, handing the inhaler to Akemy.

Akemy cocked one eyebrow up and tilted his head. "Well if you're sure? Just tell me what to do because I've never seen one of these before."

The man smiled, "Well if you had asthma, you would put the open end into your mouth and then breathe in while pushing down on the top, but since you don't, just hold it in front of you and push the top down."

Akemy did as instructed and almost dropped the inhaler when a shot of mist came out and enveloped his face.

"Oh sorry, I should have warned you to point it away from your face. Don't worry, it won't hurt you," the man said, snatching the inhaler away from the boy and carefully putting it in his pocket. "Thanks for the directions," he told Roka, hastily walking away like he had just smelled a bad fart and wanted to clear the area.

"Well that was weird," Roka said, staring after the suspiciously acting stranger.

"Yeah, it kinda was. Hey, wanna play some ball or something?"

Roka's eyes brightened at the thought. "Good idea! Let's find everyone else and get a game going."

While the two boys went searching for the rest of their friends, the stranger removed the inhaler from his pocket and tossed it into the ocean, knowing that his job was done.

Baghdad, Iraq

Fadhil Mohamed was a first lieutenant for the Iraq Police which is not a safe occupation, but as an Iraqi patriot, Fadhil felt that it was his duty to keep the citizens safe.

He had been on walking patrol for most of his shift and was looking forward to going home when he noticed a suspicious man peeking at him from around the corner of a building. Knowing how swiftly things could get out of hand, Fadhil promptly called for backup and brought his Glock-19 up to a ready position.

"Police. Step out into the open," he ordered.

Instead of the man following the instructions, he pulled the pin on a gas canister and tossed it towards Fadhil.

Thinking it might be a grenade, Fadhil dove behind a car, the smoky vapor enveloping the area before quickly dissipating.

Not feeling any effects from the vapor, Fadhil filed it away as a poor excuse for a smoke bomb and went after the man, realizing in short order that the man had already gotten away.

He got on the radio and canceled the backup before heading back to the station, glad his shift was finally over so he could take his wife to dinner.

Fadhil failed to notice the man come out from a darkened doorway and retrieve the canister, before fading back into the shadows.

DAY ONE

Eddie

Eddie Owens had grown up poor and no matter how hard he had tried, he remained poor. It came as no surprise that at the ripe old age of 31, he was in fact, still poor. While Eddie didn't mind being poor, since he had never been anything else, what he did mind was being treated like he was less of a human being just because his current address was an old delivery van in an alleyway behind a dry cleaners.

There were some advantages to being homeless, such as not having to pay rent and junk mail becoming nonexistent. For most people, the disadvantages far outweighed these advantages and even Eddie would admit this. After all, indoor plumbing was in fact, pretty damn awesome.

Very rarely will someone set out to become homeless and Eddie was no different. He had worked for a manufacturing company in Louisiana for almost eight years before being getting fired for punching out his new boss for making fun of the way that Eddie talked. He couldn't help that he was raised in the swamps and had barely passed the sixth grade.

Eddie found himself at the age of 24, unemployed with no marketable career skills. With the economy in the tank, he was unable to find a new job and was soon evicted from his rundown apartment. Not knowing what to do, he left Louisiana and hitchhiked his way to Atlanta, where his oldest sister had moved some years before, but he was still unable to find employment. Not wanting to be a burden on his family, he lived in the streets and after a while, homelessness just became Eddie's new normal. Without a phone number, address, or a shower, no one would give his job application more than a glance before putting it in the 'never going to happen' pile.

For the first couple of years, Eddie just wandered from shelter to shelter and soup kitchen to soup kitchen until he met Erik Crandall. Erik owned the dry cleaners and had approached Eddie with a job offer when he noticed him picking some trash off the street and placing it in a trash can out in front of the dry cleaners.

Eddie gladly accepted the janitorial position and in exchange for doing a bit of sweeping, window cleaning, and maintaining the restroom to an acceptable standard, Eddie could live in the old delivery van in the alley and use the restroom during business hours, in order to keep clean and take care of other bodily functions. Erik also gave him $40 a week with the promise that it would not be used for drugs or alcohol. Since Eddie had grown up with an alcoholic father and had always been against using drugs since his best friend from the old neighborhood had died from an overdose, this was a promise he could easily keep.

The arrangement worked out well and once Eddie caught someone trying to break into the dry cleaners, Erik gave him a $5 a week raise and promoted him to head of security.

Eddie might be from the backwoods but he wasn't stupid and he knew the promotion was Erik's way of thanking him and trying to help him out more without offending him. He did appreciate everything that Erik did for him and went along with the facade.

With all the money he was making and no bills to pay, Eddie was able to buy books to read, which he gave away to other homeless people after he finished reading them. Although his spoken English was broken up and sometimes hard to understand, Eddie was actually fairly intelligent and tried to read as often as he could. Hoping to improve his verbal language skills, he would sometimes read out loud. Once he had tried to get a library card, but with no valid identification or home address, it didn't go very well. He preferred to read in the park on a bench in a secluded little area he found, that had bushes that ran between the bench and the sidewalk. This is where he was when he overheard a rather odd conversation between two men walking nearby.

"...everything is moving too fast. I'm worried we could be missing something."

"I think you're worried for nothing. The big guys have been working on this for years so I doubt they are going to leave anything to chance."

"Do you know the saying 'every plan is perfect until it's implemented, then it all goes to shit'?" the first man asked, stopping to light a cigarette just on the other side of the hedge from where Eddie was sitting. "Well, it's true. I still don't get how they can create a virus that will target a certain race."

Hearing this, Eddie's mouth went dry and his throat tightened. He was uncertain of what the men were talking about but he knew, deep in his gut, that he needed to find out. He appeared to be attempting to bore a hole through the hedge with his intense stare as he completely focused his concentration on the men's conversation.

"Me either, but my buddy works for Dr. Carter and he has seen the testing and told me that it definitely works. He said every test subject died except for the white people, even though they injected them with the same stuff. You're right that this is virus appears to be spreading too fast to..." The conversation trailed off as the two men walked out of hearing distance.

"Holy shit," Eddie whispered to himself, unable to come to grips with what he heard. "They be trying to kill me."

He slowly got up, gripping his new book so tightly in his hand that it creased the cover. He followed the two men to see if he could find out more.

Having lived on the street for so many years, he knew

how to be invisible. Even if the men did notice him, they wouldn't really see him except as another homeless man contaminating the city and he would be instantly ignored.

The men walked for about ten more minutes, never once looking back to see if they were followed. Unfortunately, Eddie was unable to get close enough to hear any more of their conversation.

They crossed the street and headed to the entrance of Crouch Pharmaceuticals, one of the largest pharmaceutical companies in the world.

As Eddie stood there, shifting his weight from leg to leg and unconsciously biting his lip, he wondering what to do with the information. He needed to talk to Erik.

When Eddie arrived at the dry cleaners, there was only one customer, Mrs. Sims, who was a frequent customer. Eddie stood to the side of the door tapping his foot and taking calming breaths as he waited impatiently.

As soon as Mrs. Sims turned to walk to the door, Eddie rushed past, accidentally bumping into her, but he didn't notice in his agitated state.

"Well really?" Mrs. Sims said, looking back at Eddie. Seeing that she wasn't going to get an apology, she stomped her way out of the building.

"Erik. I be needing to talk to you about something?"

He had never seen Eddie so worried before and was instantly concerned for his friend. "Are you alright?"

"Yeah! No! I be not sure," he bleated out.

"Whoa! Slow down there buddy, take a deep breath and calm your mind."

Eddie did as instructed, feeling some of the tension and distress leave his body. More relaxed, he cleared his throat and tried again, "I be okay for now I be thinking, but I be needing to let someone know about something kinda strange I be hearing today 'n you be them. I be wanting to see what you be thinking about it," Eddie started, fidgeting with his paperback while constantly shifting from side to side. "I be hearing these two guys 'n they be talking at the park. They be talking something about a virus that only be killing the non-white folk 'n that it's spreading too fast. I be worried 'n so I be following them to Crouch Pharmaceuticals and I be thinking that they be working there. I be not knowing what to do, but I be knowing I be not wanting to die." Eddie's eyes pleaded for a magical answer that would make it all go away.

Erik could see the distress in his friend and thought for a moment before responding, "That does sound kind of odd. Do you think they could have been talking hypothetically?"

Eddie aggressively shook his head. "No ways! From the way they be talking, I be feeling it be happening now or maybe real soon like. they be saying the subjects be all dead except for the white ones. I be sure they be saying people but maybe I be remembering wrong."

"Well most likely the subjects they were talking about were mice and only the white mice lived, but I have never known you to overreact about anything so I believe you. I'm not really sure what we can do but I did go to college with a guy who is now a reporter, let me call him and see what he thinks. I wouldn't expect much since there isn't a whole lot to go on and it's all hearsay," Erik said, trying to keep Eddie's hopes from getting too high while also trying to keep him calm.

"I be really scared 'n be appreciating anything you be doing to help me."

Erik

As Erik went back to the office to call his old friend, he wondered if maybe Eddie had finally lost it. Life on the street could be hard and Eddie actually had it better than most due to Erik helping him out. This made him doubt a mental breakdown, besides Eddie had always been easygoing no matter what life had thrown at him so for him to be this upset and worried, concerned Erik. He had no doubt that Eddie believed what he had told him, but could he have possibly misheard the men in the park? The story was just too unbelievable to be real, but at the same time, Eddie wouldn't make anything like this up. He wasn't sure what to think about it himself, but if his friend believed it, he would give him the benefit of the doubt until evidence proved otherwise.

After looking up the number, Erik took a breath and then called the news outlet where his old college buddy worked.

"Thank you for calling Reliable News. Where we cover all the important local, national and international news. Watch our latest reports online or download our app to get only the news you want. Press one for subscriptions. Press two for the newsroom. Press three for...." Erik pressed two, hoping this wasn't a fool's errand.

"Newsroom. How may I direct your call?" the surprisingly friendly voice asked.

"Oh, um is Randy Elkhart in?"

"Let me check," the voice replied before a slightly muffled voice said, "Yo Randy, you here?" The person had obviously just put their hand over the receiver before yelling out instead of using the mute button.

"He's here. I'll put you through to his desk."

"Thank you," replied Erik.

After a moment, Randy was on the line. "Randy Elkhart, what can I do for you?"

"Hey Randy, it's Erik, Erik Crandall from college. How are you doing?" Eric sputtered out, now wondering if Randy would think he lost his mind. Oh well, he thought, in for a penny, in for a pound.

"Erik! I'm good. Keeping busy. How the heck have you been?"

"Doing alright. It's been a while, I wasn't sure you'd remember me," he admitted.

"Well in my line of work, you need to have a good memory but I am sure catching up on old times probably isn't why you called, so what's up?"

Erik took a deep breath as he made the sign of the cross,

even though he hadn't been to church since his parent's funeral fifteen years prior.

"Well, I think I might have some information on a possible story for you. It's probably a wild goose chase and I hate to waste your time but can we meet? I don't really want to say anything on the phone and if this really is what it sounds like...well, let's just say it will be huge and time sensitive. If you think it's nothing then I'll let it drop. No harm, no foul."

"That sounds a bit ominous. Sure, I can meet you. When and where?" Randy responded, intrigued as to what the story could possibly be about.

"Can you come to the dry cleaners over on Peachtree Street as soon as possible? There is someone here that I think you need to meet," replied Erik, relieved that Randy was at least going to listen.

"Is that the place you inherited from your folks?" he asked.

"That's the one."

"On my way. Should be there in about 20 minutes," Randy said, packing up his laptop bag and cellphone.

"I'll be here and thanks for doing this."

"No worries man. If it turns out to be nothing, we can at least catch up. C'ya in a few."

Erik hung up the phone wondering if Randy would believe them and then went to tell Eddie they would be closing shop early once their guest had arrived.

Randy

Randy wasn't quite sure what to make out of the phone call from Erik. Although they hadn't talked in several years, Erik had always been honest and trustworthy in college and wasn't one to gossip so hopefully, whatever the information was, it would be worth a story.

He managed to find a parking spot a half block from the dry cleaners. Randy grabbed his laptop bag and cellphone before going inside to meet with his old friend.

As he entered the establishment, he noticed that it hadn't changed much since his college days when Erik would occasionally help out his folks on Saturdays and Randy would sometimes come by to harass him. The same well worn floors and dinged up counter were still present as was a somewhat younger version of the original owner.

"Erik! Good to see you!" exclaimed Randy, realizing with a sense of nostalgia, that he missed his old college roommate.

"You to Randy. It's been forever," responded Erik, giving his friend a quick hug as he clapped him on the back. "Let me put a sign on the door and lock up, then we can talk in my office in the back."

After completing that, he led the way to the office. "There is someone I want you to meet and it's actually his story to tell." Erik stopped, his skin slightly pale and his heart racing, and looked Randy in the eyes before continuing, "I want you to know that I trust this man. If it was anyone else, I'm not sure I would believe it. He's had a hard life but he is also more honest than Honest Abe was. He's scared for his life and I have never seen him like this. Listen to what he has to say, ask your questions but don't just blow him off because the story sounds like an unrealistic sci-fi movie."

Randy took a moment to observe his friend. He was definitely nervous and a bit anxious, or maybe he was just plain terrified, but of what? Something was obviously going on and he was determined to find out what it was.

"Whoa. Slow down, Erik. Relax. As far as I am aware, you have never lied to me and I wouldn't be here if I didn't trust your judgment. I promise to listen and consider everything before coming to any type of conclusion."

"That's all that I ask," responded Erik with a sigh of relief.

As they entered the back room, he appraised the slightly disheveled man who couldn't seem to sit still even though his muscles appeared to be extremely tense. The man's body had a slight tremble to it as he rose to meet him. Randy briefly wondered if the man was having drug withdrawals and that this was all going to be a complete waste of his time.

"Randy, this is Eddie. Eddie, this is Randy, the reporter that I told you about. He has promised to listen to what you have to say and keep an open mind about it."

Eddie shifted his weight to his other foot as he offered his clammy hand to Randy after wiping it on his pant leg.

"Thanks for coming. I be not sure who to talk to until Erik says I be needing to tell you," Eddie said, shaking Randy's hand.

Randy continued to size him up as they shook hands. Eddie's grip was firm, eyes were clear and he didn't show any of the tell-tell signs of drug or alcohol abuse like bad skin and teeth. No, this man took care of himself the best he was able to, this was definitely something else. Erik had said he was scared for his life and Randy believed him, he just needed to know what would make someone this terrified.

"Well, hopefully I can help. Do you mind if I record this conversation or would you rather me just take notes? I just don't want to forget anything," he explained, trying to make Eddie comfortable.

"Shit no. You be recording it, but you be keeping me 'n Erik's names out of it."

"I will list you as a confidential informant. Nothing leaves here without your permission," assured Randy, turning on the record feature of his smartphone. Once he was set up, Randy said the date and time so it would be on the recording. "In your own words, just tell me what happened."

Eddie was wringing his hands and not sure how to start. "Well I be at the park, doing my own thing you know, not minding no one 'n I be hearing these two guys talking. I be not making much sense of it cause I be not trying to hears them at first, you know? Anyways, they be talking about some new virus they be making, or maybe the company made it, I be not sure which but they be all freaked out that it was spreading too fast 'n they being not able to control it. Scary part be that one of them says that the virus was race specific 'n only the white people be the ones left living. I be knowing that it be sounding like I be crazy, but I be swearing to you on everything I be holding dear, that this be the truth," he stammered, thinking about how insane he sounded, seeing the color slowly draining from Randy's face, he decided to carry on. "So then they be walking off 'n I be like, fuck that, so I be following them. Stupid fuckers didn't have no clues neither. Anyways, I be following them, like I be saying, all the ways to Crouch Pharmaceutical. That's when I be getting really freaked out that the be making all kinda stuff there 'n so I be needing to tell someone so I be hurrying back here 'n tole Er... err I be meaning my friend who says he be calling you 'n here we be at."

Randy leaned back in his chair and thought about what he just heard. A virus that could be used to target a group of people while leaving other untouched terrified him. With what he already knew, well, it wasn't going to have a good outcome. He shook the thought away and relaxed his clenched jaw.

"You said that you think the virus has already been released?"

"Um that what I be thinking from what they be saying."

"So this virus is supposed to be race specific and they were saying it was spreading to fast to control?"

"Yeah, that's what I be hearing," he confirmed.

Randy turned off the recorder, took a deep breath rubbing his hands over his eyes and said, "Well shit."

Looking up and seeing the confused expressions, he continued, "First off, I believe you. Now that being said, you both have to promise that anything we talk about, you can't tell anyone else, and I mean no one. Do not speak of this in the presence of anyone else. Agreed?"

Erik and Eddie looked at each other and then quickly agreed.

"Alright then, I guess it's my turn to talk. Over the last

few years, I've heard several conspiracy theories about a group of people who want to reduce the population. From what I've been able to gather, their theory is that the planet can only sustain about 10 billion people. In order to prevent an overpopulation problem, they supposedly have been trying to figure out how to somehow reduce it to a more sustainable number. Unfortunately, I have not been able to substantiate this rumor because it's always third or fourth hand. You know, I heard it from a friend who heard it from their aunt-in-law's third cousin twice removed who heard it from a pigeon at the park. No one ever knows who the group is or where they're from or how they plan to solve the alleged problem.

"Eddie has given me a name, Crouch Pharmaceutical, which is more than I have gotten from anyone else. Assuming that this is all true, Crouch Pharmaceutical is large enough to pull this off. I know they have researchers and scientists working for them but I don't know much about what they do, other than produce a lot of different medications and vaccines. I vaguely remember reading something about them doing genome research some time ago but have no idea what exactly they were researching it for.

"That being said," Randy continued, "I'm not sure what all I can do yet. Without any proof or someone from the inside willing to talk, Reliable News won't publish anything because they could end up being sued, but that isn't the biggest issue. The biggest issue is that we already have reports of a new virus in several third world countries right now. The first case was reported late last night and the last I heard, there were several cities with people already sick."

"Son of a bitch! You mean it's all true?" Erik asked, shocked.

"Well I can't say that yet, but from all appearances, it looks like it might be, or at least partially. Why don't you guys give me some time to see if I can find anything else out from my contacts? I'll come by tomorrow and give you an update. Call me if you remember anything else but don't go trying to find out more information on your own. If this is all true and they are willing to kill millions or possibly billions of people, they can't afford for this to get out and one more death won't matter to them in the slightest."

"Alright. I can work with that. Thanks for everything," replied a still stunned Erik while Eddie nodded in silent agreement.

DAY TWO

Jeremy

"**I** asked you a question doctor and I expect an answer that actually means something," bellowed Colonel Harker, obviously getting upset.

"Sorry sir. That's the best I can do for right now. I have some computer programs running that will give me a more precise response but it will take some time and until then, it will do no good to ask me the same question over and over again," a very frustrated Dr. Carter responded, condescendingly. He had little time for such meaningless chatter over things that couldn't be controlled.

He cared very little for the pompous bag of wind that was Col. Harker and wasn't intimidated in the least by his threatening nature. Jeremy had control of who lived and who died, the colonel would do well to remember that.

Harker released a big sigh. "You're right and I apologize for my outburst. I have others breathing down my neck, but I shouldn't have taken it out on you. Okay, best guess, how long do you think it will be before you know something more definitive?"

Jeremy had planned on making him wait for most of the day after his little outburst, but seeing that the colonel had decided it would be in his best interest to back off, he threw him a bone.

"Give me two hours, sir. The computer should have

something by then. What I can tell you is that the spread is far more aggressive than we had originally anticipated and the infection rate seems to be as well, but I can't give you anything more than that right now," Jeremy told him, even though the numbers were well within his projections. The Core didn't need to know that he had modified their plans any earlier than necessary.

"That will have to suffice for now. Would you have someone page me when you have the results?"

Dr. Carter nodded his agreement as he turned back to the workstation in his lab, effectively dismissing the colonel.

Finally, he was alone. Col. Harker had been breathing down his neck for what seemed like hours but was most likely only 20 minutes. Jeremy was glad that he had finally left, now he could do the final testing on the vaccine. This was the third and last group to be tested.

Jeremy's volunteers had arrived earlier that day and were waiting in the secure testing lab two floors down. It was a much smaller group than normal but he'd work with what he was given. Like the volunteers for the virus testing, he had no clue exactly where they came from, only that they showed up when he needed them. He suspected that they were being kidnapped from various countries and brought to the US or maybe they were illegal aliens that were supposed to be deported back to their home countries but were instead, routed to his laboratory. The subjects were all different races since the weaponized vaccine wasn't race targeted like the virus, and he needed volunteer subjects to verify that all races were susceptible. He expected that they had been more voluntold than volunteered, but that wasn't any of his concern.

Blood work on the subjects had been done when they first arrived by one of his three assistants and the male subjects were encouraged to give a sperm sample as well. Given the option of either supplying the sample or being castrated, they had yet had anyone refuse to supply the requested sample. Persuasion was so much easier without ethics governing everything. The blood and sperm samples would form a baseline of how fertile each subject was prior to receiving the vaccination.

Of course, it wasn't a real vaccine, it actually did nothing to, or for, the virus. It was just another weapon in the population war. This weaponized vaccine would cause sterilization in both men and women of all races. This would be used on the elderly, homeless, and all welfare recipients as well as anyone else deemed to be unworthy of living in the new world. There had even been talk of eliminating anyone with an IQ of less than 100. Jeremy had yet to come up with a virus that would target the less intelligent, but he was working on it.

Jeremy took the elevator down to the lab. He swiped his ID and then entered his personal 12 digit code to gain access to the lab. All of the labs were restricted and only he and his lab assistants had access. The code changed daily but was simple enough to remember. It was the last four digits of his social security number followed by his current age and then the current date using the yy/mm/dd format. He made each of the assistants use the same code layout and so far he hadn't had any breaches.

He found that his assistants had prepared both the subjects and the vaccine. Each of the test subjects had been gagged and restrained on a metal gurney where they would remain throughout their stay at the lab. On a separate rolling, stainless steel table was a number of sterile needles and two vials of vaccine labeled Steri-12. There were a total of 14 subjects covering a wide mix of races.

Approaching the first subject, Jeremy introduced himself to the subject, while the younger, slightly overweight male assistant, whom he called Chubby (he had never bothered to learn any of the assistants' names in the two years they had been with him), removed the gag.

"Good afternoon. My name is Dr. Jeremy Carter. What is your nationality please?"

"Where I be? Why do this to me?" the man yelled in broken English.

"Where are you from?" Jeremy asked again, ignoring the questions.

"I Israeli." "Good. This will protect you," he said, injecting the man with the Steri-12.

"Protect? What protect from?"

"Children," Jeremy responded quietly, waving at Chubby to replace the gag.

Continuing down the line he asked each their nationality and then injected them with the Steri-12.

During the procedures, one of the assistants would make notes on the clipboard for each of the subjects, noting the date and time of the injection, the subjects nationality, injection location, and amount of Steri-12 injected while the other two would deal with the gag and the returning of the subjects to their cells, once they had been injected.

Once all the subjects had been returned to their cells, Jeremy reminded his assistants to take blood samples every 6 hours and get sperm samples every 12 hours until further notice and then he headed to the elevator. Time to deal with the colonel.

Arriving back in his lab, Jeremy noticed the computer program had finalized the results as expected. He quickly reviewed the information and then paged the colonel who quickly arrived at the lab door. Jeremy had to go let him in since the colonel didn't have access to the labs on his own.

"You are good for your word doctor. Just under two hours. What were the results?" the colonel asked, impatiently.

He rolled his eyes. Of course he was good for his word. It was pointless to waste time saying things that were untrue. He really disliked this man more every time he spoke. Jeremy wondered if he should do something about it, maybe the colonel would get his very own One-Off. He smiled at the thought before returning to the business at hand.

"As you know, the World-Ender virus was initially released in India two days ago by directly injecting the virus into two subjects in two different cities. Within 24 hours there were only a few confirmed reports of anyone being infected. After 48 hours, the number of infected was around 120, and based on my research, that number will double every 8 hours until the virus burns itself out. As far as deaths are concerned, we anticipate a 50% initial casualty rate within ten days of the infection." He paused, giving the colonel time to write down the information before continuing.

"In Africa, we used an aerosol. Here we released it in 5 separate cities since it is such a large country. Within 24 hours, about 50 people were reported as infected, in 48 hours, the estimated infected were around 300 throughout Africa. Death rates will be about the same percentages as the direct injections, but the initial spread of the virus was slightly slower, as expected, with the different form of contamination.

"We also released a single dose in Baghdad, Iraq, simply because we could. Results were on par with both the India and Africa releases. Now we watch and wait to see how fast and where it spreads. If we feel that it's not spreading across the globe as fast as we anticipated, we will release the virus in a number of the world's major airport terminals, which was what I suggested in the first place before being overridden by The Core."

The colonel listened intently, absorbing the information before responding, "So total population decline will be about 50%? I was under the impression that it was going to be a lot higher than that."

"Well, yes and no. 50% will be about the maximum we can expect for deaths directly from the virus. I anticipate an additional 12-15% will die from complications of the virus, lack of medical care, starvation, and suicide. Around 98% of the targeted population will get the virus. The remaining 2% either being immune or more likely they will be too isolated from the main population. Since this is spreading faster than originally planned, it should burn out fairly quickly. Testing showed that a subject only remains contagious for 3-5 days after initial infection.

"The virus contains a mixture of a number of different parts of multiple viruses, mainly from influenza, rabies, and Marburg Hemorrhagic Fever. I designed it to be both aggressive and efficient. Part of its charm is that, in addition to damaging other parts of the body, it voraciously attacks the respiratory system so most of those who don't die right away, will still get pneumonia and become very weak. With most medical personnel sick with the virus themselves, medical care will be almost non-existent, causing many to die from pneumonia. Most will be too weak to eat and without someone to cook and care for them, by the time they recover enough from the pneumonia to survive, they will be too weak to care for themselves or others. Those that survive all of that will still have to live with almost everyone they know being dead, so some will commit suicide because of depression or survivor's guilt. There will also be diseases that come from the bodies decomposing all around them as there will not be anyone healthy enough to properly dispose of them all, which could account for an additional 2% to perish. Altogether we are looking at a 64-67% decrease in population in the targeted areas within 6-8 weeks of initial infection."

"Okay, I can work with that. It gives me something to appease The Core with. When does phase two begin?" asked the colonel.

"Phase two will start approximately ten days from the date of the first infection. I had to move the date up due to the overly aggressive nature of the virus. It's in the final testing right now. This will be the supposed vaccine for the virus which will instead cause permanent sterilization, anyone not part of The Elite Group will receive this. The accompanying booster shot will roll out two weeks later to anyone who became sick with the infection but managed to survive. This will end in death for the remaining targeted population. Either way, the current generation will be the last for anyone not a part of The Elite Group," concluded Jeremy.

"Very good. I'll pass the information along," Harker said

as he turned to leave.

Jeremy ignored the colonel as he left, wondering where he could get an uncontaminated sample of the colonel's DNA.

Alex

According to his alarm clock, Alex Carradine woke up at 4:34 pm. Groaning, he crawled out of bed still wearing the clothes from the night before.

"I'm getting too old for this shit," Alex complained to himself, referring to the all night bender, on his way to take a shower.

He turned the shower on as hot as he could stand it and then stripped down to his birthday suit. At 32, Alex was still in decent shape, while no longer sporting a 6 pack, he was far from being out of shape, most would call it an athletic build. You could tell he took care of himself but wasn't overly obsessive about it. He quickly showered and dried off, wrapping the towel around his waist, he headed off to the kitchen.

Opening the refrigerator door revealed half a stick of butter, a nearly empty milk jug, Chinese take-out from who knew how long ago, about a half case of beer, a partial 2 liter bottle of Coke that was probably flat, and some three day old pizza. Alex opted for the pizza and the Coke. The breakfast of college days gone by.

Hearing his roommate, Billy (not Bill and never William) Somers, come in the front door, Alex hollered out, "Hey Billy, want some pizza?"

Billy walked into the kitchen, took one look at the cold, dead pizza, before rolling his eyes and turning back towards the living room. "Nah, dude. I'm good," he said shaking his head. "I have no idea how you can eat that crap. You should at least heat it up."

"It's not as bad as it looks," Alex replied, looking at the cold, limp pizza slice in his hand, before conceding, "it's actually a lot worse."

"Why don't you throw that shit out and get dressed? We can go grab a burger or something," Billy said, turning on the TV and switching the channel over to the news.

"Sounds like a plan."

Alex tossed the pizza into the trash and then went to get dressed.

"You have to be shitting me!" Billy exclaimed from the living room a few minutes later.

Alex zipped up his pants, grabbed his shirt, and then walked into the living room. "What's up, man? You sound pissed."

"The media is at it again. They're claiming that there's a new virus that's going to cause another global pandemic. It's mostly in Africa, parts of the middle east, and India right now but they are saying that Mexico already has an unconfirmed case," Billy replied somberly.

"You mean like COVID was back in the early 20s?" asked Alex, only slightly concerned at the news.

"Yeah that's what they said, but they're also saying this could be 10 times worse. Shit! Grab your shoes. We have to go shopping before everything is gone," said Billy as he shut off the TV and headed for the door.

Billy pulled into the parking lot of the Kroger grocery store and backed the Chevy Blazer into a parking stall close to the front doors. Looking around, it seemed a little busier than normal, but no one appeared to be panicking yet.

He looked at Alex before opening the Blazer door. "Let's split up. You start at one side of the store and I'll start at the other. Get mainly canned stuff that will last for a long time but also get some meat and produce as well. Don't forget toilet paper and bottled water if it's in your area. Fill your cart and then checkout. We can load it in the truck and then decide if we can manage any more trips."

"Thank God for credit cards," Alex mumbled, still not fully convinced that this was a good idea, as he followed his best friend into the store.

Alex and Billy each grabbed a cart and then headed in opposite directions. They managed to make three trips each and were debating on a fourth trip when they noticed that the parking lot was starting to fill up and worry began to show up on people's faces. Alex went to go put the carts up, but before he made it three steps, people were taking the carts from him.

"Let's roll man. It's gonna get bad real quick," he told Billy.

"Agreed," was his friend's response.

They quickly got in the truck and just as they were pulling out, Billy glanced in the review mirror and saw people taking bags of food out of carts as people were leaving the store. "Damn, I'm glad we came when we did."

Alex chuckled nervously, "You realize that's the first time we went to the store and bought more than a case of beer and a couple of bags worth of quick to fix items?"

Billy smiled and thought for a moment before replying, "That's true, but if things are going to be worse than COVID was, we might need more than we got this trip."

The news quickly sobered Alex up. "Well, hopefully, it's just the media blowing it all out of proportion. Did they give out any information on the number of infections?"

"I might have misheard," Billy conceded, "but the number I recall is about 1,000 people have been infected so far. We need to keep in mind that they said it is spreading almost too fast to track. Since today was the first time I heard about this virus, I'm not certain how long it's been around. If it started in a third world country, it could have been around a long time before anyone figured it out and we could still have a lot of time before it reaches us. If it started recently, honestly, we could be royally screwed."

Alex nodded his understanding. "Well, there's not much we can do about it right this minute. Stop at the Burger Barn and let's get something to eat, then we can go put this stuff away and make a plan based on what happened back in the 20s."

"Alex, that actually sounds like something similar to a plan," Billy teased.

BB

"Hey BB. How's your shift going?" asked Ron as Becky Barnes trudged into the break room.

"Long. Very, very long. Thank goodness it's almost over. Just another 20 minutes unless something happens, knock on wood nothing will," Becky (affectionately known as BB) said as she knocked lightly on the wood grain Formica countertop. "I ended up pulling a double to cover for Carla. Her baby is sick and she didn't want to leave him with her mom that way. All will be well though because I am off for 3 whole days," she exclaimed happily.

"Oh wow. Big plans then?" Ron inquired.

BB laughed and then replied, "Oh definitely. I am going to go home, take a long bubble bath, get in some comfy sweats, turn off my phone, and do nothing but sleep, order food delivery, and watch Netflix for three entire days. But before I can do that, I have to finish up my rounds, check on the last few patients, and then I am out of here!"

Ron smiled. "Well, I'm just coming on shift so be sure to think of me while you enjoy yourself."

BB laughingly said, "Not a chance of that happening. I doubt you gave me one second of thought while you were off duty."

"That's true, but to be fair, I am newly married to the most gorgeous woman in the world."

"Who's gorgeous?" Linda asked as she came through the door. "You are, my beautiful bride," Ron smoothly replied to his wife of three weeks.

"Did you guys see the notice about that new African virus? It's supposed to be worse than COVID was," asked Linda.

"Not yet. I've been swamped today and have barely had a moment to myself. Anything local?" BB wanted to know.

"So far we're in the clear. There's been one possible case reported in Mexico City, but everything else is overseas," she replied.

"COVID took a few months to get around so I don't think I'll worry about it just yet. All I know for certain is that it better not ruin my three day weekend," teased BB, in order to help lighten the somewhat gloomy mood.

Ron nodded his head. "I have to agree with BB. Nothing to worry about yet. We'll just have to keep an eye on the situation and take it from there."

"Well, on that note, I'm gonna go finish my rounds. See you guys later," she said, throwing a friendly wave over her shoulder as she exited the room.

"Bye BB," Linda and Ron said in unison.

BB pulled into the parking stall next to Billy's Blazer.

"HI guys. How's it going?" she asked Billy and Alex as she got out of her Honda Accord.

"Hey BB. Alright so far. You missed a heck of a party last night," Alex replied.

"Oh sorry, I forgot all about it. I ended up working a double to cover for a coworker who had a sick baby," she admitted.

"That's alright. I drank enough for the both of us," Alex told her jokingly.

"BB, Have you heard anything about a new virus? I believe they called it the African Flu because they think it started in Africa," Billy asked her, hoping she had better information.

"Not much. Linda mentioned it in passing and said there was a notice about it at the hospital. I was pretty busy working so I didn't really get a chance to read it or watch the news. Why, what have you heard?"

Billy gave her a brief rundown on the little information he had heard on the news.

"Well that matches up to what Linda told me, but I'm not gonna worry about it yet. Sounds like the early stages and as long as they shut down air travel, we should probably be okay, at least for a while. When COVID hit, it took a few months before it made its way here, I imagine this new virus will be about the same. I'll let you know if I hear anything more about it at work though."

"Sounds good to me. Well if you get hungry, we may have over bought at the grocery store," said Billy, motioning to the still mostly full Blazer.

"Holy crap guys. If you need some freezer space, I have that small deep freezer that's pretty much empty that you can store some stuff in. Other than that, you're on your own," she told them, surprised at how much the two bachelors had bought since she didn't think either one of them knew how to cook.

Alex grinned. "We'll probably take you up on that. We bought a bunch of steaks and hamburger meat and all we have is the small freezer that's in the refrigerator."

"That's fine, but right now I'm gonna go take a long bath so give me an hour or so before you bring anything over," BB said, heading off to her apartment, located directly across the hall from the guys.

Alex and Billy

Noticing Alex watching BB walk off to her apartment, Billy asked, "When are you going to ask her out? You act like a lost puppy dog every time you see her."

Shrugging, Alex replied, "It's not that easy. She is way out of my league. BB is in her final year of residency, making her almost a doctor and I am a freaking bartender who works part time and lives off what is left of my inheritance."

"Bullshit Alex. BB is a woman and you're...well, you're almost a man," Billy said with a sly grin. "She just likes helping people. She doesn't care about how much you make so you two have that in common. Hey, if you think about it, you're kind of like a chemist and help people too."

"Yeah, help them get drunk," Alex said laughing. "Let's get this shit up to the apartment. Maybe we can hit up another store before the whole city goes crazy."

"Okay. Let's put everything in the dining room for now except for the stuff that needs to be kept cold. We can put that where it goes, then we can look over what we got and decide what else we might need before we head out again. We can use the beer coolers for the extra frozen stuff and you can take it to BB's in a little while," said Billy, giving Alex a wink.

"Cool. That should work," responded Alex, totally oblivious to Billy's attempt of teasing him about BB. "I think we should ask BB if she needs anything or if she can think of something we are overlooking. Shit! We need to fill the vehicles up before gas prices go up."

"I don't remember that being an issue during COVID, but then again, I really wasn't driving much back then so I guess it can't hurt. Good call on asking BB what we're missing as I am sure we forgot some important stuff. After all, we are just a couple of dumb bachelors," Billy said, grinning.

"That's true enough. Okay, challenge time. Who can carry the most grocery bags at one time? Annnnnd go!" Alex quickly started grabbing the plastic shopping bags, trying to get a head start on his friend.

"You're on, loser," replied Billy as he began shoving his arm through the bag handles.

Alex felt the blood circulation being cut off in his arms and fingers as he carried as much as he could up the flight of stairs to their apartment. "Shit. Doors locked."

Billy was only a couple of steps behind him. "Hurry the fuck up dude. My arms are on fire."

"No can do my friend. Doors locked and I can't really get to my keys right at the moment. Hold on. I got an idea," Alex replied, gently kicking at BB's door.

After a moment and a couple more gentle kicks, BB opened her door wearing just a robe. "Alex, I said to give me an hour and all that," gesturing to the bags Alex and Billy carried, "will not fit in my freezer."

"I know. Sorry, BB. We kinda forgot to unlock the door before bringing all this up. Would you mind opening our door for us? Keys are in my right front pocket." Alex asked, trying to hide the pain he felt from the bags cutting into his arms.

"Really guys? Nothing like planning ahead, unless this was your plan all along Alex. Are you trying to get me in your pants?" questioned BB with a sly grin.

"Umm, yeah sure. That's it," he said with a half smile, half grimace. "No, this is starting to hurt and you will probably have to amputate my arms or something if I don't set these bags down soon. Can you help a neighbor? Please?" implored Alex, now showing obvious signs of pain.

"Oh all right," BB said, knowing the joke was over.

She managed to work her hand into Alex's pocket and retrieve the keys. She found it a bit difficult since Alex had about fifteen bags on his right side that kept getting in the way and she wasn't overly comfortable putting her hand in another person's front pocket, but it was Alex, so she really didn't mind that much, although she was beginning to wonder if he was gay since all her flirting efforts seemed to fall on deaf ears.

BB unlocked the door and quickly moved out of the way as the two guys nearly bowled her over trying to get inside so they could set the bags down.

"Holy shit that hurt! Who's dumb-ass idea was it to carry everything at once? Oh, that's right, it was yours," Billy said to Alex, removing the bags he was carrying and surveying the indentations in his arms caused by the weight of the bags.

"Yeah, not one of my best ideas," Alex agreed, "but to be fair, we did get most of it in one trip."

BB laughed at the two men. "Okay guys. Glad to be of service; however, I have a bath to get to."

"Thanks, BB," Alex said. "I thought I was going to lose the use of both of my arms."

"Well, I did take an oath to do no harm. Here's your keys back or do you need me to put them back in your pocket?" BB inquired with one eyebrow raised in a questioning look.

"Well if you wouldn't mind," Alex quickly responded with a grin of his own.

"Not this time, you jerk," BB replied, laughing as she handed the keys to Alex. "Alright, I'm off to relax. See y'all later."

"Thanks BB," Billy said as she walked out the door.

Alex and Billy took their time retrieving the remaining groceries from the car so that their hands and arms could start recovering. It took roughly an hour to get things put away and a general inventory done of what they bought.

They each grabbed a cooler of food and headed over to BB's to take advantage of her freezer space and see if she could think of anything that they might have forgotten to buy.

BB answered her door, this time dressed in a set of pink sweats. "Hey guys. Get everything put away?"

"Pretty much except for this frozen stuff. Are you sure you don't mind us using your freezer?" Alex asked.

"I don't mind, I barely use it. My mom bought it for me claiming everyone should have plenty of freezer space. Not sure when she thinks I would have time to cook anything," BB said as she led the way to the freezer.

"Thanks BB. We really didn't plan this out well and to be honest, I never even thought about how much space this would require since we don't cook much ourselves," Billy responded.

"No worries. Is this everything?"

"Yep. For now anyway. Would you mind coming over and taking a look at what we bought? See if you can think of anything else we should get in case this turns out to be a long term thing like COVID?" he asked.

"Sure, no problem."

After checking over what the boys had bought, BB offered her suggestions, "Overall you're pretty set. I'd suggest you grab a big bag of rice and a big bag of dry beans. Those last forever and can actually keep you alive on their own for quite a while. Might pick up some more toilet paper and bottled water as those are items that stores couldn't keep on the shelves back in the early 20s. The only other thing I would recommend is basic medical supplies like bandages, antibiotic ointment, and some pain pills."

"Sounds good. Alright Billy, let's go hit up Walgreens and that smaller grocery store over on Walden Road. Hopefully, they will have everything we need. We also need to fill up the vehicles just in case," turning to BB, Alex added, "do you need anything? Want to come along?"

"I should be okay for the most part, but I guess it probably wouldn't hurt to pick up some extra hygiene items, just to be safe. Sure, I'd love to tag along."

Luckily Walgreens had everything that they needed except for the beans and rice. They headed off to the local family owned grocery store in the hopes it would be less crazy than the Kroger had been earlier.

Pulling into the parking lot, those hopes were dashed. People were everywhere.

"Why don't you two stay in the truck and I'll run in and see if they have the rice and beans," suggested Billy.

"No man, let's just skip it. We don't need it that bad," replied Alex.

Billy almost agreed with Alex before deciding that it was worth the risk. "Dude, it's beans and rice. I think I can handle it besides it's just crowded and no one is freaking out like earlier. I'll be back in fifteen or twenty minutes."

"Billy, please be careful," BB implored.

"Sure thing," Billy responded, stepping out of the Blazer.

Billy slowly made his way through the store. It was more crowded than Walmart on Black Friday and most of the shelves were nearly empty.

Finally locating the correct aisle, he made his way to the appropriate section where he found only one 5 pound bag of rice left and a couple of smaller bags of beans. Both items were located at the very back on the bottom shelf which was probably why they were still there. Billy had to actually get on his hands and knees to see them. He pulled out one of the bags of beans which someone quickly snatched from his hand. He glared at the bean bandit as they slowly escaped into the crowd.

Billy grabbed the bag of rice and the last remaining bag of beans and tucked them into his arms and chest like he was carrying a football. He was a fairly large guy at 6'2" and 225 lbs so he felt confident that he could deal with any other would be bean thieves.

Slowly, he made his way to the checkout counter. Realizing he was going to be there a while, Billy looked around trying to spot any trouble. Suddenly, a young man grabbed some items out of another customer's cart and quickly escaped out the exit. A moment later, bedlam broke out and a large number of people took off towards the exit with their ill gotten gains. Several people were knocked down and even more had their shopping carts ripped from their hands. The exit was jammed with everyone trying to leave at once. The staff just stared blankly at the chaos, knowing they couldn't do anything to stop it. Finally, the exit cleared enough that even more people headed that way without paying for their items. On the positive side, Billy was quickly moving up the checkout line as people left to take their chances on escaping with free food.

The store finally calmed down. It appeared that everyone who was stealing had left the building. The manager quickly locked the doors and told everyone he would let them out once they paid for their items. Billy was checked out five minutes later and as he left, he told the manager that he should close the store for a few days until the panic subsided. The exasperated manager only nodded his head in defeat.

Billy tried to open the door to the Blazer, but it was locked, so he knocked on the window instead.

Alex leaned over and unlocked the door.

"Sorry Billy. We had to lock ourselves in because that big mob was ransacking vehicles," BB told him as he got in the truck.

"Yeah, I had to show them I was armed with a tire iron to keep them from breaking the window. I think they were after the Walgreen bags because once we covered them up, no one tried to break in. They only looked through the windows and moved on," said Alex.

Billy sighed as the tension of the encounter left his body. "Let's go home. I've had enough of people today."

"Agreed," replied Alex, "but we probably need to take a look at our security once we get back to the apartment. If things are this bad today, what's it going to be like in a week?"

With that thought, they left the parking lot and headed home. Each thinking about what trouble might still lie ahead.

DAY THREE

Randy

R andy had spent the majority of the previous evening and on into the night, tapping his contacts for any information on Crouch Pharmaceutical before he had finally given up and slept for a few hours.

Crouch Pharmaceutical was turning out to be a tough nut to crack. No one would talk, which Randy thought said something in and of itself. Typically when you hit a wall of silence like he was with Crouch Pharmaceutical, it usually meant one of two things, organized crime or the US government, which was pretty much the same thing except one was legal...ish. Given enough time, he was confident that he could find someone who would be willing to talk, but time was the one thing that he didn't have, which meant he needed to focus his attention on the virus outbreak.

Unfortunately, Randy didn't know anyone in either Africa or India where the two largest outbreaks were reportedly occurring; however, he did know a reporter in Mexico City where the unconfirmed case was located.

He quickly found Raul Hernandez's cell phone number in his contacts and placed the call.

"Hola?" the voice answered after a few rings.

"Hi Raul, this is Randy Elkhart from the US."

"Hello Randy. This is very unusual to be calling so early. No?"

"Oh dang it. I'm sorry Raul, I don't even know what time it is right now," Randy explained, looking at the clock and realizing it was 5:30 in the morning. "I have been trying to chase down some information on this African flu and I heard that you might have a case down there in Mexico. You're the only person I know there so I just called without thinking."

Raul laughed, "It's okay Randy. I was already up with my granddaughter."

"What? You're not that old, are you?" Randy asked, surprised at the news.

"I must be since the baby is here, but that is not why you called. I talked to my contact at the hospital last night. They were able to confirm that the person does not have the virus. A doctor just thought the new virus could be like COVID and overreacted. He diagnosed it as an unconfirmed case merely as a precaution, and then put the patient into isolation," he explained.

"Well that's great news. You wouldn't happen to have any contacts in Africa, India, or Iraq would you?" asked Randy, pressing his luck.

"Not that I can think of, but don't you know that lady at the CDC? I imagine she could help you more than I," replied Raul.

"Well honestly, I was trying to avoid that if at all possible since her last words to me were, 'don't you ever call me again'," Randy reluctantly admitted.

"Ah yes, I can see where that might cause an issue, but sometimes a reporter must put himself in harm's way to get the story. No?"

Randy sighed before responding, "You're correct my friend, although you may read my obituary in tomorrow's paper. Oh, while I have you on the phone, have you heard any rumors about a virus that targets a specific nationality?"

"Do you think that's what this is?" asked Raul, suddenly sounding concerned.

"Honestly? I have no idea. It's just a rumor that I heard

somewhere but I thought I'd try to chase the story to see if there is any truth to it. Most likely it will just be a waste of my time," he admitted.

"It's not like you to chase a vague rumor, but no, I have heard nothing and I am not even sure if it's possible to do this."

"That makes two of us. Forget I asked and go enjoy your granddaughter," Randy said, quickly backpedaled away from the subject.

"Much easier to enjoy them when you can give them back when they get cranky," Raul replied with humor in his voice.

"True story, my friend. Well, thanks for your help and I promise to call at a more decent hour next time."

"No worries. Goodbye, my friend."

"Goodbye Raul," Randy said, ending the call.

Not looking forward to calling Lisa, especially this early, Randy decided to take a shower, grab a coffee and then head into the office. He would contact Lisa from there.

Jeremy

At one time, Jeremy had an apartment, he wasn't sure if he still did or not as he had not been there for almost two years. He thought he probably still did since The Elite Group paid for it, but he doubted he could even remember where it was. Not that it really mattered one way or the other as there was nothing there he needed nor wanted. Much preferring to stay close to his life's work, he had taken to sleeping in his office, that is, when he could actually sleep. He averaged around 3-4 hours a night with the rest of the day being spent working on his various viruses and vaccines, both real and fake.

This morning found him heading down to the subject testing lab to check on the 12 hour results of the sterilization vaccine. Previous tests showed a 25% positive result within 12-15 hours and a 100% positive result within 48 hours. He could wait a few more hours for the 24 hour results, but he was way too impatient for that.

There used to be another virologist who worked with him several years ago. Jeremy had found him to be an insufferable, self pompous know it all who somehow had 'accidentally' gotten infected with one of the earlier strains of the World-Ender virus. Jeremy had refused to work with anyone else after that and had instead, hand picked his three lab assistants, who he needed to do all the things he had neither the time nor inclination to do.

He found Chubby in the lab typing away on a computer.

"Chubby, what were the 12 hour results on the test group from yesterday? Just give me an overview, I don't need the specifics on each one"

"Out of the 14 subjects, one male and one female are totally sterile, three males have significantly decreased sperm counts, one female is inconclusive so I am rerunning that one and the remaining eight have had no change. None of the subjects are showing any other symptoms beyond some slight discomfort at the injection site," Chubby, whose real name was Fred, replied stoically.

"Excellent. That's a better percentage than the last group. Bring me the full detailed report once the results of the retest have been completed."

"Yes sir. I should have that for you within the hour. When would you like to schedule the booster shot test?" he asked.

"I'll do that tomorrow after the 48 hour mark is reached. Make sure everything gets set up for me in plenty of time, I don't want to have to wait," Jeremy said gruffly as he left the lab.

"Yes sir," replied Chubby, wishing for the thousandth time that he had never heard of Dr. Carter or The Elite Group.

Jeremy did the whole card/code thing again when he got to his main lab, then went directly to the computer.

After completing the log in sequence, he checked his

secure email looking for the latest updates of his World-Ender virus. Finding one from South Africa, he clicked on it and then waited for the encryption software to make it into something he could actually read.

The virus is now being widely reported throughout Africa with the largest concentrations within the cities of Cape Town, Oran, Mogadishu, N'Djamena, and Luanda.

The virus has been reported in an additional 23 countries on Africa's mainland.

Current infections in Africa: 2,800
Estimated one week infections in Africa: 10.5 million
Maximum infections in Africa: 1.19 Billion
Time until maximum infections occur in Africa: 9 days from the initial infection.

Current deaths in Africa: 450
Estimated one week deaths in Africa: 1.5 million
Maximum deaths in Africa: 550 million
Time until maximum deaths occur in Africa: 14 days from the initial infection.

The virus in India has largest concentrations in New Delhi and Mumbai with a few reports of infection throughout India.

Current infections in India: 1,000
Estimated one week infections in India: 4.2 million
Maximum infections in India: 1.34 billion
Time until maximum infections occur in India: 9 days from the initial infection.

Current deaths in India: 110
Estimated one week deaths in India: 600,000
Maximum deaths in India: 575 million
Time until maximum deaths occur in India: 14 days from the initial infection.

The virus spread rate to other countries is undetermined at this time.

Jeremy was pleased with the results. His own calculations put worldwide infections within 2-3 weeks and virus burnout 3-5 days after that. Total deaths at around 4.75 billion without using the vaccine or the booster shot which should take out another three and a half to four billion. Once the recruitment process was complete, less than 2% of the population will have survived. From over 9 billion people down to around 180 million in just a few months.

Now he had just one more thing to take care of. He sent off an email to Col. Harker stating that he needed him to provide a blood sample to verify that he hadn't accidentally gotten infected while he was at the lab and that if he had, his body was fighting it off the way it should.

Eddie

Sleep did not come easily and once it finally arrived, it chose not to stay long. Eddie was awake and worrying by 4:00 am. He did not understand why someone would possibly want entire races of people dead or how they figured out a way to do it. Surely the government would discover what was going on and step in to fix it unless they were the ones responsible. No, he couldn't think like that or he would go crazy believing that everyone was out to get him.

Something kept nagging at him all last evening and again this morning. He had the distinct feeling that he was forgetting something important but had no idea what it might be. Maybe it would come to him if he went for a walk to help clear his head.

He started walking with no route or destination in mind, mentally reviewing the conversation he overheard yesterday. Eddie was certain that whatever he couldn't recall had something to do with that discussion. No matter how hard he tried, he just couldn't remember what it was.

Giving up on it for the moment, he looked around to see where he was at since he had been wandering aimlessly. Realizing he was actually pretty close to the soup kitchen, he thought briefly about stopping in before remembering that it wasn't open for a few hours yet. That was too bad, his friend worked there and he had wanted to stop in and say hi. Eddie abruptly stopped walking.

His friend worked there. Holy crap, that's what one of the men had said. He said, my friend works for Dr. Cutter...Kramer....something like that. He had to get back to the dry cleaners so he could call Randy. He turned around and for the first time in forever, ran. He ran like the hounds of Hell were after him and for all he knew, they were.

Eddie waited in his van/house for Erik to show up for work. Erik always parked in the back of the building in the small parking area off the alley, right beside the old delivery van. Too excited to sit still, every few minutes, he would get out of the van and pace around the alley before returning. When Erik's car finally pulled up, Eddie was out of the van and beside the driver's door before Erik even put the car in park.

"I be forgetting but now I be remembering. Well, not everything but maybe enough for Randy. I be not sure, but Randy will be knowing, maybe," rambled Eddie excitedly as Erik climbed out of his aging car.

"Slow down Eddie. Let's go inside and you can tell me there. Remember what Randy said about talking in public?"

"You be right Erik. Let's go inside so I be telling you what I be remembering," he said, almost dragging Erik to the door.

Erik hurriedly unlocked the door and entered the back room followed closely by Eddie.

"It be the doctor who I be forgetting," he simply stated once they were inside.

"Wait, what doctor?" Erik shook his head, slightly confused.

"The doctor that those men be talking about. The one

man says his friend be working with this doctor 'n they be the ones doing tests 'n stuff," Eddie explained.

"Okay, I think I understand now. You just remembered that the two guys that were talking yesterday, mentioned a doctor who was doing testing on the virus?" Erik recapped.

"That's what I be talking about for the last five minutes!" Eddie almost yelled at him in exasperation.

Erik held up his hands in defeat, "I got it now. Sorry, it took me a minute. I'm not usually attacked like this when I get to work," he joked before continuing, "Do you remember if they mentioned this doctor's name?"

"That's the thing. I be not remembering fer sure. It be like Carver, Kramer...something like that. I be sure I be remembering it if I be hearing it again. But I be knowing it be starting with a C or K sound and weren't no long name," Eddie explained. "We got to be calling Randy 'n letting him knows about this evil doctor man."

"Alright Eddie, I'll call him after I get the store open. I doubt a few minutes will make any difference."

"Thanks Erik," responded Eddie smiling, obviously pleased with himself for finally remembering.

Randy

When his phone rang, he was sitting at his desk, staring at a blank computer screen, as he had for the last hour. He had been trying to work up the courage to call Lisa and as of yet, had zero success.

The phone rang several times before Randy shook off the stupor he was in and answered it, "Randy Elkhart. How may I help you?"

"Randy, it's Erik. We need to talk again."

"On my way," he replied as he hung up the phone, happy to be able to put off calling Lisa for a little longer.

It wasn't long before he found himself pulling up to the curb in front of Erik's business. He quickly made his way inside to hear what the news was.

"Damn Randy, you made good time," Erik noticed as his friend walked up to the counter.

"Busy day following leads or at least trying to. What's up?"

"Eddie remembered something else from the conversation he overheard yesterday. They mentioned a doctor who was doing some testing of the virus. We thought it might help you in your research," Erik explained.

"Does this doctor have a name?" he asked with a hopeful tone to his voice.

"Probably, but Eddie can't quite remember it. Said it was like Carver or Kramer. He was pretty sure it had the C or K sound at the beginning and that it wasn't an overly long name. I know it's not much to go on but maybe it will help," Erik told him, silently wishing that the information would help.

"Well it's something. To be honest, I'm finding Crouch Pharmaceutical to be difficult to get information on, maybe I can find a list of doctors who work there. Do you think Eddie will recognize the name if he heard it again?" Randy inquired.

"He said he thought so. I think he's upset with himself for not remembering it. I sent him down to the doughnut shop to get us something to eat. He should be back in a few minutes if you want to wait for him," offered Erik.

"No," he reluctantly declined. "I'd better get back to the office and start chasing down this doctor. Will he be around if I can come up with some names?"

Erik nodded his head. "Yeah, he should be. I'll just ask him to hang around just in case."

"Sounds good. I have to go make a phone call I've been putting off, it's now to the point that I can't wait any longer," replied Randy as he headed toward the door. "I'll stop by later if I find out anything."

"Later Randy," Erik said to a closing door.

Back at his desk, he spent another half hour trying to

find a list of doctors who worked for Crouch Pharmaceutical so that they could hopefully determine who the elusive doctor was. Finally, he gave up and decided to have one of the interns take over the search since he kept hitting a brick wall. He quickly explained that he needed a list of all doctors and scientists who worked for Crouch Pharmaceutical before setting the intern loose on the search.

He decided he could wait no longer and dialed Lisa's direct office number, hoping that she wouldn't just hang up on him as soon as she heard his voice.

"Lisa Johnson. How may I help you today?" a pleasant voice answered, bringing memories rushing back to Randy.

"Hi Lisa. It's Randy, please don't hang up. This is important or I wouldn't have called."

The phone line was silent for so long Randy thought she had hung up.

"I thought I made things clear to you the last time we spoke," she finally said, in a stiff, monotone voice.

"I know and you did, but this is business and if it wasn't literally life or death, I wouldn't have called," Randy quietly explained.

"I'll give you two minutes. If you haven't convinced me that somebody will die if we don't talk, then I'm hanging up and you will not call me ever again."

"Deal!" he agreed without hesitation.

"Your time started 10 seconds ago so you should start talking," Lisa warned him.

"I only need 30 seconds. I have reason to believe that the African flu or whatever they are calling it, is targeting specific nationalities and was man-made right here in the good ole USA. If that doesn't convince you that we need to meet, then you're not the woman I used to know and nothing I say in the rest of my two minutes will matter," Randy calmly stated and then waited for Lisa to respond to his statement.

"Well, that was definitely not what I was expecting. If what you are saying is true, and I'm by no means convinced that it is, then we do need to talk," Lisa agreed, accepting that this was bigger than her issue with Randy, although in her world, THAT was a major issue.

Randy sighed in relief. "Everything I have so far is circumstantial but if this is true, someone needs to do something before it is too late. That is all I am after. If you are willing to meet, I have a couple of people who you need to speak with. One of them is Erik Crandall if you remember him."

"I'll agree to meet, only because I know you wouldn't lie about something this important plus I have some reservations myself about this virus. I go to lunch at noon so just tell me where you and your friends want to meet and I will be there."

"Do you remember where Erik's parent's dry cleaners is at over on Peachtree Street? It's where Erik had that party one Saturday night when his folks were out of town. One of the party goers had a bit too much to drink and vomited all over a bunch of the clothes. He had to redo all that work before his parents got back into town and discovered what happened," Randy reminded her, hoping to at least get a small chuckle from the ice queen.

"I think I can find it." Giving no hint if she remembered the incident in question or not.

"Well anyway, Erik inherited the business when his parents passed away shortly after he graduated college. I think he keeps it open to honor their memory," Randy confided. "That's where we'll be and thank you for not just hanging up. I wouldn't have blamed you if you had."

"We will not talk about that. We are meeting specifically to discuss your claim about this virus. You guys need to convince me that there is a reason to believe you. Understood?" Lisa said giving no room for doubt.

"Got it. We'll tell you everything and maybe you might have some thoughts on it that were are missing. See you at noon and I'll bring the pizza."

"See you then," she replied, quickly hanging up the phone.

Randy was relieved that she agreed to meet and immediately called Erik to make sure both him and Eddie would be there at noon.

Lisa

She had thought her feelings for Randy were finally gone, but that phone call caused them to all come rushing back as strong as ever. Damn him for screwing things up. Well, she wasn't going to dwell on it, she had work to do, plus she wanted to talk to one of the on scene doctors in Africa or India. Both if possible. Something Randy had mentioned about nationality and the virus kept tugging at her mind since she had noticed something similar in the infection reports that were coming across her desk. Lisa needed the latest information to see if she, and by default, Randy was correct or not.

Lisa sent emails off to all the doctors that had been sent to Africa and India to let them know to be on a video conference call at 10:00 am CST, if at all possible. That would make it around 4:00 pm in South Africa and 7:30 pm in India. Lisa wasn't sure how many would get the email in time to make the video call. She knew they were busy with patients infected with the virus and wouldn't get a chance to check their email very often. If only one doctor was on the call, she would be happy.

Reviewing the latest data she had on the demographics of the victims, she noted that none of the victims were Caucasian. That didn't really surprise her as less than 8% of Africa's population was white and with only a few hundred victims as of her last report, it wasn't a large enough sample of the population to conclude that Caucasians were exempt from the virus. Sadly, the virus was spreading fast and there would be a much larger pool of victims to pull from today.

Noting that it was almost time for the video conference, Lisa logged in and patiently waited. The first doctor to come online was Nita Khatri who was quickly joined by Tim Owens, both were currently stationed in India.

"Thank you for taking the time to be on this call. I know you are all busy so I will try to make this short. I do want to wait a couple more minutes for some of our other colleagues to join us from Africa but while we wait, how are things there? Nita, you go first."

"Not good Lisa. Samples have been taken and sent to the CDC labs, but I'm still waiting on the results. Infections here in Mumbai are up to 506 with 49 confirmed deaths. I imagine that number will have at least doubled within 12 more hours. This is the fastest contagion that I have ever seen. Yesterday there were only 59 victims and 2 deaths so you can see how bad this is."

Lisa was taken aback since she hadn't realized the rate of infection was so high. "Thanks Nita. How about you Tim?"

"It's about the same here in New Delhi," Tim confirmed. "Victim count is at 489 as of an hour ago and deaths were at 58. It's like this thing doubles every 8 hours or so and if that's the case, the entire world's population will be infected within two weeks."

"That's unheard of," Lisa said as Bayron Botha from Africa came online. "Welcome to the call Bayron."

"Thank you Lisa. I will be the only one joining the call from here in Africa. I talked to all the other locations and they sent me their information."

"That should be fine, what's the situation there in Cape Town?"

"It's bad as you can imagine. Here in Cape Town, we have 612 infected victims with 82 of those deceased. All other locations here in Africa are about the same with the largest being in N'Djamena at 822 infected and 103 dead. Total numbers for Africa are 2813 infected and 472 dead," finished Bayron, obviously shaken up with the high numbers.

Running the numbers, Lisa saw that about 15% of the infected had died so far, but she knew the death rate would be much higher as it typically took a day or two after infection before deaths started to occur.

"Thanks Bayron. I know how difficult it is to be on site. Now I need to know if everyone can send me an updated breakdown of infections and deaths by race within the next hour."

"What are you thinking?" Tim asked.

"I'm not sure yet. Maybe nothing, I just have a little voice in the back of my head and I need to see where it goes," she responded without committing to anything.

"That's not a problem, but I would like to be kept in the loop if it amounts to anything. I'll get that report to you asap," replied Tim.

"You got it Lisa," Nita said.

"I'll see if I can get everyone's numbers and submit them with mine. I will send whatever I have compiled within the hour, but can't guarantee complete numbers from all locations," Bayron acknowledged.

"Understood. Let's not discuss the race issue beyond us right now. Once I have enough information compiled, I will let everyone know if race appears to play a part in this. Send me daily reports on this if you can. I'll check with the labs and see if they have any idea what we are dealing with and let you all know what I find out. Be careful everyone and take all necessary precautions until we figure out what exactly what we're dealing with," concluded Lisa as she ended the call.

She decided to stretch her legs and went down to the labs instead of calling, catching Dr. Thatcher in the hallway just outside the lab. "Hi Matt. Any word on what we are dealing with?" she inquired.

"Some. Let's go into my office," an obviously very tired scientist answered back.

Settling into the chair behind the overcrowded desk, Matt rubbed his hands over his face before he began his explanation of what he knew so far, "It's a very different virus than what I was originally expecting. For one thing, it's not solely from nature. It's what I would call a crossbreed that couldn't possibly exist without human intervention. In simpler terms, it's a man-made virus." Matt was watching Lisa and noticed she didn't seem surprised at this revelation. "You seem to know this already?"

"I have my suspicions that I will be more than happy to share with you, but please continue," Lisa acknowledged.

Matt nodded before continuing, "It was created using several genomes from an undetermined number of viruses, so far we have found traces of influenza and rabies but I suspect that there may be as many as three others. We are starting to focus on less common viruses to narrow that down, but it will take some time since we are looking for only a small segment of the original virus. This virus is not just airborne, it can also be transferred via direct touch, exchanging of bodily fluids, or even intravenously. It has a number of characteristics that make it an extremely aggressive virus both in finding new hosts and attacking the host body. If what I am seeing is correct, and I pray that it's not, this could be an Earth killer as far as humans go."

Lisa was stunned by the information she had just been given. "That's a terrifying prospect. Is there any indication of species crossover?"

"Not that we've discovered. There is a slight possibility of it crossing over to canines since they are susceptible to rabies but I don't think that will be the case as very little of the rabies virus seems to be present. It is something we are looking into though," Matt countered. "Now why don't you explain why you don't seem as surprised as you should be?"

"I can't give you everything yet. Give me until tomorrow morning on the full rundown but the short version is that I have a lead that someone in the US made this virus and it might be race specific. I'm checking into some things this afternoon and will know more afterwards. That's all I am willing to give you right now since it is all still mostly conjecture and we both prefer to deal with facts," she answered.

"You have until tomorrow morning then, but I will hold you to that," conceded Matt reluctantly.

"I promise but right now, I should be getting some reports back in my office that should help me to confirm or deny this theory, then I have a lunch meeting with a contact and some other leads to follow up on later today," she said, getting up to leave.

"Fair enough. With any luck, I'll have more for you by then as well."

Randy

He was back at the dry cleaners with Eddie and Erik. They were all waiting on Lisa. Randy was starting to worry that she had changed her mind and wasn't going to show up since it was almost 12:15. Then he saw her and she was more beautiful than he even remembered, which he hadn't thought possible. She entered the store with an air of confidence but wore a very stoic and unreadable expression on her face.

"Lisa, I'm glad you made it. This is Eddie and you might remember Erik from our college days. Guys, this is Lisa Johnson, an administrator at the CDC here in Atlanta," said Randy, quickly making introductions.

"Nice to meet you, Eddie. I do remember you, Erik. Sorry to hear about your parents," Lisa greeted them, firmly shaking their hands.

"Thank you Lisa. It means a lot," replied Erik.

"Nice meeting you to," Eddie responded shyly, obviously not comfortable around strangers of the female persuasion.

"Erik, you should probably lock the door as we won't want any interruptions," Randy suggested as he motioned for everyone to follow him. "Let's all go to the backroom and make ourselves comfortable. We have a lot to discuss."

Earlier, Eddie had set up a folding table and chairs on which sat three pizzas, some paper plates, napkins, and a variety of soft drinks.

"Lunch as promised," Lisa said with a slight tilt to her head. "So far you're holding up your end of the bargain."

"Let's eat while we talk," Erik suggested.

"Sounds good, but to streamline this, why doesn't Randy update me on what all is going on here at your end, and then I'll tell you what I know? If Randy leaves something out, you guys can bring it up afterward. Also, any questions should wait until then as well if that's okay with everyone," suggested Lisa.

Everyone nodded their heads in agreement so Randy gave Lisa the rundown on everything Eddie heard and saw as well as what little information he had been able to find out, ending with the ongoing hunt for the elusive doctor. When he was done, Lisa told them everything she had learned about the virus from the scientist and then pulled out the latest reports from the field. She only had time to briefly skim them before coming to the meeting.

"These are the reports on the demographics of those who have been infected. Overall, we are sitting at around 3,800 people infected and almost 600 dead. This is just in Africa and India within the last 72 hours. The infection rate is unprecedented as is the short time frame for deaths to occur. I have found that a wide diversity of ethnic groups have become infected and they all share one common characteristic which is medium to dark skin pigmentation. Now, before we all jump to the conclusion that this is, in fact, a virus created for the genocide of darker skinned people, remember that it just may be that no Caucasians have been exposed yet. It is unlikely, as Africa is about 8% white, but it is possible. I can't conclusively determine that until we have a lot more cases or find someone white who we know was exposed but who did not get sick. I have directed my on-site doctors to get blood samples of any white African citizens who may have been exposed, even if they aren't showing any symptoms yet so that we can test this theory," she concluded.

"So you think the virus might be designed to be active in only medium to dark skinned people instead of a specific nationality?" Erik asked, wanting clarification. "Isn't that impossible?"

"That's my current working theory and I'm not at all sure if it's possible or not. I wouldn't rule it out with all the progress we have made with mapping the human genome. I think it would be easier to make a virus like that versus making many different strains of the virus to complete the same objective," she explained to the group.

"Lisa, do you know anyone at Crouch Pharmaceutical that would be willing to talk to you?" Randy asked. "I keep hitting a brick wall and there isn't very much information available on who their personnel is, even online. I'm trying to figure out who this doctor is because I'd bet you dollars to doughnuts, that he is the one behind this virus."

"I'll check around but I'll have to be discreet. If what we think is happening is really happening, then they won't think twice of taking out anyone who tries to stop them," she replied, concerned for their safety should they learn too much.

Randy picked up a bag up off the floor and tossed it onto the table. "Lisa's right, we have to believe these people are watching for anyone who might be on their trail. I bought burner phones for everyone. Your phone has your name on the outside of the box. I have already activated them and put in everyone's numbers. From here on out, do not use any other landline or cell phone that can be traced back to you. The same goes for online research. It's best to use public WiFi, preferably somewhere busy, and don't stay online more than 30 minutes before logging off and moving to a different location. Also be very careful of who you talk to, trusting someone will be very tricky now as something this big has to have a pretty big group of people involved."

"I be thinking the doctors name be starting with a C, not the K. If you can get a list of doctor's, I be telling you which one they was talking about," Eddie claimed confidently.

"I'll also check around to see if I can find you some names," Lisa told Eddie. "Now if there's nothing else, I have to be getting back to the CDC."

"I believe we have covered everything. Everyone keep in

touch," Randy said, ending the meeting.

DAY FOUR

Latisha

"**W**hat do you mean that one of the subjects isn't sterile? It's been over 48 hours since the injection, so I have no choice but to assume that your testing must have been faulty due to incompetence!" exclaimed Dr. Carter, his cold, black eyes glaring daggers at Skinny.

"We ran the test twice, but we are preparing a new sample to test in case there was some issue with the collection of the original sample," she explained, knowing that he wouldn't care.

"Who ran the tests?" Dr. Carter demanded to know.

"Fred...I mean Chubby did, sir," Latisha replied, despising the nicknames that Dr. Carter had assigned to them.

"I want either you or Blondie to run them this time. Maybe one of you can manage to do a better job than Chubby apparently can," he replied condescendingly.

"Yes sir," she responded, thinking that she would tell Jeff that Dr. Carter specifically requested that he would personally need to rerun the test. That way, she wouldn't get any backlash when they came back with the exact same results.

"Well, at least it appears that you bumbling fools managed to get everything set up for the Booster."

"Everything is set up as per your instructions," she answered dryly.

Dr. Carter approached the first test subject. "Please make

the appropriate notations on the chart. Booster injection of 5 ccs in the subject's left bicep."

"Noted with the time of injection, sir."

They continued the process until all of the test subjects had received the Booster shot while Fred followed behind them and returned each one to their cells.

"Check their vitals every 6 hours and see to it that they are all connected to a heart monitor with the alarm turned on, so we'll know what time each one of them expires," Dr. Carter told her, abruptly turning and leaving the lab.

"I certainly hope I don't have to continue to work for him after the purge is over," Latisha said to Fred.

"Me either," he agreed wholeheartedly.

"When is Jeff supposed to be here?"

"In about an hour. Why?" Fred inquired.

"Dr. Carter is under the impression that we messed up the test on that one man who is still sterile, and he would like Jeff to retest him," Latisha said with a straight face.

"The test isn't wrong, but Dr. Carter won't ever believe that his serum could be the least bit faulty. If Jeff were halfway intelligent, he'd lie and say that the man was sterile to avoid getting his ass chewed out. Then again, I suppose that we could have done the same thing and avoided the entire mess," admitted Fred with a shrug.

Latisha laughed. "True, but you know Jeff won't do that due to it being all about the science for him."

"Better him than me, but I'm still going to suggest it to him. Do you wanna take a break and get some coffee since we're all caught up?" Fred asked.

"Sounds good to me."

Alex

He and Billy had been paying a lot closer attention to the news since the initial outbreak had been announced and today was no exception.

The TV news channel now had a ticker tape scrolling across the bottom of the screen with infection and death numbers, including the locations where they occurred. Alex noticed that the number had increased significantly since the previous night. "Hey Billy? You should probably come and see this."

"What's up?" Billy asked, entering the room.

"The numbers are, and they're still rising. According to the World Health Organization, the latest totals are 250,000 infected with 100,000 dead," Alex replied somberly.

"Anything listed in North or South America yet?"

"Not yet, but it looks like Africa and India are totally fucked. China appears to have a few cases, but knowing them it's under-reported. There are also a few cases reported in Europe, Spain, and France." His eyes widened and his heart sped up slightly at what he was seeing on TV.

"Don't forget the middle east; Iraq, Iran, Turkey, and Syria, all show as having a decent number of cases," remarked Billy as he viewed the map that was presently showing on the screen.

"Yeah man, and this is only after four days," he reminded Billy, his voice starting to crack with emotion.

"Do you still have the WiFi password for the dude downstairs?"

Alex nodded his head. "I believe so. He hasn't ever changed it, so I'd imagine that it will always be *'Ihaveabigdick!'* and his network's name is *'FBI Surveillance Van'*."

Billy laughed. "What a dumb ass. Let's connect my laptop and see if we can find one of those websites that constantly update the virus information. One of the guys at work showed me the website that he was using and it gets updated every 15 minutes. I want to be informed the minute that it hits the US."

"Well I hope to God that they shut down the airlines fast enough that it never gets here," Alex replied wistfully. "I do tend to worry that BB might become exposed while working at the hospital."

"She'll be alright. They are taking all kinds of precautions around anyone who says they aren't feeling well," he responded, hoping to keep his friend from worrying.

"Yeah, I know that you're right, but I simply can't help but worry about her," Alex admitted.

"Dude, you need to grow a pair and ask her out before everyone dies."

"Fuck you man. I don't plan on dying, but I do get your point. It's past time for me to ask her out."

"Past time?" Billy laughed. "Dude, you've been pining after her for so long that I'm surprised she's not already married to someone else."

"The time wasn't ever right," Alex complained, knowing that he was making excuses like a scared little high school student who wanted to ask a girl out for the very first time.

"Whatever you say, lover boy," replied Billy, hoping that Alex would actually ask her out this time.

Lisa

Matt sat listening in rapt attention without interrupting as Lisa explained all the circumstantial evidence that she had gathered so far. The only thing that she had factual information on was that of the updated numbers. There didn't appear to be one person that was showing any symptoms who had light colored skin anywhere in the world. With almost a quarter of a million cases, that was nearly impossible with a normal virus. The tests they had run on the blood samples belonging to the people with light colored skin who had come in close contact with someone infected by the virus, backed up her theory. Showing that the infection was present in the samples yet remained dormant for whatever reason. This was hard evidence that she didn't believe anyone would be able to refute.

"I'll start looking for a marker in the virus related to skin pigmentation. I have no idea what that might be, but maybe someone over at The Human Genome Project might," said

Matt, stunned by Lisa's news.

"Matt, please be careful on who you talk to about this. If whoever designed this horrible virus is willing to kill off most of the world's population, they won't be happy with someone trying to stop them. Also, I have no idea who funded this. It has to have taken billions of dollars and the only person I know who throws around that kind of money is our uncle," she said, with a sinking feeling in her stomach.

"I agree that Sam has been pretty free with our money, but I refuse to believe that he could be behind this. Maybe China or Russia, well probably not China if they are being targeted unless they are somehow being double-crossed," Matt noted, "but I will promise to be careful. I have a friend with who I wrote a thesis with a while back, who works at The Human Genome Project. I trust him and believe that he might be able to help us out on this."

Lisa relaxed some, "Well, alright, but don't talk to him over the phone, no telling who is listening."

"That's not a problem. We occasionally go bowling together when we both have the time. I will act like I want to get together and hang out and then casually ask about a pigmentation gene."

"That should work since that's what he does. Right?" questioned Lisa, not fully convinced.

"I think it will if I do it correctly. He loves to talk about whatever he's working on. I'll let you know what I find out," he promised as he sent his friend a quick text asking to get together later that evening.

"Sounds good. I need to get back to my office for a video conference. Let me know if you make any more headway on the virus."

"Will do," Matt answered as she left his office.

Back at her desk, Lisa logged into the video conference she had scheduled with several of the overseas doctors, finding Paul Samuels, who was in N'Djamena, Chad, already online.

"Hi Paul, glad you could make it," she greeted him with a

smile, attempting to appear as though the world wasn't in dire straights, not quite able to pull it off.

"Hey Lisa. We might have a situation brewing here in Africa, or at least here in Chad. The news is getting out that no one who's white has gotten sick so now they all seem to think that we gave them the virus. Of course, there is no such thing as a nonwhite virus, but that's what the locals here are saying. So far, we've been able to handle the people who are upset by just explaining that there are a lot fewer lighter skinned people here and that, while improbable, it's not impossible for this to occur. I also just got a report that some rebels outside the city are attacking anybody who is light complected. At least one person has already been killed so far," reported Paul.

"Wow, I hadn't heard anything about that. How's security around you?" Lisa responded, electing not to say anything about what they had discovered about the virus. She would bring that up a little later on in the call.

"We only have a couple of police officers here to keep order. If the rebels get into town, they won't be enough to stop them from attacking, especially since one of them is white and will be a target himself."

"It sounds like we may need to get you and anyone else that might be a target out of Africa. I'll send this up the ladder as a priority, hopefully, they can get someone else there to take your place, and then we can bring you home," she said, scribbling down some notes about it on her notepad and then proceeded to draw several circles around it to show it's importance.

"I'd certainly appreciate it," he replied as Albert Durbin out of Luanda, Angola and Hector Gomez, who was currently in Mogadishu, Somalia both came online.

Within thirty seconds, they were joined by Nita, Tim, and Bayron.

"Hi everyone. I know that you all are extremely busy, and these calls are intruding into time that might be utilized to help some of the victims, but it's important that we go over a few items," Lisa began. "First off, Paul just informed me that there's some civil unrest in Chad, regarding the fact that no light complected people have gotten sick from the virus. Has anyone else seen or heard of anything similar happening in your area?"

Albert, Hector, and Bayron all admitted that they had heard a few rumors along the same lines, although no one had personally witnessed anything or knew anyone who had.

"Alright, I am sending a priority message to the big guys to let them know that it's imperative that we get any of our light skinned colleagues out of Africa as quickly as possible," Lisa promised them.

"Next on the list is that all of the evidence is pointing toward a Frankenstein virus, consisting of multiple viruses. I won't go into the virus makeup since I know you all have received the latest file on what we know. What the report doesn't say is that this so called Frankenstein Virus may have been designed to target people of certain skin tones," Lisa paused a moment to prepare herself before continuing. "We have processed all the samples that we've received to date. What we found was that this Frankenstein virus does appear to be targeting people with mid to dark skin complexions. All of the samples that were taken from light skinned patients came back as being infected, but with a dormant version of the same virus, except for one, who came back as not infected. If they are infected, then they're still carriers until their body fights off the virus and clears it out of their system, so they will need to be quarantined until we get a clean blood test back."

"Do we know who designed this?" asked Hector, obviously angry that someone would do this.

"Nothing concrete, and I refuse to speculate on rumors. Rest assured that we are working hard to identify who is behind this. We are not informing the public about this new development yet as we prefer not to cause panic, but it sounds like they are figuring it out for themselves. The official line is that we are still looking into the virus and are unable to confirm or deny those allegations. Of course, that will cause everyone to automatically assume that it's true, but that is the official line that the head honchos want us to take until the government decides how to deal with it.

"I know this is quite a lot of information to take in," Lisa continued, "but we have a job to do, and I know that everyone will do their very best, just as we always do. Please get a list of any light skinned personnel together and send it to me. I will try my damnedest to get them all back home safely within the next 24 hours. Does anybody have any questions or comments?"

Everyone shook their heads, so Lisa told everyone to get back to work and that she would keep them updated, then she signed off.

She sat back in her chair and wondered just how things had gotten so bad, so fast and what the end game was for whoever planned out this genocide.

Matt

The pool hall was dingy and a little dark, which fit Matt's mood pretty well. He was waiting for Robert to show up and was starting to get impatient, although he still another five minutes left before the scheduled meet time. Just as he was about to get up and get something to drink, he saw Robert walk in.

"Robert. Over here." Matt motioned to where he was sitting.

"Good to see you, Matt. You missed our poker get together last week."

"Sorry about that. Work stuff," he explained vaguely.

"Yeah, I gotcha. Wanna beer before I sit down?" Robert asked.

Deciding he might need some liquid courage, he agreed that he would like one.

Robert returned within a few minutes with two mugs of

cold beer that he placed on the table before sitting down across from him.

"Okay, so what's on your mind? You seem a little distracted tonight," he said when Matt failed to reach for the beer and instead completely ignored it as if it didn't exist.

"I just had some things come across my desk and I'm trying to figure them out. You might be able to help me out, that is if you don't mind talking shop after hours."

"If it's not above my pay grade, I don't mind at all. What's the issue?" he inquired.

"It's not really an issue," Matt began, "I'd say it's more of a hypothetical situation at this point."

"Okay, you've piqued my interest, go on."

"Is it possible to separate an individual human gene for a specific genetic feature?" Matt carefully posed the question.

"Do you mean something like eye color?"

"Sure. Eye color, hair color, skin pigmentation, that sort of thing?"

"Theoretically it is, but to be honest with you, it would take a lot of time and effort for someone to determine exactly which gene provides which trait. I suppose that once you had it figured out, you could probably separate it, although I am not sure why you'd want to," Robert explained.

"Oh I personally don't want to, it's just that I saw something in a report and it made me wonder if it could be possible to identify genes with specific characteristics. Let's say that there was a murder and the murderer left some of their DNA at the scene. Could you determine what the suspect might look like by using specific genes of their DNA?" Matt offered as an example, not wanting to reveal the real reason for his interest.

"Wow, wouldn't that cut down on crime?" Robert chuckled. "I would imagine that at some point in the future we will be able to do something along those lines, but it's just not possible right now as far as I know. There have been a decent number of genes that have been identified, concerning singling out specific human characteristics like we were discussing. One of them that I recall off the top of my head, happened back in 2017 when some geneticists identified a few new genetic variants associated with skin pigmentation. I don't know exactly what they are as that is not the area that I personally work in."

"Is there any way that you could find out which genes control skin pigmentation?" Matt cautiously asked, trying not to push too hard.

"I'm not sure. I'll make some calls tomorrow and see what I can find out then get back to you on it," promised Robert.

"I think that would appease my curiosity if you don't mind doing it. How about a game of pool and the loser buys the next round?"

Robert laughed. "You're already buying the next round since I paid for this one, but a game sounds good."

"Excellent!" Matt exclaimed, heading towards an open pool table, feeling a bit more optimistic for the first time in several days. He could barely wait to let Lisa know what he had discovered.

DAY FIVE

Colonel Harker

Col. Harker was getting impatient, not that the calm appearance that he had honed over the years would ever give it away. He had been waiting for almost ten minutes past the scheduled time for a phone call with his latest instructions. Finally, he felt his cell phone vibrate like the thrumming beat of a roller coaster, exciting but terrifying at what unexpected thing would happen next.

"Yes?" he answered the phone.

"Peace, love," came the unknown voice.

"And dinosaurs," responded John, completing the verification sequence.

"Site three."

"Got it!" he replied and quickly disconnected the call.

John hated all the cloak and dagger bullshit. He considered it as being more obvious, but the powers above him tended to think it was a necessary evil.

Site three was a newspaper stand located at a nearby coffee shop. John headed that way on foot since it was so close. Checking his watch as he walked, noting that he would have to hasten his pace as he only had another 35 minutes before he was expected back at the Pentagon.

He was power walking as he approached the drop location. His heartbeat increased slightly as he nonchalantly scoped out the area, scanning for anything that seemed out of place. Not seeing anything or anyone who stood out, John approached the stand and inserted the required coins before opening the door. Reaching up inside, he grabbed the envelope that was taped to the top and immediately tucked it inside a newspaper with practiced ease, like a magician using sleight of hand to hide a playing card during a magic trick.

He didn't dare open the envelope or even look at it until he was safely back in his car. That would defeat the entire purpose of using the clandestine maneuvers that the government was so proud of. Once inside his car, he torn the envelope open and read the brief not inside.

Meet W @1400, site 7

Harker was curious about what Agent Warren had discovered during his investigation as he desperately didn't want to go back to Atlanta. Four days he had spent down there dealing with that insufferable prick scientist, Dr. Carter, who then had the audacity to email him with the news that he might have become infected while in the lab. Seriously? An email? He felt that information should have at least garnered a phone call if not a face to face meeting. The requested blood sample needed for testing was taken just prior to him returning to Washington D.C. and he had no desire to ever return to that God forsaken laboratory.

Randy

He had once again hit a roadblock in his investigation. Partly because he couldn't keep his mind off a certain ex-girl-friend, but mostly due to the fact that he had been unable to discover anything new. He sighed deeply and leaned back in his chair with his eyes closed, thinking.

"Mr. Elkhart?" an upbeat, happy voice sounded beside him.

Randy was jolted out of his thoughts and all but jumped out of his chair. He swiftly spun around and found Sally, the intern, who was researching the personnel of Crouch Pharmaceutical for him, standing by his desk. "Oh hi, Sally. Sorry, you surprised me. Did you have any luck with the search?" he asked, trying to cover up for his overreaction.

She had taken a step back after she, herself, had become startled by Randy's reaction. Realizing that it was more her fault than his, she moved back into place.

"Well, kinda," Sally drawled out the words slowly as if they might turn around and bite her if she said them too fast. "It's sorta weird. I was attempting to check out various websites and track down what I could on that company you asked about, trusting that a link might take me somewhere that would, in turn, link to another site. I call it 'chasing the ghost' because information can be elusive at times. You know that it's there, somewhere, but just aren't able to see it, you know, like a ghost," Sally divulged as she began to bite on her lower lip, hesitant to continue.

"Go on?" Randy encouraged her.

"Well, here's the weird part, the websites kept dropping off the grid. A whole lot of Error 404's. I mean anything and everything having to do with Crouch Pharmaceutical just disappeared, vanished into a nothingness void."

Randy nodded in understanding. "Covering their tracks I would imagine. Well, I appreciate that you tried, these guys always manage to stay one step ahead of us." He felt defeated at this point and slumped down in his seat.

"Oh, I'm not done. I did get the name of the CEO just prior to the sites going offline, a Mr. Bradley S. Crouch." His face lit up like a child seeing fireworks on the Fourth of July. "I always wonder why rich people use their middle initial, do they think it makes them sound more important?" she asked seriously, not noticing Randy's reaction to her statement.

Randy just stared with his eyes wide open and mouth agape, waiting impatiently for her to carry on with the report of her findings.

Noticing his facial expression, she understood that she

had veered off the subject a little bit. "Oh sorry, off-topic, anyway I tried searching for Mr. I'm Better Than You and the same thing happened, Error 404's popping up everywhere. Then I said to myself, self, where else would a good investigative reporter source out information? Then I thought of the library since, you know, they keep old records and stuff there. As I was about to leave to check their archives, it dawned on me that another good source was newspapers. Well, since we are working for a newspaper, I searched the records here, and what did I uncover, you might ask?" the intern teased, knowing that he was hanging on her every word.

"I'll bite. What did you find?" he asked, attempting not to get his hopes up but failing miserably.

"This!" with a flourish, she pulled a sheet of paper from her back pocket and handed it to Randy. It appeared to be a photocopy of a picture.

Randy studied the photo intently and saw that it had been taken at the groundbreaking ceremony of Crouch Pharmaceutical's lab facilities, almost 20 years prior. A man in a suit was sticking a shovel in the ground, while another man, who was wearing a lab coat, was standing beside him. He was observing the incident, yet appeared disinterested, as if he had somewhere else he'd rather be. There was a group of people standing in a group behind them, watching the event, their faces forever captured in an expression of permanent cheerfulness. Directly beneath the photo, a caption read, 'Breaking ground on the new 15 million dollar Crouch Pharmaceutical labs is CEO Bradley S. Crouch and lead scientist, Dr. Jeremy Carter.'

"I know everyone in the picture isn't listed, but I think that it's a start," she said, already anticipating that this wouldn't be enough.

"Sally, I could kiss you. This is great!" exclaimed Randy, while Sally beamed with pride at the words. "I think this Dr. Carter might be the doctor who I was searching for. I can't believe that you found this. Impressed doesn't quite cover it, you just made my day!"

"Glad I could help," she replied honestly, standing just a little bit taller, filled with pride.

"You're the best and if I ever need anything else, I'll let you know. You just became my go-to person for any and all research that I may need. Right now though, I have to go chat with some people about this doctor," he told her, preparing to leave. He needed Eddie to confirm that this was, in fact, the correct doctor.

Randy made good time returning to the dry cleaners. "Hi Erik, is Eddie around?" he asked, strolling through the doorway.

Erik glanced up from what appeared to be a pile of receipts. "Hey Randy. He's probably out in the van. Just head on back, you know the way." He motioned towards the back room.

"Thanks! I might finally have some good news to share. I'm pretty confident that I know who the doctor is, but I need positive verification from Eddie that it's the correct doctor," he explained as he walked through the building with a newfound spring in his step.

"That's great news!" Erik stated as he clasped his hands together. "Let me know once Eddie confirms it and then we can figure out where to go from here."

He nodded as he wondered where that might lead them. "I'll do that."

Randy found Eddie sitting with his eyes closed, in the open sliding door of the delivery van. Appearing to be just enjoying the beauty of the day while soaking up the sunshine. "Hey Eddie."

The man's face lit up with a huge, beaming smile when he saw Randy. He didn't often get visitors, so he was pleased when someone bothered to stop by. "Randy! Hows you be?"

He shook Eddie's hand firmly. "I'm doing good, but I'm hoping to be even better in a minute," he said cryptically. "I have a name for you and need to see if you recognize it."

"Sure thing. I be remembering," he responded confidently.

"Does the name Dr. Carter ring a bell?"

Eddie didn't hesitate, almost shouting in response, "That's him Randy! I be sure it be him."

"That's awesome Eddie. That gets us another step closer, now I just need to figure out a way to get to him," Randy lamented.

Alex

He and Billy had stayed close to home since the government had mandated, earlier that day, that they couldn't return to work as their jobs weren't considered essential. They had spent the time organizing their supplies, reading up on what happened during the COVID-19 pandemic, and watching the news.

"So, what's the plan if the rioting gets too bad?" asked Alex, after they had finished watching a documentary about the riots in 2020 and 2021.

"Not sure, but we definitely need to get out of Dallas," admitted Billy, pulling up a map of Colorado on his laptop. "I was thinking that we should head for the mountains in southern Colorado. We'll have to figure out someplace where there won't be too many people. Most likely a national park or something similar." He zoomed in on the map. "It looks like there's the Rio Grande National Forest or perhaps the San Isabel National Forest might even be better as it's a little closer and easier to get to from here."

Alex scrunched up his face in thought, "Isn't Cheyenne Mountain near the San Isabel National Forest or am I remembering that wrong?"

"Umm, it looks like it's on the south side of it, but I thought that we might want to go northwest of Colorado Springs. We don't want to be close to Cheyenne Mountain, do we?" Billy was apparently thinking that a military base might either be a target for marauding gangs or possibly become overcrowded with civilians who had no place else to go.

"We'd probably be alright. You have to remember that NORAD isn't there anymore. It's a Space Force base now and I believe that they still have a defensive bunker so we might at least consider it, although I'm not entirely sure that I want the government to control every aspect of my life. Then again, would that be a fair trade-off for them to keep us safe?"

Billy thought for a minute and then conceded, "Okay, we'll plan on going to the Cheyenne Mountain Military Complex as our primary until we can check it out, and can keep the San Isabel National Forest as a backup. I'll do some research for possible locations that we might be able to use, should we end up in the forest. We need to dig out our camping gear and get it loaded in the Blazer along with some other supplies in case we need to bug out of the city in a hurry. I bought some dark window tint for the windows in the back of the Blazer so people won't be able to see the supplies. If you'll help me install it today, we can get it packed up with a bunch of stuff and have it ready to go. We can't really put anything in your pickup until we are almost ready to leave or it might get stolen."

"I'd be happy to help. It beats sitting around here doing nothing. If we have to go anywhere in the meantime, we can use my pickup," suggested Alex, standing up and preparing to gather the needed materials for the window tinting project.

He and Billy spent the next couple of hours installing the window tint on the Blazer. It had turned out to be a bigger job than they had anticipated. Since the vehicle was older, it had quite a bit of grime built up around the window edges that had to be cleaned off, and that was taking them some time. They were just starting the last window when BB pulled into a parking spot nearby.

"Hi guys," she greeted them as she got out of her Honda.

"Hey BB. You're looking good today," Alex commented as his heart rate increased at the sight of her.

"Why thank you Alex, you're much too kind," BB said,

batting her eyes and hamming it up. "Nice job on the tint. Probably a good idea to help keep people from seeing what's inside."

Billy sprayed the soapy solution on the window as Alex pulled the protective plastic off the film. "That was the idea. I figured that we could fill it up with supplies in case we need to leave in a hurry," he replied, helping Alex place the film onto the soapy window and then wiggling it into position.

"If it gets that bad, I'll come with you guys. Of course, that would all depend on if I'm able to leave work. I'm considered an essential worker so it might be kinda hard to leave the city during the middle of a pandemic," she explained, watching the men work at removing the bubbles out from underneath the film with a squeegee.

"That's a valid concern," Alex allowed. "Let's just play it by ear for now, but I'm warning you now that if it gets too dangerous, you're coming with us regardless of what they say, even if I have to kidnap you," he told her, looking straight into her eyes and leaving zero room for argument.

She nodded her head in agreement as she watched Billy use the small utility knife to trim the film from around the window edges. "You're not going to hear me disagree with you on that. If they start rioting at the hospital, all bets are off and I'm out of there. No job is worth my life."

"Have you heard anything new at the hospital regarding the virus?" questioned Billy as he inspected their work, appearing to be satisfied with the results.

"Yeah, unfortunately it's not good news." BB's mood became a bit gloomier. "The total number of infected is now over two million. It's in multiple countries in South America and a few places in Canada so it will most likely be in the US soon if it's not already. They posted a report to all medical staff in the US from the CDC. The information is supposed to be confidential and restricted to medical staff only, but at this point, I really don't care. Besides, everyone's going to figure it out soon enough anyway," she paused to get her thoughts to line up in the correct order. "They're now calling it the Frankenstein

Virus. It's apparently man-made and contains parts of several other viruses like the flu, rabies, and hemorrhagic fever, hence the name change. The scary part is that while everyone can be infected, it only becomes an active virus in people with darker skin tones."

"Wait, what?" Billy said, shaking his head, confused and assuming that he must have misheard her.

"Basically, if you're Caucasian, you won't get sick from the virus, but you still become a carrier and can pass it on to others," she explained, knowing how unbelievable it sounded.

"Are you telling us that some asshole made this virus?" Alex asked in shock and disbelief.

"That's what the CDC is telling medical staff across the country, which is why they don't want the public to know. It would cause panic and possible race riots against whites. We have to wear hazmat suits around any infected patients and put them in isolation, not that it does much good. The virus is airborne, so nothing is going to stop it except for a cure, or a vaccine, neither of which will be discovered in time to do any good. Look at the COVID vaccine, it took a year, and that was fast-tracking it."

By now the guys were sitting on the back of the Blazer, listening intently to what she was telling them.

"They are finally restricting travel which I think they should have done sooner," she continued, "all international flights have been grounded worldwide except for government, medical flights, and relief work. Most domestic flights in the US have also been grounded. Countries around the world have closed their borders and many are shooting anyone who tries to cross. As I was leaving the hospital, I heard that masks are going to be required for everyone starting tomorrow. Since you're not at work, I assume that you already know about the stay at home order and that all nonessential businesses, as well as schools, are closed until further notice. You know, it's probably a good thing you guys stocked up when you did," admitted BB, thinking back to the crazy trip to the store a few nights before.

Billy shook his head in disbelief. "I'm not happy to be right about that, but it sounds like it could still get a lot worse before it gets any better."

"Especially in big cities," Alex nodded, agreeing with his friend.

"Well, on that somber note, I'm going to go take a shower and get out of these scrubs," BB informed the two men.

"We're done with the windows and just have to clean up," announced Billy, waving his arm towards the mess they had made.

"May I walk you to your door while Billy cleans up?" Alex asked BB, grinning mischievously.

"Why certainly kind sir and way to get out of cleaning up," BB complimented him as she smiled and accepted Alex's offered arm.

"BB, we've known each other for quite a while now and I've wasted a lot of time thinking that I wasn't good enough for you before finally realizing that just wasn't true. What I'm trying to say is that I've wanted to ask you out for the longest time, but was too big of a chicken shit. Well crap, this isn't going well," Alex admitted as they walked towards the stairs, dropping his head in disgust while thinking that he had blown his chance.

She stopped and turned toward Alex. "Just ask me," she said matter of factly.

Staring into BB's bright blue eyes, Alex got weak-kneed, before he could lose his nerve, he blurted out, "BB, will you go on a date with me?"

"Yes, Alex, I would be happy to go on a date with you, and it's about damn time you asked me, I've been waiting forever for you to get around to it. I was almost ready to give up," she said slyly.

"Really?" Alex's eyes widened at the revelation.

"Yes really. Now you have to make up for lost time and take me somewhere nice before I come to my senses," she joked, playfully punching him in the arm.

"I feel like an idiot," he admitted. "How's the day after to-morrow work for you? I'll make some reservations at that new place downtown and then we can go to a movie."

"Alex, I was joking about taking me somewhere nice. That place you're talking about is really expensive, and hon-estly, I'd be just as happy eating at the Burger Barn."

He grinned, "No can do. I want to take you somewhere nice on our first date. Burger Barn will have to wait until our second date."

"Wow! You're assuming a lot there mister," she said, lightly slapping his chest with her hand. "Day after tomorrow works for me, but you seem to have forgotten one tiny little detail."

"What did I forget?" he asked, completely confused.

She raised one eyebrow and grinned at him. "It's a simple little oversight. All the restaurants and theaters are currently closed due to the pandemic, but I'm sure that you can come up with a suitable alternative."

"Umm yeah, I'm sure that I can," he replied, not having a clue about what he was going to do.

They walked, arm in arm, up the stairs to their apart-ments, stopping in front of hers. "Well, here we are, safe and sound, at your front door."

"Thank you Alex," BB said, lightly kissing him on the cheek before unlocking her door and going inside without turning around to gauge his response.

Alex had a spring in his step and a grin on his face as he went across the landing and entered his own apartment. He had to try and figure out how he could salvage his date with BB.

"Stupid pandemic anyway," he muttered to himself, tossing his keys onto the table in annoyance.

Lisa

Lisa had spent the entire morning organizing the flight

arrangements to get her team out of Africa. Airports were closed around the globe so locating somewhere that they could land to pick up everyone had been a difficult task, but she had completed it. They would all be on their way home by this evening.

Now she was calling each location to inform them of the time and place that they would be meeting the plane. Lisa was relieved she had been able to contact everyone as she dialed the last number on her list, but of course, there was no answer. Paul must be busy, she decided, before sending an email to him requesting that he return her call as soon as possible. She would try to call again in an hour if he hadn't responded by then.

She was debating on going to see Matt, when he saved her the trip by knocking on the frame of her open office door. "Hi Matt, I was just getting ready to come to see if you had found anything out from your friend last night."

Matt closed the door and then sat down. He took a deep breath in an effort to calm his nerves. "I'm afraid that it's true. Some virologist back in 2017 found a skin pigment gene. My friend, Robert, just got back to me and sent me a file that shows exactly which gene it is. Hopefully, with this information, I can link it to the virus, and that will at least give me a starting point on how to defeat it."

"It's what we expected so I don't understand why I'm surprised," she said as she tossed her pen on the desk and leaned back in the chair. "I'm disappointed in the human race for allowing an individual to assume that it's alright to kill billions of people. For whatever reason, that's the hand that we've been dealt." Lisa sighed. "I just can't believe this is all real. It sounds like a terrible plot from a badly written book."

Matt was about to say something when Lisa's throwaway phone began to ring.

"Hello?" she answered absentmindedly as her brain was still focused on what Matt had just revealed to her.

"This is R, don't use names just in case. Found out our

elusive doctor's name. I'll text it to you, it's the first letter of each word."

"Umm okay, I'll wait for your text." Then the phone went dead.

"What was that about?" Matt inquired, just as the phone beeped.

She stared at him in an internal debate on whether she should involve her friend any further or not before shrugging her shoulders. "That was Randy, informing me that I would be receiving a text message in a basic code."

She looked at the text message and then read it out loud. "Just eat Ramen every Monday. You can, after Robert tickles every rabbit."

Matt looked confused. "What's that supposed to be code for?"

"Well, let's see what we have as she jotted letters down on a pad of paper. The first letter of every word, J-E-R-E-M-Y-C-A-R-T-E-R spells out Jeremy Carter, that's the name of the scientist who we think designed the Frankenstein virus. Ever hear of him?" she asked, wishing for an easy answer for once.

"No," he said, shaking his head, "how about you?"

"Nope but we need to find him if we want a chance to stop this thing anytime soon," stated Lisa as her office phone rang.

"Lisa Johnson, how may I help you?"

"Lisa, this is Albert Durbin in Angola," an anxious and obviously upset voice replied.

"Hey Albert. Shouldn't you be packing?" she asked absentmindedly, her mind still focused on the doctor.

"Already finished that. The reason that I am calling is that I just got off the phone with one of the doctors over in Chad, and well, there's no easy way to say this, both Paul and one of our nurses were killed by some rebels who stormed the hospital and shot every white person they saw."

Lisa felt the blood drain from her body as tears formed in her eyes. "Oh my God! Are you sure?"

"Sure as I can be without actually seeing his body. I thought you should know. I'm heading to the airport with my group of people who can't stay here. I requested that they take the bodies to the airport so we can at least bring them home," he told her somberly.

"Thank you for letting me know Albert. I'll make sure his wife is informed as well. Please be careful and I'll see you when you land," she told him, wiping her tears away with the back of her hand.

"I will. Goodbye," Albert said, ending the call.

Matt was concerned for Lisa since he had just watched her skin tone go from a healthy glow to a pale shade of death in a matter of seconds. "Now what's happened?"

"Paul Samuels is dead. He was shot and killed by rebels who are under the impression that white people are spreading the virus in order to kill everyone else. One of the nurses was also killed, but I don't know who yet. Damn it! I should have gotten them out sooner!" she complained, feeling her blood begin to boil in anger like a volcano preparing to erupt.

He leaned across the desk and took her hand into his. "Lisa, you are not to blame for what happened. You did the best that you or anyone else could have done under these extremely difficult circumstances."

"I know, but it's still not fair. He was there to help," she cried in despair, her frustration showing through.

"Come on, let's go for a walk. You need to get out of here and get some fresh air to clear your head. We'll let everyone know about the situation, one of them can make the arrangements to pick up the bodies at the airport and let Paul's wife know what happened."

Lisa smiled grimly as she stood up, "You're right. Let's let everyone know and then get out of this building for a while."

Colonel Harker

As he walked up to the Washington Monument, Col.

Harker surreptitiously looked around to make sure that he hadn't been followed, all seemed well. He located his contact from the NSA, Agent Warren, waiting outside the monument entrance. When the agent noticed Harker approaching, he turned and started to slowly walk away from the monument. His speed was such that the colonel could easily catch up, but at the same time, not appear as if he had been waiting for him.

"Colonel, nice day for a walk," the tall, muscular agent offered as he caught up to him.

"Agent Warren, I anticipate that you're bringing me good news for once," Harker replied, slowing his pace to match that of the agent.

He shook his head slightly. "Not so much. It appears that we might have a reporter digging for information where he shouldn't be. He was flagged by the NSA when he used a few keywords in a phone conversation a couple of days ago with another reporter down in Mexico City. He has also been in contact with someone at the CDC, although we're not exactly sure who."

Harker sighed. "Damn. Guess you need to go to Mexico City and find out what that reporter knows, if anything."

"What about the reporter in Atlanta?"

He shook his head while thinking that he was getting too damn old for this crap. "For now, tap his phone and bug his house and car. Let's see if we can discover who he has been talking to and if he knows anything or if he is just chasing ghosts. I'd prefer not to take out American citizens if we can help it, if he's getting too close, you may have to deal with him when you get back in the country," directed Harker.

"And what of the Mexican reporter?" the agent asked, wanting to know just how far he would be allowed to go.

"Make your own decision when you talk to him. He'll probably be dead in a week anyway, but if he knows something, why take the chance?"

"I should be back in a couple of days. I'll let you know how it goes and update you on the status of the Atlanta reporter."

"Agreed," Harker said, increasing his pace and leaving Agent Warren behind.

DAY SIX

Agent Warren

Agent Warren had flown to McAllen, Texas, along the border of Mexico. The Mexican government wasn't allowing anyone to fly in from another country, but they continued to allow people to cross the border in vehicles for some unknown reason.

The local NSA office provided him with a vehicle, a black SUV with dark tinted windows (the apparent standard for government agents regardless of the agency). He drove across the border and into Mexico before searching for the closest airport. He planned to pay someone to fly him to Mexico City otherwise, it would be a 13 hour drive.

He managed to locate a small airport about 20 miles away and quickly made a deal with a pilot. The man agreed to fly him to Mexico City and back with no name or questions asked, as long as he completed his business and returned to the airport within 12 hours of landing. It cost more than he liked, but money wouldn't matter to anyone much longer if things played out the way that The Core had planned.

Climbing aboard the small plane, suspecting that it was probably used more often for transporting drugs than passengers, he settled in for the flight.

Agent Warren had been with The Elite Group for over five years now. Initially, he just funneled information to them or deleted anything related to The Core or The Elite Group from the NSA servers. After his promotion to field agent, his responsibilities to The Elite Group had also changed. Now he was more of an enforcer that they used when a member stepped out of line, said something they shouldn't have, or attempted to leave The Elite Group altogether. Normally, a stern talking to, along with veiled threats, tended to send the offending party back onto the right path, but occasionally broken bones became involved. He had to completely remove two targets who had remained non-compliant after both the verbal and the physical warnings had been given. He didn't particularly enjoy that part of the job but felt that he didn't have a choice or he would most likely become a target himself.

As he leaned back in his seat, he began to run through the mental notes that he had about Raul Hernandez in his head. A news reporter for a local Mexico City TV station, he was married for twenty-two years with two grown children, one of whom was also married and had given him a grandchild. Neither of the children currently lived with him and his wife, although they occasionally babysat their granddaughter.

Agent Warren decided to call Raul when the plane landed and see if he would agree to a meeting. He would suggest that he had some information on the virus and was working with the Atlanta reporter. That should bring out the reporter in him and get him to consent to the get-together. He would play it by ear from there.

With a thin plan in place, Agent Warren slept peacefully the rest of the flight.

The plane landed with an initial jarring bounce, which woke up the agent, followed by two more bounces before smoothing out as the plane rapidly decreased speed.

He quickly exited the plane once it had taxied to a stop and went to the car rental office housed within the airport terminal. He rented a nondescript car under the name William James, an alias he had made for just this type of situation.

Leaving the airport, he located a store that sold disposable phones and quickly bought one.

Back in the car, he called Raul, using the untraceable phone he had just purchased.

"Hola?"

"Mr. Hernandez?" he asked.

"Yes, this is Mr. Hernandez. Who is this?"

"Hi Mr. Hernandez. I'm sorry to bother you, but my name is William James, and we have a mutual acquaintance, Randy Elkhart. He asked me to talk to you about this African virus thing that's going around. He thought you might have some insights or might perhaps be interested in co-writing a story," Agent Warren explained.

"How do you know Randy?" asked Raul, not fully buying the story.

"He dated my sister briefly and we hit it off. I work for the US government and sometimes give him information for a story he couldn't otherwise get. Occasionally, I'll help investigate a story that he's working on, which is what I'm doing now."

"Alright. I'm listening."

"I'd rather do this in person. I don't believe that it is something we should discuss on an open phone line. Would it be possible to meet somewhere? You pick the place."

The line was quiet for a moment. "Okay, I'll meet with you. Do you know where the National Museum of Anthropology is?"

"No, but I'm sure I can find it. How will I recognize you?"

"Meet me by the entrance in one hour. I will be wearing a blue shirt and a red hat. If you're late by even one minute, I will leave," Raul stated.

"I'll be there." The agent disconnected the call and wondered if he hadn't messed up by saying that he knew Randy. One phone call from Raul and the gig would be up. Oh well, too late to worry about it now. He had other things to worry about, like finding the museum.

Little did he know, at that exact moment, Raul was calling Randy, who unfortunately was preoccupied and failed to hear the phone ring. Raul left a quick message and then informed his wife where he was going and who he was planning to meet before leaving to meet the mysterious William James.

Agent Warren was at the museum 10 minutes early. He decided to stake out the place to make sure that Raul hadn't called for backup. After a few minutes, he saw Raul walking towards the museum entrance, nothing appeared suspicious or out of the ordinary. The agent noticed that Raul was also watching for him or possibly others that might be with him.

He got out of the rental car and headed directly towards Raul, making sure to act casual.

"Mr. Hernandez?" he asked with a friendly smile on his face.

"You must be Mr. James," Raul replied, shaking the offered hand.

"I am, and please call me William. Thank you for meeting with me, are we doing this inside?" he asked, nodding toward the museum's entrance.

"We can walk the grounds. Less chance of someone overhearing," Raul responded as he turned and walked away.

Agent Warren quickly caught up to him. "Randy said he had talked to you about the virus."

"He did briefly," admitted Raul, "he was wanting to know about the alleged case here in Mexico City. I told him that it was a false alarm, just some doctor overreacting. What's your interest in all this?"

"Well, to be honest, I'm not entirely sure. Randy asked me to come down here and check into the virus. Maybe he thinks the virus is here, but that someone might be covering it up," Agent Warren bluffed. "Do you think that's possible?"

"I don't know why anyone would hide it, but I suppose it could be possible. I know nothing about this virus other than what you can see on the news. I'm sorry, but I really can't help you any further," he told the man.

The agent realized that Raul was being honest with him

and didn't know anything. "Well, I guess this is a bust then. Do you know what hospital the virus patient was supposed to be at? Maybe I can get some information from there."

"Yes. It was Hospital De Jesus."

"Thank you for your help. This is my rental car," he said, approaching the spot where he had parked. "Randy doesn't usually give me much information on a story so that it won't affect my investigation. It would have been helpful to at least have a starting point of what he thought might be going on," Agent Warren replied, unlocking the door and opening it, prepared to leave.

"He did mention that he had heard a rumor that it might be designed to target certain races if that helps you any," offered Raul, trying to be helpful.

Agent Warren turned around to face Raul while glancing around for potential witnesses. No one was paying attention. "Really? I wouldn't think that could be possible, but I guess I can check into it. Thanks again for all your help," he said, offering his hand while surreptitiously removing his knife from its sheath with the other.

"No problem, not that I really helped any," Raul chuckled as he reached out to shake hands with the American.

"You've helped more than you could possibly know."

Agent Warren pulled Raul closer to him as they shook hands and deftly stabbed him in a kidney, causing Raul's body to lock up momentarily in shock. Twisting the knife as he pulled it out, he turned Raul around and shoved him backward into the car as he sliced his throat in the same movement. Quickly shoving him over to the passenger side, he got in and calmly drove off in the direction of the airport while Raul slowly bled out and died in the seat beside him.

He parked approximately half a mile away from the airport in a rundown area of warehouses that appeared to have been abandoned years ago. Siphoning some gasoline out of the tank by using a piece of hose he carried in his briefcase for just this purpose, he poured the gasoline into and onto the car, making sure to drench Raul's body thoroughly to help prevent an immediate identification once he was found. Agent Warren lit a match and tossed it through an open window.

Whoosh! The fireball blazed intensely for a moment before calming down to a small raging inferno as Agent Warren turned and casually walked away, heading towards the airport.

As he walked, he thought about the fact that Raul would still be alive had he not offered that last bit of information. Shaking his head, he put it out of his mind and wondered just how much Randy Elkhart knew, and more importantly, who else had he talked to about it.

Next stop, Atlanta.

Alex

"Hey man. I don't know how much more we can fit in the Blazer," Alex said, trying to find room for a box of medical supplies.

"Yeah, I think that's about it. We'll have to put the rest in your truck when it's time to leave," Billy agreed, shifting a couple of boxes around to make room for the one Alex was holding.

"About that, I'm not leaving without BB." Alex stared at Billy, almost daring him to argue.

Billy laughed as he clapped his friend on the back. "I didn't think you would so don't worry about it, we won't leave until she wants to."

"Thanks man, I thought I might have to fight you on that," he admitted, relieved that his friend understood.

They walked back upstairs to their apartment. Looking around at what was left, they knew that they would have to leave some of it behind.

"Let's prioritize this stuff. We already pretty much split everything in half so if we end up losing a vehicle, we'll still have food, water, medicine, a tent, and clothing. I think we can leave some of the food and clothes behind, but I want to take the rest of the water and medicine," Alex decided as he mentally began separating the supplies.

"Sounds good dude. Let's leave it for now since we can't put it in your truck yet anyway. What else do you want to do to the apartment for security?" Billy asked, leaning against the door jamb.

"I'm not sure. I'd like to find a way to block the stairs off since it's just BB and us that use it, but I have no idea how," admitted Alex.

"Me either. Plus we don't want to make it hard for us to load the truck. I'm not sure how BB would like it if we made her climb a ladder up to her balcony because we blocked the stairs," Billy replied with a smirk on his face.

Alex sat down on the couch and threw his hands in the air in defeat. "Okay, you're right. I guess we'll put that one on the back burner for now. So the basic plan is to hang out in the apartment until shit starts getting crazy, then BB will stay with us, and we'll block the front door with the refrigerator until it's time to leave the city?"

"Don't forget that we also have the guns as a backup. I just don't want to shoot anyone if I can help it," Billy admitted. Murder wasn't one of the things on his bucket list. "Luckily we're on the second floor, and there's no convenient way to get in through the windows or up on the balcony unless they use a ladder. The front door is the only easily accessible entrance," Billy deduced after eliminating the other options, "as long as we block that, we should be alright."

"That's true. Let's get the guns and make sure that they are clean and loaded. We should also check the internet and see if the virus has made it to the US yet. It was in Canada last night," he reminded Billy somberly.

While Alex went to get the guns, Billy quickly booted up his laptop and logged on. Bringing up the website that was tracking the spread of the virus, he stared at the screen in disbelief. The map of the United States looked as if it had Chicken Pox. It was pockmarked with dots of red, denoting confirmed cases of the virus. He noticed that Dallas had a red dot of its very own. Glancing down at the worldwide, infected case counter, he saw the total was now exceeding 16 million, and the death counter was just above 3 million.

"Hey man, what's wrong? You're looking a little pale," noted Alex as he walked up behind Billy's chair. Glancing down at the screen, he saw the same information that his friend was still trying to make sense of, and it made his blood run cold.

"Dude, these numbers can't be right, can they?" Billy almost whispered, his eyes widened in shock at the massive increase of reported cases.

Alex pulled up a chair beside Billy and sat down heavily as he started reviewing the information displayed on the screen. His gut began churning, the feeling in the pit of his stomach was the same sensation that he had back in first grade, when Mrs. Lix had forced him to stand up and read in front of the entire class. He ended up vomiting all over little Suzy Reynolds' desk as well as the poor girl herself. Terrified just didn't quite cover it. "I'm not sure," he finally uttered. "Wasn't it only at two million yesterday?"

"Yeah, and did you see that Dallas is showing red now?" Billy hovered the mouse over the red dot on Dallas, causing a small pop-up window to open up. It showed six infected and no deaths locally.

"Well that's not good," Alex stated unnecessarily, suddenly worried for BB's safety.

"No dude, it's definitely not. We don't leave the apartment from this point forward until we're ready to leave the city. You need to call BB and make sure that she knows to come directly here after work. Try and find out if there are any cases at her hospital." Billy had gone into command mode. He had always been good under pressure and preferred to take the lead. Alex tended to be more of a follower unless his loved ones were being threatened, and then all bets were off.

"On it," said Alex, hitting the speed dial for BB's cell phone. Realizing that she was probably with a patient, he wasn't surprised when the call went to her voice mail. "Hey BB, it's Alex. Give me a call as soon as you can. It's important." Setting his phone down, he looked over at Billy. "I need to convince BB that we have to leave and try to outrun this thing."

Billy closed his eyes while he absentmindedly rubbed his neck before he finally looked at his best friend. "At this point, Alex, I'm not sure it's even possible to outrun it."

They both felt numb after that revelation and without discussing it, they started cleaning their guns in silence. Each deep in thought, contemplating what this latest news might mean for them and those who they cared about.

About ten minutes later, Alex's phone rang, and he almost dropped his pistol trying to answer it. Glancing at the caller ID, he saw that it was BB. "Hey BB. Thanks for calling me back."

"Well, you did say it was important, so what's up?" Alex noted that her voice sounded tired, but not stressed.

"The latest infection count, it's over 16 million, and there are six reported cases here in Dallas. Are any of those at your hospital?" he asked, almost scared to hear the answer.

"Damn, it's spreading faster than I thought. No cases here yet, but they have locked down the hospital. Anyone who wants in has to call from their car and wait for a hazmat team to come out and get them. I'm not sure when I can leave since we are on lockdown, but it should be no later than tomorrow," she replied, not sounding overly concerned.

"Well, that's good news then, except for the part about you having to stay there. Promise me that you'll keep us posted and call if you need me to come and get you." Alex was feeling a lot better now that he had heard her voice.

"Alright, I will, but I need to go for now. I have patients to see, but I'll call you later," she promised him.

"Talk to you soon," Alex replied as the line disconnected.

He quickly relayed to Billy what BB had told him.

"I'm gonna turn on the local news and see what they are saying," he informed Alex as he picked up the remote.

"...cases here in the Dallas/Fort Worth area. CDC officials have informed us that they have renamed the virus, it is now being called the Frankenstein Virus. When asked about the name change, the media was informed that the virus is man-made and consists of several other viruses including influenza, rabies, and hemorrhagic fever. Further testing is required to verify what else might be contained within the virus and who may have created it. The CDC is recommending that everyone stay home unless absolutely necessary. Face masks should be worn any time you leave your house. Non-essential businesses should close and contact with others avoided at all costs. It is estimated that the entire world's population will have been exposed to the Frankenstein Virus over the next few days. At that point, the virus should start dying off. In other news, riots have broken out in Washington D.C., Los Angeles, Seattle, Philadel..."

Billy muted the TV and looked at his best friend. "We are so fucked."

Alex simply nodded in agreement, there was nothing else to say.

Lisa

The decision had been made earlier in the day to release the information that the Frankenstein Virus was man-made. The World Health Organization was forcing their hand, stating that they were going to do a press release, informing the public that the virus wasn't a product of mother nature. They spent a long time debating with WHO on telling the media that it was also designed to target anyone without a light skin tone and ultimately won a stay of execution on that argument, at least temporarily. The WHO would review that decision with the CDC again tomorrow.

Although she understood why they wanted to keep it a secret, she knew they would have to say something soon. Once people figured it out on their own, it would be too late, and the public would turn against the CDC and the government for lying to them.

She had been disappointed to learn that the plane bringing her coworkers home had gotten delayed last night due to a mechanical issue. Lisa had received an update an hour ago and was told that it should be taking off soon.

Lisa went back over the reports and was just flabbergasted at the quickly rising numbers. Matt had explained that in three or four days, there would be no one left to infect. This would force the virus to begin burning out, which he estimated, might take a week or two.

Matt had been working furiously along with other virologists, biologists, and many other scientists, trying to come up with some way to treat the virus. Lisa knew that even if they found something, there was no time to manufacture and distribute a vaccine.

She had also gotten an email from Tim Owens, who was still in India, letting her know that many members of the response teams were getting sick with the virus. Nita wasn't expected to live out the day.

"Enough of this!" Lisa declared to herself, slamming the file down on top of the desk. "Time for some fresh coffee to reboot my brain."

She went to the break room where she saw several other people who had zombie-like expressions on their faces. Slack features with dark rings under the eyes that were slightly glazed over from the lack of sleep and too much coffee. Lisa imagined that their expressions most likely matched the one on her own face. "Well at least we're all in this together," she muttered to herself.

Pouring herself a fresh cup of coffee, she decided to go back to her office and call Randy. Maybe he had some good news, Lord knows she needed some right now.

"R here."

"Hey R, it's L. I'm just calling to check-in," she told him.

"Hey L. I saw a news report about the Frankenstein Virus. It would seem as if they left some pertinent information out of their report," he said as he let the statement trail off.

"Yes they did," she admitted. "I voted for releasing that information, but the higher-ups decided otherwise. There wasn't anything I could do about it. Please tell me you have some good news for me because this has been a downer of a day so far."

"Not really, I've tried every trick in the book that I could think of, and I can't figure out a way to gain access to this doctor. At this point, I'm not even convinced that he's still in Atlanta. He may be at a completely different facility altogether."

"Well, at least it's not bad news so that's an improvement anyway," Lisa conceded, trying to find a silver lining anywhere she could.

"Oh so we're going for the whole, no news is good news, theory?" he asked chuckling.

"Heck yeah. I'll take anything at this point," she revealed, taking another sip of coffee.

"Let me take you to lunch and get your mind off work for a while," Randy suggested.

Lisa hesitated, her mind flashing back to the past before deciding that she needed the break. "Alright, pick me up out front in 20 minutes, but I do have one rule, no more bad news."

"That, I can do," declared Randy, both surprised and pleased that she had agreed.

Twenty minutes later, he pulled up in front of the CDC. A few minutes later, Lisa strolled out of the building, her long blonde hair glinting in the sunlight as it blew in the breeze.

Randy got out of his car and went around to open the passenger door, trying not to openly ogle her.

"I had forgotten that you always did that for me," Lisa said, smiling as she got into the car.

"And I always will," Randy affirmed before closing the door and walking back around before getting into the driver's seat.

"How about that hole-in-the-wall place that serves burgers with those huge baskets of onion rings?" he suggested, before explaining, "I called to make sure they were going to be open. They told me that they refuse to close unless Martial Law is declared. During COVID, they almost couldn't afford to re-open due to the shutdown, and they weren't going to take that chance this time."

"That sounds good. They always have the best onion rings," she agreed, pleased that he remembered how much she liked the place. "I don't blame them for not closing. A lot of small businesses ended up closing permanently back then."

The short drive was filled with the easy flowing small talk of long time friends, and Lisa was actually a little disappointed when they arrived at the restaurant.

As Randy parked the car, Lisa suggested, "No phones?"

"Absolutely," Randy readily agreed, pulling both of his cell phones out of his pocket. He glanced at the screen of his work cell phone and noticed he missed a call from Raul. No matter, he would call him back after lunch, he thought, placing the phones along with Lisa's in the glove box.

Over the next 45 minutes, Lisa enjoyed herself. Randy had always been good at making her laugh and keeping her entertained with silly stories about people he'd met over the years. She didn't think of work once the entire time.

Much too soon, she found herself back at the CDC, watching Randy drive away. Surprising herself, she realized that she missed being with him, they had always been good together.

Sighing, she turned and walked back inside. Returning to her office, she was feeling a lot better than she had when she left, unfortunately, the feeling wouldn't last long.

Lisa hadn't even sat down when she heard someone crying out in the hall. Turning around, she went to see what was going on.

"Sarah? Are you okay?" she asked, concerned for her coworker.

"Oh my God Lisa. It's so terrible," Sarah cried.

"What is?" Lisa questioned her, clearly confused.

"Oh no, you haven't heard. The plane was shot down over Africa. They're all dead!"

Everything went blank as Lisa collapsed to the floor, unconscious.

Randy

Randy was in a good mood as he returned to the office. Lunch with Lisa had gone very well, and he had a hard time thinking of anything else. Parking his car, he remembered that his cell phones were still in the glove box. He grabbed them before heading into the building, glad to see that Lisa had remembered to grab hers. He was in such a good mood that for the first time in a long time, Randy whistled as he walked.

Back at his desk, he saw the message about Raul's missed call and noticed that there was a corresponding voice mail. He checked the voice mail, curious about why Raul had called him.

"Randy, this is Raul. There's a man who just called me. He said that he was working on a story about this virus with you and that you asked him to meet with me. Said his name was William James. I just wanted to make sure he was on the level before meeting him. Give me a call back. I'm supposed to meet him in an hour."

Randy felt a chill come across him as he checked the time of the call. Almost two hours ago. He must have called when he was talking to Lisa before they had gone to lunch.

He dialed Raul's number, but it went directly to voice mail. "Raul, this is Randy. I don't know anyone by that name, do not meet this guy. Call me back."

Randy wondered how this William James person had connected Raul to himself. Then he realized that the only way that this could be possible was if his cell phone were bugged, and that probably meant that his house and possibly his office lines were as well. There might even be a tracker on his car.

He looked up Raul's home phone number on his phone

then dialed it from his throwaway.

"Hola?" a man's voice answered, but he could tell it wasn't his friend.

"Hi. May I speak to Raul please?" a silence followed his request. "This is Randy Elkhart, I'm a friend of Raul's."

"I'm sorry Mr. Elkhart. My Papa was murdered earlier today. My Mama said that Papa was going to meet a friend of yours, and he never came back."

"I'm sorry to hear about you father," Randy told him, offering his condolences. "Raul called and left me a message a couple of hours ago, but I only just got it. He said some guy named William James claimed he was working with me and that I had suggested he should meet with your father. I never told anyone to meet with your father, and I have no idea who this William James person is. Do you know what happened?"

"He was found in the passenger seat of a car that had been set on fire with him inside. The police think he was already dead before the fire was started. The fire department was only a few blocks away, and they managed to put out the fire pretty fast. They found Papa's wallet in his pocket. I'm sorry Mr. Elkhart, I must tend to my Mama and make arrangements to bury Papa," the man said before abruptly hanging up the phone.

Why would anyone claim to know him and then kill his friend? It just didn't make any sense unless it had something to do with the virus investigation. That was the only possible link he could think of. They had to be tapping his phone, but why kill Raul? He didn't know anything, and if they were willing to kill someone who knew nothing, what would they do to someone who knew significantly more? He felt a shiver crawl up his spine in response to the unspoken question. Randy knew he had to disappear before they found him.

He turned off his laptop and cell phone and removed the batteries before locking them in his desk. Randy then went to his editor to inform him that he was chasing a story and would be out of contact for a few days. Leaving his car, he went out the back door and made his way on foot, away from his work. Stopping occasionally to look at the reflection in store windows for anyone who might be following him, he didn't see anyone.

Flagging down a taxi, he told the driver to take him to the closest mall. He paid the driver, tipping him an extra $50.00 before asking him to drive around to the entrance on the opposite side of the building and wait for him there. The driver happily agreed.

Randy entered the mall and went to the closest men's clothing store. He bought a new pair of pants, a shirt, jacket, hat, and a pair of sunglasses. Making sure the clothes were a different color and style than what he had on currently. He went into the men's room and changed his clothes, discarding the old ones in the trash before going back outside and climbing into the waiting cab.

Not sure where to go, he gave the driver an address a few blocks from the dry cleaners. He needed to warn Erik and Eddie.

DAY SEVEN

BB

She was exhausted. BB had worked all day yesterday and well into the night. Lisa did manage to get a few hours of sleep early this morning, but it did little to stave off the tiredness she felt throughout her entire body.

The World Health Organization had held a press conference early in the morning and revealed that the virus was targeting mid to dark skinned people. Unfortunately, that news caused rioting all over the world, and the emergency room was keeping busy with victims of violence and needless bloodshed.

The hospital had also started receiving victims of the virus late last night, and they just never stopped coming. It was like a dam had burst, and the hospital was sitting at the lowest point in the path of the water, as it quickly became inundated. The quarantine area filled within an hour, causing them to have to expand it. They ended up moving two floors of patients to other levels, and now they were considering clearing a third for all the Frankenstein Virus patients, not that it would matter in the end. Many of the patients that had not originally come in with the virus, were now showing the early stage symptoms of it. Soon, the entire hospital would be a quarantine zone, and at that point, there would be very little left to do beyond waiting to see who lived and who died.

Quite a few of the hospital staff had become infected, even with wearing all the required PPE (Personal Protection

Equipment). They had run out of Hazmat suits early on, so most were just wearing two layers of gloves, a gown, face mask, face shield, and eye protection. Some were still trying to assist patients the best they could, even if they were sick themselves, but that would end soon as the virus ravaged their bodies.

Dr. Pedro Gonzalez had contracted the virus and was well on his way into the infection stage. He was still making rounds and doing what little he could for those in the same predicament.

"Dr. Gonzalez, are you alright?" BB inquired, not liking how the doctor looked. It was very apparent that he was gravely ill and should not be on his feet, let alone making his rounds.

"I doubt it. Skip the whole doctor part and call me Pedro, no need for formalities anymore," Pedro told her as he nearly collapsed. He was using the wall for support to prevent that from happening and only barely succeeding.

"Sit down and let me do a quick check," BB ordered him, knowing that there was very little that she could do to actually help him.

"No time, plus I know I have it," he replied, sounding like he was resigned to his fate. "I have a fever, chills, headache, coughing, and I just threw up in the bathroom in there, I'm sure the diarrhea will follow soon. If I'm lucky, I might have another eight hours before the internal bleeding begins, and I will no longer be able to help."

BB was upset that her colleague was sick, but attempted to not let it show. Dr. Gonzalez was the first friendly face that she had found when she had begun her residency there several years prior. She would do anything in her power to help him.

"Well, as your physician, I'm ordering you to take a ten minute break and get some more fluids in you. Take some anti-biotics and ibuprofen, and I don't care that they will do little if anything to help. Maybe some cough medicine wouldn't hurt either. You could still make it," she told him, almost pleading for it to be true. "Only about half who get the symptoms end up not surviving," BB reminded him, making her thoughts on the situation known.

Pedro absentmindedly shook his head. "While I appreciate the sentiment BB, you and I both know that once the vomiting starts, there is no getting better. The best you can hope for once that occurs is to fall into a coma before the worst of the infection takes over. Look, I shouldn't be saying this, but at this point, they can't do anything to me since I'll most likely be dead within a few days," he paused, gathering his thoughts. "You're most likely already infected, but you should remain symptom free, and we both know why, thanks to that WHO report. You need to gather up some medical supplies and leave. Get out of the city to somewhere safe, and don't look back. We have already had some issues in the emergency room from people who are blaming Caucasians for them getting sick, and it won't be long before riots break out, and the hospital gets overrun."

"I can't just leave these people!" BB declared, clearly upset at the thought of abandoning them to their own defenses.

"Yes you can, and you must. We both know that other than giving out fluids and pain medication, there's absolutely nothing that we can do for them that will make one iota of a difference. Honestly, they would probably all be better off at home, at least then they could die while being surrounded by loved ones. If you don't take this opportunity to leave while you still can, well, I don't want to think about what might happen to you. Come on, give a dying man his last wish," Pedro almost pleaded with tears in his eyes. "It will make me feel better knowing that you're safe."

BB stared at him, doing everything in her power to control her emotions and not break down crying, but she knew deep in her heart that he was right. There wasn't anything that she could do for these people except try and make them comfortable and wait to see what happens. "Alright, but under a few conditions. You will need to take a ten minute break every hour to rest and get plenty of fluids. Give yourself an IV if you have to, but get fluids in your body. Take the damn medications even if they probably won't do anything, but there's still a small chance that they will. If you don't agree to those stipulations, then I will stay here and make sure that you do," she told him, leaving no room for argument.

Pedro nodded, relieved that she agreed to leave the place that would soon become his tomb. "I will agree to that. Now get some supplies and get out of here. Be sure to change out of your scrubs before you leave. I'm sure doctors will be targets of violence if they aren't already. Call a male friend to come to get you, and don't leave this building until he arrives. Stay safe BB," he told her, squeezing her arm weakly before turning to go get the antibiotics and an IV.

"Thank you, Pedro. I'll never forget you," she quietly vowed as tears began streaming down her face. She knew that was the last time that she would ever see her friend and mentor.

BB rapidly gathered up some random medical supplies in a backpack without even paying attention to what they were before going into the women's locker room to change clothes. She grabbed her phone and called the one person she knew would come for her, no matter what.

"Hey BB. What's up?" a familiar voice asked.

"Alex, I need you and Billy to come and get me and bring your guns, just in case," she said between sobs.

Alex was immediately concerned as fear leaked into his voice, "What's happening? Are you safe?"

"Right now, I am, but I'm not sure how long that will last. Get here as fast as you can. Meet me at the emergency exit door on the south side of the building by the trash dumpsters. Call me when you're close and I'll meet you outside."

Suddenly an announcement came over the intercom system, interrupting their conversation, *'Security to the main entrance. Security to the main entrance. Code Black.'*

"What was that about?" Alex wanted to know.

"Code Black is for armed intruders. Come and get me, Alex, please!" she begged. BB had never been this scared in all of her life and wasn't sure what she should do. The only thing that she was positive about was that she needed Alex.

"We're on the way. Stay hidden until we get close. I will get you out of there," Alex promised her, leaving no uncertainty that he would do as he said.

"Hurry!" BB pleaded, obviously terrified out of her mind.

Alex

"Billy!" Alex yelled as he grabbed his keys. "Get the guns, we have to go rescue BB, and we need to move. Now!"

"Here's your Glock. What's going on?" Billy asked, tucking his Beretta 92FS 9 mm pistol in his waistband at the small of his back, covering it with the tail of his shirt.

"BB called, and she's stuck at the hospital and needs our help getting out. They called a code black while I was on the phone with her, which she claimed was the code they used for armed intruders. We have to hurry and get her out of there," explained Alex, while trying not to panic. He checked his weapon to confirm that it was loaded before following Billy's example and tucking it away.

"Well shit. Let's go dude," he said, heading towards the door.

"I'm right behind you," Alex replied as he locked the door before closing it behind them.

They hurried down the stairs, skipping several steps in the process. Alex unlocked the 4-wheel drive Chevy Silverado extended cab with his remote, allowing them to quickly jump in the cab, saving them several precious seconds.

Alex backed out of the parking stall and quickly exited the parking lot, barely checking for oncoming traffic as he headed towards the hospital. They hadn't gotten far when the truck was hit with a glass bottle, shattering on impact and leaving an impressive, albeit unwanted, dent in the driver's side door.

"What the fuck?" Alex yelled as he slammed down on the brakes. He spotted a group of people running toward the truck with hatred in their eyes and weapons in their hands. The majority of the weapons consisted of baseball bats and gardening implements, but he did see a couple of people with guns in the mix. Realizing his mistake, Alex jammed his foot down on the accelerator and quickly increased his speed. He turned onto the first side street he found, not caring where it would lead to as gunshots echoed behind them.

"That's a bad sign," Billy commented. "I wonder how bad it is downtown?"

"No idea. Side streets or interstate?" Alex threw the question out, counting on his friend to play the part of the navigator. He would need to focus solely on driving, or there might be a distinct possibility that he would get them both killed.

Billy immediately started thinking tactically. He would have made an excellent soldier in the military had he any desire to join. "The interstate would likely have fewer rioters, but we could easily get blocked in with no way off, and dude, that would suck big, sweaty donkey balls. The side streets will have more people to deal with but less of a chance of getting stuck. I vote for side streets."

"Agreed. We'll go cross country if we have to," he replied, determined to save BB at any cost.

They made their way across the five miles worth of city streets to where she was waiting, at a much slower pace than Alex had planned on. There were several streets that the residents had blocked off with cars and were being guarded with men and women openly armed with guns. Other intersections had car wrecks blocking the way, while a few had large groups of people that could either be rioters or residents. He wasn't about to approach them to find out which, luckily, there were still many streets that weren't blocked to an extent that they couldn't still be traveled on. The issue was that they were laid out in various directions, and it took them almost three times longer than it should have since they ended up backtracking multiple times before the upper floors of the hospital finally came into view.

"That's the hospital up ahead. I need you to call BB and let her know that we are only a couple blocks away," he directed Billy. "I need to concentrate on driving."

Alex worked his way through the streets as he listened to Billy talking on the phone.

"BB, we're almost there. Are you alright?...Calm down, just make your way to the exit, and we will meet you there...Were those gunshots?...Find somewhere to hide. We will come to you...Where in the hospital are you?....Okay, just wait there and we'll be there soon. Stay quiet, we're just outside the hospital now...Okay. Turn your phone to vibrate so that it doesn't ring if we need to call you back. Call us if anything changes....Alright, I gotta go. We'll see you in a few minutes." Billy hung up the phone, worry etched on his face.

Alex slammed on the brakes and brought the heavy-duty truck to a halt near a side entrance.

"Shit! We should have brought more ammo. We have 15 shots each so let's make them count," Alex mentioned as he got out of the truck, making sure to lock it but not bothering to set the alarm.

"Sorry," Billy apologized. "I didn't realize that we were going into a war zone."

Alex waved him off, knowing that he could have grabbed the extra magazines just as easily as Billy. "No worries, hopefully, we can do this without firing a shot. Pretend that it's 'Call of Duty' and we're infiltrating the enemy camp because that's exactly what we're doing. Where's BB located?"

"A bathroom on the third floor, south side of the building, across from the nurses' station," he recited, trying to mentally prepare himself for what might lie ahead.

"We're on the west side so we'll need to turn right when we enter and find a stairwell to get up to the third floor. We should be able to find the nurses' station from there. You have point since you're better at 'Call of Duty' than I am," instructed Alex, determined that nothing was going to prevent him from saving her.

"Dude, you finally admitted it, and it only took the end of the world," Billy paused, grinning stupidly at his friend. "Nothing left to do but do it. Let's go!"

"Alright man, remember that silence is the golden rule," Alex responded with a grin before opening the door.

The two men moved quickly through the doorway and up against the wall. A quick glance around showed the hallway to be clear in both directions. The hospital was eerily quiet as they moved at a fast trot down the hallway with their pistols at the ready should they find any hostile rioters, stopping just prior to the open area at the end of the hall. Shots rang out in the distance from somewhere on the main floor. They didn't sound close, so the boys chose to ignore them.

Billy peered around the corner before quietly speaking, "Two bodies on the ground, one male and one female. They're not moving and appear to be security guards. Looks to be where the elevators are at so the stairs should be close. Clear to move."

They rounded the corner and quickly located the door leading to the stairwell. Billy peeked through the window before slowly opening the door and stepping through, followed closely by Alex. They found the body of another security guard on the second floor landing. Shot in both the head and the chest. They carefully stepped over the body, avoiding the pool of blood that it was lying in. As they made their way up the flight of stairs to the third floor, loud shouting came down to meet them.

"Sounds like we have company. They're already on the third floor," Billy said as he crept up to the door in a crouch. He slowly rose up until he could see through the small window set in the door.

"Two men, both armed with pistols. It looks like they are trying to get a door open that's behind the nurses' station, most likely after drugs," Billy updated Alex in a hushed tone, not wanting to alert the men of their presence.

"Get the damn door open, Ralph. That's gotta be where they keep the good stuff," one of the men loudly told the other.

Billy watched as they attempted to kick it open, but it appeared to be a solid door and it refused to budge. The larger man pulled out his gun and shot at the lock. The bullet hit the lock and ricocheted, embedding itself in an office chair, barely missing the second man.

"Damn it!" the second man turned on the one who fired the gun. "You trying to kill me?"

"I thought I'd shoot the lock off like they do on TV," the other man replied, defending his actions.

"That shit only works in the movies. Fuck it, let's see if we can find someone to open this for us," he said, heading down the hall away from Alex and Billy. The other man quickly followed, apparently not wanting to be left alone.

"Call BB and let her know where we are," ordered Billy.

Alex pulled his phone out and dialed. "Hey BB. We're just outside the nurses' station in the stairwell. Where exactly are you?....Alright, you're in the room closest to the nurses' station off the hallway on the opposite side of the nurses' station from us," Alex repeated, so Billy would know where she was. "The two men left to see if they could find some keys. We're coming to you...Yes, see you in about a minute...Bye." Alex hung up then looked at Billy. "She's waiting on us. You heard where she's at?"

"Yep." He nodded. "Okay, this hallway is clear. Not sure where the two men are. Pay attention because they may have circled around to the other hallway. Let's move."

Billy quickly opened the door and slipped through, darting across the open area to the counter that surrounded the nurses' station, where he stopped and waited for Alex. He didn't have to wait long, Alex was beside him within seconds. They made their way to the other hallway, staying below the top of the counter before halting at the end of it.

Their destination was directly in front of them, with only a six foot wide hallway separating them from their goal.

Billy slowly peered around the corner of the counter and saw that the coast was clear. He traversed the hallway as quickly and quietly as possible. He was pleased to see that Alex didn't immediately follow him but instead waited and then did his own check before coming to meet him.

Alex promptly went to the bathroom door and lightly tapped on it. "BB. It's Alex and Billy."

"Oh, thank God!" he heard from behind the door as it slowly opened.

They heard a woman scream from the other end of the hallway, putting the two men on alert.

"I don't have a key to that door. Just let me go," a woman pleaded, getting closer to where they were hiding.

Alex and Billy went into the bathroom with BB and closed the door, leaving a small gap so that they could hear.

"How about you?" came another voice that they recognized as the larger man from before.

"Only the head nurse has the key," the man cried out as the sound of someone getting punched filled the hall.

"That's Ron and Linda. We have to save them," BB quietly begged, recognizing the voices of her newly married friends.

The group had stopped halfway down the hall while the armed men started to interrogate the man.

"Where's the head nurse at?" the man demanded to know.

"I don't know. She got infected with the virus but was still working. She could be anywhere in the hospital. We are shorthanded so everyone is working everywhere," Ron answered.

"Well you're pretty much useless," the man said as a shot rang out.

Linda screamed as she burst into tears. "You bastard! You didn't have to kill him."

"I don't have to kill you either." Another shot rang out

and the sound of a body hitting the floor quickly followed, silencing the sound of tears.

"Why'd you kill her? She was a pretty young thing," one of the degenerates asked.

"Doesn't matter, we can find others after we get the drugs. Now let's go find this head nurse. Start searching the rooms, she's probably hiding from us. Let's start down there, you take that side, and I'll take this side," he ordered his buddy.

"Oh head nurse. Come out, come out wherever you are," the man hollered, heading back down towards the far end of the hall.

BB was silently sobbing at the loss of her friends.

"We have to leave. Right now," Billy stated as he gently touched her shoulder in comfort. "Time for grieving comes later. Let's go."

The threesome came out of the bathroom, hesitating at the door to the hallway. Billy listened before easing his head around the door frame so he could see down the hall. "It looks clear, but we all need to move at the same time. We'll cross the hall and get to the end of the counter, and then I'll check to make sure that hallway is clear, then we get to the stairs as fast as we can."

Alex and BB both nodded.

"Make sure you keep your eyes forward. You don't need to see what they did to your friends," Billy instructed BB.

She nodded, trying to remain strong.

Billy checked the hallway again. "Hold. Okay, he went into another room. Let's go."

The trio hurried across the hall, but BB made the mistake of glancing over to where her friends' bodies lay. She let out a loud sob before she was able to cut it off and regain control of her emotions. Unfortunately, the man down the hall heard her and ran out into the hall, just in time to see them before they disappeared behind the counter.

"Ralph! They're at the other end of the hall. Shoot them if they don't stop," the man yelled as he started to run down the hallway, trying to catch up to them.

"Keep going," Billy said, passing the end of the counter as a shot rang out.

Billy quickly spun and returned fire as the man ducked into another room.

The three friends shoved the door to the stairs open and ran down them as fast as they could. Alex had been looking behind him for the two men and almost tripped over the body of the security guard that he had forgotten was on the landing. "Body. Just step over it and don't slip in the blood."

Each of them stepped over the body before continuing down the stairs. They were almost to the first floor landing when they heard the door slam open from above. Gunshots were hastily fired at them, but they all missed their intended targets.

"Get over by the wall. They're shooting over the handrail and down through the opening in the middle. We'll turn right out of the stairwell," Billy told BB as he yanked the door open, taking the lead.

The three passed quickly through the door, and with Billy leading, ran as fast as they could down the hall towards the exit. BB had slowed slightly at the sight of the two bloody bodies splayed out on the floor in front of the elevators before hurriedly moving on. Alex made sure that BB was between Billy and himself since she didn't have a gun. They made it to the exit and Alex was the last one through the door as more shots rang out, and a bullet struck the wall right where Alex's head had just been.

He unlocked the truck with his remote, allowing the trio to quickly pile in. Alex started the engine and immediately floored the vehicle, throwing rocks and dust up behind them as the two men came running out of the building, shooting at anything that moved. He heard a few bullets strike his truck, but they were quickly out of the line of sight of the two men as he turned out of the parking lot and into the debris strewn streets.

"Holy shit!" Billy yelled. "That was fucking insane."

"We're not done yet, we still have to get back home," Alex reminded him.

Billy quickly became serious and more attentive to their surroundings. "Oh yeah, I forgot about that."

"Was it bad on the streets?" BB asked, concerned about what they might encounter on the trip back to the apartment complex.

"A lot of the streets are blocked off. Some by rioters who are destroying everything, and some by armed residents trying to prevent the rioters from entering their neighborhoods. That's why it took so long to get to you," Alex explained while he scanned the streets, trying to find the best way home.

He turned left and was partway down the street when he saw three armed men step out from behind a parked van. "Hang on!" he shouted as he cranked the steering wheel hard to the left, crashing through a six foot tall, wooden privacy fence and barely missing an in-ground swimming pool. The truck punched through the next fence in line, taking out a small dog house and a kid's swing set before Alex turned the wheel again, and the truck rapidly removed a section of the back fence. Cranking the wheel yet again as he touched the brakes, the ass end of his truck sliding around to line up with the alley, Alex straightened the wheel as he punched the accelerator, trying to create some distance between them and the armed men.

With dust flying up behind them, they quickly lost sight of the men. Alex barely slowed down when he came to the end of the alley before speeding back up and flying down the next alley. After four blocks, he slid the truck to a stop at an intersection. Finding it clear, he turned right, quickly picking up speed.

"Sorry about that," Alex apologized. "I didn't see those guys until I had already turned. Keep your eyes peeled for others."

The rest of the trip, while tense, was uneventful. Alex backed the truck into a parking spot beside Billy's Blazer.

The trio got out of the truck and inspected the damage.

"Damn dude. You fucked your truck up!" Billy commented, emphasizing each word, as he noticed all the dents, scrapes, and bullet holes, not to mention the cracked windshield that now adorned his friend's pride and joy.

Alex sighed and shook his head at seeing all the damage. "Better the truck than us. Let's get inside, it's not safe out here, and we need to talk about our plans for leaving Dallas."

Jeremy

Jeremy hadn't had so much fun in all his life. He was just informed of the latest infection numbers, and they were outstanding, even if he did say so himself. 80 million! He was so proud of his creation, but he knew that it was just the tip of the iceberg, and within another week, every human on the planet will have been exposed. His virus had now traveled to all points of the globe. Every country in the world was reporting infected citizens. The only thing that was putting a damper on his mood was the number of deaths, they had yet to reach 10 million, but he knew that number would quickly grow.

He smiled as he realized it had been three days since the test subjects had received the Booster shot so they should all be dead by now. He decided to go down to the testing lab to confirm that there had been a 100% fatality rate. Jeremy was certain that would be the case, he had designed it after all.

Blondie had brought him the news the day before that the one subject that Skinny had said was immune to Steri-12, was actually sterile. Apparently, there had been an error in the first batch of tests, just as Jeremy had thought.

He entered the testing labs and only saw one of the assistants working, Chubby. He wondered where Skinny and Blondie were, quickly dismissing it as something not important enough for him to worry about.

"What were the results of the Booster shot?" he questioned Chubby.

"All subjects deceased within 68 hours of initial injection," Fred recited from the report he had sent Dr. Carter earlier that day.

"Excellent! Carry on," he said, dismissing Fred with a wave of his hand.

Yes indeed, this was turning out to be the best day of his life. Jeremy thought as he left the lab, failing to notice the nervous nature of his assistant.

Fred

He was still shaking, even though the doctor had left several minutes ago. Fred had never been so scared before in his life. He had just lied to Dr. Carter's face and if the doctor found out, well Fred was sure that being called a derogatory name would be the least of his worries.

Dr. Carter had lied to them. He had told them that they would be safe from the virus since they had been given the real vaccine for the virus, but now Latisha was sick. The test they ran this morning, verified that the culprit was, what is now being called, much to Dr. Carter's horror, the Frankenstein Virus.

Latisha was lying down on a gurney in one of the cell rooms. They had been discussing what to do, who they could possibly tell about the entire conspiracy. Neither one of them had believed that they weren't expendable and most likely were at the bottom of The Elite Group, Latisha getting infected just proved it.

Fred was disgusted. "I lied and told him that all the subjects had died and it made him happy. I wish he could get the virus, but we know he made it so that he couldn't. What can we do?" he asked, entering the cell where Latisha was.

Her eyes were puffy from where she had been crying. "I have a crazy uncle. I think we need to go see him," she said as she sat on the gurney.

"Why?" Fred asked, wondering how a crazy uncle could help them.

"Uncle Eddie is homeless and lives in a van behind a dry cleaners," she explained, fidgeting with the hem of her lab coat. "He came by my mama's house the other day and was telling my folks that they needed to hide from Frankenstein. Mama just shooed him away, not believing him. Knowing what we do, he may know about the Frankenstein Virus, and if he does, he has to know someone who also knows about it. I'm just not sure if it will be someone in The Elite Group or someone trying to discover the truth. You will have to be extremely careful."

Fred jerked his head up and stared at her confused. "Wait, what do you mean, I need to be careful? Aren't you coming with me?"

Latisha shook her head and hopped off the gurney. "I can't, I'm infected and one of us needs to stay here to keep anyone from discovering our little friend."

He took a deep breath. "You do realize that I'm probably a carrier right now and will most likely infect your uncle, but you're right, you're sick and you need to be the one to stay behind," Fred decided. "Where's this dry cleaners located?"

She smiled at him, pleased that she wouldn't have to talk him into doing something that he didn't want to do. "Over on Peachtree Street. I'll look up the address and text it to you. Leave now and I'll cover for you if anyone stops by."

"Do you need me to pick up any medicine for you?" asked Fred, concerned for his friend.

"Just bring me back some Gatorade," Latisha replied as Fred turned to go. "Hey Fred."

"Yeah?"

"Thanks for being my friend," she told him, giving him a quick hug before releasing him and turning away.

"Anytime," he replied, pretending not to notice the tear running down her face as he walked away.

Fred had decided to walk. He thought that it wasn't too far and it would give him time to think before confronting Uncle Eddie. He knew the general direction of Peachtree Street and headed that way at a brisk walk.

All of his thoughts kept returning to Latisha. She was his best friend and to be honest, she was also his only friend. Jeff was too standoffish and full of himself, giving off the impression that he thought he was better than both him and Latisha. He was the only other person, besides Dr. Carter, that they interacted with at work. Outside of work, Fred was too busy with college and studying to bother making friends. He didn't go to bars or clubs since he didn't drink, so no way to make friends there. He realized that he was basically all alone except for Latisha, which he found rather depressing.

He was walking by the park when his cell phone beeped, informing him that he had a text message. It was the address Latisha had promised to send him. Fred sent the address to the GPS feature on his phone and realized that he was almost to the dry cleaners.

Latisha hadn't been feeling well all morning and complained of a slight headache about an hour ago. Fred had gotten her some ibuprofen and made her rest as much as she could in the hopes that her immune system would be able to fight off the virus. He knew that she had about a 50/50 chance since he double-checked the database on it after they had run her blood test. He prayed that she survived it because he didn't know what he would do if he lost his only friend.

The GPS informed him that he needed to turn right on Peachtree Street, he did as directed and saw the dry cleaners on the next block. Remembering that Latisha said her uncle lived in a van behind the dry cleaners, he turned on the street right before it and headed down the alleyway.

He saw the old delivery van and figured it must be the right one since the only other vehicle back here was a car.

Fred knocked on the side of the van, not knowing the correct protocol for announcing ones-self to someone who lived in a van. There was no response so he looked through the windows and didn't see anyone. Now what? He wondered.

He decided to ask inside the business to see if they knew

the homeless man and where he might be. Common sense told Fred that they must know that the man was living in the van since it appeared that they were allowing him to do so, and therefore, they would know who he was.

The sign on the door stated that due to the pandemic, the business was temporarily closed. He saw some people inside the building so tried the door. Finding it unlocked, he walked in and all conversation ceased, he was obviously interrupting something important concerning the three men standing at the counter. One was probably the owner, and another looked to be either a customer or a salesman of some sort. His gaze stopped on the third man, this might be Uncle Eddie. He was clean and had shaved sometime in the last few days, but his clothes were well worn, and he had that hard life look to his face.

Fred hesitantly spoke, "I'm sorry to bother you, but I'm looking for someone. It's my friend's uncle, his name is Eddie and he lives in the van out back."

Surprised showed on the third man's face. "I be Eddie. Who's be you?"

"Umm my name is Fred Ridley and I work with your niece, Latisha, in the labs over at Crouch Pharmaceutical."

Everyone turned and stared at Fred, stunned at what they just heard come out of his mouth.

"Latisha be working for that murdering doctor?" Eddie demanded to know.

Fred backed up a step. "Umm yeah, we both do."

"Hold on a minute Eddie, let the boy explain why he is here," the salesman said.

"Well, it's kind of private," he uttered hesitantly.

"If it's about Crouch, we all need to know," the man told him. "Let me explain. My name is Randy Elkhart and I'm a reporter. You've already met Eddie and this is Erik, he owns the place. We're working on a story about this Frankenstein Virus and all roads seem to lead to a Dr. Carter who works for Crouch Pharmaceutical. Now you're all caught up and know that anything you tell Eddie, you can tell us."

Fred let out a huge sigh of relief. "Thank God. I have a lot to tell you, but I'm not sure we can do it here since it will take some time. We won't want any customers to overhear anything."

"Not a problem," Erik said, coming around the counter and locking the door. "Let's all go to the back room. Eddie, could you grab some soft drinks from the refrigerator in my office?"

"Sure thing Erik," he said, hurrying off to do as asked.

Randy quickly set up the card table and folding chairs they had used the other day and everyone was soon seated.

"Umm okay, well what have you figured out so far?" Fred asked the three men.

Randy took the lead and gave a quick rundown on their investigation. "We know the virus was designed and created by your boss by using several other viruses, including influenza, rabies, and hemorrhagic fever. It was released in Africa and India, that it spreads faster than any virus known to man and becomes active only in people with mid to dark skin tones. I think that pretty much covers it."

Fred shook his head, his eyes were wide open and mouth agape. "Wow! I'm impressed you know that much," he admitted. "As I said, my name is Fred Ridley and I am a college student majoring in virology. I need to give you my back story so you can understand exactly what you're up against."

He glanced at each of the men while taking a deep breath and slowly releasing it. "I was approached two years ago by a man who didn't give his name, even when I asked for it. He told me that he was a recruiter but wouldn't say for who. I got the impression it was the government, but it turns out that wasn't the case. I was told that they would pay for all my college and get me a paid internship with a major lab here in Atlanta, again giving me the idea that it might be the CDC."

Fred continued, seeing the interest in the faces of the three men. "In return for paying off all my student loans and giving me this well paying internship, I would agree to commit to working for them for a minimum of ten years and be well compensated for it financially. I don't know any college student who would turn this down, so I agreed.

"I had to sign a bunch of legal contracts, and once I had, I was told the truth. I was basically owned by The Elite Group," Fred paused, seeing the confusion on everyone's face.

Randy took the opportunity to ask a question. "Wow! They really have a system in place to recruit new people. I can see why you agreed, now who exactly is this Elite Group? I have never heard of them."

"I'd be surprised if you had," he told him. "It took me a while to figure that out, but The Elite Group, and trust me, they capitalize the word The, is a group that was started here in the United States by a small group of rich and powerful people. There are ten of them and they call themselves The Core. I have no idea what their names are, so don't bother asking. Now The Core makes all the major decisions for The Elite Group, they basically control everything. The media, insurance companies, hospitals, food distribution, medications, vaccines, you name it, and they have someone in the industry with power in their pocket. Yes, that does include the government. Military, senators, secret service, NSA, IRS, FBI, pick any three letters of the alphabet and they either own them outright or are able to rent them any time they want. They are everywhere and involved in everything." Fred stopped to take a drink and glanced up to see if there were any questions, but only stunned faces stared back at him.

Randy finally broke the spell. "So let me see if I understand this correctly. The Elite Group is basically like a company, and the top people who run it are called The Core. They are the ones who give out the orders and anyone who has been recruited into The Elite Group, must do what they say, no matter what it is?"

Fred was nodding his head in agreement, so Randy continued, "The Elite Group consists of people who have been recruited or tricked into working for The Core. I am assuming that they probably only recruit college students and newly recruited military personnel. Once recruited, they get them jobs in major companies and hope they rise into power. If this is true, they would have had to have been doing this for decades. How many members are in The Elite Group?"

Fred was still nodding his head as he started up the story again, "I estimate that there is well over 150,000 in the US and probably close to another half million spread out across the world. No one really knows the exact number so it could be a lot more, there's just no way to tell. As far as how long they have been recruiting, I don't know when they started for sure, but it was sometime in the mid-1800s. When a member of The Core dies, a direct descendant replaces them so there are always ten core members. Very few members of The Elite Group know the name of even one of The Core members and I doubt anyone knows them all. They are extremely secretive."

"Illuminati?" Erik asked.

Fred shrugged his shoulders. "I don't know. It could be them, the Freemasons, Skull and Bones, or the Knights Templar. Maybe none of them, maybe all."

"Who be that Skull 'n Bones?" Eddie wondered out loud.

"Skull and Bones is a secret student society at Yale, that was founded back in the early 1830s, no one really knows what they do. Might be as mundane as a book club or as evil as The Core, which is why I included them on my list of possibilities. Several US presidents have been members, as have many other high ranking members of the government and CEOs of several major corporations," explained Fred. "So that's who The Core and The Elite Group are, now I need to get back to the story or this will take all day," he said, chuckling as he warmed up to the three men.

"After I signed all of the paperwork that they gave me, they packed it all up, and when I asked for copies, I was told no. That's it, just no. They told me I had to go to the local headquarters, and then they put me in the back seat of a black SUV and blindfolded me. Let me tell you, I was scared to death, wondering what I had gotten myself into."

"They drove for a long time and took a lot of turns. I'm guessing the location probably wasn't very far from where we started, but they wanted to make it seem that way. The next thing I know is that we are in an underground garage. They kept the blindfold on me so I couldn't see, but I could tell by the way that the sound echoed. We entered an elevator and it went down, I would guess, four or five floors before it stopped." Fred again paused to get a drink.

"I did try to figure out what building it was since there could only be a few buildings with that many underground floors, but I couldn't find anything. I assume that they had someone get rid of any record of the sub-basements ever being built."

Fred stopped talking when his phone beeped. He pulled out his phone and saw Latisha had sent him a text message.

'Doc looking 4u. Said u had dentist appt n wouldn't b bak til l8r.'

Fred read the message and relayed its contents to the others before continuing.

"They finally removed the blindfold and I found myself inside a small room with just a table and two chairs. I was put in one, and another man who I didn't know, sat down across from me. That's when I was told that I now worked for The Elite Group and I was to do anything asked of me, without question. I could never leave the group, nor was I allowed to ever discuss the group or anything they asked me to do. They informed me that if I did, there would be severe penalties up to and including elimination." Fred swallowed and stared each of his companions in the eye.

"So they may kill you for talking to us?" Eddie asked, stunned.

"That's exactly what I am telling you, and not just me but Latisha too, since she knows that I came here. I'm risking everything to give you guys this information."

"We'll keep your name out of it," Randy promised.

"Trust me, it won't matter. They will eventually figure it out so I hope you understand that I am not the only one with his life on the line. Let me put it this way, if they think you know something, they will send someone to find out if you do. If they know that you do know something then it's game over." Fred decided to let that sink in.

"So we're pretty much dead if they find out we know any of this," confirmed Erik as Fred nodded his head.

"Holy chit! They be gonna kill me no matters what I be doing," Eddie exclaimed, throwing his hands up in the air.

"Okay, I think we all understand the possible consequences. There's nothing we can do about it right now, so let's just continue," suggested Randy.

"After they laid down the law, so to speak, they made me wear the blindfolded again and returned me to the college campus, taking a bunch of turns the same as before. The next day, I got a call telling me to go to an interview with Dr. Carter, so I did. Latisha was also there looking a little freaked out as well, so I knew they had also gotten to her. We were both hired to be assistants for Dr. Carter.

"At first it wasn't bad, we actually didn't do much and Dr. Carter never gave us any real responsibility. We mostly just studied for our college classes since the doc didn't trust us to do anything else. During the first summer, about 18 months ago, that all changed, at least for me. Latisha was told that she would be taking a paid leave of absence for a month. She was given no explanation, and trust me, she didn't ask for one," Fred stopped talking again before saying that he needed to take a break.

Seeing that Fred was obviously shaken up, Erik offered to order a couple of pizzas since it was well after lunchtime and none of them had eaten.

"Wanna go for a walk outside with me?" Randy asked Fred.

"Umm sure, as long as I don't have to talk for a bit," he said, accepting the offer.

"I'll talk or we can just walk and get some fresh air," agreed Randy.

"Me and Fred will be back in a few minutes. Don't eat all the pizza," he told Erik and Eddie as they headed out the back door.

"Thought you needed to get out of there for a few minutes." Randy saw Fred nod his head before continuing. "I just wanted to tell you that I think they might be onto me. I called a reporter friend of mine in Mexico and asked him if he had ever heard of a virus that could target a specific race, this was before we knew about the skin pigmentation gene, he was murdered yesterday and then set on fire. He called me before it happened, but I was on another call and didn't realize he left me a message until almost two hours later. A man had called him and said that he was working with me on a story about the virus and wanted to meet him. Raul called me to verify his story, but when I didn't answer, he went ahead with the meeting and was killed for it.

"I got rid of my laptop and cell phone, left my car at work, and bought new clothes at a random store, throwing the old ones away. I stayed here last night trying to figure out where I could go, it sounds like there isn't anywhere." Randy looked over at Fred for confirmation.

"Nope, there's not," he said, turning to go back into the building.

Randy quietly followed, realizing that he was a walking dead man.

Bellies full of pizza, the foursome sat back down to finish the story.

Fred resumed the story where he had left off, "So after the weekend, I go in the first day Latisha is off, and I'm ordered to put on a hazmat suit. They had also added a decontamination room just inside the door of the lab. Once inside, I found that they had knocked down a wall into the space next door. The new space contained 30 small, 6' x 8' rooms built into it.

Each room had a steel security door with a thick glass window that could only be locked from the outside. They were cells and they were full of people strapped onto gurneys. I was instructed to bring each subject out into the lab so that Dr. Carter could inject them with, what I now know, was the Frankenstein Virus."

Fred's eyes were tearing up, but he continued. "They brought in a new guy, Jeff, to help log the information on the subjects. Height, weight, age, sex, nationality, time of injection, and so forth. He wasn't always able to get their complete information as many did not speak English. I would bring them out, Jeff would log any information about them that he could, Dr. Carter would inject them, and I would return them to their cell. Rinse and repeat until all thirty had gotten the injection.

"Jeff and I monitored them over the next two weeks, noting any symptoms that they developed. 17 of them died within 8 days. Ten of them each developed some symptoms of varying degrees but eventually got better. The remaining three never developed any symptoms at all. Those three were all light complected, everyone else wasn't." Tears were streaming down his face at this point, but Fred didn't stop talking.

"On day fourteen, Dr. Carter came in and we did the whole thing over with the remaining 13 subjects except that Dr. Carter used a different injection. They were all dead within the hour. I have no idea what he injected them with, but I think it was an earlier version of his Booster shot." Seeing confused looks, he quickly added, "I'll talk about that later, it's not important right now.

"For fourteen days, we'd worn the Hazmat suits while in the lab and done what they wanted, then went through decontamination before removing the suits. They always tested our blood before allowing us to leave the secured lab area. In that two weeks, we murdered 30 innocent people, that was my introduction to what is now called the Frankenstein Virus, but Dr. Carter had originally named it the World-Ender. I realized they gave Latisha the time off because she could have died had she somehow come in contact with the virus. They gave me the next two weeks off. When I returned, the bodies were all gone. Everything had been cleaned and sterilized, almost as if nothing had happened." He was extremely emotional from recalling the events from his past.

Randy called a halt seeing that Fred was in no shape to continue. "That's enough for now, you need to take a break."

"Actually, I need to get back to work so they don't get suspicious. I can come back later tonight if that's alright. We don't have much time left to stop it."

"Okay, tonight then. Be careful," Randy said as Fred slipped out the back door.

Fred had stopped at a convenience store and bought some gauze and Gatorade. He walked into the lab with gauze stuck in his gums to look as if he had gone to the dentist and gave Latisha the Gatorade.

"Welcome back, how was the dentist?" she asked, letting him know they weren't alone.

"Culd of been bet'r," he mumbled through the gauze.

"Jeff, Fred's back if you want to go back to the other lab. I think we can handle things here."

Jeff came around the corner. "Next time you have to leave, let someone know ahead of time. I had to leave an important experiment to come and help her enter data in the computer because you weren't here."

"Thanks for your help Jeff," Latisha offered.

"Whatever," he said as he left the lab.

"What an ass hat," she said, leading Fred into the other room and into an empty cell. "Alright, spill it. Did you find my uncle?"

Fred removed the gauze from his mouth and quickly relayed what had happened and that he needed to return that evening.

Latisha didn't hesitate. "I'm coming with you and we

need to bring our friend as well." Nodding at the cell across from them.

Fred was surprised that she was taking the lead, it must have something to do with her contracting the virus. "Do you have a plan to get him out of here?"

She looked at him like he was an alien from another planet. "Of course I do. We'll wheel him out just like we did with all the others once we were done with them. The only difference is that you'll be driving the van and he will still be alive," she explained.

"Umm and just how am I supposed to get a van?" he asked her, not sure she would have an answer.

She was able to surprise him as she told him, "Well, I have a black windbreaker in my car you can use to help disguise you. I also believe that the convenience store on the corner sells ball caps."

"They do. I saw them when I bought the Gatorade," Fred acknowledged.

"Okay, so buy a black one since that's what the drivers usually wear. The vans aren't locked and the keys are kept in the middle console. So just get in and back up to the door," explained Latisha, like it was something that she did every day.

"Wait, how do you know they don't lock the vans and where the keys are?" Fred wanted to know.

Latisha sighed. "Not that it matters, but I briefly dated one of the security guards a while back. We took one of the vans once to go to lunch because he didn't have a car." She looked at Fred, knowing that he liked her and that he would be hurt with the information, but it couldn't be helped. "When you get to the van, call me and I will bring him out. I just need you to help me get him secured in a body bag before you go. Once he's in the van, you'll need to leave, and I'll meet you where my uncle is living."

Fred thought about it for a moment. "That should work, but we need to make sure that he is either sedated or is willing to cooperate and stay quiet or this won't work."

"I had some time to talk with him earlier and explained the basics of why he was brought here and how we plan to get him out. He has agreed to do it without sedation, he knows that it's his only chance to get out of here alive," she explained, happy that they now had a plan that they both agreed on.

"We better finish entering that data so we can leave on time," suggested Fred, putting the gauze back in his mouth to keep up with the dentist story in case they had another visitor.

It was getting late by the time they could implement their plan. Dusk had settled over the city, and Fred hurried to buy a ball cap and get Latisha's jacket from her car.

Fred decided that darkness was his friend as he managed to avoid being seen by a few workers going to their cars. He had decided to quit scurrying around, hiding behind cars, and stood up. He boldly walked over to the vans as if he belonged there and got into the first one he came to. Finding the keys where Latisha had told him they would be, he called her to let her know he was ready.

He pulled around to the loading docks and backed up to the one that was designated for van use. He got out and opened the back doors and then returned to the driver's seat to wait.

Finally, the loading dock door opened and Latisha pushed the gurney out of the building and into the van. She locked the gurney in place to prevent it from rolling around before she closed the van doors, pounding on them to let Fred know he was good to go. He wasted no time putting the van in gear and slowly driving off.

He parked in the alley to wait for Latisha and heard some muffled talking. Fred realized he had forgotten about the man zipped up in the body bag. "Sorry, hold on a second."

Fred climbed in the back of the van and unzipped the bag from around the man's face. "Sorry about that, I had to get us somewhere safe."

The man took several deep breathes before responding,

"It's okay. The girl, she warned me. Can you get me out of this bag now?"

"In just a minute," Fred replied as Latisha pulled into the alley and parked behind him.

"I'm gonna go get Randy. Don't unbuckle him yet, I want to make sure he can't run until he talks to everybody," he told her as he jumped out of the van.

He knocked on the back door of the business and waited for someone to open it.

"Hey kid. I was starting to think that you might have changed your mind on coming back," Randy told him, opening the back door.

"Umm well, I had some complications. Follow me," he directed as he headed back to the van.

Randy propped the door open with a brick that was obviously left there for just that purpose before he followed the young man.

"Who all did you bring with you, and are you sure it was a good idea to do that?" Randy asked, seeing Latisha and a man strapped to a gurney in a body bag.

"I didn't have any choice," Fred tossed the words over his shoulder as he pulled the gurney out of the van and pushed it towards the building. "That's Eddie's niece, Latisha, and this is a man who we managed to save. I don't know his name yet."

"Berto Sanchez," the man offered. "I would offer to shake hands, but it seems I am still being restrained."

"I'll let you out after we're safely inside," Fred told him, pushing the gurney through the door.

Randy followed the small group inside and closed the door, making sure that it was locked.

Fred made quick introductions and explained how Berto ended up in a body bag strapped to a gurney.

"Berto, I am going to get you out of there now, but you need to promise not to run. Once everything is explained, you can decide where you go from there. You aren't a prisoner, but I can't let you leave until everyone understands just what is going on, including you. Once this is all over, I will do everything I can to make sure that you get back home," Fred promised as Berto nodded his head in agreement.

Fred and Latisha quickly undid the straps holding the body bag to the gurney and unzipped the bag. Latisha helped the man off the gurney.

Seeing how weak Berto was from the lack of food over the past two weeks, Fred asked, "Erik, Is there any pizza left? Berto hasn't eaten much in the last couple of weeks."

"I be getting it for him," Eddie said, heading towards the refrigerator.

"Thanks, Eddie."

"I get Latisha, by why bring Berto here?" Erik asked.

Fred sighed. "Let me finish my story and it will all make sense. I promise."

"Fair enough."

After Berto had eaten and everyone had settled down in chairs, Fred continued where he had left off.

"So after the first group of 30, I told Latisha what had happened. We agreed that we had to go along with it or we would probably become one of the next test subjects. They had us trapped and there was no way out that we could see.

"Over the next six months, we repeated the tests two more times. Latisha was always given time off and the results were always the same. Ultimately, I had no choice but to become numb to it all and withdrawal my mind from what was happening. It was the only way I could deal with it and stay sane," revealed Fred.

"I'm not sure what God's rules are when you're forced to do terrible things against your will, but I don't think it matters anymore. The sheer number of people that I helped kill probably gets me an automatic one-way ticket to Hell," he stated quietly, staring at the floor as if expecting it to open up and swallow him.

"Anyway," said Fred, as he looked up, shaking off the

melancholy before continuing the story, "after that, it was pretty much back to normal for a while. Then came the Steri-12 and Booster shots. That's where Berto comes in, he was in the third and final test group, and he can fill you in on how he became a test subject after I finish my story.

"Steri-12 is not a vaccine for the Frankenstein Virus as they will proclaim, it's actually a chemical and biological sterilization formula that Dr. Carter created to sterilize both men and women. Unlike the Frankenstein Virus, Steri-12 doesn't care who they are or what skin color they may be. It also is not contagious and must be injected. I assume the plan is to sterilize those people that The Core deem unworthy of reproducing who survived the virus. Steri-12 works fast and is irreversible. Except for Berto, every test subject became sterile within 48 hours." Fred looked around and saw that he had everyone on the edge of their seats with their full attention.

"Once everyone became sterile, they were given what Dr. Carter called a Booster shot. Again, this is not a vaccine, the Booster shot must also be injected and is not contagious. Thank God! Anyone who receives this shot will be dead within 72 hours. Berto is again the exception, he survived both injections without any apparent symptoms or side effects as far as we can tell.

"I believe the current plan is to provide the Steri-12 as a vaccine sometime in the next few days with the booster shot following shortly after that, but I don't know when or how they plan on distributing it. I suspect that they may have warehouses in every major city in the world with doses of both, ready to go. A lot of this is conjecture based on tidbits of information that Latisha and I have stumbled across or overheard since we unwittingly became involved with The Elite Group," admitted Fred reluctantly.

"Okay, one final thing and then Berto can tell you his story. Part of the agreement with becoming a member of the group is that you have protection. Dr. Carter personally gave both me and Latisha injections a few weeks ago that were supposed to protect us from the Frankenstein Virus."

Fred glanced at Latisha who nodded her head slightly, allowing him to drop the bomb. "We now know that the vaccine he gave us was probably nothing more than saline. Latisha is infected and so am I, this means everyone in this room is also infected."

"What? You came here knowing that you'd infect us?" Randy demanded to know.

"Yes I did. We didn't have a choice," Fred said, raising his voice with each word spoken. "Do you think that you will somehow stay in a little bubble and never get infected? Trust me, everyone in the world will be infected within a few days. There is no way to stop that, but we are hoping that by providing this information to you, you can help us find someone to stop the Steri-12 and Booster shots from being distributed, besides, you, Erik, and I are all safe. The only ones in danger are Eddie, Latisha, and Berto. Latisha already has it and Berto had already been exposed before we discovered that we were infected. Eddie is the only one who has the right to be mad, so you can just fuck off!" Fred was standing now with both fists clenched tight, yelling in Randy's face, obviously extremely pissed off.

"Sit down!" Erik demanded in a firm voice. "Everyone needs to calm down. Fred's right, we will all get infected no matter what. Fred, you should have said something to us about this before you got close enough to infect us, at least then, Eddie would have had a choice. I would have still listened to you because we do have the best chance of stopping this. Eddie, what are your feelings on this."

"It don't be mattering none. He's be right. We be all getting it no matters what. They be not the ones to be blaming anyway," Eddie reminded the group.

Randy sighed. "You're all correct and I'm sorry for the way I overreacted, Fred."

"It's okay, it's kinda the reaction that we expected anyway, and Erik's right, I should have said something before," he admitted, feeling bad for putting them into this situation.

"I have one question before Berto starts," Erik said. "What's the end game of The Core?"

"We think that it's population control and maybe so they could take over the world," Fred confessed, nodding at Latisha, who nodded back in agreement.

Erik considered that for a moment. "Well, that makes sense in a twisted sort of way."

Randy nodded his head, "So Berto, how did you end up here?"

Berto shook his head, "Not by choice. I'm a farmer from Argentina and had just finished working in my field when I felt something pinch my leg. I looked down and saw a dart sticking out of my thigh, and then I remember nothing until I woke up in that lab, gagged and tied to a gurney. I have no knowledge of how I got there and wasn't given a choice on the shots they gave me. I'm not sure why they didn't work, but maybe there's something in my blood.

"Latisha told me what they had injected me with and that I was immune. She and Fred agreed to hide me and get me out of the lab if they could as long as I promised to help them stop it. So that's why I am here, to help. My blood might have something in it they can use to stop people from dying. If I can get somewhere that it could be tested, I am willing to go," Berto offered.

Randy ran a hand through his hair and sighed. "I can check with Lisa to see if the CDC can help, but I'll have to let her know that you're probably infected with the Frankenstein Virus."

"For now, you can stay here with Randy, since he's also in hiding," Erik suggested to Berto. "We're gonna have to find someplace better tomorrow."

"I have to get the van back to the lab before they realize that it's missing," Fred told them as he got up to leave. "Thank you all for believing us."

"Here." Randy handed Fred and Latisha each a disposable

phone. "Use these to contact us, all of our numbers have already been saved in the phone's memory."

Fred and Latisha each grabbed a phone and headed to the cars. "You think they can help us?" he asked her.

"I guess we'll find out soon enough," was the answer he received back.

Nodding, he got into the van and headed back to the lab.

Agent Warren

He was getting frustrated. There was no sign of the reporter anywhere, his car was at the Reliable News office building, but it hadn't moved in over 24 hours. The agent had even gone so far as to go inside to ask if Randy was there, before being told that he wasn't. He gave them the William James alias along with the number of a throwaway phone but doubted Randy would call even if he got the message.

Tracking the phone didn't work so he assumed Randy had pulled the battery out of it.

He checked Randy's apartment, but it was empty and none of his neighbors had reported seeing him in the last couple of days.

Randy had apparently heard about Raul Hernandez's death and figured it was in his best interest to disappear. Agent Warren couldn't fault him for that since it was true.

He had hoped that the phone records would give him the names of some friends and acquaintances, but the only calls made in the past few days were to Raul's cell and home numbers and a call to the CDC. Those had been made from Randy's cell phone, his office ran all the incoming calls through a switchboard, so there was no way to know which incoming calls were for Randy. The outgoing calls appeared to be nothing important, general business calls that seemed to be unrelated to The Elite Group. There was one incoming call from a dry cleaners that lasted less than a minute, it was a little odd and he didn't know if it was for Randy or not, but he thought he should check it out just in case, doubting that anything would come from it.

DAY EIGHT

Lisa

S he had been very rudely drugged from a deep sleep by the abrasive sound of the ringing phone. It took her a minute to get her bearings and figure out that it was the throwaway phone that Randy had given her. That ring tone really had to go, she thought, as she grabbed it off the end table.

"Yeah?" Lisa answered sleepily.

"It's Randy, I'm sorry that it's so early, but it's important and I wasn't sure what time you went into work."

"I'm actually already at work, I've been sleeping in my office because of the riots. What's up?" she asked, rubbing at her eyes, trying to wipe away the rest of her sleepiness.

"Well, I finally have some good news for you. We now have some friends on the inside of the lab and they gave us a present," Randy told her, hoping to make up for waking her. "There's a lot more going on that you're not aware of. A second and a third attack are coming in the form of fake vaccines, and I have a survivor of both sitting here with me, he's the present. I thought you might be able to test his blood or something."

The news brought her fully awake. "Matt might be able to figure out why he's immune after he does some testing. Although, we probably shouldn't be talking about this on the phone."

There was a pregnant pause on the other end of the phone before Randy finally responded, "There's an issue, he's been infected with the active Frankenstein Virus, but he hasn't shown any symptoms so far, we're sorta hoping that he's immune to that as well."

"That's highly unlikely, but I guess not impossible," confirmed Lisa. "Let me check with Matt after I get some coffee, and I'll call you back."

"Sounds good," Randy said as the line went dead.

Lisa found Matt in his office. "Hey you got a second?"

"Probably not," he admitted, looking rather haggard. "What's up?"

Lisa closed the door before sitting down in a chair on the opposite side of the desk from Matt. "Randy said there could be two more attacks coming in the guise of vaccines. He found an inside source at Crouch Pharmaceutical and also has a survivor from their testing. He thought we might be able to use the survivor to come up with something to help fight it with."

"We should be able to, given enough time, but I'm not sure that we have enough of that though," Matt disclosed as he began to yawn. "Sorry, I haven't been getting much sleep here lately."

She laughed, struggling to hold back a yawn of her own. "I can relate to that. The survivor has is infected with the Frankenstein Virus, but he hasn't shown any symptoms yet. What do you want me to do?"

Matt leaned forward in his chair, elbows on the desk and fingers steepled in front of him, like he was in prayer instead of just deep in thought. "Find out where he is and I'll have the Hazmat team pick him up and bring him in. I can put him in quarantine while I run some tests and avoid the risk of infecting anyone."

She nodded her agreement to his plan. "Okay, I'll let you know where to pick him up."

Lisa spent the next few minutes making the arrangements with Randy to get Berto to the CDC. She let Matt know where to have the team pick him up, before returning to her office.

She read the reports that had been sent to her. The infections were approaching a billion cases and would easily exceed that number by the end of the day.

Most of the teams that the CDC had sent out to help were now unreachable and presumed to be either too sick to contact anyone or possibly dead, although no one voiced those suspicions out loud.

No information at all was coming out of Africa. Too many people there were either sick, dying, or dead. Other areas of the world were also going dark. Nothing more could be done other than to just wait and see who managed to survive the virus.

Randy

Berto had agreed to go to the CDC, and Randy had the Hazmat team meet them at the end of the alley. They quickly put Berto in the back of the van and left.

Shortly after that, a man in a suit showed up at the dry cleaners and introduced himself as William James. He asked Erik if he knew Randy and, if so, had he seen him recently. Erik told the man that he didn't know anyone by that name and the man had left. Randy knew it was time to leave, or he might put his friends in even more danger. He needed to find someone in the military who could help them.

Using a new throwaway phone, he called his office.

"Reliable News, how may I direct your call?"

"Hey Jim, it's Randy. Is Charlie in yet?" he asked, praying that his plan would all work out.

"Randy, where have you been man? Some creepy guy keeps coming by looking for you. The dude's name is William James, and I got his number if you want it," Jim told him as Randy heard papers being shuffled in the background of the phone.

"I don't need it. If he comes back, pretend that you haven't heard from me," he said, drumming his fingers on the top of Erik's car. Randy was feeling a bit anxious that the man in the suit wasn't giving up.

"Will do. I'll send you on over to Charlie's desk. Hang on for the transfer," Jim said before several clicks came across the receiver, and then it rang on the other end.

"Charlie Bradford. Can I help you?"

He let out a breath that he hadn't realized that he was holding, "I hope so Charlie, it's Randy and I not only need your help but your silence as well."

Charlie straightened up, realizing that this was a serious call. "You got it. What do you need from me."

"The first thing is to forget that I called as soon as we hang up. Some bad people are looking for me, and I don't want to put anyone else in danger. The second thing is that I need a contact, someone in the military who you would trust with not only your life but mine as well," he divulged, hoping that Charlie had remained friends with some of his old Army buddies.

"That's an easy one. My old platoon sergeant is stationed at Fort Benning. He's currently a sergeant first class, but just call him sergeant and you'll be fine. If anyone can help you, it's him."

Charlie gave Randy the sergeant's name and phone number. "I'll call him and let him know that I gave you his contact information so he'll be aware that you're legit. Stay safe my friend."

"Thanks Charlie, I really appreciate this. I'll explain all of this to you later, but for now, forget that I even exist," he told his friend and coworker, not sure he'd ever see him again.

"Who is this? I don't know who you are," Randy heard before the line disconnected.

Shaking his head and chuckling at his friend's antics, he pulled the battery and memory card from the phone before breaking it in half. He pocketed the memory card and tossed the broken phone and battery in a nearby overflow drain along the curb. It was probably unnecessary to destroy a phone he had only used once, but with his life on the line, he wasn't taking any chances.

He headed back inside to let Erik and Eddie know what was going on, giving Charlie time to call the sergeant and inform him that he would be calling.

Ten minutes later, he had the sergeant on the phone. He explained that he needed to talk to him but that it had to be in person due to the nature of the information. The sergeant finally agreed, rather reluctantly, but only because Charlie had saved his life once and he trusted him implicitly. They agreed to meet just off the base at a nearby park in two hours.

"Thanks for driving me, Erik. I wasn't sure how I was going to get down here," Randy expressed his gratitude to his friend.

Erik shrugged in response. "I have time now that that the government made me close the shop. I'm not sure why Eddie didn't come along."

"I don't think he's feeling all that well. I left him a bunch of Gatorade and ibuprofen, I sure hope he survives it," Randy said, staring off into the distance. "Oh yeah, one more thing, can you make sure that everyone knows about that William James character. I'm sure that he's bad news, and I'm positive that he had something to do with Raul's death."

Erik agreed and nodded his head. "Not a problem. I'll let everyone know and give them his description so that they know what he looks like as well."

"That should work. Thanks for doing that for me," he told Erik, relieved that his friends would all be forewarned of the man.

"Well, we're here. Want me to wait in the car?" he offered, giving Randy the opportunity to have him go along for moral support or face the sergeant on his own.

"If you wouldn't mind. I'm hoping that he'll agree to hide me on the base if I can convince him everything is true. That's probably him in the Army green Hummer," said Randy, opening the door and going to sit on the pre-agreed upon bench.

The sergeant was a big and intimidating man. Standing at 6'3", he was 250 pounds of pure muscle and with a permanent scowl on his face, just looking at him would make most privates shake in their boots.

Randy watched him disembark from the Hummer, leaving his driver inside. He approached Randy and offered his hand. "I'm Sergeant Brooks, I assume you're Mr. Elkhart."

He stood and accepted the offered handshake, the sergeant's large hand completely swallowing his own. "I am and please call me Randy. Thank you for meeting with me without knowing why."

"It's not without a lot of reservation," Books confessed. "Shall we walk?"

"Absolutely."

As they made their way slowly through the park, Randy supplied the sergeant with a condensed version of everything that happened in the last week, ending with the survivor who was now in the care of the CDC. The sergeant listened without interruption, but Randy could tell he was absorbing every word that was said, whether he believed him or not was another story.

"That's quite an unbelievable story," Books proclaimed when Randy had finished. "Do you have any concrete proof or is it all hearsay?"

"Honestly, most of its hearsay. I don't have any real factual evidence, but I can get you access to the two whistleblowers who work at Crouch Pharmaceutical. The CDC has run tests, proving that it's a targeted virus and I imagine that I could get a copy of the report. There is also the survivor who was kidnapped from Argentina." He glanced at the sergeant and noticed that his facial features hadn't changed. He started to get angry, thinking that it wasn't going to be enough for him to be taken seriously. "If you want, the man who killed my friend will eventually find me, and you can have my dead body as evidence."

The sergeant stopped walking and turned to face Randy.

"Hold on there, son. I never said I didn't believe you, just that the story itself was unbelievable."

"So you do believe me?" he asked, wanting clarification.

The sergeant stared at Randy, trying to decide if he should trust the reporter. Coming to a decision, he began talking, "I've heard some things over the years that have made me question just who was actually in control. Yes, I believe you with a few reservations, but you can probably relieve me of those with some more discussion. I can tell that you left a lot out of the story, I assume for time purposes. I want you to return to the base with me where you can be formally debriefed by my superiors, and I want as much detail about that Elite Group and The Core as you can supply. If you're agreeable to that, let your driver know that you will be remaining here for a few days, and we'll take the Hummer back to the base."

A huge weight was lifted off Randy's back at the news. "I don't have any choice but to trust you, sergeant. If you are secretly working for the bad guys, well, I guess I'm dead. On the other hand, if I don't trust you, I'm probably dead anyway," Randy revealed. "I'll let my friend know that I'll be staying."

"Very good. I'll wait here for you."

Randy went to let Erik know that he was going with the sergeant to the base and that he'd call and let him know if he made any progress. He joined the sergeant for the trip back to the base, and what he hoped was safety.

Agent Warren

He had followed the target, a Mr. Robert Collins, from his residence to his workplace. This was the part that he didn't like, sitting in a hot car and waiting for the target to reappear.

The information that he had received, claimed that Mr. Collins had been requesting information about the skin pigmentation genome, which was apparently outside of his area of study. They figured that there would only be one reason why someone would be looking into that particular gene at this particular time, and so, Agent Warren was asked to pay the man a visit.

While he waited, he thought about that reporter who seemingly vanished into thin air, Randy Elkhart. The agent was beginning to wonder if someone within the government was helping him hide. Normally, he would have found at least a bread crumb that would lead him somewhere, but here he was coming up with had nothing.

He had stopped by the dry cleaners early this morning, and although it had a 'closed due to the pandemic' sign posted in the window, he had found it unlocked. When asked why he left the door unlocked if the store was closed, the man behind the counter explained that although he wasn't taking in any new dry cleaning, he wanted to give his clients a chance to pick up anything that they had dropped off prior to the pandemic. The agent asked the man if he had heard of Randy Elkhart, explaining that he was a private investigator hired to find him by an old girlfriend. The man seemed to think about it before he told him that he didn't recognize the name but admitted that it might be a past client. He could search his records if it was important, but it might take a few days as most of his computerized records had been destroyed when a power surge fried his computer a while back, and he'd have to manually go through the receipts. The agent didn't get a sense that the man was being dishonest and left his fake name and equally fake number with him on the off chance that he remembered the man.

Catching movement out of the corner of his eye, he saw Mr. Collins leaving for what he assumed was lunch. He started his car and followed a few car lengths behind. He doubted that the man knew anything himself, it was more likely that someone had asked him to look into that particular gene for them. Now he just needed to figure out a way to extract that information as quickly as possible. His gut was telling him that it would eventually lead him back to Mr. Elkhart.

Due to the pandemic, he was not surprised to follow Mr.

Collins back to his home for lunch, what did surprise him was that he was even going in to work in the first place. What could be so damn essential about working on the Human Genome Project? Oh well, not his problem, he thought, as he followed Mr. Collins right up into his driveway, parking directly behind him and blocking him in.

Mr. Collins had exited his vehicle and was now squinting at him, trying to figure out who he was and why he was in his driveway. The agent got out of his vehicle and approached the man.

"Excuse me, I hope I didn't scare you," he said smiling. "I just wanted to make sure that you were aware that the license plate off the back of your car is missing."

Mr. Collins quickly forgot about who the stranger could be and went directly to the back of his vehicle. "It's right there. I don't know what kind of game you're playing, but it isn't funny." He said, turning around to face the agent.

"Well, that's where we have a difference of opinion, Mr. Collins, or may I call you Robert?" he asked civilly. Not receiving a response from the surprised man, he continued, "It seems that we need to have a quick discussion. I prefer not to involve your family if we don't have to, but it is your choice. You may either get into my car, willingly and without making a scene, or we can take this conversation into your home and involve your family."

"What do you want me for? I ain't done nothing to nobody," came the curt reply.

Agent Warren sighed. "I am not here to cause you any problems. I work for the government and need you to give me some information. Tell me what I want to know and then you're free to go. We won't even leave your driveway if you don't want to, but make no mistake, you will give me the information that I need."

"Fine," he said as he went around the car and got into the passenger seat.

The agent got back into his car, leaving the engine running to allow the air conditioning to keep cooling the interior of the car, there was no reason for him to sweat after all.

"I'm sorry to be so abrupt, but time is of the essence on this particular matter. A couple of days ago, you requested information on a specific gene, and I need to know why," he stated, matter of factly, while staring the man dead in the eye.

"Seriously? That's what this is about?" the man said, shaking his head in disbelief. "My son is working on a project for his science class. Since I work with the Human Genome Project, he thought it would be cool to do something related to my work and asked for an obscure gene that he could include. I remembered reading something about a gene that had to do with skin and decided to look it up for him. Why is the government worried about some stupid, obscure gene anyway?"

He smiled. "Well, I'll give you an A for effort. That was a pretty good story considering that you didn't have any time to prepare. Now you will tell me the truth, who asked you to look into that specific gene?" the agent said, opening his jacket enough for his pistol to show.

"I don't know his name, it was some doctor from the CDC. He told me not to say anything to anybody so I made up that story. Can I go now?" Robert stammered out, still protecting his friend's identity.

"Was that so hard? I just have one more question before you go. What's that over there in your yard?" he asked, pointing out the passenger side window.

Robert turned his head to look as Agent Warren jabbed a needle into his thigh and depressed the plunger, causing his passenger to tense up slightly before relaxing into Death's sweet embrace.

Agent Warren put the car in reverse, calmly backing out of the driveway and heading off in the direction of downtown. As he drove, he debated on what to do with the dead man sitting beside him.

Now, how could he find out who was working on this at the CDC, he wondered as he looked for a good dumping spot for the body.

Alex

They had slept very little, spending most of the night making plans and packing up the truck to leave. He threw a tarp over the supplies in the bed of the truck and made sure it was secured tightly so that it wouldn't flap in the wind.

Billy would drive his Blazer, following Alex and BB, who would be in the pickup. BB would be the navigator and keep an eye out for trouble. They would each carry a two-way radio that the boys used once when they had gone rock climbing.

They all noticed the dark smokey haze that was hanging ominously over the city. The acrid taste of smoke in the air confirmed that they had no choice but to leave the city.

The two vehicle convoy departed the parking lot just as the sun was peeking over the horizon. The first few minutes of the trip were uneventful, giving Alex hope that the rioters were still tucked snugly in their beds with visions of destruction, dancing in their heads.

"I think we have a tail," Billy reported over the radio. "Make some turns up ahead and I'll keep an eye on them. As long as they stay back, they're not an immediate threat."

"Will do," BB replied, gazing over her shoulder to see if she could spot the car.

Alex made several turns over the next couple of miles.

"They're still trailing behind me," he verified, several minutes later.

Alex took the radio. "It might just be someone who is also trying to leave town. It's obvious that's what we're doing, and I'm not surprised others wouldn't think to do the same. Can you make out how many are inside?" he asked, not overly concerned about them just yet.

"From what I can tell, it appears to be a man and a woman. It might be a family, I just can't tell," Billy conceded.

"Let them follow for now, but keep an eye on them. After

we get out of town, we can pull over and find out their intentions," decided Alex, assuming that if they were marauders, they would have already attacked.

"Copy that," Billy replied.

"Look at all the houses that have burned down," BB said in disbelief, staring out her window at the residential streets. Some of the streets were shrouded in smoke, while others displayed houses fully ablaze and yet others held just smoldering piles of ash. Strangely, there were several houses that the inferno had left mostly untouched, while those to either side had burned completely to the ground.

"Downtown appears to be burning as well, based on the huge plume of smoke," countered Alex, who was looking the other way.

Silence settled into the truck like an unwelcome passenger as the scenery became too depressing to talk about.

It took an hour and a half of weaving through the side streets before they were finally able to exit onto US287 and head in the general direction of Amarillo. They had originally had planned to take I35 north to I40 but changed their minds since they would prefer to avoid driving through anywhere as big as Oklahoma City if they could help it. That made the decision to take US287 to US207, and then head north in order to avoid Amarillo, an easy one.

Happy to finally be clear of Dallas/Ft Worth and out on the open road, Alex decided to see what the people behind them had planned.

He picked up the radio. "Hey Billy, I'm going to pull over at the rest stop up ahead if it isn't too crowded to see if those people behind you, follow us or keep going."

"That works. I need to piss like a racehorse anyway," Billy informed him.

Laughing, Alex flipped his turn signal on and exited off the highway. There were only two semis at the rest area, and they were parked at the opposite end so Alex felt that it was safe enough for them to stop. He watched Billy signal and follow him in. The trailing car slowed down and almost stopped before also turning into the rest area. Parking on the opposite side of the road, almost directly across from them.

"Make sure you're packing," Billy relayed over the radio, parking behind him.

"Don't worry, I'll have my Glock with me. You go ahead and take your piss, but keep an eye on us. I'm gonna see what they do when we get out, but we'll wait for you to find a good position to cover us first," Alex instructed, attempting to use his peripheral vision to see into the suspect vehicle.

"On it," came the quick response.

Billy got out of the Blazer and stretched. Completely ignoring the car that had followed him for the last two hours, he headed off to find a nice tree to water since there were no public restrooms at this particular rest area.

Once Alex saw that his friend had found a good location to watch over them. He instructed BB to get out and walk around the truck, pretending to check and make sure the tarp was secure while also keeping an eye on the car, he was going to do the same on his side.

As they pretended to check the tarp, he saw the front doors of the car open. "Be careful, BB, they're getting out," he warned.

A man stepped out of the driver's side while a woman got out of the passenger side. The woman started walking over to them. "Helen wait. We don't know those people," the man yelled.

"Damn it, Harvey. Obviously, they can't be that bad if they are traveling with a woman," she hollered back over her shoulder while shaking her head.

"Hi folks. My name's Helen," she said as she approached them, "and that's Harvey. I hope we didn't scare you by following ya, but you looked like you were leaving town and we figured that there was safety in numbers. We tried leaving last night, but it was pretty bad and we turned around after only going a few blocks. Looking at the damage on your truck, I see that you've already met some of them folks, somewhere along the way. It was a lot quieter this morning so we decided to try again."

Alex waited for her to wind down. "Hi. I'm Alex, and this is BB, our friend driving the Blazer is Billy. We just wanted to make sure that you weren't a threat to us is all."

Helen cackled loudly, sounding like a witch from a Disney movie. "Not damn likely. Harvey is afraid of his own shadow," Harvey shrunk back from them as Helen announced his true colors, it was obvious who wore the pants in the family.

"Billy, we're clear," BB said over the radio.

"Alrighty then. I guess that means no target practice for me," Billy joked.

Hearing this, both Helen and Harvey took a step back, not understanding Billy's sense of humor.

"Don't worry, he wouldn't have shot you unless you pulled out a gun or attacked us in some way," Alex told the couple as Billy walked up.

"So I guess they're no threat," he stated unnecessarily as he walked up to his friends.

"Nope, just some folks trying to leave the city," BB replied, her arm intertwined with Alex's.

"Well, let's get back on the road, we still have a long way to go," Billy responded, gazing down the long highway that lay ahead of them.

"Can we keep following you?" Harvey asked timidly.

"It's still a free country so I don't see why not," he quipped at the couple as he headed to the Blazer.

"Billy, be nice," BB admonished him, knowing that he had been joking, but worried that he would scare off the couple.

Billy grinned as he lowered his head and kicked at the ground with his foot like a petulant child. "Who me?"

Alex took charge of the group. "Alright everyone. We're taking US287 until we get to US207, then we'll take that north.

That way, we can skirt around Amarillo. I'm not sure where y'all are headed, but we're going to the Colorado mountains. Follow if you want, if you have trouble, flash your headlights and honk your horn and we'll stop."

"Thank you Alex, we're going to my dad's ranch just outside of Amarillo. We will follow you up to US207 where we will part ways," disclosed Helen, seemingly happy to have others to travel with.

"Sounds good. Let's load up and hit the road," he replied, eager to get back on the road and closer to their destination.

They made good time as they passed through several smaller towns that didn't appear to have been hit by any rioters or gangs. As they approached Wichita Falls, Alex got a bad feeling in his gut and unconsciously began to slow down.

"See if you can find a way around Wichita Falls," he directed BB, handing her the map.

She scrunched up her face in confusion. "Why? The highway has been clear since we left the city," she pointed out.

"It just doesn't feel right to me," he confided, shaking his head slightly.

"Looks like you can turn at Jolly, and we can find a route around it from there," BB confirmed, her head still buried in the map.

Alex got on the radio. "Hey Billy."

"What's up dude?"

"I'm gonna detour around Wichita Falls," he informed his friend.

"What for? That's gonna add at least another 30 minutes onto the trip," complained Billy, obviously not happy about the delay.

Alex took a calming breath. "I just have a bad feeling is all."

"Do you see any smoke in the sky?"

"Well no," he admitted.

"Then it's fine. Just stay on the highway, and we'll be through there in a few minutes at most," reasoned Billy.

"Damn it Billy. Over 100,000 people live there and I know there's gonna be trouble. I'd rather lose time than have to fight," he snapped back, clearly annoyed.

"We don't know that there is any trouble to find. You're just being a nervous Nelly. Stay on the damn highway, and let's get our asses to Colorado. I'll take the lead if you're too big of a chicken shit. We made it out of Dallas/Fort Worth without any issues, so Wichita Falls should be no problem," Billy proclaimed, intentionally antagonizing his friend, having learned over the years that it was the best way for him to get what he wanted.

"Fine! I'll stay on the highway, but I am not happy about it. I'm telling you that there will be trouble there, I can feel it deep in my bones," Alex yielded as he sped back up. "You just stay behind me. I don't want to have to stare at your ugly ass the whole way."

"What? I thought you liked my ass." Billy joked, happy to get his way.

Alex shook his head, more upset with himself for caving in to the pressure than at Billy for being...well, Billy.

"In your dreams."

"More like your dreams," Billy popped off laughing.

Alex got serious. "Pay attention. We're almost to Wichita Falls."

As they entered the outskirts of the city, they saw evidence of rioting. Boarded up windows, trash littering the area, and spray painted gang tags were everywhere they looked.

"I don't like this," Alex said, "it's too quiet. Where are all the people?"

"Maybe they are staying home like the CDC said to," suggested BB, as she tried to look in every direction at once, clearly nervous.

Alex barely heard BB as he keyed the radio. "I'm speeding up Billy, this doesn't seem right. There are no people at all."

"Go for it, but don't go crazy. We still have those folks behind us and I doubt Harvey is much of one for breaking the law."

They drove past the turnoff for US277 and still hadn't seen any traffic on foot or in vehicles. "Shit this is I44. I didn't realize US287 merged with I44," muttered Alex to no one in particular.

As they topped the overpass and could see down the interstate where it ran through a business district, he saw it. A bunch of cars were blocking the exits, with a concrete center divider, and the fact that it was elevated, he realized that there was no other way off the highway and knew that they had fallen into a trap.

"We need to back up and get out of here Billy," Alex calmly said over the radio.

"Uh, that's no longer an option. They got cars behind us, blocking us in," he informed them.

"Damn it Billy! I told you that this would happen, but you always have to have things your own way and damn the consequences," he took a deep breath to try and calm his nerves, "I guess we're just gonna have to barrel through them if they try to stop us and pray that we make it. Hope the folks can keep up because I ain't stopping for nothing."

"Roger that," Billy solemnly replied, knowing that Alex was right, he had really screwed up this time.

Alex started rolling down the incline of the overpass, slowly picking up speed as he went, looking for any possible exit off of the gauntlet they now found themselves on. He noted that every exit had been intentionally blocked off with multiple vehicles. Just as he thought that they might just be herded out of town, the roadblock came into view.

They had positioned the roadblock right where the interstate came off the elevated portion, and there was no longer anything to prevent someone from driving off the road without using an exit.

The problem was that the four traffic lanes, the exit, and the breakdown lanes were all blocked with vehicles placed end to end, and the armed folks standing behind the roadblock were definitely not police.

"We're not stopping," he announced over the radio as he aimed his truck at a small gap between the two smallest vehicles in his path, knowing that he wouldn't fit. "Hang on!" he yelled as the grille guard on the front of his truck struck the quarter panels of both the two smaller vehicles, spinning them around and away from him, clearing the way for both Billy and Harvey, as he barreled through the opening.

Alex accelerated the truck as he glanced in his rearview mirror, seeing several vehicles giving chase. Billy seemed to be keeping up, but Harvey was quickly falling behind.

He focused on driving the truck while trying to figure out if there was any way that he could help Harvey out. Gunshots blasted through the air, and Harvey's car swerved and then flipped over as the rim for the front tire dug into the soft dirt in the median, rolling once before coming to an abrupt stop. It was quickly surrounded by people with guns, Harvey and Helen were lost.

Only one vehicle was still chased them. It was a pickup and two men were standing in the back holding onto the roll bar with one hand and shooting at Billy with the other.

Alex slammed down on the brakes and cranked the wheel, spinning the truck around to face back towards Billy and the pursuing truck of raiders.

"Keep going. I'm gonna give them something to think about," Alex yelled over the radio. He grabbed his rifle and carefully aimed it out his window, he relaxed as he slowly pulled the trigger. The truck immediately swerved as the front tire blew out from the impact of the slug. The truck started to tip over, tossing the men in the back like rag dolls out onto the roadway in front of the rolling vehicle, the truck didn't even slow down as it crushed their fragile bodies during one of the rolls.

Alex immediately cranked the wheel and spun his truck back around. Catching back up to Billy and retaking the lead, they sped out of town as fast as their vehicles would go.

A few miles out of Wichita Falls, Billy's voice came over the radio, sounding unusually weak, "I just thought you should know that I've been shot."

"Shit man. Why didn't you say something earlier? I'm taking the next side road, and we'll go a couple of miles in case that group decides to follow us," Alex told Billy, slowing down to turn on the next county road.

He drove slowly down the dirt and gravel road in an attempt to keep the dust down, no need to announce to everyone where they went. Up ahead he saw an old barn and figured that would be a good enough place to stop.

He pulled around to the side of the barn so he was hidden from the highway, and came to a stop.

BB had already got the first aid kit out from under the seat and was nearly halfway out the door before Alex even had the truck in park.

Billy parked the Blazer beside him and shut it off before leaning back in the seat, clutching his side while wincing in pain.

Alex could see all the blood on Billy's shirt on his left side, through the windshield. He quickly made his way around to the driver's door and helped his friend get out. He half carried Billy over to the tailgate of the pickup, which BB had already lowered.

"Get that shirt off, I need to see the wound," BB directed him as she went into doctor mode.

Alex helped his best friend take off his shirt, flinching in sympathy every time Billy gasped in pain.

"Dude, getting shot sucks," he announced.

"I don't doubt that but you're in good hands with Doctor BB. She'll have you fixed up and good as new in no time," he told Billy.

BB looked over the wound. "The good news is that it's in the fleshy part of the arm, and it's a through and through so no bone fragments or bullet to fish out."

She cleaned the wound with alcohol and told Alex to

press a bandage to the wound. "No. Press harder! Try to stop the bleeding!" she demanded.

"Billy, I'm going to give you some local numbing agent and then stitch up the exit wound first. Alex, you keep applying pressure to the entrance wound until I'm ready to stitch it up," BB ordered as she did several injections around the wound.

"So tell me how this happened," she inquired with the intention of getting Billy to take his mind off what she was doing.

"It happened so fast. I was following you guys and then you smashed through those cars. That was awesome by the way," he told Alex, sounding impressed. "Guns were going off all around me and I tried to duck down but couldn't because I needed to get out of there, and I needed to be able to see in order to do that. I heard a pop and realized that a bullet had hit my dash, and then I felt the pain and knew I'd been hit. I just floored it and followed you until you turned around. I just kept going like you told me, eventually you showed back up, and here we are."

Billy looked up at Alex. "What did you do after you turned around?"

Alex grinned. "I shot out their front tire with my rifle and got the hell out of there. We lost Harvey and Helen though," he said as his grin faded.

"Yeah, there was no way we could have done anything to save them from what I saw, it would have been suicide to try." Billy lowered his head in shame, blaming himself for their deaths since he had been the one to insist on driving through Wichita Falls.

Alex moved his blood slicked hand as BB started stitching up the entrance wound.

"That matches what I see," BB commented. "It looks like the bullet came from behind you on the driver's side, went through the muscle in your upper arm, and then into the dash. You'll have some muscle damage and a couple of scars, but it could have been a lot worse."

"Cool!" Billy declared with a big smile on his face. "Chicks dig scars."

This caused everyone to laugh, making the mood lighter.

"Well, I think we need to take a break, eat something and figure out what we're going to do from here. Billy's arm needs to be in a sling so he isn't going to be able to drive through any more roadblocks," Alex noted. "Does BB drive or do we drop down to one vehicle? Think on it while we eat, and then we can talk it out."

Alex grabbed a new shirt for Billy and then helped fit him with a sling that they had found in some of the medical supplies BB had permanently borrowed from the hospital.

Once Billy was situated, they made sandwiches and had a light lunch.

"I'm okay with driving for a while," BB started the conversation. "I'd hate to leave all these supplies behind, and Billy kinda loves his Blazer."

"Good point, I do love my Blazer. We just tinted her windows so we can't leave her behind," agreed Billy as he pet his Blazer like a puppy.

"That's good, I didn't want to lose the second vehicle either. We'd be screwed if something happened to the truck and we ended up walking," Alex pointed out.

"I hadn't thought of that, but it's a valid concern," she admitted.

"New rule, we go around every town over 5,000 people. I don't care if it takes us a week to get to Colorado, I'm not going through that again. Billy, if I ever say I have a bad feeling again, listen to me," Alex glared at him. "This could have all been easily avoided if you didn't think your way was always better."

Billy nodded his head, "Agreed. I'm sorry guys, I really fucked up this time, and I think I've learned my lesson," he said as he brought attention to his injured arm. "I think that maybe we should just take back roads from now on."

Alex thought about it for a minute before nodding his head. "We could, but then we'd end up leaving a cloud of dust in our wake, telling everyone where we are. That could be avoided by traveling at night, but then we couldn't use our headlights. Thoughts?" he asked, looking at his friends.

"I say we use the highway between towns and the back roads to go around them. If it seems like we are always on the back roads, then we can switch to just back roads, traveling at night, with no lights," BB said, giving her two cents worth.

Billy looked up thoughtfully. "Actually, that might be the best idea anyway, we're going to be backtracking a lot every time we go around a town. That's going to add a ton of miles to the trip, using more gas, not to mention the extra days of travel time."

Alex spotted BB nodding her head in silent acknowledgment of Billy's statement. "Alright then. I think it's a unanimous decision. We'll travel after dark and only when it's dark from here on out."

DAY NINE

Fred

He felt the beads of sweat slowly creeping their way down his back. If he got caught...no he couldn't think that way. He glanced around to make sure that he wasn't being observed, then, quick as he could, he reached into the small refrigerator and grabbed the two vials he desired, almost dropping them in his haste. He promptly tucked them into the pocket of his lab coat, knowing that he would have to transfer the fluids into something else and return the vials before anyone noticed that they were missing; however, unlikely that was.

"Here, use these."

Fred jumped at the words that came from behind him, letting out a small screech in the process, causing Latisha to laugh.

"Holy shit Latisha! Don't sneak up on me like that, I about shit my pants." He glared at her before noticing that she was holding out to him some of the small tubes that they used for collecting blood to send to the lab.

Changing the glare to a grin, he reached out to accept the offered tubes. A small electric shock, followed by a comforting tingle, ran through his body when his fingers grazed her hand during the transfer, or maybe it was just in his imagination. Since his emotions had been all over the place the last couple of weeks, he was no longer sure what was real and what was in his head. He was; however, acutely aware of the changes that he felt throughout his body when he saw her, touched her, smelled her...

He shook his head to clear away the thoughts that he shouldn't be having about his best friend and coworker. "These will be perfect, but you need to go lie back down and rest."

Gesturing to the cells in the back room. "How do you feel?"

Latisha sighed and looked at him. "I'm doing alright for a dead girl." Seeing the instant distress in Fred's face, she immediately tried to fix the pain her words had inadvertently caused him. "I'm sorry, I shouldn't joke about it. Honestly, I really think I should be feeling worse, I still have a slight headache, even with the ibuprofen, but it's manageable, low-grade fever, weakness, general body aches, and chills."

Fred grasped at the safety rope she had thrown. "That's good it hasn't gotten worse. Maybe your immune system can fight it off."

He saw the look flash briefly across her face before she could regain control, and he knew that she didn't think she would be one of the lucky ones. He felt a sharp pain in his chest at the thought.

"I just want to help you while I am strong enough to. Let's get the samples taken care of before someone comes," Latisha said as she went over to the workbench.

Fred watched her walk over to the table where she dug a couple of syringes out of the supply drawer before following her. She opened the package containing the first syringe and was handing it to him when he shook his head.

"I want you to do it." Setting the tubes on the table, he pulled the vials out of his pocket and handed one of them to her. He knew she needed to stay busy to keep her mind off what her body was fighting, and he was willing to do anything he could to help.

She grinned as she took the vial and looked at it before inserting the needle in the rubber stopper and drawing out a few cc's of the fluid before injecting it into one of the tubes. "This is the Booster, I'm putting it in the tube with the purple cap. We'll use the orange capped tube for the Steri-12. You need to remember which is which because we don't want to label them in case you're caught with them in your possession."

Fred admired the way she stayed calm and deftly did the task at hand as if it was just another normal day. If it was him, he'd be curled up on the floor in a dark room, bawling like a baby and crying out for his mommy. He drew off her strength and vowed to help her survive this evil scourge that Dr. Carter created. Fred made up his mind right then, that if Latisha didn't survive this, then neither would Dr. Carter. He would make sure of it.

"All done." She laid the tubes on a layer of cotton padding in a small box before adding another layer of padding. She reached into her pocket and pulled out three vials of blood, laying them on top. Closing the box that she had already labeled with another lab's name and address, she slid it toward him with a smile. "Now, if anyone stops you, tell them that you're taking the blood samples to be double-checked by that outside lab we sometimes use. You can even open the box to show them the vials of blood. Most people don't like blood so that should prevent anyone from taking a closer look under the padding. Just make sure you tell them to be careful with the blood samples because they're mine, and contain the active infection. They should probably destroy them, but if they think they can use them, that's alright with me."

Fred was impressed with how well thought out her plan was, they might just be able to pull this off after all. He had no idea how they planned to get the samples out of the lab when they had come up with the idea last night, but apparently, Latisha had.

"I'm going to go put these vials back and clean up while you run those over to Randy. When you get back, you can take me to lunch in the cafeteria," she said, grinning at him.

"It's a date," he said without thinking, then realizing his

mistake, he tried to recover, "err I meant that-" Latisha pressed her index finger to Fred's lips.

"It IS a date," she informed him before turning away to put up the vials. "Now get moving mister, I'm getting hungry," she teased him over her shoulder.

Fred hadn't moved so fast in, well, forever.

Just as Latisha had predicted, the security guard took one look in the box and promptly waved him through without further questioning. He drove as quickly as he dared, taking the side streets that hadn't yet been blocked off by residents protecting their neighborhoods or by gangs of roving rioters, intent on slowly destroying the city, block by block.

He slowed down at a stop sign before quickly accelerating away when he heard gunshots from not too far away.

Fred arrived on Peachtree Street only to find the dry cleaners in flames. Erik and Eddie were across the street, standing and staring at the fire as it consumed Erik's family legacy, apparently mesmerized by the destruction. He pulled up and stopped in front of them, hastily getting out of the car.

"Oh my God Erik. What happened?" he asked.

"Fucking rioters, that's what!" replied Erik, spitting venom with each word, "Why don't they burn down their own shit? I had nothing to do with this virus except to try and stop it."

The front of the building collapsed onto the sidewalk, as the fire continued to eat up the block with an insatiable hunger.

"I'm so sorry, did you call the fire department?"

Erik shook his head in frustration. "They said to let it burn. Too many firefighters are sick with the virus or just aren't going to work because the rioters attack them when they go out on calls. It's gone now, and there's nothing I can do about it." He looked over at Fred as if realizing that he was there, even though they had already been talking, "What brings you here anyway?"

"Randy had asked me to draw the layout of the labs for him, and I also have samples of the alleged vaccines. I thought maybe Randy could get them to the CDC, it might help their scientist to have the undiluted samples," he suggested.

Erik was shaking his head. "Randy's not in town anymore, I took him to the Army base a couple of days ago. He's trying to get the military involved."

Fred lowered his head in defeat. "Oh, so I guess I got them for nothing then."

Erik pulled out his burner phone and quickly found the number he wanted. After a moment the call went through. "Hey Lisa, it's Erik...Yeah, he's safe at Fort Benning...Well, not so good, I'm standing here, watching the dry cleaners burn...Thanks, but that's not why I called...Randy told you about Fred, right?... Well, he managed to sneak out some samples of the so-called vaccines of Dr. Carter's thinking that the CDC might be able to use them...Okay...Yeah, I'll tell him...Talk to you later."

He watched the fire for a moment before continuing. "Lisa can't leave the CDC due to the rioters, but she will have armed security come and get the samples if you can wait. If not, give me the samples and I'll make sure that they get them. As for the drawings, I can scan and email them to Randy from my house if you'd like me to."

Relief flooded through his body. "If you don't mind, I need to get back to the lab before they notice that I'm gone," he said, handing the drawings and the small box to Erik. "The samples are in the box underneath the blood vials. The one with the purple cap is the Booster shot and the orange capped one contains the sterilization drug. Make sure they know that the vials of blood are contaminated with the active Frankenstein Virus. It's Latisha's blood, we used it to hide the vaccine samples from security. Latisha said they can use her blood for testing or destroy it, she doesn't care either way."

"How she be?" Eddie asked as he coughed, either from the smoke or the virus, Fred wasn't sure which.

"As well as can be expected. She's a strong girl, she'll be okay," he said with as much conviction as he could muster.

"That be good. Her mama 'n everyone 'n the family be sick to. If she's be making it, maybe we all can," Eddie said hopefully.

Fred wasn't quite sure what to say. "It's possible, but that's one test that Dr. Carter didn't have us do so I don't know if survivors run in families or not. I'm sorry Eddie."

"You be not worrying about me. Take care of Latisha. She be the one needing you. I be not knowing where I be after this," he said, waving at the fire, "but I be having this phone that Randy got me so I be calling if I be still living to let you know."

"Sounds good and I'll let Latisha know. Can I do anything for you?" Fred asked, worried about the man he'd come to be unlikely friends with.

"I be okay. you be getting back to that niece of mine 'n taking care of her. That be giving me peace of the mind."

Fred shook both men's hands not knowing if he would ever see them again but hoping that he would. "You both take care of each other, you have my number if you need my help."

They waved him off as he got in his car and left to go back to the lab.

Colonel Harker

The never-ending meeting at the Pentagon was finally over. They had been reviewing all of the data that they had on the virus and were attempting to find a solution. The entire military force was returning home as quickly as they could arrange transport. Every time he thought they were wrapping it up, someone would start talking about something else, and the meeting would ramp back up. Thank goodness they allowed piss beaks every hour. He swore that he must have drunk about a gallon of water from the provided pitchers that were constantly being refilled during the breaks.

Unbeknownst to him, the Pentagon aide who was refilling the pitchers was part of The Elite Group and had made sure that most of the One-Offs, including the one that Dr. Carter recently made, had been added to the appropriate water glasses during one of the breaks. Unable to contaminate all the glasses, the aide dropped the few remaining capsules into a glass of water and drank it himself. As the virus was DNA target specific, he had little to worry about for his own safety. When it was time for the next break, he would be sure to stand next to the door, leading out of the conference room, infecting the air with the virus so anyone passing by would become infected themselves. Those who chose not to leave the room, he would infect just by walking past them as he exhaled while he refilled their water glasses. The majority of the people who attended the meeting wouldn't survive the next 24-48 hours.

In government buildings throughout Washington D.C., One-Offs were being distributed in water, coffee, and in one senator's case, a passionate kiss from his mistress.

Erik

It was almost two hours before the armed security team arrived to retrieve the fake vaccines. Erik made sure to call Lisa to tell her it was picked up and on its way to her. He almost forgot to tell her about the blood samples but remembered before they hung up.

He and Eddie had planned on trying to salvage what they could once the fire burned out, but there were still some hot spots inside the building. Unfortunately. he could tell just by looking, there was nothing left to salvage. The only thing remaining was three of the brick exterior walls and the skeletons of the clothes racks, dark with soot, standing sentry within the smoking ruins. Hopefully, his insurance would cover the loss, but Erik was unsure if his policy covered damage from riots.

They made their way down the alley to see if the van or his car had survived the inferno, they hadn't. All that was left were two smoldering piles of scrap metal that he would have to pay to get hauled off. Well wasn't that just the fucking cherry on top of the shit sundae that he had been given?

Frustrated, he kicked the quarter panel of what was remained of his car.

"Let's get out of here Eddie."

"Where we be going?" Eddie realized it didn't matter after he had posed the question.

"Not a clue. I just want to get away from here," he replied as he turned to walk away.

The two friends trudged down the still smoky alley, the sound of an occasional cough from Eddie, echoing behind them.

Erik unconsciously led his friend in the direction of the park, where their involvement in this nightmare had begun, as he pondered their predicament and what to do about it.

As they walked, he looked at what the rioters had done to his beloved city. A light blanket of smoky haze now covered the cities skyline. Businesses that hadn't been burnt to the ground, had their windows smashed, and looters had either taken the merchandise or damaged it beyond salvaging. Most small businesses probably couldn't sustain the loss unless it was covered by insurance. The majority would fail to reopen after the pandemic, ultimately killed by the virus.

"I be getting tired, is it okay if we be sitting for a while?" Eddie asked, obviously worn out.

He nodded his head while looking at the vandalized statues and park benches. "That's fine. It looks like the rioters have already been through the park so we should be okay."

Erik helped Eddie turn a bench upright and move it so they could sit in the shade of a large elm tree.

"I have somewhat of a plan, I'm not sure how good it is, but let me know what you think." Seeing Eddie nod his head, Erik continued, "I'm going to call Randy and see if the sergeant will let us stay on the Army base. My next-door neighbor might let me borrow a car to get us there, but if not, I'll figure something out."

"That be sounding alright except I be thinking they won't be wanting a sick infected person to be at the base. If they let you be going there, I be wanting you to be going 'n don't you be worrying about me, I be knowing some places that maybe I be staying at," Eddie told him, wiping the tears from his eyes.

Erik was touched that his friend was worried about him when he was in a much worse situation. At least he wasn't sick and he still had a home, assuming the rioters hadn't burnt it down as well.

"If they won't let you stay on base, we'll just stay at my house. I'm not going to let you go through this infection alone if I can help it. A family just doesn't do that to each other."

Eddie turned and gave him a huge hug. "Thank you Erik. You be like a brother to me to."

Trying to wipe his tears away while being hugged was too difficult of a feat for him to accomplish. Erik gave up and just hugged his friend back and overcome with emotion, he let the tears flow.

After a few moments, they broke apart, and each found themselves wiping their eyes. Seeing the humor in it, they began laughing, desperately needing the release of tension from the tragedy ridden day.

"Alright," Erik said after finally being able to regain his composure somewhat. "I gotta call Randy."

He thought the call was going to go to voice mail when Randy finally picked up.

"Randy here."

"It's Erik and I need some help if the sergeant is willing."

He relayed everything that had happened that day, ending with the suggestion that Randy ask the sergeant if he and Eddie could stay at the base until the pandemic was over.

"Sorry Erik. The base isn't letting anyone who is displaying any symptoms onto the base. They just don't have the medical staff to help that many people, especially with a lot of the soldiers already having symptoms. I'm sure that he'd allow you on base though," he offered, hoping his friend would join him.

Erik immediately refused, "I appreciate the offer, but I'm not going to leave Eddie alone while he's sick. I'll take him to my house and if it's still standing, we'll just ride out the rest of the apocalypse there."

"Are you sure? I've heard reports about how dangerous the cities are getting," Randy told him, trying to convince his old college buddy to change his mind.

Erik clapped Eddie on the shoulder and grinned at him. "We'll be okay. I have my dad's guns and plenty of ammo so we can defend ourselves if need be. Is the sergeant getting anywhere with the military in regard to resolving this insanity?"

"I'm not really in the loop anymore. They will come to ask me questions occasionally, but mostly I just sit around and stare at the walls. I did briefly chat with the sergeant this morning and he said that he's working with his base commander and a few others, but since they don't know who they can trust, it's slow going," Randy explained.

Erik sighed, he was ready for this to be all over as he wasn't sure how much more he could take. "Well that makes sense, I suppose. We've done everything that was within our means to get the information to the right people. I guess now all we can do is pray."

"Amen brother. Amen."

"Me and Eddie have a bit of a walk ahead of us so I'm gonna get off the phone. Take care, Randy."

"You too Eric."

He put the phone back in his pocket and started walking home, with Eddie at his side.

Master Sergeant Brooks

They couldn't afford to wait any longer, most of the chain of command out of Washington D.C. were now getting sick with some new flu or virus. The President had seen all the ads on the media about a vaccine being distributed and he knew that it had not gone through the FDA. He decided that the intel on Crouch Pharmaceutical was valid and for the first time, the US Army Rangers would be doing an actual raid on US soil. The target would be the labs of Crouch Pharmaceutical. The order was the last one the President signed before he was overcome with extremely painful cramps in his abdomen before collapsing to the floor.

The Secretary of Defense managed to pass the order down to several base commanders before he too, was also overcome with debilitating cramps and could no longer function. He was soon flown to Walter Reed Medical Center in Bethesda, Maryland.

When the colonel at Fort Benning received the order, he immediately called a meeting with all the top personnel on the base, to go over strategy. Newly promoted Master Sergeant Brooks was put in charge of who would go on the Op and what the infiltration plan would be.

"Alright ladies, we have a date tomorrow, and I don't want to keep them waiting so settle down."

Master Sergeant Brooks waited until everyone was focused on him.

"The target is civilian and it's right here in the United States. Crouch Pharmaceutical in Atlanta, GA, or more specifically, the labs located underneath Crouch Pharmaceutical.

"Now I know what you're all thinking, we do not operate within the confines of the US border as a general rule, but this is a special case signed by the President. It seems the alphabets might have been compromised and since they can't tell who is playing for what team, we get to play in our own house." The master sergeant watched the Rangers for a reaction and wasn't surprised when he didn't get one, they had been trained to be the best after all.

"Our intel is that Crouch Pharmaceutical is behind this virus, but they are being backed by a much larger organization called The Elite Group. This group is attempting to depopulate

the world and is doing a damn good job of it. Our job is to capture the scientist who designed the Frankenstein Virus and to
try and stop any further attacks.

"The building has state of the art security after hours,
but during business hours, it's three rent-a-cops, some cameras, ID mag strips, and a manually entered code to get into the
labs, but we have our own code breaker and its name is C-4." A
few of the Rangers gave the obligatory laugh to the well-used
joke.

"The inside source has been kind enough to draw us a
layout of the lab's three floors. As far as we know, there is no
reason to doubt this person, but bear in mind as we infiltrate
the location, that the drawings may not be accurate. The labs
we are interested in are all below ground level. The remainder
of the building is for the production of legal drugs and the employees probably aren't even aware of what occurs in the labs
below them. Normally this would be a night op, but we need to
make sure that the scientists are on-site. Entry will be made at
0900 through the front doors, the staircase will be to the right
of the elevators. This will be a coordinated attack using three
8 man squads. Charlie Squad will enter the stairwell first since
they will have the lowest level, followed by Bravo and then
Alpha. Once all three squads are in position within the stairwell, we will enter the labs at the same time. The stairwell door
requires a mag card so make sure you bring your decoder with
you. The door opens onto a small entryway that will lead into
the lab. The doors to the labs are made out of thick glass, possibly bulletproof, but a little C-4 should open them right up.

"The primary lab belongs to a Dr. Jeremy Carter. He is our
primary target along with any intel we can find on just what
the not-so-good doctor has been up to and what else he might
have planned for the future. Alpha Squad, led by Staff Sergeant
Jones, will be responsible for retrieving the doctor and his research.

"Going down one level is the secondary lab. My contact
has no knowledge of what happens within this lab but is aware

of at least one lab assistant who spends a lot of time there. He might just be watching porn, if so, confiscate it for later review." A good number of the Rangers chuckled while slapping each other on their backs. "Bravo Squad, led by Staff Sergeant Taylor, will secure any personnel and research material located in this lab.

"Finally, we have the secure testing lab. This is where the human experiments were being carried out. Charlie Squad, led by Staff Sergeant Smith, will be in charge of securing this level. There should be at least two lab assistants, one male and one female, on this level. Treat them well as they are our inside contacts. Once we have control of all three labs, they will help us in any way they can.

"Go in fast and clean. We are not expecting any hostiles as these are civilian scientists but stay on your toes. There are to be no causalities," he cautioned the Rangers.

"Staff Sergeant Jones will be in charge of the overall mission on site. Any questions?" Master Sergeant Brooks looked around the room at the Rangers.

"Good. One more thing, everyone wears a gas mask, like I said, these are scientific labs used to create viruses, and who knows what's inside. Now get your gear situated and hit the racks. There will be another mission brief at 0500 from Staff Sergeant Jones before you pull out tomorrow. Dismissed."

Jeremy

The call had gone out this morning. The Steri-12 vaccine was to be distributed to all of the military bases and medical facilities within every major city in the US. Most would be delivered by the end of the day, and members of The Elite Group would be at the facilities by morning to begin the process of administering the injections.

They were already running blitz ads on radio, TV, newspapers, and online media across the country, announcing the discovery of a vaccine for the Frankenstein Virus that would be available in the morning. While not a cure, it was being touted as both a vaccine to prevent both the initial infection, as well as possible reinfection for those who had already been infected and survived. Additionally, it was also a treatment that would alleviate some of the symptoms and shorten the overall length of time that someone would be sick.

Jeremy was bursting with pride like a father with a new-born baby. First, his World-Ender Virus was distributed and worked perfectly, and then this morning, the One-Offs were dispersed throughout Washington D.C., he was expecting to start hearing of the effects from them within the next day or so. Tomorrow they would begin the Steri-12 treatments as well as the Sarin gas that was being released in all of the major prisons. Then, in two weeks, the Booster shot would make its debut, and shortly thereafter recruitment could begin.

It was definitely going to be a very busy time and none of it would have happened without him!

The intercom buzzed.

"Yes! What is it?" he snapped at whoever was on the intercom. He really disliked being bothered unnecessarily.

"Dr. Carter, my name is Agent Warren with the NSA. We need to speak privately."

"Fine. I'll be there in a moment to open the door," he relented.

Jeremy hated to deal with people, he thought maybe that's why he loved his viruses so much. Oh well, he'd quickly find out what this imbecile wanted, and then he could get back to doing something important, like getting a fresh cup of coffee.

He had barely opened the door before Agent Warren pushed his way inside.

"You have to leave the lab and get to the bunker, I just got word that the Army is planning on raiding this building. You have two hours before the armed escort will be leaving so pack up what you can and destroy the rest. If you miss the escort, you're on your own," the agent ordered the scientist.

"Now just a minute. I can't just stop what I'm doing and pack up. I-" He was promptly interrupted.

"Shut up and start packing. You have two hours and not a minute more or I will leave you here."

The agent stared at him, almost daring him to talk back. Jeremy glared back and didn't move, nobody talked to him like that. After a couple of minutes, the agent broke the silence, "Times ticking doc," he stated flatly, tapping the face of his watch with his index finger.

"Fine! Leave so I can concentrate on packing."

Agent Warren tilted his head slightly. "Two hours," he reiterated and then turned and left the lab.

Jeremy started to tremble with anger, how dare he speak to me that way? Maybe I should just One-Off him as well, or give him a booster since I apparently don't have time to create a One-Off right now.

Looking around, he realized just how much he needed to get done in the next couple of hours. He grabbed the phone and entered the code for the secure lab. "Blondie, Skinny, and Chubby. I need all of you in my lab. NOW!" He hung up the phone and then signed off of all the computers and shut them down.

The door opened, revealing the trio of assistants, who quickly rushed inside and then stopped, waiting for instructions.

"We're leaving the labs in two hours. Pack up all the research, files, notes, samples, computers, and servers, leave everything else. Skinny and Chubby, you clear out the secure lab, if you finish in time, go help Blondie with the secondary lab. Blondie, make sure you get everything for the new project that you've been working on before you even think about touching anything else. No trace of what we've been doing here gets left behind, understood?"

A chorus of "Yes, sir," rang out across the room as they answered in unison.

"Why are you still standing here, get moving. We leave

in two hours, and if you're late, you will get left behind. Now, MOVE!" he demanded.

The assistants all turned and ran toward the door, almost tripping over each other in their haste.

Sighing, Jeremy turned and got back to work packing what he couldn't leave behind. It was probably a good thing that he had Blondie working on a backup plan. It seemed like someone had let the cat out of the bag.

DAY TEN

Staff Sergeant Jones

As he sat in the Black Hawk, feeling the thrumming of the rotors which would normally lull him to sleep, he thought about the mission. Going over it multiple times in his head and running various scenarios on what he should do if things went FUBAR as they so often did.

The three squads had been cobbled together from multiple units as about half of the men in most units were either sick, dying, or dead from the Frankenstein Virus.

Jones had just turned 30, with no children. He was married to the Army, and it still held his heart as it had for the past 12 years, ever since he had joined straight out of high school. Once he became a Ranger, he knew that he would never leave the military. He loved the men as much as he loved his own family, and in many ways, he loved them more. He trusted them to have his back and knew that they would, just as they had in the past.

The Private News Network, also known as the rumor mill, claimed that Atlanta had been overrun with gangs, rioters, and looters. Martial law had been declared several days ago but was largely being ignored. Many police officers were sick with the virus, and more were failing to go in, preferring to stay home to protect their own property and loved ones. The Governor had ordered the National Guard to stop the rioting, but unfortunately, they faced the same issues as the police department and were woefully understaffed, they had been quickly overrun by the mobs, before finally being pulled back to base. The city was now being left to its own devices until a strategy could be developed to take it back from the mobs and rioters.

Originally, the squads were to travel on the ground but with the city street rife with mobs of people and all manner of debris, the decision had been made to infiltrate by bird and fast rope to the ground should no viable landing space be available. Improvise, adapt and overcome, as his marine counterparts would say. He always thought that to be good advice and had used it to good effect many times throughout his career, but he would never say those words aloud. He was Army after all, not a Marine.

The red light on the wall of the chopper came on, giving the five-minute warning.

"Alright Alphas. That's the five-minute bell so check yourselves and the men on either side of you. Make sure everything is in order and where it should be. We should have intel in a couple of mikes if it's gonna be a hot LZ or not. That's the difference of fast-roping or taking a leisurely stroll out of this tin can we're currently in."

Everyone quickly made sure all straps were tight, and there was nothing left loose on any of the Rangers. When you did the fast rope, you didn't want a loose mag to fall and hit a friendly in the head.

"One-minute warning and it appears that fast-roping won't be necessary; however, only one bird will be on the ground at a time due to space constraints. Alpha will be first, clear and hold for Bravo and Charlie squads. Once on the ground, put on your gas masks and protect our six. Our arrival might rouse the natives so be on alert. Beat feet in three, two, one. OUT! OUT! OUT!"

The eight member squad was on the ground and clear of the Black Hawk in less than 30 seconds, a few minutes later, they were joined by both Bravo and Charlie Squads.

Alpha led the way to the entry point, weapons at the ready. Jones tried to yank the door opened but found it locked, not being aware that the building was on lock-down due to the riots. He waved Boomer up to set a charge and the door was quickly blown off its hinges, allowing Reeves, Bull, and Wilcox easy access. Reeves went to the right, Bull to the left, and Wilcox cleared the front as he yelled, "US Army Rangers! Get down on the ground. NOW!"

The stunned receptionist screamed before dropping behind the counter. One man turned to run but quickly stopped and dropped to the floor when a bullet was shot over his head and hit the wall near him. The few remaining employees, who happened to be in the lobby, initially froze before their brain caught up in understanding, and they dropped to the floor as well.

"Clear!" Wilcox called out.

The remaining Alpha Squad members promptly entered and stacked up by the stairwell entrance, Bravo immediately followed, making room for Charlie. Jones had the same three men clear the stairwell before he motioned for Charlie to proceed to their assigned target area. Bravo Squad was quickly on Charlie Squad's tail as Alpha fell in behind, Jones indicated to Reeves, Bull, and Wilcox to stay back and guard their six.

Jones heard three quick clicks on his radio followed by two more clicks, letting him know that the other two squads were in position and had a small shape charge in place, ready to blow the mag card readers and disconnect the power to the electronic locks on the stairwell doors. He finally heard one last click from Boomer, his squad's demolition expert, to let the others know Alpha was ready as well. Each squad had backed off to the landing above the doorway to hopefully prevent any injuries. Setting off any type of explosive in an enclosed stairwell was never a real good idea if it could be avoided. The squads had taken extra precautions by using earplugs and then donning sound dampening headsets to help prevent damage to their hearing.

Everyone mentally counted down, three, two, one before hearing three small explosions go off simultaneously. Jones quickly jogged down the stairs and pulled the newly unlocked door open, as smoke rose from what remained of the card reader.

Alpha Squad quickly cleared the small foyer as Jones peered through the glass door, not seeing anyone, he nodded to Boomer who quickly set up charges on the hinges and the lock of the door. The squad moved back into the stairwell and closed the door before Boomer set the charges off remotely.

The sound of the explosion was muted by the stairwell door, and was quickly followed by the loud crash of the glass door falling out of its frame and onto the floor. Alpha team promptly left the stairwell and cleared the lab.

It was empty!

Jones looked around and could tell that everything had been hastily packed up by the scattered papers strewn on the floor and the open cabinet door, where he assumed the computer towers had been kept.

"Search it. I doubt we find anything, but we're gonna try."

Pressing the button on his radio. "Bravo, you got anything?"

"Negative Alpha."

"Charlie?"

"Affirmative, we have one target in custody, no intel."

"Roger that. All squads do a quick check, then back on me and we'll regroup."

"Roger that. Bravo out."

"Lima-Charlie. Charlie out."

All teams were in the primary lab in less than five minutes, Charlie brought the captive with them.

"Where is Dr. Carter?" he asked the noticeably scared female scientist.

"They went to the bunker, but they left me here because I have symptoms, are you with Sergeant Brooks?" Latisha asked, slowly regaining her composure.

"We are. I assume that you're one of the contacts, where is the other one?"

"Fred? Oh, they made him go with them to the bunker," she told them.

"Where is the bunker?" he asked her, knowing that they wouldn't have left her alive if she had that information.

"I'm not exactly sure. I overheard someone say that they were heading to Colorado so I assume it's there. Sorry, I'm not very much help."

Jones turned away from Latisha and spoke to the Rangers, "There's nothing here, we were too late. Have Bull call the choppers back and let them know we'll be plus one."

They quickly left the building and climbed back into their respective Black Hawks as each touched down. Looking out of the helicopter at the smoldering ruins of the city, he saw muzzle flashes aimed at the bullet-resistant Black Hawks.

"Shots fired!" the copilot announced over the CVC helmets.

"Just fly higher and get us out of here. I'm not going to shoot at fellow Americans if I can avoid it. Get us back to base," Jones replied, suddenly worried for his family back in Nebraska as he felt a deep pain of loss in his heart for the country that he loved so much.

Warden Mitchell

The warden had put the Pelican Bay State Prison on lockdown early in the morning.

As part of The Elite Group, he was finally given his instructions on what he had to do to keep his family safe. He found that he was extremely troubled over what he was ordered to do, but if he failed, not only would he and his family be killed, the orders would still be carried out by someone else, meaning that he would have killed his family for nothing.

"Warden, the prisoners are angry, they want to know

why they are on lockdown, and quite frankly, so do all of us guards," the guard said, wishing another guard was here in his place.

"Tell them it's just a temporary precaution against an unknown threat. The lockdown will be lifted within a few hours if not sooner, and we will grant them some extra time in the yard to compensate for the inconvenience. Right now, I need to go meet with the Governor to get this all straightened out, so if you'll excuse me."

"Of course, warden." The guard turned and walked away, thinking that something was definitely off about the entire situation. The warden would never give extra yard time for something like a lockdown. Oh well, he was off in an hour, the next shift could deal with the fallout while he was at home enjoying time with his wife.

The warden watched the curious guard walk away before grabbing his briefcase and taking the stairs up to the roof where a helicopter was waiting for him. He needed to be anywhere but here.

In prisons across the country, a similar scene was being played out. Not all wardens were members of The Elite Group, but there were plenty of guards, nurses, secretaries, and other civilian staff who were. They had each been entrusted with placing the gas canisters within their own facilities before finding a reason to leave before the contents of the canisters were released.

At 10:00 am CST, in a coordinated effort, the Sarin gas canisters would be activated, filling all the prisons with the deadly gas, leaving no one inside alive.

Jeremy

The bus carrying the members of The Elite Group, who had worked at Crouch Pharmaceutical, pulled up to a razor-wire topped fence that enclosed the small brick building. Disguised as a remote radio antenna location, the entrance to the 150,000 square foot bunker was just inside the door.

After the fence gate and the bunker doors were opened, members were allowed to disembark from the bus and enter their new, temporary home.

Jeremy saw the 'you are here' map on the wall and quickly figured out where the lab was located. Ignoring the people behind an information table that had been set up in order to help members find out where they would be staying and what job they might be required to do, he headed straight for the elevator.

Taking it down to the third level, he exited and walked down the large hall. Seeing a sign ahead that said lab, with an arrow pointing left, he was able to find it in short order. The locks were designed using the same security procedures as they had at Crouch pharmaceutical, he found that his card and personal code worked equally well on this door as they had back in Atlanta.

Entering, he found a basic lab setup. The research that they had salvaged wouldn't be here until later in the day. It had to be loaded on a cargo plane, flown out, and then unloaded onto trucks, before finally making its way to the bunker.

Noticing the smaller lab size, he was quite pleased that they had left Skinny back in Atlanta, this lab just wasn't designed for four people.

Booting up the lone computer, pleased that his user name and password worked on it as well, he checked the status of the Sarin gas canisters as it should be almost time for them to be activated, via satellite. He brought up the map on the computer and noted the thousands of small green dots spread across the United States showing the canisters as online and ready. He watched the countdown clock above the online map count down the time to activation, less than five minutes to go.

He rubbed his hands in anticipation of the event, 2.5 million prisoners would die, along with over 400,000 guards who would become collateral damage. Jeremy had been worried that he would miss it with all the flight delays, and then they had ended up riding in a bus for over eight hours before finally finding an airport that would let a plane take off or land. Mostly because the airport had been abandoned due to the virus and the civil unrest.

He watched in gleeful silence as the timer clicked down.

10, 9, 8, 7, 6, 5, 4, 3, 2, 1, 0.

All the green lights turned red within seconds of each other as the satellite signal, triggering the release, was beamed to Earth. Red letters popped up across the screen.

CANISTERS ACTIVATED!

Jeremy yelled out and jumped for joy as almost 3 million Americans were poisoned by the odorless gas and died a horrible, painful death.

Several hours later, the trucks showed up with all of the things that they had time to salvage from the labs. He sent Blondie and Chubby to go help unload the truck from the small garage area and bring it all down to the new lab so they could start getting it organized.

He was mainly wanting his computer from the primary lab as it had a program on it that updated hourly on how many injections of the Steri-12 had been given out. Each dose was to be scanned before it was administered, and that information would then be automatically uploaded to the program.

Jeremy was curious to see if the sheeple would blindly accept that they had been able to come up with a vaccine, manufacture it, and then distribute enough for everyone in less than two weeks. It took almost a year for a vaccine for COVID-19 to be approved and another six months to a year before everyone was vaccinated, and that was considered unheard of at the time.

He was hopeful, but he realistically expected the initial numbers to be low, as most would wait to see if there were any side effects before they committed to getting it themselves. That was one reason he argued to start with the Steri-12 and not go directly to the deadly Booster shot. Had they done that, only a small percentage of the targeted population would have gotten it before people started dying, and everyone else would have refused to take it.

Blondie entered the lab, pushing a cart containing the computer towers, monitors, and other computer-related items. Chubby followed him with a two-wheel dolly that was stacked with plastic totes, full of research material.

"Blondie, put my computer over on that desk, the others can go on the counter over there. Chubby, the research goes over on the counter along that wall. We'll go through it later to get it separated out and properly filed."

He waited for Jeff to get his computer and all its components separated and on the desk before he started connecting everything up. Within ten minutes, the computer was up and running, and he was logged into the vaccine tracking program for the US, a few seconds later, he had an answer, 126,421.

Jeremy scanned the individual locations and discovered that less than 100 had been administered at military installations, and all of them had been done at only one base with the last dose given over four hours before. This was disappointing, but not entirely unexpected, the military rarely did anything without proper authorization in triplicate.

He then switched over to worldwide tracking and found that the numbers were much higher, 1,485,319. Jeremy was pleased with this and couldn't wait to check again tomorrow.

By now, every person in the world would have been exposed to the virus. The virus should start dying out, and that would be credited to the Steri-12 vaccine even though it had nothing to do with it. The virus would most likely become extinct within the next 10 days...just in time for the Booster Shot.

Lisa

Scared didn't quite cover it, terrified would be a more accurate term to describe just how Lisa was feeling, as she looked out her office window and saw the angry mob surrounding the CDC.

They had started showing up an hour ago and hadn't stopped coming. At first, it was just the picketers, demanding that the CDC admit that they had created the virus. Rioters showed up shortly after, and they soon got the picketers riled up enough to get them to join them in throwing bottles, rocks, and other debris at the building and vandalizing the cars in the parking lot.

Employees had initially tried to call the police, receiving no answer, they called the FBI, who were unable to help them as they were dealing with their own mob of rioters.

In desperation, Lisa called Randy, her fingers drumming on the desk while waiting for him to answer.

"This is Randy."

Relief washed through her body. "Randy, it's Lisa. I need help!"

"What's going on?" his concern was expressed in his voice.

"There's a mob outside the CDC, and they're trying to get into the building, 911 isn't answering, and the FBI can't help. I need you to talk to Sergeant Brooks and see if he can somehow help us."

"I can check with the master sergeant, but it will take me a little while. In the meantime, try to secure the building the best you can. I'll call you back soon," he promised her.

"Please hurry," she pleaded before disconnecting the call, only then realizing that Sergeant First Class Brooks must have gotten a promotion.

Shaking that thought away, Lisa quickly gathered everyone remaining at the CDC. Most had either gotten ill or just didn't bother to come in anymore due to the rioting. Twelve people were all that were left, including her, Matt, and Berto.

"I got a call into the Army. They're going to see if there is anything they can do, but right now, we need to lock the elevators on the top floor and fill the stairwells with anything and everything we can to prevent these people from getting up here where we are." She wasn't concerned about them getting into the labs below, the blast doors would prevent that from happening if the bio-hazard warnings didn't scare them off first.

The group quickly got busy and did as directed. Desks, chairs, filing cabinets, potted plants, drinking fountains, and other random items, were all were stacked in the stairwells, completely blocking the stairs from the main floor all the way up to the third floor. Elevators were brought up to the top floor and the doors were blocked open since they didn't have the emergency keys to lock them in place.

Her cell phone rang just as they finished up.

"Hello?"

"Lisa. There happened to be some Rangers on their way back to the base from Atlanta, they are being turned around and will be on-site in approximately 15 minutes. They need to know how many people there are and if the helipad is available?" Randy told her.

She was extremely relieved to hear the news. "There's twelve of us and I'm not sure if the pad is clear or not. I imagine it is since we haven't had anyone fly in recently."

"Alright, I'll pass that along. Stay safe and get to the roof," he told her.

"Thank you Randy, we're on the way there now."

"See you soon Lisa."

As she ended the call, she told the group that Army Rangers were coming to get them, and they needed to make their way to the roof for rescue.

Lisa watched as Matt gripped his briefcase tightly, she knew it held the samples from Fred and all of Matt's research.

No way was it being left behind.

Staff Sergeant Jones

"Incoming call for you sergeant," the pilot said over the CVC helmet as the helicopter pitched to the right making a wide turn. "I'll patch it through to your com."

"Thank you."

"Jones, you there?" Master Sergeant Brooks asked.

"I'm here, sergeant."

"Alpha's going back to Atlanta."

"What's the sit-rep?"

"The CDC is being overrun by rioters and you need to rescue the employees and scientists that are still there. The helipad should be clear, and they'll be on the roof waiting. Put the civilians on the Black Hawk and hold for another bird."

"Roger that. ETA on the secondary bird?"

"Approximately 30 mikes behind you."

"Roger. Alpha out."

Staff Sgt. Jones quickly relayed the hastily put together plan to the rest of Alpha, who had noticed the Black Hawk was now heading back the direction they had just come from.

As the Black Hawk landed on the roof of the CDC, Jones noticed the group of survivors waiting by the door that led into the CDC.

Alpha quickly disembarked from the bird, and Jones made his way over to the civilians.

"I'm Sergeant Jones. Who's in charge here?" he asked the group.

"I guess that would be me," a strikingly, beautiful woman responded as she offered her hand. "Lisa Johnson."

"Okay Miss Johnson, my men will take your group over to the Black Hawk. Keep your heads down and get inside as quickly as you can. Buckle yourselves in, there's a helmet with a headset in it that you can wear so that you can talk to the pilot. Once you're all safely in and secured, we'll close the door, and you'll be on your way to Fort Benning."

"Thank you sergeant, but aren't your men coming with us?"

"Negative ma'am. Not enough room, but don't worry about us, our ride's inbound, and we brought protection with us," Jones told her, nodding at the weapons his men carried.

It took almost ten minutes to get everyone situated on the Black Hawk before it was able to take flight. As it gained altitude, Jones heard shots being fired from the ground, and saw a spark from where a bullet ricocheted off the pilot's bulletproof window.

"Shots fired. We need to locate and take out that weapon before our ride gets here. Try to shoot the weapon, not the civilian holding it," he ordered.

The squad spread out around the perimeter of the roof, searching for any target with a gun.

Bull was the first to spot one. "Man, blue shirt behind the tan Ford pickup. I have a shot on the man but not the weapon. Anyone else got eyes on him?"

Wilcox spoke up, "I got a shot on the weapon."

"Take it!" ordered Jones.

Bull watched as the rifle jumped sideways out of the man's hands, the stock blowing apart as the sniper round entered it just in front of the man's head.

"Good shot. Weapon down, continuing to search,"

Two other men were found with rifles, Bull was able to take out one of the weapons, but no one had a shot on the other one.

"Shoot to wound," Jones gave the order, not wanting to kill any Americans.

"I got the shot!" Wilcox called out before pulling the trigger.

"Target down. Left-arm. Flesh wound only. Taking out weapon now." Another shot rang out. "Weapon out of commission."

"All clear."

"Keep a watch on them in case more weapons show up."

The building shook slightly as an armored van slammed into the front doors of the building before backing up and trying again. Three hits later and the mob swarmed into the building.

"Bull and Boomer, check the stairwells and elevators. Secure them if possible. Take out a section of stairs with C-4 if nothing else. Our ride should be here shortly."

Alpha team continued to watch the mob for additional threats.

"Alpha Three to Alpha Six Actual?"

"Go for Alpha Six Actual," Jones replied.

"Stairwell secured by civilians prior to our arrival. It looks like they threw the contents of the building into the stairwells. We can't get any lower than the third floor. Elevators were also secured. On our way to your position."

"Roger that Alpha Three. Alpha Six Actual out!"

"Alpha Three out!"

Jones was impressed with the group that they had just rescued. Most people wouldn't think to block access from the lower floor or do so effectively.

"Hunter One to Alpha Six Actual."

"Go for Alpha Six Actual."

"Be on-site in five mikes. Just wanted to give you a heads up."

"Roger that Hunter One. Be advised we have retired three shooters."

"Understood Alpha Six Actual. Hunter One out!"

"Alpha Six Actual out!"

Bull and Boomer exited onto the roof and waved Jones over. "Just a heads up. The mob set fire to the pile of furniture in the stairwells. The stairwells are concrete so I doubt it will be an issue other than some smoke," Boomer told him.

"Roger that. We'll be gone in a few." Nodding his head toward the horizon where a Black Hawk was quickly approaching.

As the Black Hawk settled onto the helipad, smoke began to billow from around the edges of the stairwell door.

"Alpha Squad, prepare to board. It's time to go home."

Within a minute, the Black Hawk was airborne and heading south toward the base, leaving the CDC to the fate of the rioters.

Alex

So far they had managed to drive about 550 miles, all of it at night except for the first 150 miles. At their current pace, they should reach the Cheyenne Mountain Complex that housed the military base before morning, if they didn't run into any problems before then.

The first night of travel, they realized immediately that they needed to remove all of the exterior bulbs from both vehicles. They took it one step further and removed the interior bulbs as well. That way if they stopped and opened the doors, their position wouldn't be revealed to anyone who happened to be in the area and paying attention.

They had been back on the road for almost an hour before the first sign of trouble showed up.

"Hey Alex. It looks like we might have someone following us with their headlights off. I keep seeing what I believe is their brake lights reflecting off the grass alongside the edge of the road. They're about a half-mile back," Billy told him over the two-way radio.

"Okay. I'll circle around them to see if they continue to follow. If not, we will end up behind them."

Alex turned right on the next crossroad and sped up a few more miles per hour. He couldn't go very fast or he'd stir up too much dust but he wanted to put a bit more space between them, if possible. He watched in the passenger side mirror as BB followed him. A few moments later, he also saw the red glow of taillights as the vehicle slowed down and turned to follow them. Coming to the next intersection, he turned right again, finding himself on pavement. He floored the truck. He glanced in his mirror and saw BB follow suit. Quickly arriving at the next road, he slowed down and turned right again but had to keep his speed down due to it being another dirt and gravel road. Arriving back at the original road they had been on, he turned right once more.

"Any sign of them Billy?"

"Not yet. I'll keep an eye open for them just in case."

Alex turned left a few miles later wanting to get a bit further west and closer to the highway. They would need to get gas soon so they were going to have to take a chance and check out some small towns for a place to get fuel.

"They're back!" Billy exclaimed, interrupting Alex's thoughts.

Alex sighed, wishing people would just leave them alone. "Alright, I'm going to turn at the next intersection, go about a quarter-mile and flip a U-turn and stop, facing the intersection. I want BB to go straight and then do the same thing. We'll see who they follow. If they follow BB, I'll get behind them and then we both turn on our brights to blind them. If they turn behind me, BB can get behind them and we'll do the same. Make sure you have your guns ready."

"Let's do this," Billy replied, seeming relieved to be doing something about the vehicle.

At the next intersection, they followed the plan to see who the car followed. Alex watched the vehicle as it slowed slightly before continuing on, following BB and Billy.

"They're headed your way, I just turned in behind them," Alex told them as he sped up slightly before turning on his bright lights, flooding the mid-sized car from behind with blinding white light. The car started to accelerate until BB turned on her brights, blinding the occupants temporarily as they slammed on their brakes and swerved to avoid what appeared to them as an oncoming car, ending up sideways in the ditch, passenger side facing the road.

"Now what?" Billy asked, as Alex stopped, angled on

the road with the truck facing the car. The truck's headlights, lighting up the car.

"Have BB turn and face the Blazer towards the car with the brights on so they can't see where you are. I'd suggest getting behind the Blazer in case they try to shoot y'all."

Alex stood beside his truck to keep out of a possible line of fire. Seeing movement in the car, he called to the occupants, "Why are you following us?"

"Fuck you!" the response came as Alex saw the barrel of a rifle come out of the passenger window closest to him.

"Drop it or die!" he yelled, as the rifle barked out a round, missing completely.

"Die it is. Fire!" Alex yelled loud enough for Billy to hear him.

The two friends began firing, filling the passenger compartment full of holes. As their clips emptied, he asked, "Anyone still alive?"

Not hearing a response, he crouched down and fast walked to the rear of the car and peered in through the back window. The two men inside appeared to be dead. He walked along the passenger side and saw that the men both had multiple gunshot wounds and each had suffered at least one head wound. They were both dead.

Alex reached in and took the rifle. He quickly searched the rest of the car and found a box of ammo as well as the driver's rifle, which he handed to Billy, who headed back to the Blazer to check out his new toy. Alex grabbed the keys from the ignition and opened the trunk.

"BB! Get over here!" he yelled, shocked at what he had found.

She jogged over in a huff. "What's so damn important that you need to yell at me?" she demanded to know.

"Them," he said, pointing at the two young girls who were bound, gagged and terrified, lying inside the trunk.

"Get them out of there, why are you just standing there?" she admonished Alex.

He grabbed her gently by the arm and looked into her eyes. "BB, these girls were kidnapped by men with guns. How do you think they would react if I, a man with a gun, tried to get them out of the trunk?"

"Okay, good point." Turning her attention to the two girls. "Hi there. My name is BB and I'm a doctor. This is my good friend Alex. He was the one who saved you from those men. He killed them so they can't hurt you anymore. I'm going to take the gags out of your mouths and untie you. Is that okay?"

Both girls were still obviously terrified but bravely nodded their heads.

"Hey Billy. Bring a couple of bottles of water over here and leave your gun," Alex directed his friend in a conversational tone so as not to upset the girls.

"Sure thing but I'm not sure why you have the cripple bringing you two lovebirds drinks," he teased.

"It's not for us," Alex said, nodding towards the open trunk where BB was now busy untying the two girls.

"Son of a bitch. I was feeling bad about us killing those guys, but now I want to kill them again, only slower," Billy growled, not being able to instantly control his emotions.

The girls flinched at the anger in Billy's words. "It's alright girls. That's my other friend, Billy. He helped Alex shoot those bad men." She held out her arms to the older of the two girls, who couldn't have been more than 12. "Let me get you out of there, Billy brought you some water to drink. What's your name sweetie?"

"Emma," she replied hesitantly as she allowed BB to pick her up and remove her from out of the trunk.

"That's a beautiful name. Would you like some water, Emma?"

Seeing a slight nod of her head, BB took a bottle of water from Billy and handed it to Emma who gulped it down greedily.

"Slow down a little or it will make you sick. Don't worry, we have more if you want it," BB promised her as Emma took smaller sips.

The smaller girl was now sitting up in the trunk, crying

silently.

"Aww, sweetie. Let me get you out of there and get you some water too."

The girl almost leaped into BB's arms in an effort to leave the confines of the small prison.

"What's your name, little one?"

"Jen'fer," the girl responded shyly.

"Well Jennifer. How about some water?" she offered.

The girl eagerly nodded her head as BB opened the other bottle and handed it to her. "Drink it slow. Yeah like that. Good job!"

"What do you guys say we go over by that big pickup, would that be okay?" BB asked them, wanting to get them away from the car that they had been held captive in.

Both kids nodded in the affirmative as each clutched one of BB's hands and carried their water bottle in the other.

Alex and Billy both backed off a few steps to give the girls some room so they wouldn't frighten them any more than they already were.

BB comforted the two girls for the next twenty minutes, slowly getting the story from them before she motioned him and Billy closer.

"Hey girls. I'm going to talk to my two friends real fast. I'll be right over there," she said, pointing to the two men.

The girls nodded their heads while keeping a wary eye on the two men.

"They haven't been sexually assaulted as far as I can tell without doing an actual examination. Apparently, the two are sisters and their parents were trying to get them all to their grandparent's house but were stopped by those men." Nodding at the bullet-ridden car. "The men shot the dad, probably raped and killed the mom since all I could get out of them is that they had hurt their mom and then killed her. The bastards tied the girls up and put them in the trunk. The girls weren't sure what time it happened, Emma said the sun was starting to go down so they've been in that trunk for at least four hours."

"Any idea where the grandparents live?" Alex asked, wanting to get the girls to a relative as soon as possible.

"Well I don't have an address, but Emma said they live near Trinidad and she's pretty sure she can find their farm."

"I'm not sure what else we can do but try to find them. Do you think the girls will ride with you if Billy is in the car?"

"I think so as long as he's up front and they can sit in the backseat, they should be alright. If not, he'll just have to ride with you," she told him unapologetically.

"I agree, but I'd prefer to have Billy with you in case you run into any trouble. He's injured but can still shoot a gun," Alex pointed out.

BB turned. "Hey girls, we're going to see if we can find your grandparent's farm. Would you be alright riding with me and Billy in the Blazer?"

Emma quickly replied, "We know they aren't bad men so we can ride in either car, but we need to be together."

"Thank you Emma," Alex said smiling at the young girls. He squatted down to be at their eye level. "This big truck is mine and I'll be driving in front, making sure we're safe. BB is driving Billy's Blazer since he hurt his arm and Billy is riding with her to help keep her safe. They will be following me. You two can choose who you want to ride with."

The two girls turned to each other and whispered back and forth a few times, coming to a decision, they turned and faced the trio. "We're gonna ride with Alex because he reminds us of our Uncle Ray and I need to be in front so I can show him where to go."

"That's a good point. I hadn't considered that and I think you could be my radioman if you want," he told her as she started to laugh.

"I can't be a radioman, I'm a girl," she told him seriously.

"Oh goodness. That's right, how about you be my radio-girl then. You can hold the radio and talk to Billy and BB if we need to tell them something," he explained.

Emma quickly nodded her head. "I can do that."

"Alright, the job is yours. Are you girls hungry? I think we have some sandwiches left," he offered.

"Yes please!" the girls squealed.

Alex was fairly certain the girls wouldn't suffer any long term effects from their imprisonment but wasn't sure how they would be once the reality of their parent's death set in.

"Okay everyone, load up. We have sandwiches to eat and grandparents to find," he declared with a huge grin, making the two girls laugh.

Alex ended up having to pick up the girls one at a time and putting them into the truck as it sat just a little too high for them to be able to scramble inside by themselves. He told them the sandwiches were in the cooler on the back seat and to help themselves, before closing the door.

He walked back over to BB and Billy. "Trinidad is only about 20 miles away. I was planning on trying to find some fuel there so we could fill up." He looked at BB and watched as her eyes kept flittering over to the girls. "They'll be alright, you did great with them."

"Thanks Alex. I love kids, just so you know," she said grinning as she turned and walked back to the Blazer.

"Woohoo. Already talking about kids. You lucky dog," Billy said, lightly punching him in the shoulder before following BB.

Alex stood there staring after BB before shaking his head and going back to his own truck.

He started his truck. "Alright girls, let's go find your grandparents."

As they made their way to Trinidad, Jennifer curled up in the backseat and fell asleep. Emma stayed up front and told Alex what she could remember about where her grandparents' farm was. It wasn't a lot.

He now knew they needed to get back onto the highway and a few miles before getting to Trinidad, there would be a small airport on the left side of the road. He had to turn left after the airport and then make a quick right. Emma said she

11ERNIE J SINCLAIR

could direct him from there.

Following the instructions that Emma had given him, it hadn't taken long before they were turning off the highway. Alex saw another road immediately to their right, just as Emma had said. Feeling better about the vague directions, he followed the road as Emma watched intently out the window to make sure they didn't miss any turns, and soon they were pulling into the long driveway of a farm.

Alex turned on his headlights so that it would seem more normal to anyone at the farm. Hopefully, they wouldn't shoot before making sure they weren't there for nefarious reasons.

"Is this the right place?" he asked Emma.

"Yes, this is my grandparents' house," she said, bouncing in the seat, eager to see her grandparents.

He shut off the truck. "Okay Emma, I need you to stay in the truck until I talk to your grandparents."

"Why can't I go?" she started to complain.

"For one thing, it's the middle of the night and it doesn't look like they're expecting company. Just to be safe, can you please wait here."

"Fine!" she replied, crossing her little arms in defiance.

Alex got out of the truck and took his weapons to the Blazer. Placing them in the back seat. "BB, I need you to come with me. Billy, watch my six."

"You got it. You're going unarmed?" Billy asked, looking concerned. "Are you sure that's a good idea?"

He shrugged his shoulders, "Not really but it's the middle of the night and I'm about to wake an older couple up. I'd prefer them to think I'm harmless so they will at least talk to me before filling me full of lead."

"So that's why you want me to go with you?" BB asked, realizing that a male with a female was considered less of a threat than a male by himself.

"One of the reasons," he admitted as he started walking to the house.

206206206206
206206206206
206206206206

They got as far as the bottom of the steps that led to the porch. "That's close enough!" a man informed them from the darkened doorway. "I have my shotgun aimed at you so don't do anything more stupid than you already have. I've been watching you since before you turned on your lights. Mighty suspicious if you ask me, driving around in the dark without any lights on. Now, what's your business here?"

"Do you have a couple of granddaughters, Emma and Jennifer?" Alex asked.

"What do you know about my gran-kids? Answer me before I pull this trigger," the man barked, concerned that complete strangers knew his granddaughters' names.

"They're fine. They're in my truck but I'm sorry to tell you that their parents are dead. They were killed by some men who kidnapped the girls. We inadvertently ended up saving them when the men started following us and we had to ambush them. They're dead," Alex quickly explained, glossing over the gory details.

The older man had lowered the shotgun, his eyes glinting with tears. "Agnes, come on out. These folks mean us no harm and they brought the girls to us."

An older woman pushed the man out the door. "Where's my gran-babies and where are their parents?" she demanded to know.

"Agnes, the girls are all that's left. These folks found them and brought them to us," he said hugging his wife before looking at the younger couple. "Please go bring them in."

Alex immediately turned and jogged back to the truck. He barely opened the passenger door before Emma jumped out into his arms. He set her down, watching her quickly scamper off to see her grandparents. Looking up, he saw Jennifer waiting for him to hold up his arms before she committed to jumping down as her sister had.

He lowered her to the ground, and she hurried after her sister as fast as her little legs would go.

"Emma, wait for meeee," she pleaded with her older

sibling.

Laughing, he closed the door and waved Billy forward. "We're safe. Let's go check and make sure that everyone's alright and leave your pistol in the Blazer."

Billy went and put the gun back in the Blazer before returning and walking with his friend back to the house. Everyone was already inside so they politely knocked.

"Come on in, no need for knocking," Agnes hollered at them.

They entered the well kept home. "Sorry for bringing them by in the middle of the night," Alex started to apologize but was quickly cut off.

"Oh nonsense, we were up waiting for them anyway. One of our neighbors called to let us know that you were headed our way with your lights off so we turned ours off in case you were up to no good," Agnes explained. "I'm Agnes, by the way, and that hunk of a man is my husband, George."

"I'm Alex, this is my best friend Billy, and you've already met BB," he introduced them, holding his hand out. Agnes slapped it away and pulled him in for a big hug. "Thank you for bringing us our babies," she whispered, trying not to cry in front of the girls, before finally releasing him and then turning to Billy, giving him a less powerful hug, due to his injured arm. "We appreciate what you did for the girls. Do you know where their parents were left?" George asked quietly so that the girls wouldn't hear.

Alex shook his head, "I'm sorry we don't. They tracked us for about five miles before we created our own ambush. BB talked to the girls, and other than being bound and gagged, the men didn't touch them, just so you know," he explained. "I can probably show you where we noticed them the first time if you want. We think they were in that trunk for hours before we discovered them so there's no telling how far they drove in that time."

"Well, thank you for making them pay. What can we do to help you, you must need something?" George asked, wanting to repay the men for the kindness shown to his grand-daughters.

"If you could point us in the direction of somewhere we could buy some fuel, that would help us tremendously. We still have a fair distance to travel, but gas is getting harder to find," he admitted to the farmer.

"I got about 200 gallons of it in the tanks out back. Diesel too, if you need some of that. Y'all are welcome to take what you need and I don't want to hear any argument about it. It's the least we can do after you saved the girls." Seeing the slightly confused look on the guys' faces. George explained, "I'm a farmer. I can't be taking the farm equipment down to the local gas station, now can I? Most farmers have an above-ground tank of fuel just for that reason. Now, where are you heading?"

"We thought we'd go to the military base at the Cheyenne Mountain Complex," Billy told him.

George shook his head, "Not a good idea, there have been a lot of shootings up that way from what I hear. Some folks tried to fight their way onto the base and it ended in a gunfight. We heard that about 50 people died, including some soldiers. They're not allowing any civilians on the base now."

"Okay, good thing we made a backup plan then. We're going to the San Isabel National Forest to get away from all the craziness," Billy corrected.

Overhearing the conversation, Agnes joined in, "Non-sense boys, you'll stay right here with us until all this silliness is over. We have plenty of room and I won't hear one word of argument from either of you."

"We wouldn't want to impose," Alex told her.

She raised one eyebrow and glared at him while she pointed her finger at his chest. "I told you no arguments. Do I need to take you over my knee young man?"

"Uh, no ma'am. We'd be honored to stay with you, as long as you will let us help out where we can. We'd also like to help protect the farm while we're here if you'll allow us the honor," he quickly backtracked to get himself out of trouble with Agnes.

"Now that's more like it. If you're asking if you can carry guns, we have no problem with it as long as you can manage proper gun safety," Agnes explained.

Billy started to laugh. "Sorry, ma'am, I don't mean any disrespect by laughing, but it's just that we're from Texas and gun safety is bred into us. In fact, you have to pass a gun safety course before they will even let you start kindergarten," he joked.

This caused the older couple to laugh as well.

"Well, I hate to break this up, but we really need to get the girls to bed. There's an extra bedroom through that door and then a couple of couches in here."

"Ma'am, if it's all the same to you, Billy and I would prefer to sleep in the barn loft. It gives us a higher vantage point to spot any trouble heading our way. BB can take the bedroom."

She waved him off. "That will be fine as long as you don't mind the smell. Normally breakfast is at 7 am, but we'll make it 9 am for just this once. See everyone in the morning."

"Goodnight."

Billy looked at Alex, shaking his head. "The barn, really, Alex? You do know that I only have one good arm to climb with don't ya?"

"You'll be fine," he said, pushing Billy out the door.

DAY ELEVEN

Erik

He was extremely concerned about Eddie. After walking several miles to his house following the blaze that destroyed the dry cleaners, Eddie more or less collapsed from exhaustion. The virus had taken a toll on his body and made him unusually weak. Erik managed to get him into the house and onto the couch where he remained, not having the strength to get him up the flight of stairs to one of the bedrooms.

Erik stood vigil, doing what he could for his friend. He was feeding him soup, ensuring that he was drinking plenty of fluids, and helping him to the bathroom when needed.

All he could do was keep him company and try to treat the symptoms the best he knew how. Tylenol and ibuprofen for the body aches, fever, and headache. Calamine lotion for the rash and cough syrup for the uncontrollable, constant coughing. He kept expecting the more severe symptoms to show up but so far, they hadn't, and he prayed they never would.

While Eddie was sleeping, Erik took the opportunity to do security sweeps throughout the house, securing windows with furniture and blocking the doors to help prevent looters from breaking in. He had cleaned and loaded his Mossberg 500 pump action, 12 gauge shotgun, as well as the Sig Sauer P365 9 mm pistol, in case it became necessary to protect Eddie or himself from intruders. So far, it hadn't been required, and for that, he was very thankful.

There was hardly any food in the house. Being single, Erik tended to utilize the drive-thru restaurants as much as possible. He thought they would be able to stretch what little there was for another week, perhaps a bit longer if they rationed it. He had filled the bathtub and most of the pots and pans with water in case it quit working. Candles had been located and placed strategically in every room in the house for the inevitable power outages that were sure to come.

Most of the TV and radio stations had quit broadcasting. He had no idea if it was due to power failure in those areas, rioters destroying the broadcasting equipment and buildings, or if the employees made the conscious choice to stay home with their families. Perhaps it was a combination of the three or maybe none of them, in the end, the reasons didn't matter, the results remained the same. Civilization was beginning to crumble and the odds were stacked against them for it to get better anytime soon.

Randy

Nearly a week had passed since he had last seen Lisa, and he was thrilled that she was now on the base. Last night Master Sergeant Brooks had delivered the news regarding the failed raid on the labs and the details of the successful rescue of the CDC personnel. He had been promised that he could meet up with Lisa sometime this morning, once she had been cleared by the medical staff, but Randy was starting to get impatient.

"Mr. Elkhart, good morning," came the booming voice from behind him.

"Good morning Sergeant Brooks," he replied as he turned his head to face him, "and it's Randy, not Mr. Elkhart. How many times do I need to remind you?" he said, shaking his head.

The master sergeant waved the comment off as he took

residence in a seat directly across from him. "As many as it takes, I suppose. Your friends will be out of medical soon. I apologize for the delay, but with so many soldiers sick or dying from this virus, well, to be honest, our ranks have been disseminated. The entire command structure has gaps in it, and we can't promote fast enough to keep it intact."

He stared off into space as he continued. "The Command Sergeant Major passed away this morning. That's 40% of our base command either dead or incapacitated right now. Heck, I have platoons being temporarily being led by privates, over 50% of the enlisted men are currently out of action, but I guess that there's not really much to lead anymore."

The master sergeant sighed as he turned to face him. "I guess you're probably wondering why I'm telling you all of this."

Randy slowly nodded his head as he was indeed confused.

"I need you to understand just how bad the situation has gotten here. Martial Law has been enacted country-wide, although I am not sure who is going to enforce it. Without enough healthy personnel to feed, guard, organize and treat everyone, something had to give, and right now, that's the cities. The decision has been made that all military bases are to go on lockdown until this virus runs its course. No one in and no one out. Miss Johnson's group was the last of the civilians that will be allowed onto the base for the time being. We also won't be allowed to go chasing your Doctor Doom across the country until we have concrete evidence of exactly where he is or enough of our people have regained their health so that we can mount a proper search. I'm sorry," the master sergeant finished as he glanced away, unable to look him in the eye.

"Even though they know what he's planning to do with the fake vaccinations? How many American lives is this going to cost?" he retorted, rubbing his hands over his face.

His small group had tried so valiantly to prevent this. They somehow managed to discover who created the virus along with obtaining information on the original group of people who designed the plan for the entire thing. Now everything was grinding to a halt, and there was literally nothing they could do about it.

"It wasn't my call, but honestly we don't have any intel on where they fled to, other than 'something was said about Colorado' and that doesn't narrow it down enough to warrant risking the lives of the few healthy men we have remaining. I didn't say we were quitting and giving up on ever catching the doctor. Trust me, we are tracking every lead that we find and rumor we hear, no matter how absurd it may be, it's just that we can't afford to send our men out on a wild goose chase while the country is in complete turmoil," the master sergeant told him, attempting to explain the reasoning behind the decision.

Randy understood the point and was aware that the master sergeant was doing everything in his power to help stop this, but he felt defeated. "I get it sergeant. I really do, but have you considered that this might be one more part of The Elite Group's sick twisted game? They probably own members high up in the military's chain of command and they could be the ones behind the tying of your hands? Something to think about and maybe discreetly check into, the US military that I know wouldn't quit against any odds, especially with an attack on US soil."

"Mr. El...Randy, that's something we've discussed ad nauseam. We have our suspicions on a few who may be involved, but we have to have some evidence that they are actually guilty, even if everything points to them being a part of the conspiracy. Of course, we can't get that unless we track down the doctor, so it's a catch-22 right now. Give me time to work some things out and in the meantime, keep checking with your contacts. Maybe we'll get lucky and can figure something out between our two groups, otherwise, there may not be an America left when the dust settles."

On that somber note, the master sergeant stood up and walked off, leaving Randy to wonder if their efforts to stop this catastrophe were like using bubble gum to plug a hole in a collapsing dam. Too damn little, too damn late.

Jeff

He was on a mission, the same mission he began almost 15 years earlier when he was nine, and his mom died from Rabies. Jeff was determined to prove that his father, Dr. Jeremy Carter, was solely responsible for causing his mother's death.

Jeff had understood early on, that his father belonged in some super-secret group, but he had no knowledge about who they were or what they did. Once, right after the death of his mother, his father had been drunk while celebrating the death of his ex-wife and Jeff had overheard him congratulating himself on how much better and more important he was than she had ever been. He had been the one that had been chosen to secretly join The Elite Group by being one of the best students in college, not her. He held the fate of the world in his hands, not her.

This had made Jeff's blood boil with rage, and that was when he first suspected that his father had murdered his mother, he only needed to find a way to prove it.

To achieve this goal, he had to stay close enough to his father in order to figure it out. He began by telling his father that he wanted to change his last name to his mother's maiden name. This would allow him to prove that he could become as great of a scientist as his father but on his own merits. Jeff didn't want anyone to think that he was riding on his father's coattails. Of course, the real reason was that he was ashamed to be the son of a murdering psychopath, and he didn't want anyone to discover that they were related.

He had decided to go into the same field as his father and convince him to work together, playing off of his father's ego and getting him closer to his father's research.

For years, he had dedicated all his time and energy to studying and learning everything that he could about microbiology and virology, forgoing friends, parties, and his social life. It had all paid off one day in college when he was approached and offered to join the same exclusive group as his father. This, in his father's eyes, made him worthy enough to work together and he was eventually hired on as a lab assistant. On the first day of work, his father had called him Jeff, luckily they were alone at the time and he was able to point out that the other assistants all had nicknames. He wanted to be treated exactly the same as the others, from that point forward, he became known as Blondie.

Unfortunately, none of the assistants were allowed to work in the primary lab. This limited the possibility that he would be able to find any information that would irrefutably connect his father to the murder of his mother. Dr. Carter had given him a special project to work on, possibly to help The Core in their depopulation efforts, unfortunately, this gave him even less of an opportunity to snoop.

He didn't trust Latisha or Fred enough to ask for their help, and besides, they weren't allowed in the primary lab either unless Dr. Carter summoned them.

When they had been forced to move to the bunker where there was only one lab, Jeff knew that this was his opportunity to finally discover the truth. There had to be incriminating evidence within his father's records that he kept stored on his main computer. Jeff just had to wait until he could be alone long enough to access them or figure out a way to access his father's computer without his knowledge.

It was a mere two hours later when Jeff found himself alone in the lab. Dr. Carter had sent Fred back down to the garage to look for a missing box of research before he had left to get something to eat in the cafeteria and then take a quick shower. He told Jeff to expect him back in approximately 45 minutes and that he needed to work on getting his special project set back up while he was gone.

The second the door closed behind him, Jeff ran over to

the doctor's computer and entered the user name and password he had found on the underside of the keyboard when he was moving the computer. He was in. Jeff plugged in an external hard drive into a USB port and started copying as many of the research files as possible. He ignored the ones that he already knew what they did, like the World-Ender, Steri-12, and the Booster.

"I wonder what One-Offs are?" he mumbled to himself and began to download those files as well.

He had been so absorbed in what he was doing, that he had lost track of time and hadn't heard the door to the lab open. He nearly jumped out of his skin when a voice asked, "Just what do you think you're doing?"

Jeff's heart stopped momentarily before he turned around and was relieved to find Fred standing behind him instead of his father. "Look I'll explain later, but right now, I need to get this information off his computer before he comes back. If you decide you don't like my explanation, you can always rat me out later."

Fred studied him for a moment before finally responding, "You don't like him either, do you?"

Jeff shook his head, admitting it for the first time. "I actually hate him more than you can possibly ever imagine. Look, I promise to tell you everything later tonight, but I need you to watch my back for a few minutes while this downloads, it's almost done." Adrenaline was coursing through his body and he felt like he might throw up. "Please?" he begged, his hands clasped in front of him. He had never felt so vulnerable in all of his life.

Fred must have sensed his panic. "Alright. Assume you have less than ten minutes. I saw him leave the cafeteria and head towards the housing wing a few minutes ago. What can I do to help?" he asked, setting the tote down on the floor that he had brought up from the garage.

Jeff jumped at the offer. "Can you set up for my project? Start by booting up my computer. User name is '*Jcaldwell*' and the password is *'Dr. Carter is a murderer!'* with no spaces, capitalize Dr and Carter, and an exclamation point at the end. Also, pull a bunch of research out of that green tote and make it look like I was separating it and throw a few beakers and stuff on the counter as well."

He kept glancing between the progress bar and the lab door, knowing that he could be caught at any minute. Finally, the download signaled that it was complete. Jeff removed the hard drive from the USB port, placing it inside his pocket as he logged off the computer.

"Damn, the computer needs to be asleep or he's gonna know that something happened. Fuck it!" he unplugged the server, causing all the computers to shut off. "Shit! Hope I didn't fry anything," he said as he plugged it back in. Two seconds later, Dr. Carter opened the door.

"What happened? Why are all the computers booting up?" he demanded to know.

Seeing the deer in the headlights look in Jeff's face, Fred lied to help to cover Jeff's ass. "It must have been a power surge or something. Me and Blondie were working over here when the lights flickered and all the computers shut down, right before you walked in."

"Well we better not have lost any data or tech support is gonna lose some heads," Dr. Carter vowed.

A small shiver ran down Jeff's back as he wondered if his father might actually cut off their heads, not putting it past him.

He quickly started organizing his research and getting everything ready to try the next process in his experiment as he gave a slight nod of thanks to Fred, his new ally against his poor excuse for a father.

Lisa

She had been unable to sleep well the previous night. It could be due to being in a new place or might have been caused by the crash of all the adrenaline that had been coursing through her body during the escape from the CDC. It didn't matter why she hadn't been able to sleep, just that she hadn't.

They had been ordered to report to the medical team, first thing this morning so that they could be tested for the active virus, before finally being released and allowed to roam the common areas of the base. It had seemed to take forever for her to get processed and receive a clean bill of health.

Lisa drug her feet as she headed to the cafeteria. One of the soldiers told her that it was actually called the DEFAC, or dining facility, right now she was too worn out to care what it was called. She just needed some coffee to help her get motivated and figured that was the most likely place to find some.

She entered the DEFAC and found a huge urn of coffee which caused her to grin. Quickly pouring herself a cup of that liquid gold, she took a moment to glance around and was surprised to see Randy at one of the tables with Matt.

"Hey guys. Mind if I join you?" she asked, not waiting for a response before sliding in next to Randy.

"Finally got cleared, huh?" he asked.

She nodded her head after taking a drink of her coffee, causing her eyes to close in ecstasy as the warmth spread throughout her body, reinvigorating her.

"So I heard they raided Crouch's labs but that it didn't go so well."

He shook his head. "No matter how close we get, they somehow always seem to stay one or two steps ahead of us."

"It does seem that way. They still have Latisha in quarantine, but it looks like she's gonna make it," she told her two friends, happy to give out some good news for once.

Randy smiled, instantly cheered up at the news. "That's great! I'll call Eddie later and let him know, hopefully, it's something that runs in the family."

Lisa shrugged. "We still don't know, she found out that her dad passed away just before the Rangers located her in the lab, unless it is something passed from mother to child, it

won't be. That's one reason she stayed at the lab when everyone left, she didn't want to go home and watch her family die.
I plan on keeping tabs on her family, if everyone else survives
then it increases the likelihood that it does run in families and
Eddie could be okay since her mom is Eddie's sister."

Matt finally spoke up, "Lisa, do you remember me telling
you about my buddy Robert?"

She nodded her head as she recalled who he was. "Isn't
he the guy who got you the information on the skin pigmentation gene?"

"Yeah, that's him. I found out that he was murdered, his
body was found behind a dumpster somewhere downtown.
I'm certain that he was killed because I brought him into this
investigation," he admitted as he stared at the floor.

"Okay everyone, that's enough doom and gloom," Randy
interrupted. "Matt was just telling me Berto escaped with you
guys and he might have found something contained in his
blood that could potentially prevent the virus and the alleged
vaccines from triggering," Randy said, gesturing to a con-
flicted-looking Matt.

He shook the cobwebs out of his head. "Well it's a starting point, but it could still be months or more likely years before we're able to create something to stop Dr. Carter, especially
now that I don't have my lab at the CDC."

Lisa smiled at her colleague. "That's temporary. Once the
virus burns out, things should get more under control, and we
can go back to the CDC. Tell me about your discovery," she encouraged him, knowing that he needed to get his mind off the
death of his friend.

"Latisha had sent us samples of her blood, which were
contaminated with the active virus, with the samples of the
alleged vaccines that Fred managed to smuggle out of the labs.
I compared her sample against Berto's, looking for any differ-
ences between the active and inactive viruses. I discovered a
gene sequence that appears to act as a switch or trigger when
combined with certain skin pigmentation genes, it changes

slightly when triggered." Matt looked at her and Randy to make sure they were following what he was saying. Confident they were, he continued.

"I found that gene sequence missing in both of the smuggled samples, which makes sense because Fred told us that they weren't designed to be race-specific. Berto's immune system appears to have some kind of a blocker that makes his immune system act differently than how the average person's immune system will. He claims that his entire family rarely gets ill and when they do, it's with very minor symptoms that never last long." Matt paused to take a drink before continuing.

"This is where it gets interesting. Berto claims that when he first met his wife, she would constantly get sick with whatever cold or flu was currently in favor at the time. Shortly after they were married, she quit getting sick. This tells me that whatever Berto has flowing in his veins that makes him immune is communicable. I haven't figured out exactly how, but I assume it's transferred via body fluids because if it was airborne, there would be a lot more people immune."

Lisa was excited as the understanding of what this could mean, began to sink in. "So if you can figure out which genes in Berto's DNA are causing this blocker effect, it might be possible to use them to create a generic, one-time vaccine, that would essentially, prevent anyone from ever getting sick."

Matt nodded his head. "It should work in theory, but I still need to isolate the correct gene sequence and then create a way to infect everyone with it."

Randy looked at him sharply. "Now hold on a minute, what do you mean infect them? I thought you were talking about a cure, not a virus."

He smiled at his friend. "It would actually be a little of both, a virus that contains the cure. It would basically be an inert virus that would become the delivery mechanism for the cure. The virus would infect human DNA by adding a few extra strands of genes, thus infecting the body with the cure."

"That's amazing news, Matt. Exactly what I needed to

hear right now," Lisa confided. "I was beginning to think Dr. Carter and The Elite Group were going to beat us, but now I have hope there still might be a future for mankind."

Fred

He opened the door to the small room he now called home, allowing Jeff to slip inside before firmly closing and locking it.

"Were you followed?" he asked Jeff, concerned that someone might discover that the two were meeting in secret.

Jeff shook his head. "No one saw me, I was extremely careful." He paused. "Why did you help me today? I was under the impression that you didn't like me."

Fred sat down on the bed and motioned Jeff to sit in the small chair by an equally small table. "To be quite honest with you, I didn't. You come off as a pompous, arrogant asshole, who thinks they're better than everyone else," he stated in a matter of fact tone as he watched Jeff's face slowly turn beet red in embarrassment, "but when I saw you at Dr. Carter's computer, I had to take a chance that you were against what he has been doing. You do realize that he lied to us about the alleged vaccine that was supposed to protect us from his World-Ender virus, don't you? Latisha has the active infection which is why she was forced to stay behind, not that they would have allowed her in the bunker anyway since she's the wrong color," he spat the words out in contempt.

Jeff stared at him as he admitted, "Actually, I'm not surprised to hear that at all. You will probably go back to hating me once you hear my story and why I was on his computer, but I can't do this alone anymore. I need someone to help me, and I'm hoping that we can at least be allies, if not friends, and try to find a way to fix all the damage that he's done. Well, not all the damage, we can't bring my mom back from the dead."

"Wait, what? Dr. Carter killed your mom?" Fred asked, shocked at this revelation.

"It gets worse." Jeff bowed his head and took several deep breathes to steel his nerves enough to explain to Fred exactly what was going on. "My birth name isn't Jeff Caldwell, it's Jeff Carter, and Dr. Carter is my biological father."

Fred's eyes popped open wide as his mouth dropped open in shock. "Holy shit!" he finally managed to say.

"I've never told anyone that. After my mom died, I started using her maiden name to distance myself from him," Jeff told the rest of his story while he stared at his hands in his lap, too embarrassed to look Fred in the eye, but he left nothing out. It took almost an hour before he finally stopped talking, and he was able to scrape up enough courage to look up at Fred. He appeared to be expecting a guilty verdict and to be told to leave. Instead, Fred grabbed him up in a bear hug and held him tight while they both began to cry.

After a few minutes, the two men sat back down. Now exhausted and with their emotions spent, they wiped their tears away.

"I'm so sorry that happened to you, and I'll do anything I can to help you find the truth. Latisha and I have some other allies on the outside who are trying to stop Dr. Carter and The Elite Group from completing their plans. Let me tell you about what we have been up to."

It was another hour before they finished comparing notes.

"Okay, I think that's enough for us to think on for tonight. Let's meet back up tomorrow after work and figure out a plan to bring justice to your mom and the world," Fred said, happy he was no longer alone in his quest.

Jeff readily agreed. "I'm going to review some of the files I downloaded and see if there is anything we can use against him when I get back to my room. If I find anything, I'll let you know tomorrow."

"That sounds good. I'm glad I caught you snooping today," Fred half-joked as he smiled at his newfound friend and accomplice.

Jeff returned the smile as he opened the door to leave. "Me too," he said as he slipped out the door.

Billy

Alex had spent most of the day unloading and organizing the contents of the two vehicles. He put everything that they didn't plan on using back into the Blazer to keep it out of the way. All the food was being taken into the house for Agnes to use as she saw fit.

Billy was busy supervising from the loft door, overlooking the yard and driveway while still keeping watch for anything that might be trouble.

Alex thought it was a good idea for someone to keep watch 24/7, and everyone else had instantly agreed. They were keeping one of the radios in the loft and one in the house so that they could communicate without having to leave their post.

With Billy's arm still out of commission, he mostly pulled the over-watch duty since he wasn't good for much else.

Emma and Jennifer, the two girls they had rescued, would bring him drinks and food when he wanted, and Emma would sometimes stay to keep watch while he took a quick restroom break. Emma didn't know that Alex would become more alert when she was on watch by herself, on the off chance that trouble would choose that moment to strike.

She wasn't allowed to touch any of their guns, even when on watch, but she did have a pellet gun that she now carried. Billy thought that it probably made her feel safer since the kidnapping. He wanted to talk to George and Agnes about training Emma on using a real gun. Maybe a .22, but he hadn't worked the courage up yet since Agnes still scared him.

Billy thought she was trying to make up for being unable to do anything when her parents were killed but didn't say anything to her about it. She would work it out in her own way and in her own time.

It was on one of his breaks as he entered the house on his way to use the restroom that BB told him she wanted to talk to him and Alex and would meet them in the barn loft in a few minutes.

After he emptied his bladder, he went to find Alex.

"Yo dude. BB wants to talk to us up in the loft in a few minutes, be there or be square."

"Oh wow, that's a super old one," Alex commented. "I guess you can't always be original."

"I'm bringing square back. Just wait, in a few weeks, it will be all the rage, all the cool cats will be hip to be square," he said, acting completely serious.

Alex laughed. "You must have watched some TV shows from the '50s recently. Go on up and I'll be there in a minute."

Billy chuckled. He enjoyed making people laugh, especially when they were stressed. He carefully climbed up the ladder to the loft, it was slow going wearing the sling, but he powered through.

"Hey kiddo, I'm back. Did you see anything?" he asked the aspiring sniper.

Emma grimaced. "No, is it always this boring?"

He laughed. "Most of the time it is, but if we didn't keep watch and some bad men showed up, we might not be able to fight them off."

"Like my mommy and daddy?" she sniffed.

"Yeah," he whispered as he put his good arm around her, "like your mommy and daddy. That's why I'll stay up here and be bored forever if it keeps you and your sister safe."

"Grandma and grandpa too?"

"Yes, grandma and grandpa too. Now you need to run along and see if your grandma needs any help," he told the youngster, who was having to grow up way too fast.

"Okay Billy," she replied with a smile before heading over to the ladder.

He watched the girl scramble down the ladder and scamper off into the house.

Using the binoculars, he did a scan of the area and noted a dust cloud in the distance but quickly realized that the cloud was dissipating and wasn't an indication of an oncoming threat.

Alex soon joined him, followed shortly by BB.

"Alright BB. You called this meeting, so the floor is yours." Billy waved his arm at the hay-strewn loft.

"Ah, thank you kind sir." She curtsied, causing the three friends to laugh. "Alright guys, time to get serious. It's nothing overly important, but I did want you guys to be aware of what they are saying on TV. The first thing is that a lot of prisoners were murdered using some kind of chemical gas. The information was rather sketchy, but supposedly entire prisons were affected. They didn't specify which prisons or why they were targeted though."

"That's kind of an odd target. It's not like they can do anything from prison," Alex observed.

"As I said, I just thought it was odd enough to mention. The more important thing is that they are offering a vaccine for the virus," she stated without any fanfare.

"Well, that's good news," Alex said until he saw the scalding look that BB shot his way. "Okay, maybe not."

"No, it's definitely not good news," she clarified. "There is absolutely no way that anyone had time to develop and test a vaccine for this virus. Not unless they knew that the virus existed years ago and had time to study it."

"If that's true, wouldn't that mean that the vaccine was a good thing?" asked Alex, obviously confused on what BB was trying to get them to understand.

"Well you would think so, wouldn't you. My question is, if they knew about the virus and already had the vaccine, why wait almost two weeks before releasing it to the public?" she tossed the question out to see if they would figure it out on their own.

Both men came to the realization at the same time.

"Oh shit!" Alex uttered as the color drained from his face.

Billy quickly leaned back against the wall as a cold sensation invaded his body and settled in his stomach. "Damn! Someone released it on purpose, and they wanted people to be infected."

"Now you guys are getting it. Alright, time to think a little deeper. Ask yourselves, why release the vaccine now? The entire world has already been exposed, and the vaccine can do little good at this point," she asked, knowing they would put it all together.

Half a heartbeat later, Billy answered, "It's not really a vaccine, is it?"

BB shrugged. "I honestly don't know, but I seriously doubt it. I do know that I am not getting it and I don't want you guys to either. I'd rather take my chances without it."

The two friends nodded in agreement.

"Damn! If you're right, that's completely fucked up," Alex said, confirming what the others were also thinking.

DAY TWELVE

Agent Warren

He wasn't surprised when the new directives came down the pipeline. The writing had been on the wall since almost the beginning of the outbreak. He had been surprised that The Core had allowed it to continue for as long as they had.

The group from Atlanta would need to be eliminated. Dr. Carter had changed the plan at the last minute and brought too much attention to The Elite Group. Too many people were trying to figure out who was responsible for the planning and the execution of this nefarious crime against humanity so The Core was going to give them Dr. Carter instead, not breathing of course, but all roads would definitely lead back to him.

Unfortunately for everyone else in the bunker, they would become collateral damage. The vast majority of whom had never even heard of Dr. Carter but just happened to be assigned to this particular bunker. The evidence that he would plant on Dr. Carter's computer would imply that they were the only members of The Elite Group and that he was the one and only member of The Core, wrapping everything up with a nice neat bow.

All of this would be good news for the health and well-being of that reporter and his friends. There would no longer be a need to remove them from the equation. Agent Warren was slightly annoyed at this, he had never failed to complete an assignment and wasn't keen on starting now, but sometimes assignments needed to be changed, this was one of those times. The agent knew that if he didn't do as ordered, he could be the next one on the elimination list, regardless of who his father was. He would continue to keeps tabs on the reporter for a while to make sure that he wasn't still on the trail, just in case.

The good news was, the plan required him to plant the incriminating evidence on the doctor's computer and set the timer for the release of the gas, then he could leave the entire mess behind him.

The bunker had been designed and constructed for every eventuality, including the need to kill everyone inside without destroying the bunker itself. The Sarin gas was already held in tanks that were connected to the HVAC system and once activated, would release the gas to be carried through the air with the air-conditioning. The entire bunker complex would be contaminated within minutes, killing everyone inside.

He also needed to add a fail-safe. The Core didn't want the bunker to fall into the government's hands, but they also needed them to find enough evidence to convince them that Dr. Carter was behind the whole population control conspiracy. A small tracker would be attached to the doctor's computer, and once the computer was moved more than 1,500 feet from the bunker's entrance, it would trigger the automated self-destruct sequence for the bunker complex. 3,000 pounds of explosive would ensure that nothing would remain except for one giant hole in the ground.

It was still early, around 5 am when he snuck into the lab. Dr. Carter believed that only he and his assistants had access, but Agent Warren had full access to every part of the bunker. Being the son of one of The Core members and next in his family's line to become one of the ten, gave him special privileges.

He quickly logged into Dr. Carter's computer and had the

incriminating information downloaded within a few minutes. He quickly logged off before attaching a small transmitter to the back of the computer server.

Agent Warren had spent less than five minutes in the lab and was now on his way to the utility maintenance room, where he would set the timer for the dispersion of the gas.

His footsteps echoed down the concrete halls as he approached the maintenance door. He felt like he was being watched but didn't see anyone when he checked behind him. Trying to ignore the feeling, he entered the code to unlock the door and hurried through the opening.

What the hell was that about, he wondered as the feeling of being watched began to dissipate as the door started to close. He shrugged it off and walked into the large room, failing to realize that the door hadn't latched behind him.

He was in the lowest level of the bunker where it was darker and had a slightly abandoned feel to it as few ever went down there. Agent Warren quickly made his way through the maze of equipment required to keep the bunker running smoothly.

There were a vast number of electrical panels, water tanks, a host of servers controlling most of the automated parts of the facility, including the heat and A/C. He bypassed all of that before reaching a large breaker box, that coincidentally matched the dimensions of a normal sized door. Opening the panel, he flipped two breakers to the off position releasing a latch, allowing the entire panel to swing open on hinges, revealing a small room located behind it.

He entered the room and booted up the computer held within. The agent scrolled through the menu until he located the Sarin Gas protocol. After typing for several minutes, a pop-up window appeared.

Protocol 7: scheduled to initiate in 48 hours,
zero minutes, zero seconds.
Press OK to confirm.

He pressed OK, and the pop-up box disappeared, being

replaced by a countdown timer.

47:59:59

47:59:58

47:59:57

Satisfied, he left the computer running and left the room, closing the panel behind him. He would make sure that he was long gone before the gas was released.

Lisa

She was worried about the Steri-12 vaccine. Fred had told them what it would do, but the military refused to do anything without proof.

At Lisa's insistence, the master sergeant had found Matt a small workspace to continue his research. Luckily, he had run every test he could think of on the Steri-12 vaccine back at the CDC before they had evacuated since they didn't have the necessary equipment here on the base. He just needed time to review the mounds of data and interpret what it all meant.

After several hours, he emerged from the room, looking beaten and worn from the combination of too little sleep and too much work.

"Hey Matt. Get it figured out?" she asked, her fingers were literally crossed.

"I can prove that Steri-12 is not a vaccine and that it will, most likely, cause sterilization in whoever takes the shot," he said, confirming what they had already been told by Fred.

It took her almost 30 minutes to locate the master sergeant, but less than five to convince him that the vaccine was, in fact, another virus.

"I agree it's probably another virus, that's why I won't let anyone here get the shot. In fact, I had them destroy every dose that was delivered here. We sent word to all the other bases to do the same, I'm not sure what else you think I can do?" he said, starting to get exasperated.

"Sergeant, I appreciate what you have done, but there are

millions of Americans who are lining up to get this injection. We have to let them know that it's not real, that instead of curing them, the vaccine will sterilize them. Everyone thinks that the number of deaths is decreasing because of the Steri-12 vaccine, but that's not why. Fewer people are dying because the virus is burning out because there is no one left to infect. In a few more days, almost no one will be dying from the Frankenstein Virus," Lisa was almost begging him at this point.

Master Sergeant Brooks shook his head. "Miss Johnson, you seem to forget that there is a chain of command that I have to follow. I will pass the information along, but I still don't know what we can do, the vaccine is already out there."

She glared at the master sergeant, knowing that he was right, "If we could somehow get the media to announce it, let everyone know of the danger of getting the shot. I could at least feel like we tried."

"I'll talk to the colonel but I can't make any promises," he conceded, raising his hands in defeat. In his experience, arguing with a woman always seemed to be a futile act.

"Make sure he's aware the CDC is recommending no one gets the injection, maybe it will sway him our way," she suggested.

"Do you have the authority to speak for the CDC?" he asked her with one eyebrow raised.

"Honestly, probably not, but since I have no idea who is still left alive, theoretically I could be," Lisa gave a small grimace as she offered her last-ditch effort.

The master sergeant smiled. "Okay, I'll tell them that it's a recommendation from the CDC, hopefully, it will work."

Lisa gave him a quick hug before turning to leave. She wanted to update Matt and Randy on what was going on.

Jeff

After spending most of the night reading through all the research from his father's computer, he was finding it ex-

232

tremely difficult to focus on what he was supposed to be doing in the lab. Luckily a lot of it was computer work, and he could at least appear as if he was working hard.

Dr. Carter had informed him that the number of the Steri-12 vaccinations had already doubled from the previous day. It disgusted Jeff that he took such extreme pleasure from other people's pain and misery.

He really needed to show Fred one of the files that he found in the download, but he hadn't seen him yet today. Jeff was sure he had found the smoking gun for his mom's murder, but he wanted a second opinion on what he had read to verify that he wasn't misinterpreting the information.

It was odd that Fred was late, a cold finger of fear slide down his spine, what if they had been discovered and Fred had been murdered? Was he next? He pondered that as he rubbed the back of his neck. He shook his head as he thought. No, I can't think like that. He's only three hours late so he probably overslept or just got lost.

Twenty minutes later, Fred walked through the door.

"Sorry I'm late, Dr. Carter. I started feeling sick after I ate breakfast so I went to medical. They said it might be food poisoning, so I'd watch what you eat for the next few days," Fred suggested as he walked over to his workstation.

Dr. Carter glared at him before turning and going back to work without saying a word.

Fred looked at Jeff, grinned, and shrugged his shoulders before turning on his own computer, starting his workday.

When Dr. Carter left the lab for lunch, Jeff immediately turned on Fred. "Don't do that to me! When you didn't show up this morning, I thought we'd been found out and that you'd been murdered."

"Sorry, I found some stuff out this morning and had to come up with a reason for being late, so I faked being sick and went to medical just in case he checked my story," Fred quickly explained.

"What did you find out?" he anxiously wanted to know.

"We'll talk tonight. We can't give him any reason to suspect anything until we decide what we are going to do."

"Okay, agreed. I have something to show you tonight as well."

He decided to make a concerted effort to get the project back up and running before leaving the lab tonight. It would keep his mind occupied if nothing else.

The remainder of the day went by, albeit rather slowly. Nothing much happened of note except that his father had let a man in a black suit come into the lab. They spoke in hushed tones for a few minutes before his father turned away from the man and refused to acknowledge him anymore, finally, the man gave up and left. His father told him and Fred to leave a few minutes later.

The two boys had immediately shut down their computer terminals and left.

"What do you think that was about?" he asked Fred.

"Grab us something to eat and then meet me in my room. Don't say anything until then," Fred responded without even glancing his way. "I need to check something out."

He started to object, then changed his mind. It was obvious that Fred knew some information that he didn't. "Okay. I'll see you in about thirty minutes with some pizza and my laptop."

Fred nodded as he turned down a hallway Jeff had never used. He fought off the desire to follow Fred and see what he was up to, instead he headed off to the housing wing to get his laptop before hitting the cafeteria for the pizza.

Thirty minutes later, he was standing in front of Fred's door, laptop in one hand and pizza in the other. He had to kick the door instead of knocking since his hands were full. Thankfully, Fred almost immediately opened the door and pulled him into the room.

"Easy there. I almost dropped the pizza," he said, setting

it down on the small table.

Fred was pacing the floor, clearly agitated about something.

"Sit down and relax. I'm not sure what has you so worked up, but you seriously need to calm down. Grab a slice and talk to me," he said, motioning to the pizza on the table.

Fred sat down but appeared extremely worried as beads of sweat formed on his brow.

"Just tell me what has you so worked up. You were fine an hour ago," Jeff told him, placing his slice of pizza back down on the table.

"You know the guy that was in the lab?" Fred asked, standing back up and resuming his pacing.

Jeff nodded, watching his friend move back and forth across the small room. "You're talking about the dude in the suit?"

"Umm yeah." Stopping suddenly, Fred looked Jeff in the eyes. "Any idea who he is?"

He started shaking his head. "Nope, I've never seen him before. Why?"

"Well I have," he said, resuming his pacing once again. "He was one of my recruiters. I've heard stories about him doing a lot of the dirty work for The Elite Group. His description also fits the man who killed a reporter down in Mexico and has been looking for one of my friends to kill as well. I didn't put it together until just now."

"Okay, so what does that have to do with us?" Jeff asked, not understanding where all these pieces were supposed to fit in the puzzle.

"For one thing, if we get caught, that's who will be coming after us," Fred pointed out. "Also, I went to the lab really early this morning to check on something I thought I had seen in one of the totes. While I was in there, that same man showed up, he logged onto the doc's computer and either uploaded a file or downloaded one, whichever it was, it only took him a couple of minutes. Then he did something to the back of the server before he left. I was lucky I didn't turn on the lights when I got there, so I was able to remain hidden in the shadows behind the stack of totes, or I might have gone missing this morning for real."

Jeff was having a hard time wrapping his mind around what Fred was telling him. "Are you serious?"

"As a heart attack. So now I'm wondering just what the fuck he was doing there, so I decided to follow him and ended up in some sub-basement maintenance room with all kinds of equipment that I don't have a clue what their purpose might be for. He stopped in front of this large electrical panel and somehow got it to swing open, like a door, revealing a secret room that was hidden behind it. I couldn't get very close or he might have seen me so I couldn't tell what he was doing in there, but I doubt it was anything good." Fred sat down and grabbed a slice of pizza, trying to calm his nerves down.

"Shit! No wonder you're freaking out," Jeff told him, impressed that his friend was keeping his shit together so well, under the circumstances.

"I stayed down there after he left and tried to figure out how to get into the room but eventually gave up. That's the real reason that I was late," he admitted.

"Wow! I'm not sure what to say. Any idea what's in that room?" Jeff asked him, curious as to what the man had done.

"Not a clue. It sounded like he was typing on a keyboard, but I won't swear to it."

"That's alright, you did good. What were you looking for in the lab this morning? You said you were looking for something," he asked.

"Oh yeah. I remembered hearing you say something about One-Offs when I found you on the doc's computer yesterday. After you left last night, I recalled seeing a paper file in one of the plastic totes, labeled One-Offs, and I couldn't get it out of my mind, so I decided to see if I could find it this morning."

"Did you?" Jeff asked, curious.

"No. I kinda forgot about it when I started chasing Mr. Black Suit through the bunker."

"That's alright. I think I found what I needed. Look at this file," he said, turning his laptop around so that Fred could see it. Half worried and half excited.

"Umm, if I am reading this right, it's instructions on how to create a mutated rabies virus but with a specific person's DNA."

"You are, but keep reading," he encouraged his friend.

"Okay, it sounds like he ran a test to make sure it worked by infecting the target subject's child with it to see if it would transfer over to the target subject." Jeff watched his friend's face as the truth dawned on him. "Oh, Shit! Your dad infected you so that you would infect your mom? That's some fucked up shit!" Fred exclaimed, shocked at the depths of the doctor's depravity.

"Yep. Now you know why I hate him so much. Not only did he murder my mom, but he used me to do it. At least now we have some proof," he admitted.

"I think we should leave tomorrow and try to get a hold of my friends. Maybe they can get the Army to come down here and capture him if they know exactly where he is. I still want to try to get that paper file in case it has any of his handwritten notes on it," Fred told him.

"Okay then, I guess I can suffer through one more day. Any idea on how to get out of here without anyone noticing?"

Fred started laughing. "Funny you should ask, I went to see if I could find our mystery man while you went to get us pizza. I followed him to what appears to be an emergency escape hatch and watched him leave. If that doesn't work, I'm sure we can find a way out through the garage area somehow."

He nodded his head in agreement. "I'm glad that you're on my side because I don't know what I would have done without you here, probably would have just injected him with his own Booster shot, but I'd rather not become him," he admitted, as a shudder ran through his body at the thought.

"One more day and then we can get the authorities to come and get him. He's killed billions of people, not just your mom. I would think that they would do everything in their power to capture him and make him pay for his crimes."

"Thanks. You're right, but I better get to my room and get some sleep, sounds like tomorrow is going to be another long day," Jeff predicted as he gathered his laptop up.

"Alright, I'll see you in the morning."

"Goodnight!"

DAY THIRTEEN

Fred

Dr. Carter had already arrived at the lab by the time he and Jeff showed up. Fred hadn't anticipated this, causing him some difficulty locating the file since he wouldn't have free rein in the lab.

"Chubby, you need to fix this mess. Figure out where everything needs to go and get rid of all the empty totes. This is a lab and it must be organized," Dr. Carter demanded.

"Yes sir. I'll get started right away." He couldn't believe his good fortune now he just needed to find that file for Jeff.

He spent the entire morning and most of the afternoon emptying, organizing, and filing before he hit pay dirt. The file was labeled: *One-Offs – Testing and Targets*.

Fred set it to the side along with another file he found that was labeled, *Up in Smoke*. He hadn't gotten a chance to look at it and figure out what it was about, so he had chosen to take it for later review in case it turned out to be something important.

Picking up the now empty tote, he headed off to put it on the stacks that needed to be taken to storage. As he passed by Jeff, without breaking stride, he whispered, "Found it." He received a quick nod in response.

"Are you done yet?" Dr. Carter asked him.

"Just one more tote to empty sir," he replied, mentally reminding himself that he only had to deal with the insufferable doctor for a few more hours.

"Finish it up and then get rid of all that?" Dr. Carter said, waving his arm at the stacks of empty totes. "Have Blondie help you and then you two are both done for the day."

Fred quickly emptied the tote, barely even looking at the files. He shoved them into a random filing cabinet drawer before picking up the two files he had previously set aside and placed them inside the now empty tote.

"You ready to help me take the totes to storage?" he asked Jeff loud enough for Dr. Carter to hear.

"One second. I just need to finalize this result and..... done. Alright, let's get them moved," Jeff replied, logging off his terminal, eager to see the file.

With each of them using a two-wheel dolly, they managed to get both stacks of totes in one trip and quickly moved them into the storage area located beside the garage.

Fred grabbed the two files and tucked them into his waistline, behind his back so that they would be hidden by his lab coat.

"I'm going to grab my laptop, and then I'll meet you in your room," Jeff informed him.

"Sounds like a plan. I'll go get us some food from the cafeteria, I'm not sure when we will get a chance to eat again," he mentioned.

"That's a good point. I'll stop and grab some things as well and some extra bottled water to take with us when we leave."

The two young men split up and within thirty minutes, were reunited in Fred's room.

"Hey Jeff, have you ever hear of something called 'Up in Smoke'?"

"Sure have. That's one of the projects that I've been working on, basically the goal is to make it so that a live virus can be added to cigarettes during the manufacturing process. When they get smoked, the smoker gets infected and then through the secondhand smoke, infects those around him,"

Jeff explained. "Doc wasn't having much luck with it and couldn't overcome the two major obstacles. How to keep the virus alive in the cigarettes and how to prevent the heat from causing the virus to die and burn up as the cigarette is smoked. I think I figured it out though, they already make a cigarette that you have to break open a capsule that is embedded in the filter to add more flavor, just add the virus to the capsule to keep it from drying out and dying. The heat would be too far away to initially affect it when the cigarette is lit, by the time the cigarette burned down to the filter, the infection would have already occurred," Jeff explained matter-of-factly.

He stared at his friend for a moment. "Damn! That's diabolical."

"Yeah, it is. To me though, it was just a mind puzzle to be solved, but it should never be implemented in the real world, although I could see where it might come in handy," Jeff conceded.

"In what world would that be okay?" asked Fred, appalled at the thought.

"Let's say there's a terrorist that someone has ordered to be taken out due to crimes against humanity. It's either too dangerous or they're too well protected to send in someone to shoot them, and they can't use a missile without killing innocent bystanders. So send in tainted cigarettes to do the job for you. The only issue is how to get the cigarettes to the targeted subject, but that's a problem for someone else. Not everything has to be for evil purposes," Jeff reminded him.

"Fair enough. I guess that I could see where the government might like something like that," he said, yielding the point to his friend. "I also grabbed that file since I didn't know what it was."

He handed Jeff the One-Offs file. "The doc did list your mom as the first test subject and that he used you as the carrier to get it to her. It's in a handwritten notation at the side of the first page. The next few pages are information about the virus design and various modifications that he did to it. The last few pages are lists of targets that he made One-Off viruses for. We need to get this information to someone who can stop it, assuming that it's not already too late."

Jeff nodded in agreement. "Let's get this stuff packed in a bag and find a way out of here. No one will miss us until tomorrow morning, and we should be long gone by then."

Fred grabbed his backpack and filled it with the food and water they had taken from the cafeteria, as well as the two files and the cell phone Randy had given him. "Done. Let's go," he said with a new determination in his eyes.

They passed a few people on their way to the emergency escape hatch that he had seen the man in the suit use the day before. Fred was surprised that there wasn't a need to enter a code or swipe a mag card in order to open the door before realizing that if it was a true emergency, people would be too panicked to deal with those types of things. Besides, a bunker's purpose was to keep people out, not in. He did note the keypad on the opposite side of the hatch as they left, so a code was needed to open it from the outside.

The hatch led to a concrete-lined tunnel that slowly curved and angled upwards, back towards the surface. After walking for what Fred estimated to be about a mile, the tunnel ended with a ladder leading up to a hatch in the ceiling.

He climbed the ladder, opened the hatch, and exited into a small gardening shed, Jeff quickly followed. They peered out the door and found themselves on an old abandoned farm.

Without knowing where they were and no clear destination in mind. They struck out cross country in the hopes of coming across a town where they could find some help.

Alex & Billy

He noticed that they had all fallen into a routine since arriving on the farm. BB helped Agnes take care of the girls, most days by working in the large garden or helping with the chickens and rabbits. George kept Alex busy, moving hay and water for the cattle, fence-mending, or just patrolling the property fence line, looking for trouble. Sometimes they would go visit the neighbors to see if they had seen anything suspicious or needed any help. Billy mostly just stayed on overwatch.

It seemed like forever, but it had only been six days since they had fled Dallas and half of that time they had spent on the farm. Word around the area was that some unsavory characters were roaming the back roads looking for food and women. Delivery trucks had quit running in most areas of the country, some due to the riots, but mostly it was because of the virus having swept across the country, incapacitating factory workers, truck drivers, and everyone else.

Grocery shelves were empty from coast to coast, and people were beginning to starve across the country. Hunger would make sane people do insane things that they would have never considered before. These were some of the people that Billy watched out for.

His arm was doing better, and hopefully, the stitches could be pulled out in another week or so. BB had done a pretty good job of stitching him up, and by keeping the wound cleaned, he had avoided infection. The constant climbing up and down the ladder to the loft had caused him some minor pain. Now he just stayed in the loft and used empty water bottles when the need to relieve his bladder showed up, cutting down on the number of times that he needed to use the ladder by quite a bit and had helped to ease the pain in his arm.

Seeing some movement out in the north field behind the house, he picked up the binoculars to get a better look. As he adjusted the focus, two figures came into view, odds were that they were both men.

"Alex?" he called over the radio.

"What's up man? Need a break?"

"No dude, I'm good, but we have movement in the north field. They're still too far away to make out details, but it looks like a couple of guys, maybe a little younger than us. They're walking and headed our way."

"Any weapons?" Alex wanted to know.

Billy took a moment to scrutinize the men through the binoculars. "None visible, but it looks like one is carrying a briefcase or laptop bag. If you ask me, that's kind of a weird thing to carry around when the whole world's gone to shit. If they maintain their current pace, they should be closing in on us in about five minutes."

"Alright, keep them in your sights. George is going to take up a position inside the house, and I'll go introduce myself when they get a bit closer," Alex explained his hastily put-together plan.

"Be careful dude, and leave your mic open on the radio so I can hear what they are saying," Billy advised his friend.

"No worries. How close are they now?"

"About the length of a football field. Young guys, early to mid-twenties, one has a backpack and the other a laptop bag. Maybe their car broke down because they aren't dressed for hiking and don't appear to have any weapons."

"Alright. I'm heading out to meet them. Keep them in your rifle scope in case you need to take them out, I'll leave the mic open."

Billy watched his best friend walk out from the side of the house and to the edge of the field, the two men slowed down slightly before committing themselves to continuing forward.

When they were about 50 feet away, Alex hollered out to them, "That's close enough boys."

"Please help us," the blonde guy begged.

"What are you doing trespassing on private property?" Alex asked them.

"We're looking for some help. We have information that the authorities need," the blonde continued, obviously the leader of the two.

Alex still held his rifle with the barrel pointed down, but he could easily bring it up if needed. "Not much left in the way of authority nowadays. Come forward slowly with your hands up."

The other guy glanced at the blonde and finally spoke, "I told you this was a bad idea. We need to get into a city."

"Damn it Fred, just do what the man says," the blonde replied, raising his hands and walking slowly forward. The other man soon followed suit.

When the gap closed to ten feet, Alex spoke again, "Stop and drop your bags."

The blonde responded without hesitation, "I won't drop it, but I will set it down. It's too important to take a chance on it getting damaged."

Alex nodded his assent. "Once the bags are on the ground, you'll need to step back a few steps, lift up your shirts and do a slow 360-degree turn so I can make sure that you don't have any weapons. Try anything stupid, and you'll get a bullet for your trouble, I'd just as soon avoid that as I'm a bit too tired to dig another grave."

The men quickly complied, apparently terrified and wondering what they had gotten themselves into.

"Lift up your pant legs," Alex commanded.

"Billy, they appear to be weaponless. I'll need to pat them down to be sure they don't have any knives so watch my six." Turning his attention back to the two men. "I want each of you to come to me, one at a time so I can pat you down for weapons. It's either that or you strip, your choice, but keep in mind that there are at least two other rifles pointed at you so don't even think of trying anything."

The blonde moved forward slowly with his hands in the air until he was directly in front of Alex.

"Okay, turn around."

The guy complied and allowed Alex to thoroughly check him for weapons before being waved to the side.

"Your turn," he said to the other man, who didn't hesitate to do as his friend had.

Once he had checked both of them for weapons, Alex

had them sit on the ground while he went to inspect the bags. Finding nothing of interest, he slung them over his shoulder and motioned the men toward the front of the barn.

"Coming to you, Billy," he said, giving his friend a heads up.

Billy climbed down from the loft and met them outside.

"Before we go any further, you two are going to answer some questions," he said to the two men.

The shorter one raised his hand reluctantly.

"This isn't high school, just ask your question," Billy told him.

"Sorry, it's my first time being captured, or I guess it's technically the second," he said, shaking his head. "Can we get something to drink? We've been walking forever and ran out of water a couple of hours ago."

Alex headed off to the house. "Hey! Have BB come and do overwatch while we have a conversion with these two gentlemen," Billy called after him, getting a wave in reply.

He invited the men into the shade of the barn and had them sit on some bales of hay. "You got names?"

"Umm, I'm Fred. Fred Ridley and this is Jeff Caldwell," the shorter man replied.

Alex came back with some bottled water and was followed by BB, who headed up into the loft with only a glance at the two men. He handed each man a bottle and allowed them to drink.

"Now, would you care to explain just why you two are wandering the countryside, carrying a laptop, a cell phone, and a couple of paper files in the middle of a pandemic?"

Fred looked up. "It's a long story."

"Aren't they always?" Billy retorted. "Now, start talking."

Taking a deep breath, Fred began his story. He started with his recruitment into The Elite Group and stopped when he walked in on Jeff breaking into the doc's computer.

"I think Jeff needs to finish the rest."

So Jeff picked up where Fred had stopped, explaining

everything, up until Alex approached them in the field.

"And that's how we ended up here and why we were carrying what we were," he finished, relief flooding his body now that he had told the whole story.

"Well, that's a bit more than I was expecting," admitted Billy.

Alex nodded his head and was grinning. "Yeah, me too. I figured that they ran out of gas and were looking for a ride."

"Let's say that we believe you. You work for, or are related to, the mother fucker that created this virus, and we're just supposed to believe that now, once half the world is dead, you want to do the right thing?" he demanded to know, glaring at the two young men.

"Umm, well yeah, kinda. Look, we didn't choose to help them do this. If we'd refused, we would have been killed and probably still will be, once they figure out that we escaped," Fred told them. "If you can get me a charger so I can charge up my phone, then you can call Randy, he's staying with the Army and can verify some of my story. Jeff can show you files on his computer and the paper files, and that will verify the rest. We need to stop him from killing even more people, don't you get that?"

"Yeah, I get that! I'm just pissed the world was pretty much destroyed to satisfy one man's inflated ego," he said, throwing a bottle of water across the barn in anger. He watched it explode against the wall, sending water flying in every direction. "Let's get you inside to charge the phone, and you both can get cleaned up. Agnes will have dinner ready soon and until then, you can show us what's in those files."

The two men quickly cleaned up, and the group was soon enthralled by the information contained in the files.

It wasn't long before it was time to eat and they were able to fill in George and Agnes while they ate.

"Sounds like you two have been busy," Agnes said. "I for one, believe you. Your story also matches what I heard on the radio earlier."

Billy looked at Agnes, surprised. "What did you hear?"

"The Army is telling everyone not to take the vaccine, that it's not as effective as first thought and that it might cause sterilization as a side effect."

"So they either don't know it's a fake virus, or they don't want the public to know that it is. I'd assume that they are trying to keep it under wraps to prevent further rioting," Alex stated.

Billy agreed, "Okay Fred, you're calling your friend Randy after we finish eating. Hopefully, the Army can stop this madness from continuing."

"This is Randy," the voice answered, nearly 1,300 miles away.

"Randy, it's Fred."

"Oh my God Fred. What happened? The Army raided the labs, but everyone was gone except Latisha," he told him.

"Is Latisha alright?" Fred asked, holding his tears back.

"Last I heard, she was recovering nicely from the virus. She's in quarantine here on the base, but you didn't answer my question," Randy reminded him.

"Well, you remember the man in the suit who was asking around about you? He showed up and warned of a raid that was being planned on the labs. Everything was packed and moved in two hours, forcing us all to go to a bunker in Colorado. Jeff and I escaped with proof that Dr. Carter designed, created, and unleashed the virus on the world. He also made some people-specific viruses, we have a list of names, and the President is one of them," Fred declared. "We're hoping the Army can stop this from happening."

Randy was silent for a moment. "The President died this morning. They plan on announcing it later today."

"Shit! That means we're too late," he exclaimed.

"To stop that attack, yes. But they still need the proof, and they want to capture Dr. Carter alive and bring him to justice."

"Jeff has most of the proof on his computer, and I also

have a couple of paper files I took. We know where the bunker is and the location of at least two entrances. I can also draw the layout for them like I did for the labs in Atlanta. We just don't have any way to get to Fort Benning," he revealed.

Randy sighed. "Well, I need to talk to the sergeant major and let him know what you have. The Army has locked down all the bases, so I am not sure what they will do. Do you think Jeff can email some of the files so I can show him at least some of the evidence you have? Maybe that will be enough to convince them to do something."

Fred checked with Jeff before responding, "He said that he could send a few. Most of the files are too big for a standard email. Send me your email address on a text message, and we'll get that over to you asap."

"No problem. Give me a little time to talk to the sergeant major and show him what you sent me, and then I'll get back to you on what the plan is," Randy said, his voice betraying his excitement at the information that Fred had just disclosed.

"Okay. Can you please let Latisha know that I'm alright and that I've been worried about her?" Fred asked, exposing some of his feelings.

"I'll make sure that she gets the message, and I'll get to work on the sergeant major as soon as I receive those files," Randy promised as he ended the call.

Within a minute, Randy's email address was in hand, and Jeff was sending all the files that they could. Now the only thing left for them to do was wait.

Sergeant Major Brooks

Brooks had been promoted again, three times in as many days. He was a first sergeant for less than three hours before his latest promotion to sergeant major, and he could be less thrilled since it meant that they had lost another good man to the virus.

He was headed back to his barracks to try and get in a

quick nap when Randy caught up to him. After listening for a few minutes, he forgot about his nap and headed back to command headquarters, bringing Mr. Elkhart and his computer with him, this was something that couldn't wait.

The colonel was still in the conference room, turned war room, and the sergeant major wasted no time having Randy explain what Fred had told him before showing him the files.

He had known Colonel Baker for a good many years. Their paths had crossed at various times throughout their careers and they held a mutual respect and trust for one another. Over the last week, they had vetted all of the senior personnel on the base. They were now confident that there was only one member of the senior staff on base who might have been corrupted by The Elite Group. This man was not included in any of the briefings and was kept on a very short leash.

The colonel had requested a conference call that included most of the base's senior staff along with Fred and Jeff so that they could ask their own questions about who all might be involved and what else was still being planned.

Eventually, it was deemed necessary to retrieve the data that was currently in Fred and Jeff's possession. They also needed to infiltrate the bunker and capture Dr. Carter and anyone else that may be involved.

The military bases were all still on lockdown, but the colonel decided that this was too important of a chance to pass up. Since they had no idea who might be involved with The Elite Group higher up the chain of command, they chose not to share the information with anyone who was not at Fort Benning. They believed that this was necessary due to the fact that someone had warned the doctor about the raid on Crouch Pharmaceutical's labs, the only ones who knew about that were the Rangers who carried out the raid, a few of the higher-ranking officials on base, and those higher up the command structure. The only ones the colonel couldn't vet out were those who not on the base. The logical conclusion was that the leak was higher up in the command structure.

A hastily put-together plan called for the three squads of Rangers to fly out to the closest airport they can find, that was large enough to land a fully loaded C-17. They would then drive to the farm in Colorado in the Flyer 72 Ground Mobility Vehicles that they would bring with them in the C-17. The Rangers would get any intel that they could from Fred and Jeff regarding the bunker, including the location, layout, entrances, and the number of possible personnel inside before finalizing their plan.

DAY FOURTEEN

Underground Bunker North-East of Trinidad, CO.

Deep in the bowels of the bunker, where few have reason to venture, in a small hidden room, sits a computer. The monitor was throwing just enough light to create shadows that would frighten small children and keep them shaking in fear under the covers. Had anyone been in the room, what they would have seen on the screen would have probably terrified them even more as the counter continued counting down.

00:00:04
00:00:03
00:00:02
00:00:01
00:00:00
Protocol Seven: Sarin Gas has been initiated
Automated Venting will begin in:
00:60:00
00:59:59
00:59:58
00:59:57

Dr. Carter had just walked into the lab as the first micron of the Sarin Gas disbursed through the vents, propelled throughout the facility by the A/C fans. He would never know what killed him since the gas was odorless and colorless.

Within a few minutes, bodies littered the floors

throughout the bunker. The last to die was one of the cooks who happened to be inventorying the contents of the walk-in freezer, and he did not come into contact with the gas until he left the freezer fifteen minutes after the last body had dropped. He lived for another three minutes and twelve seconds, then nothing was left except for the buzzing of fluorescent lights and the humming of the air conditioning until the Automated Venting began less than an hour later. Loud clangs rang through the bunker as huge vent fans began replacing all of the air in the bunker. The venting would continue for one hour, completely replacing all the air over and over again, once every five minutes, until the cycle completed, making the bunker safe to occupy once more.

Staff Sergeant Jones

After landing at the Pueblo Memorial Airport and offloading the Flyer 72's, the Rangers were now heading towards Trinidad on I25. The farm was approximately 90 miles from Pueblo.

He had called after they landed to get final directions, and Billy and Alex had agreed to meet them at the US350 and US160 junction to lead them in.

So far, they had only run into one attempted roadblock by some road warriors looking for easy prey, they took one look at the GAU-19/A three-barrel rotary heavy machine guns that were mounted on each of the vehicles before they tucked tail and headed for the hills. Staff Sgt. Jones thought that was a mighty smart move on their part.

They turned off onto El Moro Road, just north of Trinidad, and followed a few other county roads before coming out on US350. They hadn't passed any vehicles the entire way except for one lone pickup on County Road 75.1, and they had quickly turned off and given the Rangers a wide berth.

Making good time, they approached the junction of the two highways, he could see two men standing outside a lifted

Chevy pickup. They were armed but holding the weapons in a non-threatening manner.

The GMVs were brought to a stop and Jones dismounted the rig and stepped forward to meet the two men.

"Howdy! I'm hoping that you're Sergeant Jones, who was sent here by Colonel Brooks," the one not wearing an arm sling greeted the small convoy.

"That would be an affirmative, but it's Master Sergeant Brooks and Colonel Baker who sent us," he corrected the man.

"I'm Alex and this is Billy. Sorry about the mix-up on the names. You can follow us back to the farm, it's kind of a maze to get to it so that's why we wanted to meet first," he explained to the Ranger.

The staff sergeant looked Alex in the eye. "Really? I figured you just wanted to make sure we were really with the military and not some bandits, pretending to be military, hence the intentional name mix-up."

Alex grinned. "Well, I guess you got me there. You can't be too careful these days. Follow us," he said as he motioned to someone in the field next to them that it was safe to come out.

Jones grinned as an older man revealed himself, he had been their backup. Not bad instincts for civilians, he thought, as he headed back to his GMV.

Everyone loaded back up into their respective vehicles, and the journey continued with the pickup maintaining the lead, arriving at the farm about fifteen minutes later.

Leaving two men to guard each vehicle, the Rangers followed Alex and Billy into the barn where a table and some chairs had been set up, a map of the area hung on the wall behind it.

Every one of the rangers had noted the overwatch that being done from the barn's loft, Jones' respect for the group went up another notch. These may be civilians, but they had excellent survival instincts.

Two gentlemen were sitting at the table who were obviously the scientists they had come to meet.

"Fred, Jeff, this is Staff Sergeant Jones and some of the Rangers the Army promised you," Billy said as they approached the table.

The two men started to get up, but Jones waved them off. "Don't get up on our account. We have a lot we need to go over so I'd like to get right into it if you don't mind."

"Umm, sure thing staff sergeant," Fred agreed, before being interrupted.

"While I am a staff sergeant, please address me as sergeant. For future reference, any staff sergeant, sergeant first class, or master sergeant, you should address as sergeant when speaking directly to them. You give their entire title when they are not present and you're referring to them," Jones explained, hoping to clear up some confusion.

"Umm, okay. Thanks for clarifying that. I didn't mean any disrespect," Fred said as the staff sergeant waved it off. "I drew out a diagram showing the layout of the bunker the best that we can remember. There are three occupied levels underground, built like an inverted pyramid with each level is slightly smaller than the one above it. The top-level contains the public areas like the cafeteria, recreation space, food storage, and things along those lines. The second level is where all the housing is, along with communal showers and laundry facilities. The lowest level contains the lab and some of the bunker's mechanical workings. We know of three entry/exit points. The first is hidden inside a small building next to an antenna, we believe that its location is right here," he pointed at a small, red 1 that Jeff had placed on the map. "The number 2 denotes the exit that we used when we escaped. It's hidden in a small storage shed on an abandoned farm about 20 miles due north of here. The final entry point that we are aware of, is the garage. Neither of us have used that particular entrance, so we can't be positive of its location; however, based on satellite maps of the area, we believe that it's most likely in one of the two sites marked with a 3 on the map. Those are locations where there is a large structure, but no habitable houses close by," he explained.

"Any armed guards? How many people are in the bunker?" Jones rattled off his questions.

"No guards that we saw. The only person we saw armed the entire time we were there was a man in a black suit, but he left the bunker the day before we did. He might have returned, but he wasn't there when we left. As for how many are there, I'd guess right around 350-400. The bunker was designed to hold over 1,000 people," Fred told them, happy to be able to provide them with the information.

The staff sergeant nodded his head. "Where are the most likely places for Dr. Carter to be?"

Jeff promptly answered, eager to give any help to those who wished to take down his father. "The lab, and if he isn't there, then he is either in the cafeteria getting something to eat, or he's sleeping in his quarters, which is unit #180. All three locations are marked on the diagram with red X's"

Jones turned toward Fred. "You said occupied levels, are there any unoccupied levels that you're aware of."

"Yeah, there's at least one sub-level that I know of. Its entrance is right here," he said, pointing to a spot on the hand-drawn bunker layout. "It's pretty much just a short hallway and one large room containing a bunch of mechanical equipment. There's a small hidden room inside there, but I wasn't able to get into it."

"You can show us where it is once we have secured the facility. I'm sure we can find a key to open it with," he mentioned as several Rangers gave a slight chuckle. "Anything else that you think we should know about?"

Fred shook his head, but Jeff chose to respond, "Just remember that most of those people have no idea who's responsible for making and releasing the virus. They are unwittingly caught up in this, against their will, like me and Fred."

"No worries there. Our goal is to secure Dr. Carter and any information regarding biological weapons without hurting anyone. Once we get what we came for, everyone else is welcome to remain in the bunker or leave if they wish," he briefly explained the goal of the raid.

Jones continued, "Alpha will take entrance one and will focus on the lowest level. Bravo, you have entrance two and the middle level and Charlie, which leaves you with the garage entrance and the top level. Each squad will send a two-man team to scout their assigned entry points. Since we don't know for sure where the garage entrance is, I want Charlie to go and scout both of the two possible locations and determine if one of those is what we are looking for, if neither are, see if you can locate it before sundown. Regardless of what you find, I want everyone back here on-site, 30 mikes after sundown. We can review what everyone sees and make adjustments to the plan as needed. We'll camp here tonight and move out at 0530. Any questions?"

The Rangers shook their heads, and Jones released them to do what was needed before nightfall.

"That was a good briefing you gave," he complimented the two scientists. "When we leave to go back to Fort Benning, Colonel Baker has requested you accompany us for an official debriefing, if possible. It's your choice of course, but there are a few folks from the CDC to whom you might be able to provide some valuable information."

Jeff looked at Fred, who nodded his assent. "Sure, no problem as long as you keep me as far away from my father as possible."

"Agreed. Now where is a good place to set up our camp and be out of everyone's way?" Jones asked, looking around the property.

"Along the side of the barn. We'll make sure the girls know not to bother your men," Billy offered.

"I'm sure they'll be fine. Thanks for everything you've all done. Hopefully, by tomorrow night, this nightmare will have ended, and no further damage will be done by the doctor once the Frankenstein Virus completely dies out."

"I sure hope so because Alex still has a date to go on, and

he's not getting any younger," Billy teased as Alex shook his head at his goofball friend.

Lisa

"We need to talk," she said, sitting down across from Randy in the DFAC without waiting for an invitation.

"I haven't heard anything else from Fred. All I know is that the Rangers left for Colorado sometime last night or early this morning."

She shook her head. "That's not what I mean. We need to talk about what happened between us."

"I screwed up and I've regretted it every day since. That's what happened," he stated pointedly.

"Truthfully, I'm to blame. Technically, you didn't do anything wrong. I told you that we were on a break, and that meant that you had every right to go out with someone else. It was wrong of me to get mad about it and cut you out of my life," Lisa told him, admitting to what she had come to realize over the last few years.

"I only did it to make you jealous, I didn't even kiss her goodnight," Randy confided to her.

"That wasn't the story I heard." Seeing him about to object, she waved it off. "Looking back on it now, I understand what happened. I wanted you to fight for me, that was the whole reason for the stupid break in the first place, and you know what makes it worse? That She-Devil of an ex-best friend was the one who talked me into it in the first place, and then she went out with you. I should have known that she just wanted to break us up. It wasn't you who I was really mad at this whole time, it was myself for being so stupid and buying into her bullshit," Lisa confided.

Randy wasn't sure what to do with this revelation based on the confused look he wore on his face. "I still should have never agreed to the date. She asked me to go out to dinner and told me that it was a good way to make you jealous. I knew it was a mistake the minute that I said yes, but I was too weak to admit it. I went through the motions on the date, drawing the line at giving her a goodnight kiss. My heart belonged to you and she and I both knew it. I never spoke to her again, although she called and left me several messages over the next few weeks."

"Damn it! If I hadn't been so damn stubborn and bullheaded and just talked to you instead of shutting you out, we could have figured all this out years ago. Instead, we lost all that time when we should have been together," she complained, more to herself than to him.

Randy smiled. "I guess that's one good thing to come out of this mess, we can both stop feeling guilty. How about, after things get back to normal-ish, we go out on a date? No strings attached, just to test the waters and see if we still make sense together."

Lisa batted her eyes. "Why Mr. Elkhart, I believe that would be a mighty fine idea."

Erik

It had been quiet in his neighborhood over the last few days. The power had gone out the previous night, and Erik had opened the upstairs windows that couldn't be reached easily from the ground to allow the heat to escape and prevent the house from getting too stuffy.

The looting and rioting had stayed downtown and in the more affluent residential areas. That came to an abrupt halt as gunshots from the house next door shattered the peace of the night.

Erik left his 9 mm pistol with Eddie, who was still extremely weak but could shoot if necessary. He took the 12 gauge pump action shotgun as he roamed the house, prepared for trouble.

Over the next half hour, he heard men yelling at each other, although it didn't sound like an argument, more like instructions. Erik had been unable to make out most of the words but clearly understood that these people were looking for food and were willing to kill to get it.

It wasn't long before there was a loud pounding on the front door. "Open up and give up your food and you get to live, don't and you'll die," a gruff voice yelled from the front porch.

"Move on! We don't have any to spare," Erik replied and then quickly ducked into the hall in case they shot through the door.

"It wasn't a request. Now, OPEN THE DOOR!" the man demanded.

Erik snuck back towards the front door and peeked out the sidelight window to see where the man was. He could just make out the figure of a man on the darkened porch, he carefully aimed and waited to see what the man was going to do. He didn't have long to wait as the man almost immediately reared his leg back to order to kick in the door. Erik pulled the trigger, not waiting to see the results, he quickly pulled himself back into the hallway. He chambered a new round without really thinking about it as bullets began flying through the door and windows.

"He shot Donald!" someone yelled.

"I'll shoot you too if you don't leave right now," Erik countered.

"Fuck you! You shouldn't have killed my friend."

"He was warned just like I warned you. Now go, or your group will have one more less person to feed," he quickly crossed the living room so that they couldn't pinpoint his location by tracking where the sound of his voice came from.

Peering through the small gap in the curtains, he could make out three more looters in the moonlight, so he knew that there were at least four left. He saw one of them heading around the house, probably headed for the back door.

Erik squat walked over to the couch. "Eddie, I have to go take care of one of them who's going to the backyard. You need to stay down low and shoot only if they try to enter the house and you have a clear shot. I'll be right back."

"I be okay. You be going on back 'n I be shooting them if they try to get in the house," Eddie replied quietly, while gripping the pistol. Although still weak, he could walk with assistance since his legs weren't currently strong enough to support his body. Eddie rolled off the couch and crawled to a more defensive position that would also have sight lines to all the access points at the front of the house.

Nodding, Erik headed to the kitchen just as someone tried to open the door. It was locked, and the refrigerator had been placed in front of it, making it much more difficult for someone to gain entry. He ducked into the laundry room, which had a small window facing out onto the deck. Raising his head just enough to see over the window sill, Erik surveyed the area. The man picked up what looked like a flower pot and threw it through the window of the back door. That was enough for Erik, he raised the shotgun and shot for center mass, the slug blowing a fist-sized hole through the man's chest, causing him to twist and fall against the door jamb. The man lived long enough to wonder what the hell happened before his brain finally realized that he was dead.

He quickly returned to the hallway off the living room. "Your friend in the back is dead now as well. More food for the rest of you, now leave and don't come back. This is your last warning, try again, and you all get to die."

Hearing murmuring voices out front, he tried to make out what they were saying, but they were too far away. He kept his head on a swivel, checking every access point into the house that he could see from his position. Erik hoped that the men would just leave, but apparently they weren't that smart as he saw movement out the dining room window. They were circling the house.

He caught Eddie's attention and indicated that he was going to check the rest of the house, then slipped up the stairs. Figuring that the men were probably focused on the lower level, he took the high ground. He was rewarded with seeing the darker shadows of two men against the white siding of the house. They were creeping along and checking the windows.

Glad that the window was already open, he pushed out the screen and bought the shotgun's muzzle to point in the direction of the two men and quickly shot twice before ducking down and changing windows. He only had two shots left before needing to reload, but he had to make sure that the men were dead before he could leave his position. He looked out the window and saw that one shadow was not moving while the other was trying to crawl away, Erik carefully aimed and finished him off.

He heard glass breaking downstairs and cursed himself for not carrying any extra shells. He only had one shot left before the shotgun would become a club. The box of shotshells was still sitting on the kitchen table where he had cleaned the guns. He quickly headed down the stairs to try and retrieve them before he needed them. As he reached the bottom of the stairs, a shot rang out, and a bullet struck the wall by his head. Erik reacted instantly and promptly shot in the direction of the front door where the gun flash came from. Hearing a yell and someone cursing, he knew that he had hit them, but it hadn't been a kill shot.

Erik's mind was focused on getting to the shells at this point, and he failed to realize that one of the men had gained entry into the house from another room or possibly the basement. Just as he turned to go towards the kitchen, another shot rang out. Erik dropped to the floor.

He heard the sound of a body hitting the floor behind him, along with the clatter of a gun. He looked back and understood immediately that Eddie had just saved his life. He nodded his thanks to his friend and scrambled back up and into the kitchen.

"You get him Bo? I heard a shot," the injured man on the porch asked.

Erik wasted no time reloading the shotgun and rapidly made his way to the window, searching the darkness for any other threats beyond the injured man. Not seeing any, he glanced down at the bleeding man and pointed his shotgun at him, "No, he didn't."

"Oh shit!" The man struggled to bring his pistol up, but his damaged arm, where Eric had shot him, wasn't allowing it.

"Drop it!" Erik ordered.

The man hesitated before comprehending that Erik had the drop on him and lowered his weapon. "We just wanted to feed our families," he said, trying to justify their actions.

"I don't care. You were told to move on and you should have listened. How many of you were there?" he asked, glaring at the man.

The man said nothing.

"Do you want to die?" Erik asked as he raised one of his eyebrows.

"No. I want to go home to my family," he said, beginning to sob.

"How many? Don't make me ask again."

"Six. There were six of us. How many did you kill?"

Erik pulled the trigger before responding, "Six."

He had never killed anyone before, and it suddenly hit him that he had personally murdered five men. Erik leaned against the wall and slid down to the floor and started to cry.

"You be okay?" Eddie asked quietly.

Erik took a moment to compose himself. "Yeah buddy, I am. I just never killed anyone before."

"I be not killing before either, but you be needing to remember that they be animals, not people. Animals that would have killed you 'n me both for a few cans of corn. Them or us and I be picking us every time."

"That's wise advice, Eddie. Thank you for watching my back and saving my life."

"You be knowing that I be always getting your back, besides, you be taking care of me 'n probably saved me too," Eddie acknowledged.

"Well that's what friends are for. Now let's get you back

on the couch and then I'll take out the trash." Nodding at the dead man lying on the floor.

Making quick work of removing the body, he decided to find the vehicle that they came in. It wasn't hard since there was a pickup and a suburban parked directly in front of his house. Realizing that they also needed food, Erik hesitantly grabbed the boxes of stolen food that were in the back of the pickup, taking them into the house. He decided not to feel bad about it, whoever it had originally belonged to was probably killed by the men, and it would only go to waste otherwise.

Erik checked to make sure that keys were in the ignitions and donned a pair of work gloves before loading all six bodies into the back of the pickup. He drove it several blocks away and left it parked on the side of the street before walking back and moving the suburban as well, leaving the keys inside the vehicles.

He decided to keep their weapons, no sense in leaving them lying around for someone else to find and use against him or some other unsuspecting person. He took those into the house along with the ammo that he had found inside the vehicles.

Once back at the house, he rounded up some cleaning supplies and cleaned the blood off the floor inside the house and off the porch and deck outside, he'd wait until morning to secure the broken windows.

It turns out that surviving was hard work and not for the weak-minded. Erik had never wanted to kill anyone, but he now knew that not only could he do it, but that he would do it. With that thought, he laid down and tried to go to sleep, assuming that it would be an evening full of nightmares. He wasn't wrong.

DAY FIFTEEN

Staff Sergeant Jones

It was too damn early to function without any coffee. They had left the farm at 0530 with plans to have all three squads make entry at 0630. Charlie Squad had located the garage entrance at the second location that they had checked the previous evening, and all teams had looked for cameras and other obstacles that might hamper their gaining entry, they would check again this morning in case anything had changed overnight. All the entrances had well-concealed cameras, but Jones didn't much care about them since he knew that they would already be in the bunker within thirty seconds of coming into camera view.

They had already breached the fence, and Boomer had his shaped charge ready to be stuck onto the door. All he had to do was run in, place it, run back, and then press the button to remotely detonate it, and then Alpha Squad would have no problem walking through the newly unlocked door. Bravo and Charlie had their own demo experts and were set up in much the same way.

Jones counted down over the radio using the throat mic, leaving his hands free.

"Three, two, one. GO! GO! GO!"

Boomer was fast and had the explosive set in place and was back in eight seconds and the door lock blown off at nine, by 27 seconds, the last of Alpha Squad entered the bunker.

They found themselves in a large entrance hallway. Jones saw a bank of elevators at the end of the hall and quickly made his way there. Finding the stairwell door on the right, he motioned his entry team forward. Reeves went first, followed by Bull and then Boomer. "Alpha Squad, stairs are clear. Descending," Reeves said over the radio.

A half a moment later. "Charlie Squad, inside the tunnel. Moving toward the garage."

"Bravo Squad. Stairs clear. Entering level two."

Alpha squad almost ran down the stairs since they had the furthermost location to secure, just as they were preparing to enter the third level.

"ALL SQUADS! MASKS! MASKS! MASKS! Probable contamination. Bodies on the floor."

Jones wasn't sure who called the warning, but every Ranger reacted without pause and immediately donned their gas masks.

"Alpha Six Actual to all squads. The goal remains the same. Secure the target, do a quick sweep of your area for any survivors and move them outside. Do not touch any of the bodies or the survivors. We don't know what we are dealing with yet."

"Roger Alpha Six Actual. Bravo out."

"Roger Alpha Six Actual. Charlie through the garage and moving into level one."

"Alpha Squad on level three. Setting off charge on lab door," Boomer said a second before the small charge went off. "Alpha entering and securing lab."

Reeves almost tripped over the body on the floor. "Body. Someone confirm if it's the target or not," he said, as he stepped over it, checking the lab for threats.

"Alpha has located the target. Target deceased. Bravo and Charlie, continue a quick sweep for survivors. Everyone needs to be out of the bunker yesterday. Wilcox, you and Bull pull the computer server," Jones ordered.

"Bravo Six Actual to Alpha Six Actual. Bravo is headed to

the surface. No survivors located."

"Roger Bravo Six Actual."

"Charlie Six Actual to Alpha Six Actual. No survivors. Charlie heading out."

"Roger that Charlie Six Actual."

The two men made quick work of retrieving the server and Alpha Squad headed back to the stairwell. "Alpha Six Actual. No survivors. Returning to the surface."

"Bravo Six Actual to Alpha Six Actual. Bravo Squad has ex-filled back to the GMV. En route to your position. Bravo Six Actual out."

"Roger Bravo Six Actual," Jones replied just as he exited the bunker.

Alpha squad headed back to their GMV but that hadn't gotten far before a loud siren went off followed by a message.

Self-destruct sequence initiated. 30, 29, 28, 27,...

"Alpha Six Actual to all squads. Get to your GMV and ex-fill as far away as you can. ASAP! This mission just went FUBAR."

Alpha Squad was quickly in their vehicle and headed away. Jones could still hear the countdown as it slowly faded in the distance.

...11, 10, 9, 8,...

"Alpha Six Actual to Charlie Squad. You guys make it out?"

...3, 2, 1.

The ground shook violently as a huge, dirt geyser sprung up out of the Colorado landscape. The sound was deafening and seemed to carry on for several minutes as multiple explosions went off. A gigantic dust cloud pushed through the surrounding area with the explosive waves of air caused by the implosion of the bunker. The dust cloud quickly caught up to, and then engulfed, Alpha Squad, who stopped and waited out the man-made dust storm.

"Alpha Six Actual to Bravo Six Actual. You guys alright?"

"We're five-by. A little hard of hearing and dusty, but

otherwise no complaints. Bravo Six Actual out."

"Roger Bravo Six Actual. Alpha Six Actual to Charlie Six Actual. Status?"

Jones waited but didn't receive a callback. "Charlie Six Actual, do you have a copy?"

Still nothing. "Bravo, you pick up anything from Charlie? I might be too far away if they drove the other way."

"Negative. I'll see if I can rile them up. Bravo Six Actual to Charlie Six Actual. Status?" Nothing. "Bravo Six Actual to anyone on Charlie Squad. We need a status update."

"Ch.....int....com....ut."

"Alpha Six Actual. Did you copy that?"

"If it was a garbled mess then yes, I did. Bravo, meet us at Charlie's last known position."

"Roger that Alpha Six Actual. Bravo on the move to Charlie's last known position. Bravo Six Actual out."

"Roger Bravo Six Actual. Alpha Six Actual out." Jones, like most Rangers, seldom showed any worry or fear on their face or in their voice, that didn't mean they didn't feel it. He needed to find Charlie Squad and make sure they were safe.

"Wilcox. Get us moving. Back to Charlie's position."

"Roger that." Wilcox cranked the wheel and headed back into the dust as he skirted around where the bunker used to be. Visibility was only about ten feet so they weren't able to go very fast. 30 mph was about all he was willing to push it, afraid that a huge hole or very large rock might appear in front of him at any moment and ruin the rest of their day.

"Alpha Six Actual to Bravo Six Actual. Let me know the instant you have eyes on Charlie."

"Roger Alpha Six Actual. It's slow going due to the dust and concrete chunks littering the ground. GPS shows us about a klick away from his entry point. Bravo Six Actual out."

"Roger that Bravo Six Actual. We have the same issue. Looks like we'll converge on Charlie's position at about the same time so watch for us as well. Alpha Six Actual out."

"Roger that."

"Slow down Wilcox. We still need this vehicle to get back to the farm," Jones told him after they nearly hit a chunk of concrete the size of a washing machine.

Seeing the lights from Bravo Squad's GMV, Wilcox slowed down and stopped beside them.

"Alpha Six Actual to anyone on Charlie Squad. We are at your last known location. Anyone copy?"

"Charlie Three to Alpha Six Actual. We're coming back to you. Charlie Six Actual got slammed in the head with some debris, and something took out the antenna on the GMV so our radio range is for shit. Be there in two mikes. Charlie Three out."

Relief swept through the men at hearing those words, knowing their friends were alive and safe.

"Roger that Charlie Three. Glad to hear you're mostly in one piece. We'll hold for you at our current position. Alpha Six Actual out."

He was thankful that he hadn't taken his mask off when he had exited the bunker or he wouldn't be able to breathe. As it was, the filter was starting to clog up with the fine dust particles. He wiped the dust off the glass so he could see better.

Climbing out of the GMV, he walked closer to where the bunker had been. Through the dust that was still hanging in the air, he could see the edge of what had to be a huge crater. There was no way they would be able to salvage anything from the rubble. He was glad he had thought to grab the server, otherwise, they wouldn't have anything at all to show for their efforts, returning empty-handed would have sucked.

Charlie Squad pulled up beside them, and Jones took a moment to check on Staff Sgt. Smith, the leader of Charlie Squad. He was conscious, but there wasn't anything he could do for him in all this dust.

"Rangers, load up. We're headed back to the FOB."

Thirty-five minutes later, they pulled up to the farm. Everyone was still wearing their gas masks, per procedure, until they could be decontaminated. In this case, decontamination would consist of getting spayed down thoroughly with a garden hose.

He raised a hand to let Alex know not to come forward. "We need to get hosed off first in case there are any contaminates on us."

Alex pointed him to a water spigot on the opposite side of the barn that had a coil of hose beside it.

Nodding his head, he started in that direction with a line of Rangers following. "Rangers, listen up. Charlie Six Actual needs to be priority decon so we can get him looked at by Dr. Barnes."

Once Staff Sgt. Smith had gotten the dust hosed off him, he was taken into the barn where BB was able to examine him. She found no lasting effects from the head injury and determined he probably received a mild concussion. She gave him some ibuprofen for the headache and released him back into duty.

"Ah, Ranger candy. Just like an Army doc," he told her, grinning as he left the barn.

Confused, she asked Jones what he had meant. Jones laughed, "Army docs all think that ibuprofen can cure anything. They give you a few pills and send you back to duty for pretty much anything that doesn't require amputation. It's prescribed so often that everyone started calling it Ranger candy."

Forty-five minutes later, all of the Rangers had thoroughly rinsed off the dirt and dust from the bunker explosion. By that time, George had a cooler of bottled water, soft drinks, and beer set out for them in front of the barn, along with a large pile of sandwiches that Agnes had made for the men. The Rangers made quick work of devouring the food, much to Agnes' delight.

"So how'd it go?" Alex asked.

"Honestly, not as well as we had hoped. Everyone in the bunker was dead before we arrived, most likely poisoned with gas, it looked like they died where they stood. Hence, the wearing of the masks which turned out to be a good thing. When the entire bunker blew up, we were still able to breathe even with all that dust in the air," Jones explained.

"So my father's dead and you got nothing?" Jeff asked in disbelief.

"I never said that. We can confirm that Dr. Carter is dead. I saw him myself and even took a photo on my phone if you want to see it," he paused but only received a subtle head shake from Jeff. "We also managed to get the server from the main computer in the lab. Hopefully, there will be some information on there that will help us."

Fred perked up. "Wait. When did the lab blow up? Were you still inside?"

"We had just left it and were almost to our vehicle when a siren sounded and announced that the self-destruct had initiated. Why?"

"Umm, I think you might have set off the explosion when you removed the computer server from the bunker," he explained, as it dawned on Jeff what he was talking about.

"Oh shit! The beacon thingy the dude in the suit did to the computer."

Fred was nodding his head. "That's what I'm thinking."

"Wait a minute, the whatsit with the whosit?" Alex said, not having a clue what the boys were talking about.

"Remember when I told you that the man wearing the suit came into the lab when I was there looking for that file. He got on the computer and did something, and then after he logged off, he reached down and stuck something on the back of the server. I bet that was a beacon of some sort that caused the explosion when it got far enough away from the bunker. I meant to check and see what it was before we left, but I got caught up in other stuff and forgot," Fred divulged to the group.

Jones walked over to the computer server that was still in the GMV and inspected it. He pulled a small transmitter off the back of it and threw it on the ground, stomping it into pieces. "God damn it! I almost got everyone killed because I wanted to get the server right away instead of waiting like I should have."

"There's no possible way for you to have known about the transmitter," Alex told him.

"That's not true. I listened to the briefing that Fred and Jeff had given us over the phone. Fred mentioned that he thought something had been placed on the back of the server. I fucked up!" Jones stated, pissed at making a mistake that had almost killed his men.

Jeff looked almost constipated. "Shit! They wanted the server to be discovered and inspected but nothing else. That means that the information on the computer could be compromised and worthless." He kicked the ground in disgust.

"Not necessarily Jeff. We know when he was on the computer because Fred saw him. We just need to have a computer expert get into the computer and see what was done during that time. If he erased stuff, it could still be recoverable, and if he added stuff, we know not to trust it," Billy explained to the confused group. Shaking his head, he added, "haven't you guys ever watched 'Forensic Files' on TV?"

"Billy's right, it actually helps us that Fred saw him. If he hadn't, we wouldn't know that the information might have been tampered with. George, do you have a trash bag that I can put this server in? They will have to clean all the dust out of it before they can turn it on, and in case there are some contaminates in the dust, it's probably best to seal it up the best we can."

"I can go grab one for you. I'm sure we have some in the kitchen," George replied as he headed off to the house.

"As soon as we wash out the vehicles, we need to get loaded up and head back to the airport. I want to get this server to Sparky as soon as possible, he should be able to handle it without any issues. We'll call the sergeant major as soon as we get in the air and give him a status update." Jones turned toward the two scientists. "You guys coming with us?"

Jeff nodded. "We talked about it and both agree that it's a good idea. We should be able to understand anything that my father put on the computer in regards to viruses and gene splicing. Plus, Fred really wants to see Latisha," he teased his friend.

Fred turned red but didn't disagree with Jeff's rather astute assessment.

The Rangers quickly washed the GMVs and then broke camp. Thanking everyone for their help and hospitality, Jones promised to update them when he had news, making sure he got their phone numbers.

Within the hour, they were on the road and headed back to Pueblo, where their plane, pilot, and small security detail, awaited them. The server was securely strapped in the GMV, they couldn't afford to lose that or the mission would become a total write-off.

They met a little resistance near Walsenburg. Four pickups and half a dozen men started to shoot at them when the Rangers ignored the poor attempt at a roadblock. The marauders were quickly reminded not to bring a rifle to a Gatling gunfight. The Rangers were careful not to kill anybody, but the .50 BMG rounds quickly took care of the marauder's trucks.

A few more vehicles were on the roads than they had seen the day before. Probably people who were running out of food, looking for something to eat.

It took almost 2 hours to get to Pueblo instead of the hour and a half that it should have, but Jones had wanted to be extra careful. No chances were being taken with the irreplaceable server on board.

Shortly after arriving at the airport, they had the vehicles loaded and the server secured on the plane. They immediately taxied out on the tarmac and took off, leaving Pueblo and Colorado behind them.

Using an encrypted satellite phone, Jones called Sgt. Maj. Books and gave him a rundown of what had happened, informing him of the doctor's death and the subsequent bunker explosion, taking full responsibility for not checking the server for a transmitter before leaving the lab. The sergeant major quickly brushed that off and told him not to bring it up again.

SGM Brooks assured him that he would have Sparky standing by when the plane landed. Hopefully, they would have some answers tomorrow.

Agent Warren

He had been smart enough to hack into the bunker's security cameras as it had given him a front-row seat for the raid that the military had done on the bunker. He was pleased when he saw that one of them had taken a picture of Dr. Carter's body before removing the computer server. This would be proof enough that the doctor was, in fact, dead since there would be no physical remains due to the explosion.

Agent Warren was equally, if not more thrilled, that they had taken the server and immediately left the bunker, triggering the explosion. He had tried to cover all his tracks at the bunker but knew that his fingerprints would eventually be found there if given enough time. With the bunker now in a gazillion pieces, that small worry had been eliminated.

The one thing he had been debating was if he should do anything about the two scientists that he spotted leaving the bunker prior to the explosion. On the one hand, they had been in the bunker and might have potentially seen him there, and since nobody had seen him leave, it would be assumed that he had perished along with everyone else. On the other hand, they most likely didn't know anything, and if he killed them now, it would possibly give the military a reason to keep looking into The Elite Group, and the cover-up would have been for naught. He finally decided to leave them alone for now, should they become an issue in the future, he would deal with them then.

Glancing at the clock, he saw that it was almost time to

check in with his father to inform him of the success of using Dr. Carter as the fall guy for the cover-up. His father could then pass the information along to the other members of The Core. The agent also wanted to discover if there were any more loose ends that he needed to tie up that he wasn't currently aware of. He couldn't think of any, but that was because he left very little to chance and always cleaned up any possible loose ends as he went along.

DAY SIXTEEN

Sparky

It had taken a little over two hours to take the server apart, clean all the dust out of it and then reassemble it. He had done that last night as soon as Staff Sgt. Jones had given the computer server to him. He had explained what they needed to know and how vital the information on the hard drive was.

Sparky had started the actual investigation into the contents of the hard drive this morning at 0430. First, he made a mirror image of the hard drive and that was the one he used. The original was left intact and untouched. He felt like he had barely started working on it when he discovered the files that had been downloaded on the computer, early in the morning hours, four days prior. Sparky could find nothing that had been deleted during the suspect time frame.

He spent the next six hours checking every file for anything to do with viruses, vaccines, The Elite Group, The Core, Sarin Gas, and many other keywords. He felt he had enough to give the sergeant major sufficient information that a decision could be made on how to proceed. So he went in search of the sergeant major and found him and Staff Sgt. Jones in the cafeteria.

"Just the two men I need to talk to," Sparky said as he invited himself to sit at their table.

"We were just wondering if you found anything out,"

Jones told him.

"Sergeant major, sergeant," he said, nodding at the two men, "there were some files that had been downloaded during the time frame I was given. I am assuming that information was probably planted and can't be relied upon; however, I think you might want to know what it is anyway. The short version is that the files show Dr. Carter as the sole conspirator. Funneling his research money from Crouch Pharmaceutical into making weaponized viruses that he then had released in several countries. He basically names himself as the one and only member of The Core and called all the people that died in the bunker with him, The Elite Group. The way it was all put together was a pretty decent attempt at a cover-up and it might have succeeded had it not been for Fred seeing the unknown male as he was downloading the file. The file timestamps had been digitally altered by a hidden computer virus that he downloaded at the same time as he did the file. It was quite brilliant actually, and had I not been looking specifically for what occurred during the suspect time frame, I would have easily missed it, and these files would have appeared to be several years old."

He paused to see if there were any questions thus far. Hearing none, he continued his brief. "Now the non-suspect files. These go way back. I'm talking well over two decades' worth of research. The doctor did create a rabies virus that specifically targeted his ex-wife's DNA. He injected it into his 12-year-old son, Jeff, not knowing for sure that he wouldn't become infected since he has his mother's mitochondrial DNA. Obviously, he didn't get infected since he's still alive, but he did become a carrier. Passing the virus on to his mother, causing her death."

"If Dr. Carter wasn't already dead, I think I'd kill him myself," Sgt. Maj. Brooks admitted as he grew angrier over the many heinous acts the doctor committed throughout his life.

"Well, he didn't stop there. The DNA-specific viruses that he called, One-Offs, in the last decade, he's made a lot of them. There is a list of 143 names, tagged with different types of viruses or virus combinations in the earlier files and that doesn't include the more recent file containing another 126 names, including the President, Chief of Staff, and a decent number of pentagon officials. It's fair to say that he murdered all of them by using these One-Offs. We now have proof that he was the creator of the Frankenstein Virus, which he called the World-Ender. A bit of good news there, once you have been infected with the Frankenstein Virus, you can't get reinfected, it has built-in autoimmunity. We also have proof of the Steri-12 fake vaccine that he designed to not only cause permanent sterilization in both men and women, but for it to pass on to any sexual partners they may have for at least the next five years and possibly longer," he explained to the two stunned men. Sparky had already become numb to the atrocities Dr. Carter had committed in the name of science.

"Damn! That means anyone who got the shot, thinking it was a vaccine, will need to be aware that they will cause permanent sterilization in any future sexual partner, and then that partner will be a carrier and so on. Potentially, this could eventually end the human race if someone doesn't figure out a way to cure it or create a vaccine for it." Jones found it hard to believe that someone could be that callous about human life.

"That's it exactly. Now we move on to what he called the Booster shot, this is basically a shot of liquid death. Take it and you'll be dead within 72 hours. I saw the reports on all the test subjects that Fred talked about. 90 were infected with the Frankenstein Virus and another 74 with the Steri-12 and then the Booster. The reports show that all of them died, but we know that there was one survivor that Fred and Latisha managed to save. Hopefully, he will be the key to saving the human race."

Brooks nodded his head. "That's the hope. The CDC was running tests until their facility became overrun. He has agreed to help them come up with a cure if they can. Mr. Sanchez is our best and possibly last hope for the future of mankind."

Sparky hoped for the sake of the human race that this would be the case. Otherwise, within the next 100 years or so, mankind would become extinct.

Jones popped off, "We need to make sure we do our best not to scare Berto off. I don't know about you, but having the fate of mankind placed on your shoulders would be a terribly heavy burden, psychologically speaking."

Sparky nodded his head, but he hadn't finished yet. "There are a few other viruses that he was working on, but as far as I can tell, he never completed them. One of them was to be released via cigarette, and if that doesn't make you stop smoking, then you probably deserve to die just for being a dumb-ass. I believe that Jeff was working on the delivery mechanism of this particular monster if you're interested in the details."

He handed a thumb drive to Brooks. "This contains all the locations throughout the world where Steri-12 and the Booster shot were made and stored, along with every location that they were to be delivered to. Hopefully, we can get this out to the appropriate people and get them all destroyed."

Brooks took the thumb drive, feeling the weight of the world it held within. "The only issue is keeping some of these countries from keeping a stockpile of them to use on someone else in the future. Hopefully, they will become ineffective at some point and turn out to be useless. Oh well, that's a headache for another day and above my pay grade."

"I really hate this doctor. So far, I can account for 432 deaths that he was directly responsible for, just with his human testing and the One-Offs he created. That doesn't even touch the billions he murdered with the Frankenstein Virus. Hitler and Stalin were like Mother Theresa compared to him." Sparky shook his head to clear his mind, knowing that he was getting angry. "There is a lot of information about how he created all his viruses on the hard drive that might be useful to the CDC. I'd recommend getting them a copy. I imagine that there is a lot of information that I missed on the hard drive, this was just what I found in a few hours. Other than that, I don't have anything else for you."

Sparky wished someone else had drawn the short straw and had to search the hard drive. He doubted he would ever have a decent night's sleep ever again, knowing the depravity of some people's minds.

"Thanks Sparky. I'm glad there's nothing else. I think what you've told us already will give me nightmares for years to come and I'll be damned if I ever get another vaccination," Jones said, only half-joking.

"I appreciate it too, Sparky. You outdid yourself on getting this information compiled so quickly. I'll get this thumb drive to the colonel and brief him on everything that you discovered. I'm warning you now, he'll want a written report before morning."

"Understood, sergeant major. I'll get to work on that after I get some chow and take a nap."

Brooks stood up. "I'll also let the CDC people know what you found and that we will give them full access to the information. Maybe it will bring a ray of sunshine into this craptastic clusterfuck of a situation. Oh, I almost forgot to ask, did you find anything on The Core or The Elite Group?"

Sparky shook his head. "Nope. I specifically searched for them and found nothing, not even a hint that they exist, except for in the planted file, and we all know that was just a bunch of bull shit they used to fertilize the cover-up."

"Well damn! I guess that's also a problem for another day," he said, shaking his head as he walked away.

Sergeant Major Brooks

He spent the next two hours with Col. Baker, going over the information and trying to come up with a strategy to destroy all of the Steri-12 and Booster shots. Once that was done, the colonel sent the recommendation to all the military bases and up the chain of command. Now they would have to wait and see what the powers to be, decided to do. He figured it was probably 50/50 on if they would destroy it all or save it for a rainy day.

Having left the colonel, he was now on his way to see Dr. Matt Thatcher, the virologist that the Rangers had rescued from the CDC a few days before. He remained hesitantly optimistic that the scientist would be able to come up with something that would save the world, even with all the information that they had gleaned from Dr. Carter's computer hard drive.

He wasn't surprised to find the scientist in the makeshift lab, reviewing reports on his computer. Rapping his knuckles on the door frame before walking in uninvited. "Mind if I bother you for a few minutes?"

"Oh, hi sergeant major, or did you get another promotion that I'm not aware of?" Matt joked.

Brooks laughed lightly. "Not that I've been told, but at this rate, I'll be Commander in Chief by the end of the week," he teased back.

"What can I do for you? It's a little late for a social visit," he noted, leaning back in his chair while chewing on the end of a pen.

"We were able to get into Dr. Carter's hard drive and retrieved quite a bit of information on the viruses he created. Sparky is going to download everything onto an external hard drive for you. Hopefully, this will help you figure out how to either reverse or stop everything. You should have it sometime tomorrow," Brooks told him.

Matt sighed. "I appreciate it but honestly, until I get back to my lab at the CDC, I'm not sure how much I can really do with it. The sterilization is permanent and irreversible, all we can do is try to stop the Steri-12 injections."

Brooks shook his head, hating to break the bad news to the scientist, "We have a bit more to worry about than that. According to Dr. Carter's testing on the Steri-12, if you get the injection and become sterile, you then become a carrier and can infect others that you have sexual intercourse with."

"Oh shit. That could end us all, surely he had taken that into account and had some kind of vaccine for it so that he couldn't get infected himself," then realizing who he was referring to, quickly amended that statement, "but then again, why would he care. He wasn't going to have any more children, and he obviously could have cared less about the future of mankind."

"Sparky didn't read every file so there may be something in his files that will shed light on a possible vaccine. You'll need to go through them all, I guess, but one thing you might consider is bringing Fred, Jeff, and Latisha on board to help you. They have some insider knowledge and would most likely be willing to help," suggested Brooks, thinking that the kids would jump at the chance to try and right some of the wrongs they unwillingly helped create.

Matt smiled at the idea. "That's not a bad idea, They can help me go through the data off the hard drive, and maybe together we can develop something to help fix some of this. I just won't know until we get into it."

"I won't keep you any longer, I just wanted to touch bases and let you know where things are currently standing."

"Thank you sergeant major. I appreciate being kept in the loop and I'll do my best to do my part," Matt replied as he shook Brooks' hand. "There is one thing you might want to know about the Frankenstein Virus or perhaps not, now that I think about it. Either way, I found something strange in the makeup of the virus itself. I am not sure what it means exactly as I need to do more research in a proper lab, but I believe that there is another trigger switch within the DNA of the Frankenstein Virus that has yet to be activated. This might be a two-for-one and we are still waiting for the other shoe to drop or it may have just been a mistake within the virus and nothing will ever come of it."

Brooks felt the blood drain from his face. "Damn! That's just fucking wonderful! It just keeps getting better and better, doesn't it?" he said, his shoulders slumping as he began to feel defeated. "Well, keep me posted."

"Will do. It makes me wonder just how many layers there are to this conspiracy onion and how many we have yet to discover," Matt confided to him.

The sergeant major shook his head as he left the room. Not sure how to respond to Matt's theory, but knowing that it didn't end with the death of Dr. Carter.

DAY SEVENTEEN

Fred

He'd finally gotten to see Latisha yesterday. She remained in quarantine but would be released in the next day or so since all her symptoms had gone away. Fred had wanted to hug her but settled for placing his hand over hers with a pane of glass separating them. He had been stoked to see her and it had lifted his spirits to see her so healthy, considering everything she had gone through. She wouldn't be back to full strength for a couple of months while her body slowly recuperated. Latisha had told him the good news that her Uncle Eddie was also going to survive, as well as everyone on her mother's side of her family.

Fred was in a good mood as he made his way to get Jeff. They had been called to a meeting with Dr. Thatcher from the CDC to see if they might be able to help him with researching ways to fight all the damage that Dr. Carter had done.

"Hey Jeff," he said, seeing his friend leaning up against the wall, waiting for him.

"Hey yourself," he replied as he peeled himself off the wall and started walking alongside Fred. "So what do you think about everything that has happened over the last couple of days?"

Fred pondered the question for a few moments before responding, "I feel lucky," he admitted. "If I hadn't walked into the lab and encountered you playing around on the doc's computer, my honest assessment is that we would both be dead right now."

Jeff nodded in agreement. "True, but I still wish that the Rangers had gotten him out alive. He was still my father no matter how much I may have hated him. I was hoping for justice, and it feels like that was stolen from me, and he got off too easy."

Fred clapped his friend on the back, offering his support. "I can understand that. I feel the same way but to a lesser extent. Mostly I'm just happy that he's finally gone and that this nightmare is almost over."

Jeff grabbed his friend's arm and pulled him to a stop. "Is it? Over, I mean. Think about it. The man in the suit wrapped everything in a nice neat package. My father, who I freely admit was a terrible human being, is being made out to be the fall guy for the entire conspiracy. So The Core and The Elite Group get off scot-free and fade off into the background, free to kill another day. No evidence was found that proved that they even existed even though we know they do because they recruited us, but we can't prove it. So what will they do five or ten years from now? Are we still in danger because we escaped the bunker? Are they hunting us down as we speak? I'm not so convinced that it's over, at least for us," Jeff finished as he released his friend's arm and stared off into the distance.

"Wow, I hadn't even thought about any of that. Do you really think they will come after us?" Fred asked, clearly worried about the possibility.

Jeff shrugged his shoulders as he began walking again. "Honestly, I have no idea but if you were them, would you allow us to live knowing what we do?"

Fred shuffled his feet, now deep in thought. "We need to figure out a way to expose The Elite Group."

"We will," Jeff assured him, "just not today. Let's hurry, I don't want to be late."

They arrived at the meeting with a few minutes to spare, surprised to find that most of the people they knew on the base were already there, waiting on them.

"There they are. Come on in boys," Staff Sgt. Jones hollered at them from across the room. He was standing next to the sergeant major and the colonel.

In addition to the military men and Dr. Thatcher, Fred saw that both Randy and Lisa were also here. So much for this just being a meeting concerning them helping out Dr. Thatcher.

"I wasn't expecting this many people," Fred admitted to no one in particular.

"Sorry, that's sort of my fault," Randy told him. "I asked if we could all be kept in the loop, and I guess they took it to heart."

"If everyone can find a seat, we can begin," the colonel said, motioning to the seats around the table. Once everyone was situated, he began. "First, I wanted to thank all of you for your part in helping us combat this unprecedented disaster that we have been facing. As you all know, Dr. Carter was found deceased inside the bunker. His computer server was retrieved just prior to the bunker imploding, destroying everything contained within it."

The colonel turned toward Jeff. "I know he wasn't a very good father to you, but I am sorry for your loss on a personal level. I just wanted you to know that."

"Thank you sir," he replied, overcome with a wide range of emotions. Jeff was holding back tears that he was surprised to have. Never in a million years would he have thought it would be possible to shed tears over his father's death.

"There is still a lot of work ahead of us. We know where all the Steri-12 and Booster shots are supposed to be. Right now, all across the world, they are being tracked down and destroyed. Here in the United States, this is being handled by the military, including the National Guard."

The colonel took a drink. "Unfortunately, approximately 10% of the world's remaining population received the Steri-12 injection, causing them to become sterile. What wasn't known until we retrieved the doctor's hard drive was that these people are now carriers of the sterilization virus. That means that anyone they exchange bodily fluids with could potentially become both sterile and become a carrier themselves. We assume this was planned intentionally by the doctor as a final farewell 'Fuck You' to the world. Personally, my feeling is that he made these terrible viruses just because he had low self-esteem, it made him feel important and better than everyone else, basically it fed his ego."

Both Jeff and Fred were unconsciously nodding their heads in silent agreement with the colonel's assessment.

"I promised Sergeant Major Brooks I would be honest and tell you everything I knew, even if I didn't think I should. With that in mind, I need each of you to promise not to speak to anyone else about what I am about to tell you. Can you all do that for me?" he asked the group, surveying their faces for any hint that they wouldn't follow through with the agreement.

A lot of "No problem" and "yes sir" responses sounded around the room.

"Alright. Dr. Thatcher made a discovery in regards to the Frankenstein Virus. Apparently, there is an anomaly contained within the DNA of the virus, that might be another trigger for a secondary infection. As I understand it, the Frankenstein Virus is like two viruses in one, a buy one and get one free, so to speak. We can't be certain who will become infected, what the infection may be, or what can trigger it to happen, at least not without further study being done in a well-equipped laboratory. With that in mind, Matt's team will be solely responsible for working on all of Dr. Carter's viruses with the government's full backing. That team will include Jeff, Fred, and Latisha, once she is out of quarantine, of course," he said, cracking his first smile of the day.

"In addition, his team will also be working with Berto Sanchez and his family, who we will be flying in from South America, to try and find out why his family appears to remain immune to most viruses. The hope is that they will come up with a generalized vaccine, capable of preventing people from ever becoming infected in the first place," he announced, allowing hope to show through his stern-looking facade.

Everyone applauded, happy to hear some good news for a change.

"One last thing. The military, after securing and destroying the fake vaccines, will be taking control of the country back from the gangs, rioters, and looters. The plan is for it to be safe for everyone to return home within a few weeks. Now any questions?"

Lisa raised her hand. "Do we have causality numbers yet?"

"The latest estimates are that the world's population has been decreased by 62% or just under 6 billion people dead, nearly two-thirds of the population. Of the remaining 3.5 billion or so, 350 million of those are sterile. This does not take into account all those killed during the riots, who died from starvation, lack of proper medical care, suicide, or those who become ill and died from other diseases caused by being exposed to so many decomposing bodies. That could easily add another several million to the death toll."

The room was dead quiet while everyone took the opportunity to absorb all the information.

Fred raised his hand. "Sir, Jeff and I have been talking and were wondering about The Elite Group and The Core. Is anyone going after them?"

"Well gentlemen, that one is a bit harder to answer. While I believe everything you said about them, the problem is the lack of proof that they even exist, let alone being the ones who were pulling the doctor's strings. We are actively looking for anything that might point us in a direction to find them, but honestly, unless someone high up in the organization defects and turns against them, there is very little that we can do. They insulated themselves extremely well and were able to make it appear, rather convincingly I might add, as if Dr. Carter was the one behind all of this. I should warn you, the official story will be that Dr. Carter was the mastermind behind the entire plan. This is to help quell any anger and distrust that our citizens may harbor towards the government and the CDC. We have to stop the rioting, and by offering up Dr. Carter and using the planted file we found in his computer as proof, we can save lives and stop further rioting. I wish I had better news for you because I would personally like to put them all in the grave myself for what they have done to humankind, I can only imagine how you feel," the colonel told them sincerely, the pain he felt, showing in his eyes.

"One of our personal concerns is that if they discover that we escaped the bunker, that they will come after us?" Fred admitted to the group, who he now considered as his friends.

"That's a possibility, but highly doubtful. Think about it from their point of view, you really don't know anything or have any proof of what you know or suspect. Is it worth the chance of bringing unwanted attention to themselves, just to remove a couple of small fish from the ocean? I can't see it being worth the risk," the colonel pointed out to them.

Breathing a sigh of relief, "Thanks. That does make sense and I do feel better."

"So you don't think I'm in danger anymore, either?" Randy asked.

"As long as you don't actively pursue looking into them, you should be safe. I'm sure that they will watch you for a while to make sure that you have dropped the investigation. The government; however, will not drop the investigation, so don't think that we're trying to brush them under the rug. Trust me that I want this scourge of society to be held accountable for what they have done."

"Alright, I'll drop it for now," he agreed, albeit with some reservations.

"If there's nothing else, then this meeting is adjourned."

289

Lisa

After the meeting, Randy asked her if she would join him for a walk around the base, to which she happily agreed.

"So what do you think?" he asked, offering his arm, which she happily accepted.

"It's a lot to take in," she admitted. "Once the CDC is secured, and we're back to some semblance of normal, Matt will be able to work on what he needs to, with the right equipment and with the trio joining his team, I really think we have a chance."

He grinned at her, causing her heart to do a slight flutter. "While I found that fascinating, I was thinking more along the lines of us being together again."

Lisa laughed as a small thrill coursed through her body. "Oh, I thought we'd already decided to give it a go."

"We did. I just wanted to give you an out in case you had changed your mind," he confessed, "but you're right, I agree that Matt and his team of nerds will probably be our best bet to save what remains of mankind."

She stopped suddenly, quickly turning to face him. "You're dropping the investigation into The Core?" she asked, but it sounded more like a demand.

Randy nodded his head, he couldn't afford to bring any attention to himself that might get Lisa hurt. "Yes. As long as they don't do anything to bring themselves to my attention, I'll let the Alphabets in D.C. handle it."

"The alphabets?" she questioned.

"You know, CIA, FBI, NSA, etc."

Her laughed traveled off into the night. "It sure does feel good to feel joy and laugh again," she said to no one in particular.

Randy found that he couldn't disagree with that assessment.

Alex

He had utilized the morning for planning, and the afternoon was spent executing said plan. Alex had roped Billy and Agnes into helping him. The plan was to surprise BB by taking her on a date. The one they were supposed to go on, before being so rudely interrupted by a riot, had never occurred and he wanted to make it up to her.

BB was put on overwatch, Billy told her he needed a break from it for a while. This allowed Agnes to cook up some fried chicken, roasted corn on the cob, potato salad, and fresh bread, along with some strawberry cheesecake drizzled with chocolate.

It was all set up in the back yard where it was out of the view of BB. They strung up Christmas tree lights and set up a small dining table on top of the rug out of the living room using an old card table covered with a nice table cloth and a couple of kitchen chairs. George had agreed to do overwatch during the date, allowing Billy to act as the waiter.

Emma and Jennifer had wanted to help with the secret date so they had spent some time making up a playlist on George's laptop.

When the sun started to go down, George made his way to the loft and sent BB off to the house. Agnes met her at the door and directed her to go take a shower and dress in the outfit laid out on the bed. Looking confused, BB did as asked and then allowed the two girls to help her with her hair. No matter how many times she asked, no one would tell her why she was getting pampered.

She heard a knock on the bedroom door.

"Come in," she called out.

"No BB. You have to go open it," Jennifer said with her little hands on her hips and a stern look on her face.

"Well, okay then." Properly chastised, she walked over to the door.

As she opened the door, she saw Alex standing there, dressed in blue jeans, a black t-shirt, and a sports jacket that George must have bought some 20 years prior. His jet black hair had been trimmed, and he had shaved, leaving his mustache and goatee just the way she liked. Bright blue eyes twinkled as he smiled at her, holding out a handful of flowers that had obviously come from Agnes's flower bed.

She took his breath away, dressed in blue jeans and a plain, white, sleeveless blouse. A simple necklace completed her ensemble.

"Good evening Miss Barnes. I am here to pick you up for our date. You look amazing if you don't mind me saying," he told her, happy to notice that she was pleasantly surprised to see him, based on the huge smile currently plastered across her face.

"I don't mind at all, Mr. Carradine. I must say you look quite handsome yourself," she complimented him as she accepted the flowers.

Jennifer quickly procured a vase that had been stashed under the bed for just this reason. BB placed the flowers in the vase before Jennifer took them away to add some water.

"Thank you. Are you ready to go?" he inquired.

"Absolutely." Alex led her out to his truck and opened the passenger door, he helped her climb inside before carefully closing it behind her. He knew that she was trying to figure out where he was taking her, but he had no plans on spoiling the surprise.

Getting in on the driver's side, he started up his truck and drove forward two feet before stopping and getting back out.

BB was shaking her head as her eyebrows scrunched up in confusion when he opened her door and helped her get back out.

Without saying a word, he led her back into the house where Billy was waiting for them, wearing a black jacket and a white towel over his injured arm.

"Good evening," he greeted them. "Do you have reservations?"

"Yes, under the name Carradine," Alex replied seriously.

"Ah yes, here we are. Carradine, party of two. We have a very special table for you. Follow me please." He turned and headed further into the house, towards the kitchen, and then out the back door. Alex could tell that BB was surprised at what they had done as she clasped her hands together, bringing them up to her face.

The sun was just beginning to set in the background, casting a slight orange glow to everything it touched, Christmas lights were lit overhead and all around the back yard, the table was set with the finest fake china. The vase containing her flowers had been strategically placed in the middle of the table, along with a small candle that was gently flickering in the slight breeze. The music that the girls had picked out, was playing softly in the background, from the laptop on the back porch.

"Alex, this is absolutely perfect. How did you get this all set up without me finding out," she said quietly, in awe of what he had managed to accomplish without her knowledge.

"I have my ways," he replied mysteriously as he pulled the chair out for her.

"Thank you," she told him as she sat down.

Once he confirmed that she was comfortably seated, he made his way to his own chair.

Billy cleared his throat. "For our specials this evening, we have your choice of fried chicken, roasted corn on the cob, potato salad, and fresh-baked bread or, if you prefer, we also have fried chicken, roasted corn on the cob, potato salad, and fresh-baked bread," he stated, attempting to sound like a waiter.

"Oh, I think the fried chicken sounds wonderful. I'll have that," BB said, laughing, clearly enjoying herself and putting a smile on Alex's face.

"An excellent choice. And to drink, we have a fine selection of water, soda, or beer, if you have your ID," Billy told her seriously.

"Darn it. I forgot my purse. Water please," she said in mock dismay.

"Bottled or tap?" came the quick response.
"Bottled, please," she responded, thinking that Billy made an excellent waiter.

"And for you, sir?" Billy asked, turning to his friend.

"I'll have whatever she's having," Alex confirmed, unable to take his eyes off BB.

"I'm sorry, we seem to have just run out," Billy teased him. "Oh wait, I was just informed that we do still have that available. Sorry for the misunderstanding," he said, bowing as he slowly backed away from the table, making the couple laugh.

Billy quickly returned with their water and a small garden salad. "Umm, sorry I forgot to tell you about the salad so just go with it. It's my first time being a waiter, and I don't want to get fired," he told them, glancing over his shoulder as if worried.

The meal was pleasant and relaxing. Billy cracked jokes almost every time he came to the table, but BB and Alex only had eyes for each other, barely even paying him any attention. After they had finished the dessert, Alex asked her to dance. So they did.

"I'm sorry. I promised you dinner and a movie, but the VCR is apparently broken and they haven't moved into the 21st century yet. Instead, we'll be watching mother nature's lights and do some star gazing from the haystack," he explained as he walked her to the pile of hay that he had strategically placed there the day before, just to the side of the barn and out of the view of the overwatch.

"That sounds perfect. I still can't believe you managed to pull this off. It's the best first date ever," she remarked as she settled into his arms. BB was content, lying in the hay and staring into the night sky while Alex pointed out the various constellations that he knew, the rest of the world forgotten in that moment.

As a falling star streaked across the sky, they each made a wish. Interesting enough, it was the same wish.

THE AFTERMATH

Two Years Later

Alex

Nearly two weeks after arriving at the farm, Alex and Billy took George to find the girl's parents. After several hours of driving around, they finally located their remains. They carefully bundled them up and returned to the farm, where they were buried under the shade of an old oak tree.

Billy, BB, and Alex stayed at the farm for another two months before deciding to head back to Dallas and reassess their lives. Deciding that they had given the military plenty of time to contain the rioting and bring civility back to their city.

Before leaving, George and Agnes offered to give them each a few acres of land close by if they decided they would like to stay. They had politely refused but were told that the offer would remain open should they get back to Dallas and find it to be a place they no longer wished to live.

As they drove on the interstate through the city, they were stunned at the destruction left behind. It looked like a war zone, wrecked and abandoned vehicles lined the streets, untold city blocks had been completely destroyed by fire, and it seemed as if everything had been tagged by gangs. Alex had never seen so much spray-painted graffiti in his life. Most of the windows that had been broken during the riots, were now boarded up in an effort to keep the weather out and would eventually get replaced. The city looked desolate, and alone, it felt like it had lost its heart and soul, and perhaps it had.

Alex made quick time in getting back to their apartment complex, only to discover that their apartments had been looted of anything of value before being set on fire. There was nothing left to salvage.

BB checked at the hospital to find that it was boarded up. Most likely it would stay permanently closed due to the shortage of doctors. Her little Honda that she had for years, had been destroyed by the rampaging mobs. The only good news was that she found that due to the lack of qualified medical personnel, she was going to be allowed to graduate and become a full-fledged doctor without completing the last few months of her residency. She would only need to pass her medical boards to become a licensed doctor.

Finding nothing left to keep the trio in Dallas, they returned to the farm back in Colorado with a heavy heart and were welcomed with opened arms.

Once BB became a licensed doctor, she opened a practice in the nearby town of Trinidad and quickly became well-liked and respected by the residents of the town.

Alex took odd jobs helping out the neighboring farms as the need arose. He enjoyed working outside and preferred not to be tied down working a 9-5 job, plus he still had his inheritance to fall back on should the need arise.

Billy was an excellent mechanic and had soon opened up his own shop in Trinidad. He found out that all the mechanics in the area had died, either from the virus or marauders. The town welcomed him with open arms, happy to have a qualified mechanic again. The second day his shop was open, he met a local teacher whose fuel filter had gotten clogged. They had their first date the next day and quickly became inseparable.

Upon hearing what the trio had done when saving the girls, all of George's neighbors had gotten together and did an old-fashioned barn raising. Instead of raising a barn, they built a couple of small houses on the property that George had deeded over to the three heroes. This was in appreciation for what they had done for the girls, and George had threatened to have Agnes bend them over her knee if they didn't accept. They had no choice but to graciously accept the offer, Agnes wasn't one who they wished to trifle with. The boys lived in one of the houses while BB stayed in the other, at least until Alex and BB were married, at which time, Alex switched houses.

On weekends, Alex and Billy taught the girls proper gun safety and how to shoot. Emma was given a .22 rifle on her 13th birthday, which she carried everywhere she went on the farm. She would never be a victim again.

The trio couldn't remember being happier and found that they really didn't miss the hustle and bustle of the city.

They realized that they were home.

Erik

Atlanta was slowly coming back to life as were most large cities whose population had been decimated by the virus and the riots. After the military had regained control, the police returned to work, as did the firemen, and other essential workers, albeit shorthanded. Power was restored throughout the city within a few weeks, along with basic services like water, gas, cable, and internet. Marshal Law remained in effect for almost a year before finally being lifted.

With the only goal of saving the life of his homeless friend, Eddie, he had somehow managed to survive the madness.

No charges were ever filed against him for the murder of the men that occurred at his house. The government gave everyone a pass for anything they had done while protecting their lives or property. They were still going after those who had intentionally gone out and murdered, raped, stolen, or destroyed during the riots, but there had been few arrests.

The insurance company paid his claim for the fire at

the dry cleaners since they couldn't prove what had actually caused the devastating fire. Erik decided to use the money to repair his house and purchase the one next door, which he let Eddie live in, rent-free. The man had saved his life after all, and it was a small thing that he could afford to do for his friend.

At first, he wasn't sure what he wanted to do now that he no longer had the business to tend to. In reality, he had never needed to keep it open in the first place but did so to honor his parent's memory. When his parents had died in a car wreck many years before, he had inherited the dry cleaners, the house, cars, along with everything they had owned. In addition, he was the beneficiary on both of their life insurance policies totaling more than a million dollars.

He eventually decided to purchase the entire block where the dry cleaners had once stood and open up a homeless shelter and community center on the property. The sole goal would be to help those less fortunate get back on their feet. Drugs and alcohol would not be allowed, but job training, GED classes, and other self-help classes would be. Physical fitness would also be worked in, and he had plans for a basketball court and a gym that clients could work out in for free. They would be given clothes, food, shelter, and education as long as they were willing to try to better themselves. Eddie had agreed to help him and was as excited at the endeavor as Erik was.

This would be Erik's small way of giving back to the city that he still loved.

Randy

Knowing the truth, but having to lie and go along with the government's official version was extremely hard for him. It was what he had to do to keep Lisa safe, so he did it, hoping that one day, he could tell the world the truth behind Dr. Carter and The Elite Group.

So many people had needlessly died for nothing. It was all blamed on Dr. Carter, and rightfully so, up to a point. While he had been the creator of the deadly virus and subsequent sterilization treatment, he had not been the one calling the shots, nor was he financing it.

The government had posthumously tried and convicted Dr. Jeremy Carter of a variety of crimes. Including crimes against humanity, global terrorism, the murder of over 6 billion humans, illegal sterilization of over 350 million people, kidnapping, and many other heinous crimes. They had released the file that was found on his computer, after his death, as proof that he and the group of people that died in the bunker alongside him were solely responsible for the pandemic that nearly destroyed mankind.

This had essentially let The Core off the hook for their involvement in the crimes. As much as Randy wanted to chase that story, he wanted to leave it alone equally as much. It was a rabbit hole that he would never escape, and it could cost him, not only his life but Lisa's as well. The risk just wasn't worth it to him.

They were both in a good place now, both back to work and dating exclusively again. That was the one good thing that the virus had done. Lisa was back in his arms where she belonged, and he was loving it.

Jeff

He was as happy as he felt he could be, considering who he was. Luckily, very few knew who his father had been, and those that knew the truth weren't telling anyone so that secret was safe.

It had been frustrating work and taken quite a while, but they had finally located the exact gene sequence from Berto's blood that caused his immunity. The team had spent most of the following days segmenting it and inserting it into a group of benign cells that would attach themselves to the host DNA, thereby infecting the host with the cure.

Over the next couple of months, they had tested it in the

laboratory in Petri dishes, and the vaccine had prevented every infection from taking hold, effectively stopping it in its tracks.

The vaccine had quickly moved into the testing phase, and only volunteers were being accepted into the trials, Jeff had been the first one to sign up. It had worked perfectly, just as expected. After the six-month trials were over, production was allowed to being and FDA certification was received.

The biggest hurdle that they faced, was getting the public to trust a vaccine. After the news had broken about the nefarious nature of the Steri-12 vaccine, humanity's faith in allowing others to inject substances into their body had collapsed. Very few people had been willing to take the vaccine that would provide them with a cure to most human illnesses. It sounded too good to be true so it couldn't be real. Right?

Back to the drawing board they went, looking to determine if they could make it transmittable by air. Surprisingly, Dr. Carter had unintentionally provided the answer in his notes on how he designed the Frankenstein Virus. Within weeks they had an aerosol version of the cure that could be quickly spread all over the world. Surprisingly, they ended up using another one of Dr. Carter's ideas. By utilizing the cigarette method that Jeff had perfected, they were able to send cases of sample cigarettes around the world containing the special flavor capsule as a supposed marketing gimmick. For the first time since the invention of cigarettes, smoking was actually good for you. They were able to infect enough of the remaining population that within a year, every man, woman, and child was infected with the now airborne cure. Stopping the secondary release of the Frankenstein Virus and putting an end to the Steri-12 strain that had caused so many to become sterile.

This was why Jeff was so happy, he had helped save the world from his father's evil. Jeff would now be able to finally put his father's ghost to rest, knowing that no more harm could come from his father's past deeds.

The world was officially safe from Dr. Carter.

Akemy

He had become extremely ill and watched many of his friends and family die, including his beloved grandfather, but Akemy had finally recovered. His home of Luanda, Angola was nearly wiped out. The virus killing a much larger percentage of their population than in other parts of the world for some unknown reason.

No one knew where the virus had come from or where it had gone once it fled the village, but Akemy remembered the strange man with the inhaler. He was sure that was where it had come from. Akemy would never speak of it as he felt that he was personally responsible and had caused the virus to be released. He had been the one to press the canister, releasing the monster into his village, no matter how unintentional it had been. Forgiveness was not in his future.

After two years, life had slowly returned to the village and Akemy was now 14. He had taken over many of his grandfather's chores, and fishing became one of his favorite things to do. Mostly because he no longer trusted strangers as he had two years before. The virus had not only stolen his grandfather and a multitude of other family and friends from him, but it had also stolen his innocence and trust.

He kept a very watchful eye on the shoreline as he fished, hoping that one day, the stranger would return to finish what he had started. This time, Akemy would be ready. He had become hardened by death and would avenge his family should he ever get the chance.

Agent Warren

The agent did not have a pleasant time during the first year after the event. All of the government agencies were being thoroughly vetted. The rumor was that there were spies from other countries that had become employed by the government, but he suspected the truth was that they were looking for members of The Elite Group. Every employee was going through a rigorous vetting process before being allowed to return to work.

The problem was that none of The Elite Group had managed to get in a position to sway any of the results, revealing a good number of The Elite Group members, who were then taken into custody and interrogated. Agent Warren decided that he didn't want to take the chance of getting caught and chose to disappear instead. He would reinvent himself and return as someone else. It wouldn't be the first time, Warren wasn't even his real last name.

Maybe it was time for someone new to take the reins, he thought as he left the Washington D.C. area. While in the bunker, he had confiscated a vial of the Booster shot from the laboratory without anyone's knowledge. Thinking at the time that it might come in handy at some point. His father would be an easy, unsuspecting target as he would never believe that his loving and faithful son would ever turn against him. What wasn't understood, was that The Core had turned him into an unfeeling killer who would do whatever he felt was necessary to achieve his goal. Once his father was removed, it would be a simple process to arrange to meet the remaining members of The Core and execute them, one by one.

It was definitely something worth thinking about, he decided. Doing the bidding of others, just wasn't what he wanted to do anymore. He had his own plans for the future...

EPILOGUE

The members of The Core were meeting once again. Nine of the ten had arrived, and it was decided to start the meeting without the tenth, they would catch him up once he arrived.

Dr. Jeremy Carter had not followed the agreed-upon plan and ended up paying the ultimate price for his betrayal. In the process, he had set their plan back a good number of years, possibly decades.

They reviewed what the original plan with the virus had been. The virus was supposed to only have been introduced in one town or village in Africa and allowed to spread slowly, all on its own. The virus Dr. Carter had used was much too aggressive, it should have taken at least an entire year to make its way around the world instead of just two weeks. Dr. Carter had also made it less lethal than was originally intended.

The sterilization drug should not have been introduced for well over a year after the initial release of the virus, with the booster shot following behind a month later. The One-Offs had been part of the original plan but were supposed to have been spread out over a year with the cause of death appearing to be a natural death, like heart attacks, strokes, brain aneurysms, and the like.

The nine men agreed that Jeremy had probably become mentally unstable towards the end, but he did make a good scapegoat as there were no ties that would lead back to them.

Although, they did have to deal with the loss of one of their bunkers and several hundred members of The Elite Group. Looking at the big picture, they determined that those losses were acceptable.

Should anyone bother to investigate, the land that the bunker was on had been legally owned by Dr. Carter, although he hadn't been aware of that fact. They did this with most of their properties, just in case they had to let someone take the fall, just as Jeremy had.

The current estimates of the total reduction of the population, after all the variables were considered and future deaths, whose underlying cause could be attributed to the Frankenstein Virus, would be right around 65%-67%. Far less than the initial goal of 95%, bringing the population back down to 1960s levels. They had bought themselves some time, maybe 75 years worth. The Core knew that they would have to wait a while before trying again, and try again they would, it was just a matter of how and when.

The door opened as the newest member arrived. Unfortunately, one of their long-time members had passed away unexpectedly the week prior and his son was his replacement. Time to bring him into the fold, or so they had thought, as a gas canister was tossed into the room and the door quickly closed behind it. Sarin gas quickly filled the room and took the lives of the nine men.

Their families would soon follow...

SURVIVING THE UNSURVIVABLE: MUTATION

an apocalyptic thriller by Ernie J. Sinclair

Read on for a free preview

Prologue: What's going on with the scans?

Dr. Michael Zimmerman, an astrophysicist with NASA, was pouring through the data from the latest scan of sector 26 when he noted what appeared to be an anomaly. Pulling the data for the same sector from three weeks prior, he checked to determine if the information was the same. Finding it was different, he input the data into the supercomputer and let it crunch the numbers.

While waiting for the computer to process the information, he checked the data for sector 25 from the last two scans. Encountering the same discrepancy as he had in sector 26, he thought there might be an issue with the scanner.

"What's going on with the scanner?" he silently asked

himself, his eyebrows crinkling up in concern.

He decided to check with an associate in Canada to see if they could review their data to either confirm or deny the abnormality.

"Dr. Pearl Krisle," a pleasant voice said over the phone.

"Hi Pearl. It's Michael Zimmerman from the US. How are you today?" he asked, while subconsciously pushing his black plastic-framed glasses back into position with his index finger.

He looked like the epitome of a stereotypical nerd. Short dark hair, parted to one side, large black plastic-framed, coke-bottle thick glasses, and a complete lack of style in how he dressed. Anyone looking at him would naturally assume he was exceedingly intelligent, and they would have been right. Dr. Zimmerman was a member of Mensa and had a tested IQ of 142, which placed him within the genius category, although he never cared about such things.

"Ah Michael, it's good to hear from you. I'm doing wonderful and yourself?" she asked cheerfully.

He was glad she was in the office, since he didn't want to wait any longer than necessary for an answer. "I'm good, but I was hoping you might double-check some information for me. There appears to be an inconsistency in the latest scans we took of sectors 25 and 26. I thought you could verify if the data is accurate or not. It might just be a problem with the scanner," he admitted before taking a few minutes to explain what the data he was receiving was showing.

"That seems rather odd," she admitted. *"I should be able to check it for you, but it will take me a little while so I'll have to call you back."*

"I understand. The sooner I can figure this out, the better," he admitted.

She laughed. *"Isn't that always the way it is?"*

"I guess that's true. Thanks for helping me with this. I'll owe you one," he said, confident she would substantiate the theory that the data was corrupt.

"Not a problem. I'll get back to you in an about an hour," she

promised.

"That sounds good. Thanks for the help," he said, relieved he'd have an answer soon.

After hanging up the phone, he started looking for any current photos of the area in question. Not finding anything recent enough, he sent off an email to all the major astronomical observatories in the United States. In the email, Dr. Zimmerman explained what he was seeing in the information from the scans and asked for some help in locating any photography from the same area taken within the past two to three weeks. All he could do now was wait for someone to get back to him.

The phone rang 20 minutes later. "Zimmerman here," he answered before the first ring completed, in a hurry to settle his mind.

"Hi Michael, it's Pearl. I checked our data and it's showing similar results. Whatever it is, it isn't because of a scanner error. Any idea on what it might be?" she asked, thrilled to be part of a new discovery, if only from the sidelines.

Dr. Zimmerman took a deep breath as he leaned back in his chair. "I do have a theory," he admitted. "I think it's a massive dust cloud, caused by two large asteroids colliding head on into each other as opposed to a glancing blow. That's the only thing that makes sense of the data, but I'm trying to get photographic evidence from an observatory to confirm my theory."

"That would definitely explain the data," Pearl confirmed. *"Let me know what you find out. It could be a significant find,"* she told him excitedly as his computer dinged to let him know he had a new email.

"Hang on a second, I just received an email from a place in California," he said as he quickly opened the attachments and saw what he expected, a very large and dense cloud of space dust.

"Pearl, it's confirmed. I just received the photos of a dust cloud, an extremely large one. I need to track the trajectory to see if it poses a danger to our satellites or if it will safely pass us by."

"That sounds like a good idea. Please keep me informed if you don't mind," she requested, a slight hint of concern creeping into her voice.

"Absolutely. I'll let you know of my findings. Thanks again for the help and I'll talk to you later," he said as he disconnected the line without waiting for a reply.

Six hours later, there was no doubt the Earth would pass right through the middle of the cosmic dust cloud in about three months. It was time to let his boss know so they could inform the government. Hopefully, there would be sufficient time for them to come up with a viable plan to protect the satellites orbiting the planet.

Day 1: The beginning of the end...

Three Months Later

Stan Wright & Ben Williams

"What are you doing after work?" Stan asked, trying to kill some time.

Ben shook his head before replying, "Nothing special. I'll probably mow the damn yard again. I swear it grows a foot a week. Why? Do you have some plans you need to fill me in on?"

Stan laughed. "Nope. I was thinking about watching 'Prepping for the Apocalypse' on TV with Sally."

Ben's eyes widened. "That stupid show? Man, I thought you had some taste. You know those folks are all whacked in the head, right?" he asked, tilting his head to the side, questioningly.

"Hey now. I have great taste otherwise you wouldn't be my friend now would you?" replied Stan, looking a little butt hurt as he took a step back from his friend.

"I'll admit you have a valid point there," he said, smiling.

"I think it's stupid for those people to spend tons of money on something they'll probably never use, but then again, it's their money. Maybe I'm just jealous since I don't have enough money to waste on stupid shit like they do," Ben explained, shrugging his shoulders.

While Stan agreed with what Ben was saying, he still enjoyed watching the show. Mostly so he and his wife, Sally, could make fun of them. Everyone knew it was stupid to prep for an apocalypse because the likelihood it would ever happen was pretty much zero.

He walked back over to his cubical before responding, "It's the only time Sally and I get to spend together since she's working evenings right now. It's nice to sit and do nothing together," he replied, knowing that even if it made little sense, it was the truth.

Stan worked Monday through Friday from nine to five, as a customer service tech for a computer software company in downtown Dallas. He had the privilege of sitting in a tiny cubicle all day, answering emails and talking on the phone. It was extremely boring, but it paid the bills. It was something the blonde-haired, blue-eyed, 36-year-old had never imagined doing, but here he was, behind a desk, letting his waistline slowly expand from sitting all day. Not that he was overweight. He had more of what people referred to as a dad bod. A slight paunch with minor love handles, while still keeping the illusion of working out occasionally.

His wife, Sally, was working at Walmart. A job she disliked immensely, but in this economy, she considered herself lucky to even have a job.

Sally earned a business degree in college and used to manage a local bank, but when the economy tanked, the bank closed several of their brick-and-mortar locations and steered their customers to do more business online. Sally's was the last one they closed and at the ripe old age of 32, the sandy blonde-haired, blue-eyed bank manager found herself unemployed. After six months of chasing leads for a job that would use her business degree, she gave up and took the first job that was offered to her. They had bills to pay, after all.

Stan previously worked as a mechanic until five years ago, when the shop filed for bankruptcy because of the owner taking all the profits to feed his cocaine habit. Luckily, Tech-U-Serve hired him on shortly after.

"It's about time to head home. You're more than welcome to come and hang out at my place tonight as long as you bring the beer," Stan told Ben, grinning.

Ben starting logging off his station before he replied, "Nah, I think I'll go to the bar for a bit and then head home. Make it an early night."

After getting their stations logged off and shut down, they headed to the elevators. They rode the elevator in silence, along with about six other people. Since they worked on the 5th floor, the elevator would normally stop a couple of times on the way down. It must have been their lucky day, as the elevator only made one stop and only two people got on.

The two men headed their separate ways after reaching the lobby. Stan always parked in the attached parking garage next door, and Ben took the metro bus since he'd lost his driver's license when he received his last DUI.

Ben wasn't a heavy drinker, but would occasionally binge during a tough time. The last time he did was when he received the DUI. His girlfriend had left him for some rich, muscle-bound jerk in a Porsche, and he hadn't taken it well. This led him to making a poor decision and driving home after drinking away his sorrows.

Stan had parked his truck on the second level of the garage and he felt like he had run a marathon by the time he reached it, even though he was walking at a normal pace. His head was hurting, his muscles were aching, and he was beginning to sweat.

"Great! Just what I need right now. Why can't I get sick before work and not after?" Stan muttered to himself as he wiped the sweat off his brow before starting his trusty Chevy.

Over the years he'd customized the five-year-old, 4-wheel drive, extended cab pickup. He added running boards, a roll bar, heavy-duty brush guard, blacked-out head and tail lights, new wheels, and larger tires along with an 18-inch lift kit.

As Stan drove the thirty minutes home, he sensed his entire body getting weaker. He wasn't sure if he would make it home safely, but being the stubborn guy he was, he toughed it out and arrived home just before he had to throw up. The good news was he got home safely, the bad news was he threw up before he got his truck door open. At least most of the vomit was contained to the passenger-side floorboard. Ignoring the mess, Stan tumbled out of the truck and stumbled into the house, collapsing onto the couch where he promptly passed out.

Agnes Overbay

"I don't like peas. I keep telling them but they keep buying them for me," Agnes told her son, Darren, when he stopped by for his weekly visit.

"I'm sorry, mother. I'll tell them again, but do me a favor, if it happens again, don't throw the can at them. Give them to your next-door neighbor or throw them away. Poor Barry is going to have a knot on his head because of you," he said, gently admonishing the 82-year-old, spirited woman.

"It's your fault, you know. I didn't want to live in a damn nursing home."

"Mother, it's not a nursing home, it's called assisted living. You have your own apartment so it's just like being home," he told her, knowing it would do no good. It was the same argument every week. Sadly, she had early stage Alzheimer's and needed someone nearby in case she became confused or tried to wonder off. Assisted living was the best compromise Darren could come up with.

"Whatever you call it, I don't like it here," she told him again.

"Let's go outside for a walk," he suggested as he stood up and offered his arm to his mother.

Agnes smiled at him as she rose easily out of her chair and took his arm. She was still quite healthy and spry. It was her mind that was failing her.

"That sounds wonderful," she said.

They walked out to the garden and sat at a table with an umbrella to shade her with. Darren was enjoying the visit. His mother was having a good day, and those were getting scarcer as time went on. Suddenly, everyone on the garden patio became ill in varying degrees.

Agnes and her son were both affected, but to a lesser extent than some of the other residents. A few of the caregivers came outside to help the sick residents and became ill as well. After twenty minutes, almost everyone's symptoms went away except for most of them retained a slight headache and were physically exhausted. Agnes and Darren were among them.

Darren decided to spend the night at his mom's apartment and informed the staff. This helped the staff out since so many residents were ill. Agnes was one less worry for them.

Shortly after dinner (he made sure there were no peas on her plate), Agnes retired to bed. Darren stayed up to watch some TV, since seven o'clock was just too early for him to go to sleep, before eventually falling asleep on the pullout couch.

An aneurysm that had been slowly growing inside Agnes's brain burst an hour later. Two hours after that, Agnes was dead. 12 hours later, she opened her eyes and was hungry...

Ethan Mayer & Topher Yoder

"So am I going to see you tonight?" Ethan asked his boyfriend, Christopher 'Topher' Yoder. Topher was 23, 5'11" with light brown hair, bright hazel eyes, a clean-shaven face, and an athletic body, but it was his free spirit that had first attracted

Ethan physically to his childhood friend.

"It depends on what you mean by see," Topher winked as he replied. He loved to mess with Ethan while they were at work.

Ethan was a lot more serious than Topher, and always worried about what others might think when the two men were out in public together. When it was only the two of them, the 24-year-old, 6' 2" Ethan, lightened up and was a lot of fun. What drew Topher to him was how Ethan's bright blue eyes contrasted with his jet black hair, his black mustache and goatee balanced out his face and gave him the appearance of a model. To top it off, Ethan worked out four times a week and was muscular and physically fit. Most people who saw him would think he was vain and full of himself, but nothing could have been further from the truth. He was extremely down to earth and well centered. He did like to look his best but only for Topher, and he kept physically fit because it made him feel good, not to mention he could take his frustrations out during his workouts.

Ethan looked around the car dealership, checking for anyone who might have overheard Topher's comment. "Keep it down. Charlie's still here," he gently berated Topher while biting at his lip nervously.

"When are you going to tell your stepfather about us? I'm tired of sneaking around," said Topher, throwing his hands in the air.

"It's not that easy for me, Topher. You know that," replied Ethan, sighing. He knew he was repeating the same thing he said every time Topher brought it up. "My stepfather freaked out when he found out you were gay. Imagine what he'd do if he knew I was, too," he said, trying to explain his thought process to Topher, yet again. "Charlie didn't want us to hang out together because he was afraid I might 'catch it' from you, as stupid as it sounds. It took me nearly a month to get him to understand it isn't like the flu. You can't catch homosexuality from being in close proximity to a 'homo', as he so eloquently put it. The only reason he let me hire you was because I told him he could get sued for discrimination if he didn't. I can only imagine what he'd do if he discovered we were seeing each other as anything other than friends. He'd probably fire both of us and he could get away with it, since I'm your direct boss and it's against company policy to date someone at a different level within the company. Charlie's not as open-minded as your parents, but you already know all this," he replied, his muscles rigid with frustration as he sensed a wedge being driven between Topher and himself.

"Ethan, I'm not pushing you to do anything you're not comfortable doing, you know that. I'm simply saying it would make it easier for us to be together if we could be open about it with everyone. I hate having to sneak time with you. If you remember, my parents didn't accept I was gay easily either, and it was only after I explained that I was the exact same person who I've always been, the only difference was they now knew a secret about me that I had been keeping from them," he explained for the umpteenth time. "You're an excellent manager, and I'm one of the best sales agents Charlie has. We can always find new jobs at another dealership," Topher said, almost begging but knowing it would probably only irritate Ethan more.

Ethan sighed as he dropped the subject, hoping to ease the tension. "I know, Topher. Can we talk about this later tonight?"

Topher nodded his head. "Let's meet at Mike's Bar & Grill after work."

"Sounds good," he replied, leaning back in the chair in resignation. Some motion in the parking lot caught his eye as he glanced out the dealership's front window. "It looks like Mr. Hawkins is back again to check out the SUV for the fourth time. Why don't you go work on that sale and see if you can get the tightwad to release some of his money?" he suggested, happy the topic of conversation had officially changed.

Topher groaned as he rolled his eyes. "Him again? I think he likes to find things that don't meet his expectations just so he can bitch about it and try to get a better price."

"I know, but he buys a new vehicle every year and every time it's the same thing. Last year it took him seven visits before he finally bought one. The good thing is that he always buys eventually so it's not a total waste of our time," Ethan pointed out, trying to look on the bright side.

As Topher strolled towards the front doors to meet Mr. Hawkins in the parking lot, he watched as the slightly overweight and balding man stumbled and nearly fell, catching himself on a vehicle in the lot. Topher pushed through the doors and ran the rest of the way. "Mr. Hawkins, are you alright?" he asked, concerned for the older man.

"Do I look alright?" Mr. Hawkins gruffly replied as he glared menacingly at Topher.

"Let me help you into the office where you can sit down and rest for a moment," he responded, ignoring the question while trying to keep the anger out of his voice as he helped the grumpy old man to his feet.

Mr. Hawkins pulled his arm away from Topher. "I can walk by myself. Do I look like a damn cripple? I don't need you to help me like some doddering old fool," he reprimanded the salesman condescendingly.

Topher rolled his eyes as the man turned away from him. "Certainly sir. My apologies," he said, trying to calm the man down.

As Mr. Hawkins walked unsteadily towards the dealership, Topher also felt lightheaded, but managed to get Mr. Hawkins inside the lobby and seated before passing out onto the floor.

Ethan ran to Topher's side when he saw him collapse. "Topher! Topher! Wake up, buddy."

Topher's eyes fluttered. "What happened?" he groaned as he attempted to sit up.

"You fell and almost hit me," Mr. Hawkins retorted. "What the hell is wrong with you people? Is this how you treat your best customer?"

"I'm sorry, Mr. Hawkins," Ethan said, helping Topher to his feet. "I'll have someone with you in just a moment."

"Don't bother, just get me something to drink. I'm going home and then calling your father to tell him how terrible you've treated me today," Mr. Hawkins responded, glaring at Ethan as if he hoped the young man would burst into flames. "I might have to rethink where I buy my cars from if this is how you handle your best customers."

"Actually Mr. Hawkins, it's my stepfather who I was going to have help you since you are one of our most valued clients," Ethan said in a calm voice, even though he really wanted to tell the old curmudgeon to fuck off and die. "Please wait here and I'll be back with a bottle of water and my stepfather."

Mr. Hawkins just glowered at Ethan as he helped his friend over to his desk.

"Sit down Topher. Relax for a minute while I go get the dumb ass a bottle of water, find Charlie and somehow convince him to take care of the pain in the ass. I'll be right back," he said, concern etched in his voice.

"Ethan, I don't feel so good," uttered Topher, looking extremely pale.

"Dude, you don't look good either. Let me take care of Mr. Hawkins and then I'll take you home," he promised, worried sick about his boyfriend.

Ethan ran to his stepfather's office, bursting through the door without knocking. "Charlie, I need you to talk to Mr. Hawkins. He nearly fell in the parking lot, and when Topher was helping him into the building, he collapsed, nearly falling on Mr. Hawkins. He's now insisting you be the one to help him," he said in a rush, wanting to get back to Topher as quickly as possible.

Charlie Mayer looked at Ethan sternly for a moment before responding, "What the hell, Ethan. Can't you manage a simple sale by yourself? Fine, I'll take care of Mr. Hawkins and you go deal with your inept salesman," he spat the words out as if they were tainted with venom.

"Thanks, Charlie," Ethan said, ignoring the tone of Charlie's voice as he turned to leave. He wished he could tell his stepfather what he was really thinking at that moment, but knew it would just create a huge blowup and right now, he was more concerned about making sure his boyfriend was okay.

Ben Williams

Leaving the office, Ben started thinking about how nice it would be to get his license back later in the week. Although taking the bus was annoying, it really wasn't much of an inconvenience for him and saved a small fortune in gas. The bus stop was less than a block from his office building and only a few blocks from his two-bedroom bungalow, but he still missed the freedom that driving gave him.

As he approached the enclosed bus stop, he suddenly became quite weak and had the beginnings of a headache, which was unusual for the physically fit, 39-year-old, African-American. Ben leaned against the outside of the bus shelter, his bald head resting against the sun-warmed Plexiglas as he nearly passed out. Slowly, he made his way around the edge of the shelter and pulled himself up onto the bench. Still extremely weak, he leaned against the Plexiglas as he looked around and noticed many of the pedestrians had fallen to the ground or were now leaning against buildings, parked cars, and signposts, most groaning in pain. The few who seemed to be fine were either helping others or just standing around, taking video of the incident with their phones.

After a few minutes, Ben felt well enough that he didn't think he would pass out, but he could see others were getting worse as several began vomiting. He quickly decided he was going home and taking a nap instead of going to the bar.

Holly Sanford

She was tired. Her body had been battling stomach cancer for over a year. At first, Holly had been optimistic after the initial shock of hearing the dreaded 'C' word. She originally hoped they could do surgery and remove it. Unfortunately, by the time her doctors had diagnosed the cancer, it had progressed to the point where surgery was no longer a viable option. Over the past year, they had tried radiation therapy, chemotherapy, and immunotherapy at various times to try to reduce the cancer and extend her life. Each time, the cancer would come back with a vengeance. Holly finally told her doctor today that she was done with all of it. If God was ready for her, then she wouldn't fight Him anymore.

Holly enjoyed life, and at 54 she wasn't ready to give up and die, but the treatments were wearing her body down and she couldn't deal with all the side effects anymore.

After informing her doctor she would no longer do any further treatments, she went to the park. Seeing an ice cream cone vendor, she smiled and bought one on a whim. She hadn't eaten ice cream in years and doubted her stomach would be happy about getting it now, but she didn't care. Holly found an empty bench overlooking the playground and sat down to enjoy her ice cream and watch the youngsters play.

She was only a few licks into her cone when she felt a headache coming on. Almost simultaneously, her body became weak and as her grip strength gave out, she dropped the ice cream cone on the ground. Seconds later, her body followed. Holly could barely move and thought for sure the cancer was taking her. Smiling briefly at the thought of Him not wasting any time once she quit treatments before realizing that people were screaming and yelling nearby. She found the strength to turn her head to where she could view the playground and was shocked at what she saw. Almost everyone had fallen to the ground. Kids and adults both were sitting or laying down. There were only a few people who seemed unaffected.

It was nearly five minutes later when she finally felt well enough to sit up and another ten before Holly was confident that she could walk without collapsing. She eventually made it back to her car and drove home.

Holly took a shower to get the dirt and ice cream out of her hair, and since she still wasn't feeling well, she went to bed. Dying peacefully in her sleep three hours later.

Mrs. Ewing

"Now what on Earth is going on outside?" the 63-year-old flower shop owner wondered out loud as she flipped the open sign on the door to closed. Mrs. Ewing noticed that nearly everyone outside her shop had either fallen to the ground or were leaning up against parked cars, signposts, or buildings.

She exited the front door and stood just outside the entrance, looking for any sign of danger. Not seeing anything, she took another hesitant step before fatigue suddenly overcame her, along with the beginnings of a headache. She quickly turned and stumbled back into her shop, making it as far as the counter before collapsing to the carpeted floor.

The elderly shop owner clutched at her chest as her heart gave out, her body not being able to handle the stress of what everyone would soon refer to as the Super Flu.

'This carpet smells. I need to get it shampooed,' was her final thought as she slipped into unconsciousness and passed away.

Sally Wright

Today should have been Sally's day off, but of course, Walmart had called her in. She reluctantly agreed to work, but only until five, as she planned to hang out with Stan later that evening. A few minutes before her shift was to end, her supervisor asked if she could stay another hour as several other associates called in sick. Against her better judgment, Sally agreed. She didn't really like her job, but it beat unemployment and she could always use the extra hour of pay.

To entertain herself and to help from going insane at her mindless job, Sally liked to people watch and sometimes name customers who reminded her of a TV or movie character. Right now, she was helping a middle-aged woman with three kids. The lady was tall and thin with her hair pulled up on top of her head, similar to Marge Simpson, so the woman became Marge in Sally's mind. She noticed Marge wasn't looking healthy. She was quite pale and kept raising her hand to her head as if she had a headache.

"Are you okay?" asked Sally, concerned about the woman's health.

"I just don't feel very well," Marge responded as she brought a hand up to her face and covered one of her eyes. "I have a headache and feel feverish all of a sudden."

"I know the flu is going around. Several associates called in sick today," replied Sally, hoping whatever the woman had wasn't contagious..

Just then, baby Maggie started to cry and Sally noticed that neither Bart nor Lisa were looking very well, either. She rushed to finish up with Marge and then waited on the next few customers as quickly as possible.

Sally motioned for her supervisor to come over and told her she wouldn't be able to stay after all.

"But I need you here! We're very shorthanded today. Everybody scheduled to come in at five, called in sick. Apparently, there's some kind of flu going around," her supervisor replied, exasperated. Her face looking haggard under all the stress.

"I know, and I'm sorry. I'm just not feeling well and I only agreed to stay until five in the first place," Sally told her supervisor as she tried to fake looking sick.

"Fine! Just finish up helping these customers and we'll close your register," she spat out, obviously pissed off. Sally didn't care, she just wanted to go home.

Sally hurriedly finished up with the customers and quickly left to clock out, not feeling the least bit guilty about leaving. As she made her way to the minivan, she noticed several people in the parking lot were looking extremely ill and should probably be at home in bed.

By the time she arrived at her minivan and got buckled in, Sally seemed weaker as a headache started coming on. It only got worse as she drove home. Sally rolled her window down, hoping the fresh air would help. It didn't. She actually thought it caused her symptoms to become worse.

She pulled into the driveway and parked beside Stan's truck, noticing his driver's door was open. Sally thought this to be quite odd as she got out of her car and closed the door to his truck, getting slapped in the face with a wall of odor from Stan's vomit. Suddenly concerned about her husband, she raced into the house and found Stan asleep on the couch. He was pale and his forehead was hot and sweaty.

Still not feeling well herself, Sally ran into the bathroom and threw up into the toilet. Wiping her mouth, she opened the medicine cabinet to look for some Pepto-Bismol and she saw her reflection in the mirror. Her normally tan skin was now a pale, milky-white color and dark rings had formed beneath her eyes, making her look as if she hadn't slept in several days. She shuddered at how ill she looked, but ignored it as she continued her search for the familiar pink bottle. Luckily, Sally found a half-full bottle of the pink medicine. Not bothering to measure it out, she took a large swig of the thick liquid and then another for good measure. She also found the bottle of Tylenol and took a few of those to help fight her headache.

Taking the medications with her, Sally entered the kitchen and grabbed a bottle of water out of the fridge. She assumed Stan hadn't bothered taking anything before lying down and woke him up to give him the appropriate doses of the two medications.

"Stan honey. Wake up," Sally said as she gently shook him. "You need to take some medicine."

"Huh? Wha... what?" Stan mumbled as he slowly revived. "Oh hey, Sally. What happened?" he asked as he rotated his body into a sitting position, using one hand to push himself up while the other hand cradled his pounding head.

Handing him the dosage cup of Pepto-Bismol, Sally explained, "We both seem to have the flu. They called me into work today and there were so many people I saw who were in just as bad of shape as you. The odd thing was, I didn't have any issues until I went outside to get into my car. Then it hit me all at once. It was like a freight train slammed into me. I don't think I've ever gotten so sick, so fast before."

"That's weird. I was fine at work too, but got sick after I left the building. It must be some kind of airborne virus or something," Stan commented, trying to figure out what happened as he choked down the Pepto-Bismol.

"I think you're right, but I find it strange that there was nothing on the news about it about it this morning. Have you seen the boys today?" Sally asked, referring to Kent and Preston, Stan's teenage sons from his first marriage.

"Not since this morning. Kent said something about having to work tonight, and Preston is probably over at Sarah's house. Give me a few minutes to get my head back together and I'll call them to make sure they're alright," responded Stan, after taking the Tylenol Sally had given him.

She shook her head. "You go lie down in the bedroom and get some rest. I'll call the boys. You seem to have it a lot worse than I do."

Stan shuffled off towards the back of the house as Sally pulled out her cell phone. She tried Kent first, but ended up leaving him a voice mail to call her back when he got a chance. It didn't surprise her that Kent didn't answer since McDonald's didn't allow their employees to use cell phones while working. Preston; however, answered on the second ring.

"Hey Sally."

"Hi Preston. Your dad and I were wondering where you were and if you're feeling okay."

Preston paused slightly before answering, *"I'm over at Sarah's, but neither of us are doing very well. How did you know I was sick?"*

"Your dad and I are both sick, as well. I heard it was some

kind of fast acting flu so we wanted to check and make sure you boys were alright. When are you coming home?"

"Uh, I'm not sure. I thought I would wait a bit to see if I started feeling better before trying to drive home if that's okay?" Preston replied, sounding tired, which was out of the ordinary for the young man.

"That's fine. If you don't get better soon, call us back and we'll come get you. Check with Sarah and see if her parents have any Tylenol or anything you can take. It seems to help," she suggested.

"Will do Sally. Bye."

"Bye Preston."

Sally made some toast, believing it might to help settle her stomach and then went into the living room to eat it while she watched the news to see what the officials were saying about this unusual flu outbreak. After locating the remote between the couch cushions, Sally settled into the recliner and turned to the local TV station.

"...ing this Super Flu is not a regional problem, nor is it a national problem. Reports show this is a worldwide phenomenon affecting every country in the world. The Centers for Disease Control is currently working with the World Health Organization to determine the cause of this worldwide outbreak. This is what Justin Cook, a spokesperson for the CDC, had to say."

"The CDC has very few facts on this new 'Super Flu' outbreak. The outbreak seems to have occurred like a tsunami wave traveling around the world. It happened so fast we don't even know where it originated. From what we have been able to tell, this 'Super Flu' is just that, an extremely virulent and widespread flu. The CDC recommends that the public take over-the-counter medication for any symptoms and stay in bed until it runs its course. Those citizens who are in the most danger are the elderly or those with compromised immune systems. Those folks should check in with their doctor or seek treatment at an emergency care facility. Everyone else should just stay home and treat this as you would any other flu."

"*Excuse me Justin. Ryan Palmer, RNN News. So no one knows why billions of people around the world are sick? Could this be some kind of biological terrorist attack?*"

"*Ryan, there are absolutely no signs to indicate that this is a terrorist attack. Frankly, it appalls me you would even suggest such a thing. It appears to be a highly contagious and aggressive strain of the flu that affects people much faster than normal. We know those who have been indoors all day, show fewer and less aggressive symptoms than those who have been outdoors. This makes us believe it's related to our environment, but as of right now, we don't know how.*"

"*Jane Jeffers, News for You Magazine. Mr. Cook, what are the CDC's thoughts on the theory given by Dr. Michael Zimmerman, the astrophysicist, about the Earth passing thru a cosmic dust cloud at the time this epidemic started?*"

"*Ms. Jeffers, the CDC is looking into the theory based solely on the time frame aspect. Most scientists seem doubtful this could be the cause, simply because any dust particles would burn up in our atmosphere and would have no chance to filter down to the Earth. We haven't ruled it out, but it seems to be highly unlikely. It's most likely a coincidence that these two events happened simultaneously. That's all the time I have for questions, but the CDC will keep everyone updated as more information becomes available.*"

"*Once again, that was Justin Cook, spokesperson for the CDC. We need to break away for a comer...*"

Sally turned the TV off, catching the news anchor in mid-sentence. She hadn't really learned anything helpful except to stay indoors and treat the symptoms, which was exactly what they were already doing. She decided to go lay down for a few minutes to let the worst of the symptoms pass, heading to the bedroom to check on Stan before lying down herself.

Jerrell Gustafson

When the Super Flu hit Jerrell Gustafson, he didn't know

it. He was too stoned on heroin to realize anything was wrong. He had just shot up with some heroin he had scored off a hooker. So what if he had to beat her up to get it? She had a whole kilo of the shit and he only took a little of it so he didn't think it was that big of a deal. When he was depressing the plunger of the needle, he knew it was worth all the trouble he went through to get it. As it entered his bloodstream, he leaned back against the brick wall in an alley and took in a deep breath tainted with the Super Flu virus.

He was tripping balls right until the minute his heart shut down from the unintentional overdose. The heroin he had stolen earlier hadn't been cut yet and was four times more potent than what he was used to. Jerrell was dead in less than two minutes, but it was three minutes too late to save him from a fate even worse than death.

Day 2: Zombies only exist in the movies...

Stan & Sally Wright

Stan woke up to the alarm going off at 6:30 am and leaned over to shut off the blaring noise as quickly as he could. Hoping the alarm hadn't woken Sally up, but as soon as he hit the off button, he heard her stirring on her side of the bed.

"How are you feeling this morning?" asked Stan as he rolled over to give her a kiss on the cheek.

Sally opened her eyes and rubbed the sleep from the right one before replying, "Better. I don't have a headache or feel nauseous anymore. How about you?"

"I'm good. No headache or anything, but I am hungry. Why didn't you wake me up for dinner?"

"Oh crap. I didn't even think about fixing dinner last

night. I felt so miserable that I went to bed. I'll fix you some breakfast while you get ready for work," said Sally as she crawled out of bed.

"Are you sure?" Stan asked. "I can just pick something up on my way in."

Sally shook her head slightly as she climbed out of bed. "I'll fix you something. I want to see what they're saying on the news, anyway."

Stan nodded his head as he headed toward the bathroom to shower. "Did you get a hold of the boys yesterday?" he hollered at her as he turned on the shower to let the water warm up.

"Preston was sick, so he ended up staying at Sarah's last night. I left a message for Kent but fell asleep before he called back. Let me check my messages real quick," she replied as she picked up her cell phone. "Kent texted me saying he was going to stay at Tim's because he didn't want to get what we had, so I guess he didn't get sick."

"That's good to hear. I'll be down in a few minutes," he replied, stepping into the steaming shower.

Sally went into the kitchen and turned on the small TV they kept on the counter before getting everything ready to make pancakes. Her mind was drifting as she stirred the batter until the newscaster mention the Super Flu.

"...ports have been coming in across the globe. Every country is being affected by this Super Flu. Does the CDC have any idea what caused this flu and can you tell us anything about the flu itself?"

"I understand everyone's frustration. We at the CDC are working non-stop to get this figured out."

Sally glanced at the TV and saw it was the same CDC spokesperson as yesterday, but she couldn't recall his name.

"As you can probably tell, I'm suffering from the same flu as everyone else. As of right now, we don't have any proof indicating where this flu originated; however, because of the way it spread and the fact the Earth was passing through a cosmic dust cloud at *around the same time, there is some speculation that perhaps it is extraterrestrial in nature, meaning not from this planet. Please remember that this is just a theory and is probably irrelevant since any contaminants from the dust cloud would burn up on entry into Earth's atmosphere. Now, as for the flu itself, it would seem that approximately 90% of the Earth's population was directly affected and suffered at least some symptoms. That being said, most of those people recovered within ten to twelve hours, with no adverse effects. Infants, the elderly, and those with compromised immune systems are having a harder time in dealing with the illness. As of two hours ago, there have been 426 confirmed deaths in the United States directly related to this Super Flu, and we expect that number to go higher as the day progresses.*

"This Super Flu doesn't appear to kill on its own but it is exasperating other respiratory issues. Based on the latest information from around the globe, we anticipate only a slightly higher fatality rate worldwide than normal, less than 10%. In the United States, we are looking at approximately an additional 750 people per day dying while the Super Flu remains active. Those numbers will be higher in third world countries due to the lack of proper medical care."

"Hold on a minute, Justin. Let me see if I understand you correctly. If you have a compromised immune system or any type of respiratory problems, get to a medical professional as soon as possible if you're showing symptoms. If not, all you need to do is treat the symptoms and you'll be fine in a few days?" the reporter inquired, obviously surprised by the news.

"That's correct," the CDC spokesman continued. *"Treat the symptoms and get plenty of rest and you should be fine unless you are elderly, an infant, or are already suffering from respiratory issues in which case you should seek medical care. Hopefully, since the entire world's population has already been exposed to this virus, it should burn itself out over the next few days."*

Sally couldn't believe what she was hearing. 750 people a day sounded like a lot, but after thinking about it, she realized it really wasn't considering there are over 328 million people in the US.

"*Thank you, Justin,*" the reporter said. "*Let me reiterate for those who may have just joined...*"

Sally turned off the TV just as Stan walked into the kitchen, frowning. "Are you burning the pancakes?"

"Oh my gosh. I'm sorry. I was listening to the news report and forgot about your breakfast," she replied, tossing the burned pancakes into the trash. "Let me make you some more."

Stan shook his head. "That's okay, I'll just stop and pick something up on the way to work besides, you look like you've just seen a ghost."

"Can you believe 750 people a day are dying because of this flu? That's just insane," she told him, relaying what she'd heard on the news report.

"I guess on the bright side, it's short-lived and we seem to build up an immunity to it fairly quickly," he replied as he kissed his wife. "Okay, I'm off to work. I'll see you when I get home tonight."

Sally waved halfheartedly at Stan as he headed out the door, then began to clean up the breakfast mess.

"Oh man, this is bad!" Stan said to himself as he opened the door to his truck. The smell of day-old vomit overwhelming him. "Why couldn't I throw up outside my truck?" he lamented.

Stan walked around his truck and carefully removed the floor mat, glad he spent the extra money on the deeper floor mats that could hold more debris than the flat ones that had originally come with the truck. He was able to get the majority of the vomit out just by doing that. The rest would have to wait until he came home from work. He drove to work with the windows down to dispel some of the offensive odor, hoping the smell wouldn't permeate his clothing and leave him smelling like vomit all day.

Tanya Mayer

Tanya looked at the clock, noting that she would end up being about ten minutes late if she left the house now. "Oh well, they'll just have to deal with it," she mumbled to herself. Truth be told, she didn't feel like going in at all. Yesterday's flu bug still had her feeling slightly under the weather, but she no longer had a fever and the headache was almost completely gone, so there was no reason she shouldn't go to work. After all, the deceased wouldn't autopsy themselves.

Tanya was 42 and had been an assistant to the county medical examiner for the past three years. Before that, she had been an intern for two years. While she enjoyed trying to figure out the mysteries of how and why people died and helping the surviving family members understand the reasons behind why their loved ones passed away, she didn't like her boss, Brian 'the asshole' Lieberman. He was arrogant and treated Tanya like she was a dumb blonde, but nothing could have been further from the truth. Tanya was blonde, no denying that, but she had a Doctorate of Medicine (MD) degree and held undergraduate degrees in biology and organic chemistry. One look into her sparkling green eyes would tell anyone she was quite intelligent and not to be trifled with. She had been offered the county medical examiner position in two other counties, but she didn't want to move. No, scratch that. Charlie, her husband, didn't want to move and what Charlie wants, Charlie usually got.

The coroner's office used a rotating shift of ten staff members. Brian, Tanya, Gabriel Lowery, and Jillian Hernandez were all able to perform autopsies, and each of them had an intern. Brian's intern was Jeff Decker, Tanya's was Becky Smalls, Gabriel had Anthony Gomez, and Jillian worked with Ralph Arenz. The two remaining staff members were Hugo Vasquez and Dennis Claremore, who did investigative work and made the runs to pick up the deceased.

She was almost fifteen minutes late and was both surprised and relieved to see Brian hadn't made it in yet. He would probably still admonish her for being tardy, but at least she could throw his being later than her back into his face. Checking the autopsy docket, she noted that she only had two autopsies scheduled. Brian had three, and Jillian one. Today was Sam and Anthony's day off and Jillian was required to appear in court for a murder case for which she had autopsied the victim six months prior. She assumed they would be busier. After all, people don't stop dying just because the coroner's office is short-staffed.

Strolling into the butcher block, a nickname given to the autopsy room decades ago, Tanya saw both Jeff and Becky had the two autopsy tables that she and Brian would use, set up and the first two 'clients' of the day were laid out and ready for inspection.

The autopsy room had four stations. Each station was equipped with an autopsy table, a counter with cabinets both above and below, as well as an industrial size sink. A scale hung beside each station that was used to weigh any organs removed from a cadaver. Everything was made from high-grade stainless steel for easy cleanup. Tanya's station was the furthest from the door by choice, since Brian always used the one closest, and the more distance between them, the better, in her opinion.

"Good morning guys," Tanya said, more cheerfully than she felt. "How are you two today?"

"Ugh, I feel like someone hit me with a sledgehammer," Becky replied, obviously still not back to her normal chipper self. She carried a few extra pounds on her already big-boned frame but was always very cheerful, so her glum attitude gave credence to the story of her not feeling up to par.

"I'm about the same," admitted Jeff, his voice dull and tired sounding.

"Let me guess, you both got the flu yesterday?" Seeing them both nod an acknowledgment, she continued. "Me too. I think they said on the radio that the infection was currently active in about 90 percent of the world's population by this morning and around 10% seem to be immune. I imagine business will pick up over the next few days..."

"I'm glad you could make it in, Ms. Mayer. I noticed you were almost twenty minutes late this morning," interrupted Brian rather rudely as he strode into the room.

"I was only twelve minutes late and still arrived before you," she replied curtly.

"My tardiness was because they called me to the hospital to speak with the chief physician, not because of sleeping in," Brian retorted, taking some wind out of her sails. "He's very concerned about this flu and warned me they have three cases there that we will probably end up with later today and one that Hugo and Dennis are already on their way to pick up."

Jeff frowned. "I thought we only did autopsies on unattended deaths or those who died under suspicious circumstances, not on people who died from the flu."

"Wouldn't you say that billions of people getting the flu within hours of each other suspicious?" he questioned smugly. "I would and the CDC does too, so they have opted to have any deaths attributed to the flu, autopsied. Besides, the flu isn't what these people died from, it's just the instigator." Turning to face Tanya, he continued. "I'll be handling the flu case after I take care of this one, so I moved the suspected heart attack I was slated to do this afternoon, onto your docket. Now let's get scrubbed up, it's going to be an exciting day."

Tanya almost laughed when she saw Becky roll her eyes as Brian turned away, but hid it with a smile. "Yes, a very exciting day. Man, I wish Brian would have gotten a more severe case of the flu, but I think he scared it off," she whispered to Becky as they headed over to the sink to scrub up.

Their first case was an automobile accident. The man hadn't worn his seat belt and was thrown from his car. Unfortunately, the car ended up coming to rest on top of him, causing him to sustain numerous lacerations, internal injuries, and broken bones. Brian tended to give Tanya the messier autopsies, as they required more time and paperwork to process them. They were required to document every cut and scrape, as well as any cracked or broken bones. Tanya secretly believed it was so he could complain about her taking longer to do an autopsy than it did him. By the time she officially determined the man died due to hemorrhaging out from internal injuries, specifically from a tear in the inferior venae cavae vein that brings blood back into the right side of the heart, Brian finished up with his brain aneurysm. Jeff cleaned and sterilized the worktable and the tools and was already wheeling in the suspected flu death that had arrived a few minutes earlier.

Tanya wrote out her notes on the accident victim while Becky finished closing up the chest cavity and returned the man to the refrigeration room. Tanya helped Becky clean and sanitize the table and tools before she scrubbed up again, before donning a fresh set of gloves. Becky went to go get their next case, a woman who was found in the river. Tanya wasn't looking forward to this case, as the woman had been dead for several days and was now swollen up like a balloon from all the decomposition gases built up inside her abdomen, but it had to be done.

She helped Becky transfer the woman onto the autopsy table and then filled out the form with the woman's information while Becky got all the necessary tools ready. Once she had all the known information, she began the autopsy by giving the body a visual examination, verbalizing what she saw into a digital voice recorder she would later use to transcribe her notes. Tanya had got into the habit over the years of ignoring everything around her while performing an autopsy. There was usually at least one other autopsy going on, and this was probably why she didn't realize anything was wrong until Becky screamed.

Ready to yell at Becky for the interruption, Tanya looked up and saw total fear and panic on her face. She turned to look behind her to see what had Becky in such a state and found it difficult to comprehend what she was seeing. The flu victim had a Y incision in his chest and Brian had opened his chest cavity up so he could check all the various internal organs for abnormalities. This was all normal. What wasn't normal was the dead man was sitting up and biting Brian's arm and he was screaming at Jeff to help him while Jeff just stood there, frozen in shock.

Becky was the first to react by running across the room and grabbing the man by the shoulders, trying to push him back down onto the table. She was yelling at Jeff to help her and he finally did after what seemed like hours, but was in reality only a few seconds. Brian was hitting the dead man in the face with his fist, trying to get him to release the bite. After several blows, the man bit off a chunk of Brian's arm and immediately turned and grabbed Jeff's left arm and tried to bite it as well. Jeff jerked back as he tried to break free of the hold. His foot slipping in the blood that had drained out of the corpse and onto the floor when it sat up, causing Jeff to fall, dragging the newly reanimated corpse off the table and on top of him.

Tanya ran over to help, but by the time she arrived, the flesh-eating monster had already bitten a sizable chunk of Jeff's ear off and was currently attempting to go in for seconds. Looking for something to subdue the man with, Tanya grabbed the fire extinguisher off the wall and slammed it into the side of the dead man's head, crushing the skull like a bat hitting a Jack-o'-lantern. The re-alive man was now re-dead and Tanya's first thought was that she was going to jail for murder. Her second thought was, what the hell happened? She glanced around and saw that Brian had fled the room after getting bitten by the dead man. Becky was now sitting on the floor in a puddle of blood, rocking back and forth while sobbing. Jeff was attempting to crawl out from underneath the twice dead man while also trying to stem the flow of blood from what remained of his ear.

Suddenly, two of the building's security guards rushed into the room, one after the other. Unfortunately, the first guard stopped, his brain unable to process what he was seeing, triggering the second guard to slam into him and causing both guards to crash to the floor like dominoes. Brian came in behind them but avoided the pileup.

"What did you do?" Brian demanded to know when he saw the bloody fire extinguisher in her hand. "You didn't kill him, did you?"

"What is wrong with you?" Tanya countered. "This... this thing attacked you and Jeff and you're mad at me because I killed it? How can I kill something that's already dead?"

"Well obviously he wasn't dead because he was moving under his own power," Brian retorted. "You murdered him and I'll make sure you rot in jail for it."

Tanya threw the fire extinguisher to the floor and stormed around the table, reaching into the scale and pulling out the man's heart that Brian had removed from the man's chest cavity shortly before being attacked. "And I suppose this is a figment of my imagination? You were the one who cut out his heart so there is no way I could have killed him because he was already dead!" her voice rose in anger as her face flushed red.

By this time, the security guards had untangled themselves and were now trying to assess the situation. One of them finally found the courage to speak. "Folks, I don't have a clue what happened in here, but for everyone's safety, I'm going to put you all into separate rooms until the police arrive. They can sort this mess out."

"You can't make me stay here, I'm injured and need to get to the emergency room before I bleed to death," Brian said with as much authority as he could muster as he shoved his wounded arm into the man's face..

The guard shook his head at Brian's arrogance and then replied, "I can, and I am. You will all go to your own offices and you will remain there until the police and paramedics arrive."

Becky looked up and timidly spoke, "I don't have an office and neither does Jeff."

"That's alright miss, I'm sure we can find a couple of empty rooms for you two to wait in," the guard replied kindly.

Tanya set down at her desk in disbelief of the events she had just witnessed, or rather, took part in. Did she really kill someone? She wasn't quite able to wrap her head around what had transpired. Luckily, she had little time to dwell on it as the police and ambulance arrived within a few minutes of her getting to her office. They didn't come to her office right away as the wounded took priority, but she heard bits and pieces of the conversation from whoever was talking in the hall just outside her door. From what she could decipher, they were as confused as she was.

After the police took Brian and Jeff's statements, they let the paramedics take them to the emergency room to get treatment for their bite wounds. Although Jeff's condition concerned her, the relief of having Brian gone took a tremendous weight off her shoulders. She didn't want to have another run-in with him today.

A knock on the door startled her. It opened to reveal two uniformed police officers.

"Miss Mayer?" an officer inquired.

"Yes officer, I'm Dr. Mayer," she gently corrected him. "Are Brian and Jeff okay?" she asked before he could say anything else.

The officer nodded his head as he entered the room. "They should both be fine. We sent them to the hospital to get them checked out, but what we need from you is a statement about what happened earlier."

Tanya took a deep breath and gathered her thoughts for a moment before she explained what happened. As the words flowed from her mouth, she realized it sounded absurd, even to her. She did her best to not leave anything out, including hitting the reanimated corpse with the fire extinguisher. When she finished, she could see the look of doubt on the officers' faces, although they both tried to hide it.

The first officer cleared his throat before he spoke. "So you're trying to tell us a dead man attacked two of your co-workers and to stop the attack, you killed, or rather, re-killed him? You do understand how absurd that sounds? This is not a joke, Dr. Mayer. I would appreciate the truth and not this bizarre fairy tale everyone here seems to have cooked up."

Glancing at the officer's name tag, Tanya responded, getting angry, "Excuse me, Officer Bowers. I told you exactly what happened. I understand what I've told you may be hard to wrap your mind around, but it's what happened. The corpse attacked Brian and Jeff, and I did what I needed to do to stop it. Medically, I don't understand how someone who had their internal organs removed from their body could do what that man did, but somehow he managed it." Pausing for a moment, she then thought of something and grinned. "I can prove what I am telling you is the truth."

"And just how are you going to do that?" Officer Bowers replied, with no emotion in his voice.

"When we perform an autopsy, we use digital voice recorders as we work so we're not constantly having to stop and write things down. There are voice recordings of everything that happened on both mine and Brian's recorders. There is also a security camera in there that should have recorded the incident as well."

Officer Bowers looked relieved. "Dr. Mayer, I'm not trying to be the bad guy and I apologize if it sounded like I was. We'll need a copy of both voice recordings and the video recording. As long as they corroborate what you've told us, I don't think any charges will be forthcoming, but I also don't have the final say. Can we review the recordings and get copies now?"

"We'll have to get with Brian about the security video, since I don't have access to it, but I can get the audio ones for you now. I want to apologize to you as well. I shouldn't have gotten angry but this whole thing is so unreal and I think my nerves are fried."

Tanya went back to the Butcher Block, escorted by Officer Bowers since she had to cross the crime scene tape to re-trieve the recorders. She quickly copied them onto a flash drive once she was back in her office. Tanya played the audio files for the officers, first Brian's and then hers. All three of them were still in disbelief at what they were hearing.

She called Brian and told him the police wanted a copy of the security video from the Butcher Block and he told her to get the key from Jennifer and make a copy for them.

After getting the key and gaining access to the security room, it took her a few minutes to familiarize herself with the system. Soon she was able to download a copy of the video onto a thumb drive for the officers, taking the extra time to make a copy for herself as well.

Thankfully, the officers left her alone after she wrote out a statement of what happened and gave them a copy of the video They told her the autopsy room was a crime scene and it would be after five before they would return control of the room back over to her. Tanya had some reports to catch up on but told everyone else to take the rest of the day off since there was nothing further they could do until the investigation was finished.

Charlie Mayer

Charlie pulled his BMW into his personal parking space behind his car dealership, noticing several employee's cars were missing.

"Great! What a bunch of worthless pieces of shit. Prob-ably all at home faking getting the flu. At least Ethan and his fruity friend both showed up," Charlie muttered to himself as he eased his 305-pound body out of his current pride and joy.

Glancing at his Rolex, he saw it was 7:50 am so there wouldn't be any customers in the showroom yet since they didn't unlock the doors until eight.

"Ethan!" Charlie bellowed as he entered the back door. "My office. NOW!"

"Okay Charlie," he hollered back. "On my way."

Ethan walked into the office just as Charlie settled his hefty body into his chair. "Morning Charlie. What's up?" he asked as he wondered for the thousandth time how Charlie's chair hadn't collapsed under all his weight.

"What's up? You want to know what's up? I'll tell you what's up. Not sales that's for damn sure. What kind of crap was your buddy pulling yesterday by attacking Mr. Hawkins? We almost lost his business over his little stunt. I had to give him a huge discount and I should take it out of both your commissions since I had to sell at just above cost," complained Charlie.

"I'm sorry Charlie. Topher got the Super Flu that everyone seems to be getting. It won't happen again," he responded, holding back his anger.

He'd learned as a small child not to raise his voice or be the least bit confrontational to his stepfather, since it would only escalate the problem and make Charlie angrier. Ethan was used to the emotional abuse and had conditioned himself over the years to ignore all the yelling and just listen to the words, pretending they were said in a nice calm voice, otherwise it could easily turn into physical abuse. His stepfather hadn't hit him since he was a junior in high school when Ethan started to hit back, and he wanted to keep it that way.

"I don't want to hear you're sorry. I want you to control the staff. That's your job as the sales manager and if you can't do it, I'll find someone who can. Understand?"

"Yes sir," Ethan said, trying to look properly reprimanded, but wishing he could punch his stepfather in the nose.

Charlie nodded. "Good, now that we have that out of the way, I want you to personally make sure Mr. Hawkins's Cadillac Escalade is cleaned and ready for pickup by noon. He bought the silver metallic one out in the front row. The keys and paperwork should already be on your desk. Mr. Hawkins will be in at one o'clock to pick it up, and I don't want Topher to be here when he does. Send him on a late, extended lunch. Hell, tell him to leave at noon and you'll call him when he can come back after Mr. Hawkins leaves. Is that understood?"

Ethan nodded his head. "I'll take care of it. Anything else?"

Charlie glared at Ethan for a moment. "Not right now, but if Mr. Hawkins sees Topher here today, this will be your last day as sales manager and Topher's last day working here. Now get those doors open and tell whoever bothered to show up for work that they need to sell some damn cars."

"Will do," replied Ethan, heading out of the office door.

Oliver Sanford

He called his mom every day since she found out she had stomach cancer, and today was the first day she had failed to answer. After several tries without getting ahold of her, Oliver drove to her house to make sure nothing was wrong.

"Mom? Are you here?" he hollered into the house after entering Holly Sanford's duplex when she failed to answer the door.

He thought he heard her moving around in the bedroom, but she hadn't answered him. Oliver walked down the short hallway to her bedroom and knocked on the door.

"Mom? Are you okay?" he asked again.

Again Holly failed to respond, which was very unlike her, so Oliver opened her bedroom door to check on her.

"Mom. I'm coming in. I hope you're decent."

Oliver entered the bedroom and saw his mom tangled up in her sheets, thrashing around. Fearing she might injure herself, he hurried to her side and tried to help untangle her. During the confusion, his mom somehow scraped her teeth on his arm, drawing blood. He barely acknowledged the injury as he finally got the sheet untangled from Holly's body.

He turned to leave so his mom could get dressed in private. As he walked to the door, Oliver heard her groan as she climbed out of bed, tripping over the cover lying on the floor and falling, striking her head on the bedpost, rendering her unconscious.

Unable to find a pulse, Oliver dialed 911 and informed them of his mom's death.

Grief stricken, he waited outside in his car for the police and paramedics to arrive. Oliver failed to notice as Holly walked out the front door he had inadvertently left open and disappear around the side of the duplex.

When no body was found, the police opened an investigation regarding Holly's disappearance with Oliver named as the prime suspect. After six hours of interrogation, he was finally released and allowed to return home to his family.

Oliver was physically exhausted and mentally drained from dealing with everything. He wanted nothing more than to put the day behind him. Afraid his nerves would make him puke if he ate anything, Oliver skipped dinner, took a hot shower, told his wife and two kids goodnight, and went to bed. By midnight, Oliver was in a coma as his heart slowed down to an unbelievable six beats per minute. Had his wife awoken in the middle of the night and checked on him, she would have believed him to be dead. Unfortunately for her, that wasn't the case.

Kent & Preston Wright

Kent was at his locker, digging out his algebra book for his next class, when his brother slapped him on his back.

"What's up, bro?" Preston asked him, leaning against the bank of lockers beside him.

"Nothing. Getting ready for algebra class, you?"

"Study hall, but I'm thinking about ditching it to go check on Sarah," Preston confided to his brother.

He looked at him with an evil grin. "You better be careful. If dad and Sally find out you're ditching classes, they'll ground your ass into next year."

"I'll take my chances. I'm the favorite son anyway," he

teased his slightly older brother.

Kent was 17 and a junior, by some weird twist of fate and how the school district determined when you started school, his 16-year-old brother ended up in the same grade as him. There was just over seven months' difference in their ages since Preston had been born two-and-a-half months premature and his parents apparently didn't wait to have sex after he was born. Because of this, most people thought they were twins.

It used to bother him when he was younger, but he kinda got a kick out of it now. They didn't look or act a lot alike. Kent was 5'8" with light brown hair and dark brown eyes and was the more serious of the two while Preston was 5'7", with blonde hair and blue eyes, and he was more of a jokester.

"Did you get that flu thing yesterday?" he asked Preston, finally pulling the algebra book from the bottom of the stack.

"Yeah, but Sarah got it a lot worse than I did. How about you?"

"Nope, but I heard that almost anyone who went outside got it and since work didn't need me, I went over to Tim's house and we were down in his basement playing Call of Duty the entire day."

"You're such a geek," Preston said, punching his brother lightly in the shoulder. "Come ditch with me. No one will care since half the school didn't even bother to show up."

Kent shook his head, but his brother wasn't finished. "Bro, you're a 17-year-old junior who has never ditched a class. Live a little while you're young enough to enjoy it. If we get caught, I'll take the blame and say you were trying to stop me."

He looked at his algebra book and sighed. "Fuck it," he said, tossing the book back into his locker and slamming the door. "Let's go before I come to my senses."

The two boys went out a side exit and jumped into Preston's fifteen-year-old piece of crap Chevy pickup. She was beaten to hell and had over 250,000 miles on her, but Preston loved his truck and took excellent care of her mechanically. It started as soon as he turned the key, and they were soon driving away from the high school.

"Damn it! I'm a teenage delinquent," moaned Kent as he tilted his head back and rolled his eyes. Now that they had left, he worried about it hurting his chances of getting into a good college if they got caught.

"Bout time, bro. You're always doing the right thing. I'd hate it if you looked back on your life twenty years from now and wondered why you didn't have more fun when you were a teenager. As a teen, we're expected to screw up every now and then, besides, it's not like we're out robbing a bank or anything," Preston told him, laughing about how nervous Kent was over something as minor as ditching a class. He tapped out a rhythm on the steering wheel as if he didn't have a care in the world.

"It's different for you," he explained to Preston. "You get away with pretty much everything because you're the miracle baby who shouldn't have survived. That's why you've always been given anything you wanted while I've had to work my ass off to get anything."

"That's not true..."

"Shut up, Preston! It is too." Kent was pissed off, and he glared at his brother. "Take this truck, for example. Dad literally gave it to you, but not only that, he saved it for you for nearly four years after he bought his new one until you turned 16 and got your license. You know what he did for me? He loaned me $500 for a down payment and then charged me interest, and that was only after I practically begged him to help me. Not only that, but I had to sign a contract like he didn't trust me to pay it back."

"Shit, bro. I didn't know it bothered you that much. I think they treat you differently because they see you as more of an adult, always doing the right thing and never getting into any trouble. He gave me the truck to control me," he admitted. "How many times have they threatened to take your car away?"

"None, but I've never really done anything to warrant it, either," countered Kent.

"That's true, but since they gave me the truck, it's constantly being held over my head as something they can take away should they decide to. I've been saving up money so I can pay dad for it just so he would know I can be responsible too." admitted Preston.

Kent deflated in his seat. "I guess I never looked at it like that before. Now that you mention it, I see how they treat us differently." He sat up quickly and grinned at his brother. "Let's ditch the rest of the day and you can teach me some of your bad boy ways."

Preston started laughing, slapping Kent on the shoulder. "I like how you're thinking, bro."

They drove down the street and didn't look back.

Darren Overbay

It was nearly eight in the morning, and his mother was still sleeping. He really should have gone to work but with his mother not feeling well last night, he called in sick. Darren would spend the morning with her and maybe stay for lunch, but after that, he would need to leave. His great-grandchildren were coming over in the afternoon to spend the night, and he wanted to spend some family time with them.

The doorbell rang, causing Darren to jump. He hadn't been expecting the loud noise.

"Good morning. How may I help you?" he asked the young lady at the door.

"You must be Mr. Overbay, Agnes's son. She speaks of you often. My name is Meg and I'm one of the nurses here," she replied.

"I'm sorry. Mother is still sleeping," he told her, smiling.

The nurse glanced at her watch and frowned. "What time did she go to bed last night?"

Darren stroked his chin as he thought. "It must have

been around seven. She wasn't feeling well and went to bed early."

"It's almost ten now. I think I need to go check on her. Fifteen hours is a long time to sleep," she said as she pushed her way past Darren and headed to his mother's bedroom.

He thought about berating her for being so rude, but changed his mind. She was going to check on his mother and honestly, he was worried about her still being in bed. Darren had been mentally arguing with himself for almost two hours about checking on her, but his mother had a temper and he didn't want her mad at him for waking her up. Letting the nurse wake her was a better choice for him.

The nurse entered the bedroom and he followed her.

"Mrs. Overbay, it's Nurse Meg. How are you getting along today?" she asked in a friendly voice.

The only response was a groan, which caused him to cringe. Darren knew his mother was going to yell at the nurse, but he said nothing to warn her.

"Mrs. Overbay. It's time to wake up. You've been sleeping for fifteen hours and your son is here."

The nurse touched Agnes's forehead. Shaking her head, she pulled out digital temporal scanner and placed it against her forehead.

Agnes didn't appear to be completely awake. She seemed really groggy to Darren and her skin was ashen. She must still be sick, he thought.

"Mother, are you feeling okay?" he asked as he approached her bedside.

The scanner beeped, causing the nurse to look at it funny. The nurse slapped it against her hand a couple of times and put it back up to his mother's forehead.

"What's wrong?"

The nurse shook her head. "I think the battery might be loose or something. It was reading 72 degrees and that can't be right."

The scanner beeped again.

"Hmm, same thing. I guess it needs a new battery."

Agnes's arms were under the cover and she was trying to move them as she snapped her mouth at the nurse.

"Sir, help me hold her down. I think she's having a seizure," the nurse said as she tried to hold the elderly woman down, surprised at how strong she was.

Darren was pushing her shoulders down as the nurse struggled to control her legs. Worried she was going to hurt herself, Darren reached up to keep her head still when she bit his fingertip.

"Calm down, mother. Everything will be fine in a few minutes," he said, trying to soothe her.

"I'll be right back. I need to get some help," the nurse said as she scurried from the room.

A few minutes later, two men brought a gurney in. Rather than remove her blanket, they tucked it under her to prevent her hands from escaping and put her on the gurney. With practiced hands, they strapped her down.

"What are you doing?" Darren demanded to know.

"Calm down, sir. We're taking her over to the doctor's office over in the main building. They will take good care of her there," one of the men promised him.

Darren followed them and waited for thirty minutes before the doctor came out to speak with him.

"How is she, doctor?"

The man shook his head. "I'm not exactly sure. It seems like she might have what they call a convulsive status epilepticus seizure, which is basically a seizure that lasts over ten minutes. There's nothing I can do for her here so an ambulance is taking her to one of the local hospitals."

Darren sank into a chair. "Is she going to be alright?" he asked quietly, fearing the answer.

"I'm afraid I don't know the answer to that. They'll run some tests at the hospital and then they should be able to tell you more. I'm sorry I can't be of more help. I'll have the nurse get you the hospital's information," the doctor said as he turned to leave.

Three hours later, the doctors at the hospital informed him she wasn't coming out of the seizure. They had put her into a medically induced coma to prevent her from injuring herself and hopefully give her body time to heal.

Darren broke down and cried for a few minutes before finally gathering himself and going home to his wife and great-grandchildren. He had forgotten about the small bite on his fingertip until he bumped it on a table and briefly thought about cleaning the wound and putting some antibiotic ointment on it. Shaking his head at the horrible memory, he went back to playing with the three-year-old twins. He'd worry about the finger getting infected later.

All across the country, similar scenes were being repeated. In the United States, over 8,100 people die each day from various causes. Most of those were now reanimating and attacking unsuspecting family, friends, doctors, and other strangers. The bite victims would treat their wounds and go home to their families, only to fall into a coma and wake up as something else. No one had put the pieces together to understand exactly what was happening, allowing the virus to spread unencumbered...

Ben Williams

He'd thought about calling in sick, but decided he needed the money more than he needed the rest. Ben almost had enough saved to buy himself a new car, or at least one that was new to him. He was excited to be getting his license back and wanted to have a car with no payments. Ben had been putting money away for the last eighteen months for this very reason, and his paycheck on Friday would supply the last couple hundred dollars he needed.

Although Ben was thirty-nine, he looked ten years younger because he took good care of himself. He enjoyed the extra bit of exercise he got each morning by taking the stairs to his fifth-floor office, but today he opted for the elevator since he still felt a little weak from yesterday's flu. There were only three other people in the elevator, and all three looked worse than Ben did, so he was glad he had come in. After all, he wasn't a little wussy boy, and something as simple as the flu wasn't going to stop him.

As he stepped out of the elevator, Ben saw that only about half of the staff had arrived. Hopefully, more people would show up, otherwise it would make for a long day. He noticed Stan coming out of the break room, sipping a cup of coffee, and headed his way.

Ben and Stan had been best friends for almost five years, ever since Stan was hired on at Tech-U-Serve. Ben had been his trainer and they hit it off from day one.

"Good morning, my friend," said Ben as he approached Stan.

"What's good about it? I feel like crap because I got that flu crap everyone else seems to have. You're looking a lot better than most everyone here. Were you one of the lucky bastards who didn't get sick?"

Ben chuckled. "It hit me right after I left work yesterday, but I guess I just had a mild case. I still have a minor headache, but I took a few ibuprofen this morning, and it seems to help."

"I'm glad for you, man. I almost didn't make it home last night and ended up puking in my truck, so I have that to look forward to cleaning up after work. Preston and Sally got it as well, but we all seem to be on the mend. I guess that's something to be thankful for," replied Stan as they arrived at their work cubicles.

"You think you're still going to be able to take me car shopping Friday after work? I got my eye on a used Camry down at Mayer's Auto Emporium."

Stan grinned, happy to see his friend excited. "Sure thing. Are you ready to be mobile again?"

"More than you could possibly ever know," he admitted, grinning from ear to ear.

Ethan Mayer

Ethan sat with his elbows on his desk and his head in his hands as Topher knocked on his office door.

"You wanted to see me, boss man?"

"Yeah. Close the door and have a seat."

"Oh, one of those conversations. Okay Ethan, let me have it," Topher said as he sat in the chair in front of Ethan's desk. "What's step-daddy dearest done now?"

Ethan shook his head as he took a deep breath. "That fat fucker is blaming us for the whole Mr. Hawkins fiasco from yesterday. Now I realize it wasn't your fault that you got sick, but you know how Charlie is. Anyway, he said you need to leave at noon and not come back until I call you after that grouchy fuck Hawkins picks up his SUV. If Hawkins sees you here today, not only will he demote me, but you'll be unemployed."

"What the fuck, Ethan? Seriously?" Topher snapped back. "I didn't even do anything wrong."

"I know that and you know that, but I'm between a rock and a hard place on this. Just do it for me, please. I plan to make it up to you this weekend by taking you to that new club you keep asking me to go to. I heard it's going to be neon night on Saturday with the black lights and fluorescent paint. We can get good and dirty," he teased, winking at the man he loved.

Topher grinned. "I heard about neon night. Water pistols with fluorescent paint and everyone in their bathing suits. That's going to be so much fun. You know I would do this, anyway. It just pisses me off the way he treats you."

"I know. I keep hoping he has a heart attack and dies. That sounds terrible and I'll probably go to hell for even thinking it, let alone saying it, but I'm honestly not sure how much longer I can handle his bullshit," he said, tossing his pen onto the desk.

"Don't worry about it, man. He's an asshole who eats and drinks too much. I'm not sure how your mom puts up with his shit, but whatever. We still have each other and we'll get through this, so fuck him!" Topher replied. "Anyway, it's almost noon, so I better get out of here. Call me when the coast is clear."

"I will. See you later."

"Later," Topher said as he walked out the door.

Russell Sherling

He was going to be late for the meeting at the bank. Russell needed to secure the loan for his company's expansion or his investors were going to bail on the project and he would end up bankrupt.

The bank was only a few blocks away from his office, so he was walking, since finding parking was usually a hassle. As he approached an alleyway, he noticed a homeless man wrestling with another person while two others tried to break up the fight. Russell wanted nothing to do with the ruckus and tried to skirt around the group as quickly as possible. Just as he thought he was in the clear, the homeless man broke free of the others and knocked Russell to the ground.

"Son of a bitch!" he yelled, kicking the man away from him as he scrambled backwards.

Russell's pant leg had slid up his calf and exposed his leg. The homeless man, who looked very ill, grabbed his leg and bit his calf.

Screaming in pain, he got his other foot under the man's chest and pushed as hard as he could, using his leg muscles. The force of the shove threw the man back against the corner of the building, cracking his skull and pushing a bone shard into his brain. The homeless man went still.

"Dude! I think you killed him," said one of the guys. His eyes widened in shock.

"It was self-defense! You saw him attack me!" yelled Russell, fear in his eyes.

"The guy had to be mentally ill," said another man as he

held his arm. "I was just walking, and he just started attacking me. I thought I was getting mugged, but he kept biting me." he said, staring at his bloody arm that had several bite wounds on it.

"Dude! The fucker bit me too," the younger man said, showing off a small bite wound where the man's teeth had barely broken the skin. Russell assumed the guy was on drugs by the way he was talking and acting.

"Are you okay, mister?" the girl who was apparently with the younger man asked him.

Russell checked his leg and saw that the man's teeth had punctured his skin, causing the wound to bleed, but not too badly. He tied his handkerchief around his calf and struggled to his feet. "I'm alright. What about you?" he asked, seeing her hand had blood on it.

"Yeah. It's more like a scrape. He tried to bite my hand, but I yanked it away from him before he could. His teeth raked across my skin though," she said, staring at the injury like she couldn't believe it was there.

The first man spoke up. "I called the police and told them what happened. They said an officer would be here soon."

"Dude, we gotta go," the younger guy said, looking at the girl.

"Wait! You need to give a statement to the police and tell them it was an accident," Russell said as they started to walk off.

The man shook his head. "No can do. I'm too fucking high right now and I don't want to get busted."

The girl shrugged her shoulders as an apology before turning away and following her drugged up friend.

Russell watched the pair walk away and then remembered his meeting.

He pulled out his phone and called the bank to inform them he had been the victim of a mugging, since he didn't want to tell them what really happened. Thankfully, they rescheduled the meeting for the next afternoon.

The police eventually arrived and after interviewing Russell and the other man, they determined it was a case of self-defense. The officer offered to call the paramedics to come and look at the bite wounds, but the two men refused and went their separate ways.

The zombie-mutant virus was slowly spreading as incidents like this occurred throughout the city.

Stan Wright

"Ready for lunch, Ben?"

"Sure am. Where do you want to eat today?"

"Burgers and More?" Stan asked, already knowing the answer since it was Ben's favorite burger joint.

"Sounds great to me. I heard they might have emu meat today," responded Ben excitedly.

Stan laughed. "You always go for their exotic burgers when they have them. What did you get last time?"

"I think it was crocodile but it might have been alligator. Either way, it was some damn fine eating."

Stan and Ben walked, since it was just around the corner from their office. As they turned the corner, they noticed an ambulance and a couple of police cars at the flower shop across the street from Burgers and More.

"Wonder what happened there," Ben said as they approached the restaurant.

"I'm not sure but I bet someone in the burger place knows."

As Ben opened the door to Burgers and More, the paramedics brought out the stretcher with a sheet pulled completely over the body.

"Well, that doesn't look good," stated Stan, following Ben into the restaurant.

"What can I get you fellers today?"

"An emu burger and fries, if you have it, Sam," replied Ben.

"Sure do. It came in this morning, and for you?" the man asked Stan.

"I'll have the same."

"And to drink?"

"Coke is fine with me," responded Ben.

"Same here," Stan echoed.

As Sam rang up the order, Ben asked, "So what happened across the street?"

"Mrs. Ewing, the old lady who owns, or I guess I should say, owned the shop, died. About an hour ago, a lady went to pick up some flowers and found the closed sign on the door. When she looked in the window, she saw Mrs. Ewing laying on the floor. She came in here all distraught, so we called 911. Guess they couldn't get her back. I heard they think she died last night. It's too bad, she was a sweet lady," Sam responded, shaking his head. "I guess you just never know when it's your time. Anyway, your order should be ready in a couple of minutes and we'll get it right out to you."

"Thanks Sam," Stan told him as he turned to find a table.

Just as they sat down, a few customers started talking loudly and pointing out the window. Stan turned to see what the commotion was about and noticed a paramedic appeared to be struggling with the old lady on the stretcher.

"Looks like she made it," Sam said as he set the tray of food down.

Just then they heard a scream, and it stunned Stan to see that Mrs. Ewing had one of the paramedic's hands in her mouth as the guy was hitting her with his other hand.

"What the hell is he hitting her for?" someone yelled.

Stan watched a few people get out their cell phones and start recording what was happening. Several police officers rushed to help the paramedic and got his arm out of the lady's mouth, but she was still trying to bite him. Luckily, they had strapped her down on the stretcher, and she couldn't do any further damage. The other paramedic immediately went to her aid and tried to calm her down, but she tried to bite him as well. He ran to the ambulance and came back a few moments later with a syringe, which he used to inject her with something. After a couple of minutes, she appeared to have calmed down. The police helped secure her inside the ambulance while the injured paramedic was treated by his partner.

"That was pretty freaky," said Ben as he took another bite of his burger.

Stan nodded his head. "She probably woke up and panicked since they had her face covered and she was strapped down. I would freak out too if it happened to me."

"I guess you have a point. Damn, this burger is good," he said as he took a drink from his Coke.

Stan laughed at his friend. "I can't believe you were eating while watching that."

"Gotta eat it while it's hot," he replied, stuffing some more fries into his mouth.

Stan glanced back out the window as the ambulance pulled away with its siren blazing away. He shuddered at the thought of waking up like Mrs. Ewing, strapped to a gurney with a sheet over his face.

Tanya Mayer

Tanya had just gotten in her SUV when her cell phone rang, groaning internally as she saw it was her boss calling.

"Hello?"

"Where are you and why aren't you at the office?" Brian barked at her through the phone.

"Hi Brian. I was getting ready to head home because the police told me the Butcher Block is a crime scene and we won't have access to it for the rest of the day while they collect the evidence," replied Tanya, a lot nicer than she wanted to be. "How's your arm?"

"I'm sure it will be fine. You need to get back to work because someone from the CDC is on their way to meet me and I'm stuck here at this so-called hospital, waiting for them to stitch me up.

Since I may not be there before they arrive, you need to be."

"I'm still here, just outside. I'll go back inside and wait for them so no need for you to hurry."

"Like I have a choice to hurry? Just keep them there until I get back. They should be there at any time," Brian told her.

This confused Tanya. "It's only been a couple of hours. How did they get here so fast?"

"I don't know and I don't care."

Tanya heard Brian disconnect from the call. "What an asshole," she muttered, putting her phone away before going back into the Medical Examiner's office.

She had been in her office for less than ten minutes when her office line buzzed.

"Yes Jennifer?"

"I have Dr. Carlock from the CDC to see Brian, but he's not back yet."

"Brian called and asked me to meet with him. Can you show him to my office, please?" she asked as nicely as she could.

"Of course Dr. Mayer."

Tanya took a deep breath and again wondered how the CDC showed up so fast. Before she had time to contemplate the question, Jennifer was walking in the doorway. "Dr. Mayer, this is Dr. Carlock, from the CDC."

"Thank you Jennifer," replied Tanya as Jennifer turned and left the room.

"Dr. Carlock, it's nice to meet you," she said as she stood and offered her hand.

"I'm sorry, I don't shake hands, too many germs. I'm sure you understand," Dr. Carlock stammered, obviously disgusted by the gesture.

"Not a problem. I completely understand and please call me Tanya," she told him, ignoring his discomfort, but wondering how he could work for the CDC if he detested germs so much.

"I am supposed to be meeting with your chief medical

examiner, a Mr. Brian Lieberman, so I don't understand why I'm talking to you."

"I apologize. Brian is still at the hospital, getting the bite wound looked at. He should be back in a little while, but he asked me to meet with you until he returns. Please have a seat and let me know what you need from us," replied Tanya as professionally as she could.

"Bite wound?" Dr. Carlock asked, confused. "No one said anything to me about a bite wound."

"I'm sorry. I guess I should have asked what you were here for. I just assumed it had to do with the earlier incident."

"Dr. Mayer..."

"Please, call me Tanya," she invited him.

"Tanya, my name is Dr. Travis Carlock. The CDC has sent me here to help investigate this, so-called Super Flu. They felt it was important to have someone on the front line in many of the country's largest cities to see how this Super Flu was affecting different parts of the United States. They are interested in the cause of death findings for those who died with this flu. I would like to be present during some of the autopsies and take some of our own blood and tissue samples to send back to our labs. We, at the CDC, are very interested to find out what caused this outbreak."

Tanya sighed. "Well, I guess it's a good thing you're here. I should probably explain what happened earlier since it had to do with one of the flu victims, even though it doesn't make much sense."

"What do you mean, it doesn't make much sense?" Dr. Carlock inquired.

"You probably won't believe me, but earlier Brian was doing an autopsy on the first known death of a flu victim here in Dallas. In the middle of the autopsy, the victim attacked him."

"Excuse me?" Dr. Carlock interjected. "What do you mean, the victim attacked him?"

"Brian had removed the victim's heart and was weighing

it when the body sat up and bit him on the arm. I know it sounds crazy, but I saw it with my own eyes. I had to hit the man in the head with a fire extinguisher to keep him from attacking everyone else."

"Wait, what? Okay, now I am confused. You're trying to tell me that a dead body attacked your chief medical examiner in the middle of the autopsy?" Dr. Carlock asked in disbelief.

"That's exactly what I'm saying."

"I don't have time for your games, Dr. Mayer." Dr. Carlock stood up and glared at Tanya. "Obviously, I need to wait for Mr. Lieberman."

As Tanya was about to reply, there was a knock on the door frame. "Excuse me, Dr. Mayer. I'm with the crime scene unit, we're still gathering evidence but I wanted to inform you we'll need everyone's fingerprints before we leave and if they're not here, they'll need to come by the station either today or tomorrow."

"That shouldn't be a problem," Tanya replied. "Did you discover anything to explain what happened?"

"Not really," the officer said, scratching his head. "I watched the video of the attack, and to be honest, I don't think we'll ever be able to explain exactly what happened in there. That was some crazy shit and quite frankly, it creeped me out. I just want to hurry up and get the hell out of here." The man visibly shook as a shiver ran down his spine. "I better get back to it."

"I can't blame you for wanting to be done. Most everyone has left for the day, but I'll let them know about the fingerprints," she promised him.

"Sounds good," he said, turning to leave.

Dr. Carlock just stood there, slack-jawed, until the man had left, then his body slowly deflated back into the chair. "Maybe you should show me that video."

Ethan Mayer

He made sure the Escalade was completely detailed, inside and out, and he even filled the tank up with gas before Mr. Hawkins arrived to pick up his new vehicle.

After spending almost two hours dealing with the gruff old man when it should have taken less than one, it thrilled Ethan to watch him drive off, glad he wouldn't have to deal with that particular pain in the ass for another year.

He pulled out his cell phone and quickly called Topher. "Is he finally gone?"

Ethan sighed before responding, "Yeah, it's safe for you to return."

"I'm not sure I want to," admitted Topher. "Maybe it's time I find a job somewhere else. As much as I love being around you all day, I'm tired of dealing with all of your old man's bullshit."

Half expecting this old conversation to rear its ugly head, Ethan conceded the point. "I understand your frustration, believe me. I'm just as pissed at the whole situation as you are. Maybe we should both find new jobs and screw me eventually taking over this place. Come on back and we'll go to the bar and talk about it after we get off work."

"Really?" Topher couldn't contain his excitement. "Do you mean it? I know how badly you wanted to take over. It's not something you should give up on a whim, even to make me happy."

He nodded his head, even though Topher couldn't see him do it. "Actually, I think I do," admitted Ethan, surprising himself. "He's finally gone too far. Charlie's not planning on retiring anytime soon and he's too damn stubborn to die. It could be another twenty years before he hands over the reins and even then, he may decide just to sell it and not let me have it because he's that big of a dick."

"Wow! I wasn't expecting this. Have I told you recently

just how much I love you?"

Ethan laughed. "Not in the last thirty minutes. Get your butt back here and sell some cars."

"Yes sir," replied Topher, happy at the thought of getting Ethan out from underneath his stepfather's influence.

The rest of the workday seemed to both fly by and crawl ever so slowly, but eventually it was over and the boys headed to Mike's Bar & Grill.

They sat at a table towards the back so people entering and leaving the popular hangout wouldn't disrupt them.

Topher started the much-anticipated conversation. "I'm stoked that you're willing to leave Charlie's business and come with me to find another job, but I don't want you to rush into anything and then regret it later."

"The more I think about it, the more it makes sense. Charlie's never going to give me the business willingly, at least not within the next few years, and I hate the way he treats you. It might be easier to be with you in public if I wasn't always afraid that word would get back to Charlie and then he'd fire both of us," Ethan told him, fidgeting with the label on his beer bottle.

Nodding his head in agreement, Topher suggested, "Why don't we take it slow, we can brush off our resumes and I can start looking around to see what might be available for jobs in the area. If I find something that sounds promising for both of us, then we can take the next step and apply. This way, it's less likely for Charlie to find out until we're ready for him to. What do you think?"

"I like it. There's no major hurry so we don't have to take the first thing that comes along, but if we happen across the right job opportunity, then it won't be an issue to move forward with it either," Ethan said as he sat up straighter in his chair, more confident in their decision than he had been earlier.

Topher reached across the table and clasped Ethan's hand in silent agreement. Ethan didn't pull away as he normally did when in public. Maybe things really were changing, he thought as he smiled at his boyfriend.

Ethan got up to get them a couple more beers. A feeling of peace had settled within him and he felt good about the future, even though it was still uncertain. He knew they had made the right decision because he no longer felt stressed out.

"Hey Mike. Can I get two more Buds in the bottle?" he asked the owner of the bar, who always seemed to be working.

"Sure thing, Ethan," came the response. "How's the car business going?"

Shrugging, he replied, "Meh, it's about normal for this time of year."

Mike laughed as he sat the two opened bottles of beer on the counter. "I know what you mean. I thought this Super Flu might slow business down some here, but thankfully it hasn't." he leaned in towards Ethan as he lowered his voice. "I heard a rumor that a corpse came back to life and attacked the coroner this morning."

"You're shitting me!" Ethan exclaimed as his eyes widened in surprise.

Shaking his head, Mike continued. "I shit you not. One of the coroner's assistants stopped in here earlier, all shook up and with a bandage wrapped around his head. When I asked him what happened, he told me that in the middle of an aut-opsy, the dead guy attacked the county coroner, who had just removed the man's heart. When the assistant went to help his boss, he got bit, and it about ripped his ear off. Someone ended up crushing its skull in with a fire extinguisher in order to stop the attack. They're trying to keep it all hush, hush until they can figure out exactly what happened. I'm telling you it freaked the man out, and he was stone-cold sober when he got here and told me about it."

"That's crazy. I'll have to check with my mom. She works there so she would know about this. Assuming it's true, I'll need to pay closer attention to the news in case it's not an isolated incident. Thanks for the heads up Mike," he told the bartender.

"Let me know if you hear anything to corroborate the guy's story. I hate to spread misinformation if I can help it. I've only told a few of my regulars about this so they can keep their eyes and ears open and inform me if they find out anything to either dispute or confirm the story. Will you do the same?" Mike asked.

"Sure will Mike," he said as he laid some cash on the counter to pay for the beers before turning to head back to the table where Topher was impatiently waiting.

"That took a while," Topher said as Ethan set the beer on the table and sat down. "What's got Mike looking so agitated?"

Ethan repeated the story the bartender told him, still not sure if he was ready to believe it or not.

"So we're talking about zombies?" came the unbelieving response. "Pretty sure I'm not going to buy into that. You know how all these conspiracy theory nuts are. The dude probably got hurt because he was on drugs and made up the entire story. After all, zombies only exist in the movies."

Laughing, Ethan agreed, "You're right, there's no way people can come back from the dead, especially if their heart has been removed from their chest."

Their conversation moved on to other things, leaving the thought of zombies behind them, at least for the moment.

Dr. Travis Carlock

He couldn't wrap his mind around what he'd seen on the video, but he knew it was real. He saw the evidence, after all.

After returning to his hotel, the doctor called his supervisor, Dr. Lee Parish, at the CDC office in Atlanta.

"Hey Lee, it's Travis."

"Hi Travis. How's Dallas treating you?" came the friendly voice across the receiver.

"I think we have a problem. I sent a video to your email, it's a security tape from the local medical examiner's office.

You need to watch it and then call me back," directed Travis.

"Let me check to see if I have it yet," he replied as Travis heard a keyboard rattling in the background. *"I do. I'll call you back in a few."*

"Thanks," Travis said as the line went dead.

He grabbed a beer from the six-pack he'd bought on his way to the hotel. Travis felt he needed it after what he learned today. It wasn't long before he cracked open his second one. He knew he should slow down, but he needed to get his nerves calmed down first.

About halfway through his second beer, his cell phone rang.

"This is Travis."

"Travis, it's Lee. I need samples from the body, and I'm reassigning you to the infectious disease department at the John Carver Hospital in downtown Dallas," Lee told him, sounding a little worried.

"I already sent you samples. They should be on a flight arriving there later tonight. I'll email you the flight details," he said, taking a deep breath before continuing. "Any idea what this is?"

"I'm not sure yet. We've been receiving scattered reports from across the country about people coming back to life and biting others, but this is the first video evidence I've seen," Lee admitted. *"Whatever it is, we need to get on top of it and figure out just what's causing it and find a way to prevent it from spreading.*

"You'll need to get ahold of Dr. Aaron Lahusky over at the hospital, first thing in the morning. Although they normally just treat infectious diseases, he has a team who are working on this issue as we speak. They allegedly have one victim secured in their facility and are running tests on her," Lee told him.

"Maybe I should head in tonight then," he suggested.

Travis heard Lee sigh before replying, *"No. Get some rest tonight, no telling when you'll get another chance."*

"Alright, I'll send you daily reports on anything we find. Maybe we can get in front of this before it's too late."

"That would be nice," responded Lee after a slight hesitation that didn't go unnoticed. *"Don't forget to send me the flight information,"* Lee reminded him as he disconnected the call.

Travis sent another quick email with the needed flight information before wondering if he might need something stronger than beer.

ABOUT THE AUTHOR

Ernie J. Sinclair

Born in the midwest, Ernie spent his early years on a non-working farm before moving into town. Barely graduating high school due to a lack of interest, he worked a variety of jobs while getting married, having two kids, and getting divorced before eventually joining the military. He currently resides in the midwest with his constant companion, Spice.